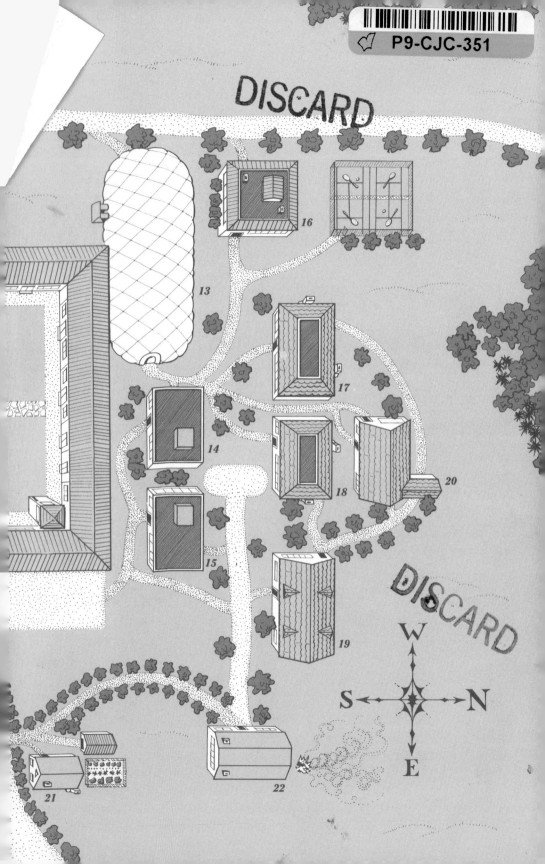

Well-Schooled in
MURDER

ELIZABETH
GEORGE

BANTAM BOOKS
NEW YORK • TORONTO • LONDON • SYDNEY • AUCKLAND

WELL-SCHOOLED IN MURDER

A Bantam Book / July 1990

Library of Congress Cataloging-in-Publication Data

George, Elizabeth.
    Well-schooled in murder / Elizabeth George.
       p.   cm.
    ISBN 0-553-07000-2
    I. Title.
PS3557.E478W 1990
813'.54—dc20   90-117
                                      CIP

Published simultaneously in the United States and Canada

Bantam Books are published by Bantam Books, a division of
Bantam Doubleday Dell Publishing Group, Inc. Its trademark, con-
sisting of the words "Bantam Books" and the portrayal of a rooster,
is Registered in U.S. Patent and Trademark Office and in other
countries. Marca Registrada. Bantam Books, 666 Fifth Avenue, New
York, New York 10103.

PRINTED IN THE UNITED STATES OF AMERICA

BVG   0 9 8 7 6 5 4 3 2 1

For Arthur, who wanted to write.
TIMSHEL

I have shot mine arrow o'er the house,
And hurt my brother.

HAMLET

AUTHOR'S NOTE

Although there are many independent schools in England, Bredgar Chambers is the product of my imagination and should not be confused with any existing educational institution.

I am, however, extremely grateful to a number of schools, headmasters, staff members, and students who played a large part in allowing me to gather information that provided such useful background material for my book. I must particularly thank Christopher and Kate Evans of Dauntsey's School in Somerset and Christopher Robbins of the same; Robin Macnaghten of Sherborne School for boys in Dorset; Richard and Caroline Schoon Tracy of Allhallows School in Devon, as well as John Stubbs and Andy Penman whose classes I spoke to; Simon and Kate Watson of Hurstpierpoint College in Sussex; Richard Poulton of Christ's Hospital in West Sussex; Miss Marshall of Eton College in Berkshire; and most of all the students who opened their lives to me with such engaging candour: Bertrand, Jeremy, Jane, Matt, Ben, Chas, and Bruce. My time spent with all these people in England enriched my understanding of the independent school system more than any other sort of research I might have done.

In the United States, I thank Fred VonLohmann for generously carrying out the initial stages of research for me at Stanford University; Blair Maffris, Michael Stephany, Hiro Mori, Art Brown, and Lynn Harding for fielding questions on a variety of topics; and Santa Barbara criminalists Stephen Cooper and Phil Pelzel who kindly opened their laboratory to me.

Most especially I am grateful to my husband Ira Toibin who has borne all things well, and to Deborah Schneider who has been my Gibraltar.

1

The rear garden of the cottage in Hammersmith's Lower Mall was set up to accommodate artistic endeavours. Three slabs of knotty pine stretched across six battered sawhorses to function as work stations, and they held at least a dozen stone sculptures in varying stages of completion. A dented metal cabinet near the garden wall contained the artist's tools: drills, chisels, rifflers, files, gouges, emery, and a collection of sandpaper with differing degrees of abrasion. A colour-splodged painter's dropcloth—smelling strongly of turps—made a dispirited lump underneath a partially broken chaise.

It was a garden completely without distractions. Walled in against the curiosity of neighbours, it was thus also protected from those insistent and largely mechanical noises of river traffic, of the Great West Road, of Hammersmith Bridge. Indeed, the high walls of the garden were so expertly constructed, the cottage's position on the Lower Mall so well-chosen, that only an occasional waterfowl in flight overhead broke into the superb stillness that the site afforded.

Such protection was not without one disadvantage. Since cleansing river breezes never found their way through the walls, a patina of stone dust covered everything from the small oblong of dying lawn, to the crimson wallflowers that bordered it, to the square of flagstones that served as a terrace, to the cottage windowsills and the building's pitched roof. Even the artist himself wore fine grey powder like a second skin.

But this pervasive grime did not bother Kevin Whateley. Over the years, he had become quite used to it. Even if he had not been accustomed to operating perfectly well in a cloud of grit, he would not have noticed it while he laboured in the garden. This was his haven, a place of creative ecstasy in which convenience and cleanliness were not required. Mere discomfort meant nothing to Kevin once he gave himself over to the call of his art.

He was doing so now, taking his latest piece through the final stage of buffing. He was particularly fond of this current effort, a reclining nude rendered in marble, her head raised on a pillow, her torso twisted so that her right leg was drawn up over her left, her hip and thigh an unbroken crescent that ended with her knee. He ran his hand down her arm, round her buttocks, and along her thigh, testing for rough spots, nodding with satisfaction at the feeling of stone like cold silk beneath his fingers.

"You do look a bit daft, Kev. Don't believe I ever once saw you smiling like that over me."

Kevin chuckled, straightened, and looked at his wife who had come to stand in the cottage doorway. She was drying her hands on a faded tea towel, laughter drawing deeply at the wrinkles round her eyes. "Then come right 'ere and give it a try, girl. You just weren't paying attention last time."

Patsy Whateley waved him off with, "You're crazy, you are, Kev," but her husband saw the pleased flush appear on her cheeks.

"Crazy, am I?" he asked. "Not what I recall you saying this morning. That *was* you, wasn' it, sneaking up on a bloke at six A.M.?"

"Kev!"

She laughed outright, and Kevin smiled at her, studying her dear, familiar features, admitting the fact that although for some time she had been surreptitiously colouring her hair to preserve a semblance of youth, her face and figure were decidedly middle-aged, the one lined and no longer firm at jaw and chin, the other filled out in places where once he had found the most delicious curves.

"You're thinking, aren't you, Kev? I can see it on your face. What?"

"Dirty thoughts, girl. Enough to make you blush."

"It's these pieces you're working on, i'n it? Looking at naked ladies on a Sunday morning! It's indecent and that's all there is to it."

"What I feel for you's indecent and that's a fact, luv. Step over here. Don't mess me about. I know what you're really like, don't I?"

"He's gone mad," Patsy declared to the heavens.

"Mad the way you like." He crossed the garden to the cottage door, took his wife into his arms, and kissed her soundly.

"Lord, Kevin, you taste all of sand!" Patsy protested when at last he released her. A streak of grey powder tinted the side of her head. Another smeared against her left breast. She brushed at her clothing, muttering with exasperation, but when she looked up and her husband grinned, her face softened and she murmured, "Half crazy. Always was, you know."

He winked and went back to his work. She continued to watch from the doorway.

From the metal cabinet, Kevin brought out the powdered pumice that he used to condition the marble prior to signing his name to a finished piece. Mixing this with water, he smeared it liberally onto his reclining nude and worked it against the stone. He gave his attention to legs and stomach, breasts and feet, taking the greatest care with the delicate work upon the face.

He heard his wife move restlessly in the doorway. She was, he saw, looking behind her into the kitchen at the red tin clock that hung above the stove.

"Half-ten," she said reflectively.

It was a statement she intended to sound self-directed, but it didn't deceive Kevin with its pretence of detachment. "Now, Pats," he soothed her, "you're just making a fuss over nothing. I can see it dead clear. Leave off, can't you? The boy'll ring home as soon as he can."

"Half-ten," she repeated, regardless. "Matt said they'd be back by Eucharist, Kev. Eucharist surely would've ended at ten. It's half-past now. Why's he not rung us?"

"He's busy, no doubt. Unpacking. There's schoolwork to be faced. Tales to be told about the weekend's fun. Then lunch with the rest of the boys. So he's forgotten to ring his mum for the moment. But he'll do it by one. Wait and see. Not to worry, luv."

Kevin knew that telling his wife not to worry about their son was as useful as asking the Thames to stop rising and falling every day with the tide just a few steps away from their own front door. He'd been offering her variations of that admonition for the last twelve and a half years. But it rarely did the slightest bit of good. Patsy *would* worry herself over every detail of Matthew's life: over whether his clothing was correctly matched; over who was cutting his hair and seeing to his teeth; over the polish on his shoes and the length of his trousers; over his choice of friends and the hobbies he pursued. She studied each one of his letters from school until she had it memorised, and if she didn't hear from him once a week, she worked herself into a state of the jitters that nothing could quell save Matthew himself. He usually did so, which made his failure to telephone after his weekend adventure in the Cotswolds all the harder to understand. This was something that Kevin would not admit to his wife, however.

Teenagers, he thought. *We're in for it now, Pats. The boy's growing up.*

Patsy's response startled her husband, who thought himself not so easily read. "I know what you're thinking, Kev. He's getting bigger. Won't want his mum fussing over him all the time. There's truth to it. I know."

"So . . . ?" he encouraged her.

"So I'll wait a bit before I ring the school."

It was, Kevin knew, the best compromise she would offer. "That's my girl," he replied and went back to his sculpture.

For the next hour he allowed himself the bliss of complete absorption into the delights of his art, losing track of time entirely. As was usually the case, his surroundings faded into insignificance, and existence was reduced to the immediate sensation of marble coming to life under his hands.

His wife had to say his name twice to return him from the twilight world he inhabited whenever he was called there by his particular muse. She'd come back to the doorway, but this time he saw that she held a black vinyl handbag in place of the tea towel, and she was wearing her new black shoes and her best navy wool coat. She had inserted a coruscating rhinestone pin haphazardly into the lapel—a sleek lioness with one paw raised and ready to strike. Its eyes were tiny specks of green.

"He's in the Sanatorium." She spoke the last word on a high note of incipient panic.

Kevin blinked, eyes drawn to the dance of light diffracting from the lioness rampant. "Sanatorium?" he repeated.

"Our Matt's in the Sanatorium, Kev! He's been there all weekend. I've just rung the school. He didn't ever go to the Morants' at all. He's sick in the San! That Morant boy didn't even know what was wrong. He hadn't seen him since Friday lunch!"

"What're you up to, girl?" Kevin queried shrewdly. He knew full well what the answer would be and sought a moment to ponder how best to stop her.

"Mattie's ill! Our boy! Lord knows what's wrong. Now, are you coming with me to that school or planning to stand there with your hands on that woman's flipping crotch for the rest of the day?"

Kevin hurriedly removed his hands from the offending part of the sculpture's anatomy. He wiped them down the sides of his work jeans, adding white abrasive cream to the dust and dirt already embedded along the seams.

"Hang on, Pats," he said. "Think for a minute."

"Think? Mattie's ill! He'll be wanting his mum."

"Will he, luv?"

Patsy worked on this thought, her lips pressed together as if in the hope of keeping further words at bay. Her spatulate fingers worried the clasp of her handbag, snapping it repeatedly open and shut. From what Kevin could see, the bag was empty. In her rush to be off, Patsy had thought nothing about putting inside a single belonging—a pound coin, a comb, a compact, anything.

He pulled a piece of old towelling from the pocket of his jeans and rubbed it along his sculpture fondly. "Think, Pats," he gentled her. "No boy wants Mum flying out to his school if he's got a bit of flu. He's liable to be a bit choked over that, isn't he? Red in the face with Mum hanging about like he needs his nappies changed and she's just the one to do it."

"Are you saying I just let it be?" Patsy shook her handbag at him to emphasise her words. "Like I wasn't interested in my own boy's well-being?"

"Not let it be."

"Then what?"

Kevin folded his towelling into a small, neat square. "Let's think this out. What did San Sister tell you's exactly wrong with the boy?"

Patsy's eyes dropped. Kevin knew what that reaction implied. He laughed at her softly. "They've a nurse right there on duty at the school and you've not rung her, Pats? Mattie'll have stubbed his toe and his mum'll go running out to West Sussex without a thought given to ringing up to see what's wrong with the boy first! What's to become of the likes of you, girl?"

Hot embarrassment was climbing its way up Patsy's neck and spreading onto her cheeks. "I'll ring now," she managed to say with dignity and went to place the call from the kitchen phone.

Kevin heard her dialling. A moment later he heard her voice. A moment after that, he heard her drop the phone. She cried out once, a terrified keening that he recognised as his own name wailed in supplication. He flung his ragged towel to one side and flew into the cottage.

At first he thought his wife was having an attack of some sort. Her face was grey, and the fist at her lips suggested that a shrieking-out in pain was being withheld by an act of will. When she heard his footsteps and swung to face him, he saw that her eyes were wild.

"He's not there. Mattie's gone, Kevin. He wasn't in the San. He's not even at the school!"

Kevin struggled to comprehend the horror that those few words implied and found he could only repeat her own statement. "Mattie? Gone?"

She seemed frozen to the spot. "Since Friday noon."

Suddenly that immense stretch of time from Friday to Sunday became a breeding ground for the sort of unspeakable images every parent must confront when first acknowledging a beloved child's disappearance. Kidnapping, molestation, religious cults, white slavery, sadism, murder. Patsy shuddered, gagged. A faint sheen of perspiration appeared on her skin.

Seeing this, fearing she might faint or have a stroke or drop dead on the spot, Kevin grasped her shoulders to offer the only comfort he knew.

"We'll be off to the school, luv," he said urgently. "We'll see about our boy. I promise you that. We'll go at once."

"Mattie!" The name rose like a prayer.

Kevin told himself that prayers were unnecessary at the moment, that Matthew was only playing the truant, that his absence from the school had a reasonable explanation which they would laugh about together in the time to come. Yet even as he thought this, a vicious tremor shook Patsy's body. She said their son's name beseechingly once again. Against all reason, Kevin found himself hoping that a god somewhere was listening to his wife.

Thumbing through her contribution to their report one last time, Detective Sergeant Barbara Havers decided that she was satisfied with the results of her weekend's labour. She clipped the fifteen tedious pages together, shoved her chair back from her desk, and went in search of her immediate superior, Detective Inspector Thomas Lynley.

He was where she had left him shortly after noon that day, alone in his office, blond head cupped in one hand, his attention directed towards his own section of the report which was spread across the top of his desk. The late Sunday afternoon sun threw long shadows against walls and across the floor, making perusing typescript without artificial light next to impossible. And since Lynley's reading spectacles had slipped disregarded to the end of his nose, Barbara entered the room noiselessly, certain that he was fast asleep.

That would not have surprised her. For the past two months Lynley had been burning the candle not only at both ends but right through the middle. His presence at the Yard had been so unceasing— generally requiring her own reluctant presence as well—that he'd been jokingly christened Mr. Ubiquitous by the other DI's in his division.

"Go hame, laddie," Inspector MacPherson would roar when he saw him in a corridor, in a meeting, or in the officers' mess. "Ye're black'ning the rest o' us. Hearkening aifter a super's position? Canna rest on the laurels o' promotion if ye're deid."

Lynley would laugh in his characteristically affable fashion and sidestep the reason behind this sixty-day stint of unremitting toil. But Barbara knew why he remained on the job long hours into the night, why he volunteered to be on call, why he took other officers' duty at the first request. It was all represented in the single postcard that lay at the moment on the edge of his desk. She picked it up.

It was five days old, badly creased from a hard journey across Europe from the Ionian Sea. Its subject was a curious procession of incense bearers, sceptre-wielding officials, and gold-gowned, bearded Greek Orthodox priests who carried a bejewelled sedan chair upon their shoulders, its sides made of glass. Resting within the chair, his shrouded head leaning against the glass as if he were asleep and not more than a thousand years dead, were the remains of Saint Spyridon. Barbara turned the card over and unabashedly read its message. She could have guessed before doing so what the tenor of the words would be.

> Tommy darling, Imagine having your poor remains carried
> through the streets of Corfu town four times a year! Good Lord,
> it does give one pause to think about the wisdom of dedicat-
> ing one's life to sanctity, doesn't it? You'll be pleased to know
> that I've made my bow to intellectual growth with a pilgrim-
> age to Jupiter's Temple at Kassiope. I dare say you'd approve of
> such Chaucerian endeavour.   H.

Barbara knew that this card was the tenth such communication from Lady Helen Clyde that Lynley had received in the last two months. Each previous one had been exactly the same, a friendly and amusing commentary upon one aspect of Greek life or another as Lady Helen moved gaily round the country in a seemingly endless journey that had begun in January only days after Lynley had asked her to marry him. Her answer had been a definitive *no,* and the postcards—all sent to New Scotland Yard and not to Lynley's home in Eaton Terrace—underscored her determination to remain unfettered by the claims of the heart.

That Lynley thought daily, if not hourly, about Helen Clyde, that he wanted her, that he loved her with a single-minded intensity were the facts which, Barbara knew, comprised the heretofore unspoken rationale behind his infinite capacity for taking on new assignments without protest. Anything to keep the howling hounds of loneliness at bay, she thought. Anything to keep the pain of living without Helen from knotting steadily, like a tumour within him.

Barbara returned the card, retreated a few steps, and expertly sailed her part of their report into his In tray. The subsequent whoosh of air across his desk, the fluttering of his papers to the floor, woke him. He started, grimaced disarmingly at having been caught sleeping, rubbed the back of his neck, and removed his spectacles.

Barbara plopped into the chair next to his desk, sighed, and ruffled her short hair with an unconscious energy that made most of it stand on end like bristles on a brush. She spoke. "Ah yes, do ye hear those bonny bells of Scotland calling to ye, lad? Tell me ye do."

His reply made its way past a stifled yawn. "Scotland, Havers? What on earth—"

"Aye. Those wee bonny bells. Calling ye home to that land of malt. Those blessit smoky tastes of liquid fire. . . ."

Lynley stretched his lengthy frame and began to gather his papers together. "Ah. Scotland," he replied. "Do I imagine this sentimental journey into the thistle is an indication that you've not tipped into your weekly allotment of alcohol, Sergeant?"

She grinned and sloughed off Robert Burns. "Let's pop round to the King's Arms, Inspector. You can buy. Two of the MacAllan and we'll both be singing 'Coming Through the Rye.' You don't want to miss that. I've the very devil of a mezzo-soprano sure to bring tears to your lovely brown eyes."

Lynley polished his spectacles, replaced them on his nose, and began an examination of her work. "I'm flattered by the invitation. Don't think I'm not. A proffered opportunity to hear you warbling touches me right to the heart, Havers. But surely there's someone else here today into whose wallet you haven't dipped your hand quite so regularly as mine. Where's Constable Nkata? Didn't I see him here this afternoon?"

"He's gone out on a call."

"More's the pity. You're out of luck, I'm afraid. I did promise Webberly this report in the morning."

Barbara felt a twinge of exasperation. He'd dodged her invitation more adroitly than she'd managed to phrase it. But she had other weapons, so she trotted out the first. "You've promised it to Webberly in the morning, sir, but you and I know he doesn't need it for another week. Get off it, Inspector. Don't you think it's about time you came back to the land of the living?"

"Havers . . ." Lynley didn't change his position. He didn't look up from the papers in his hand. His tone alone carried the implicit warning. It was a laying-down of boundaries, a declaration of superiority in the chain of command. Barbara had worked with him long enough to know what it meant when he said her name with such studied neutrality. She was barging into an area off-limits. Her presence was not wanted and would not be admitted without a fight.

Well and good, she thought with resignation. But she could not resist a final sortie into the guarded regions of his private life.

She jerked her head towards the postcard. "Our Helen's not giving you much to go on, is she?"

His head snapped up. He dropped the report. But the jarring ring of the telephone on his desk precluded reply.

Lynley picked up the phone to hear the voice of one of the girls who worked reception in the Yard's unfriendly grey-on-black marble lobby. Visitor below, the adenoidal voice announced without preliminaries. Bloke called John Corntel asking for Inspector Asherton. That's *you,* I s'pose? Though why some people can't ever keep a body's proper name straight . . . even when a body takes to stringing names together like some flipping royal *and* expects reception to know each and every one so's to sort it all out when old school-mates come calling—

Lynley interrupted this verbal tally of woes. "Corntel? Sergeant Havers will come down to fetch him."

He hung up upon a martyred voice asking him what he thought he'd like to be called *next* week. Would it be Lynley, Asherton, or some other dusty family title that he thought he'd try out for a month or two? Havers, apparently anticipating his request from what she had heard of the conversation, was already heading out of his office for the lift.

Lynley watched her go, her wool trousers flapping round her stubby legs and a scrap of torn paper clinging like a moth to the elbow of her worn Aran sweater. He contemplated this unexpected visit from Corntel, a ghost from the past, to be sure.

They'd been schoolmates at Eton, Corntel a King's Scholar, one of the elite. In those days, Lynley recalled, Corntel had cut quite a figure among the seniors, a tall and brooding youth, very melancholy, favoured with hair the colour of sepia and a set of aristocratic features reminiscent of those endowed Napoleon on the romantically painted canvases by Antoine-Jean Gros. As if with the intention of holding true to physical type, Corntel had been preparing to take his A-levels in literature, music, and art. What had happened to him after Eton, Lynley could not have said.

With this image of John Corntel in mind, part of Lynley's own history, it was with some surprise that he rose to greet the man who followed Sergeant Havers into his office less than five minutes later. Only the height remained—two inches over six feet, eye to eye with Lynley. But the frame that had once allowed him to stand so tall and sure of himself, a promising scholar in the privileged world of Eton, was round-shouldered now, as if protecting him from the potential of physical contact. That was not the only difference in the man.

The curls of youth had given way to hair close cropped to the skull and peppered with premature grey. That miraculous amalgamation of bone, flesh, contour, and colour that had resulted in a face speaking of both sensuality and intelligence now bore a pallor usually associated with sickrooms, and the skin looked stretched across the bones. His dark eyes were bloodshot.

An explanation had to exist for the change that had come upon Corntel in the seventeen years since Lynley had last seen him. People did not alter so drastically without a central cause. In this case it looked as if a burning or a freezing at the core of the man, having destroyed that interior substance, now pushed forward to decimate the rest.

"Lynley. Asherton. I wasn't sure which name to use," Corntel said diffidently. But the timidity seemed studied, a decision about salutations made well in advance. He offered his hand. It was hot, and felt feverish.

"I don't use the title much. Just Lynley."

"Useful thing, a title. We called you the Viscount of Vacillation at school, didn't we? But where did that come from? I can't even remember."

Lynley preferred not to. It stirred up memories. How they assaulted the protected regions of the psyche. "Viscount Vacennes."

"That was it. The secondary title. One of the joys of being the oldest son of an earl."

"Dubious joys at best."

"Perhaps."

Lynley watched the other man's eyes sweep over the office, taking in the cabinets, the shelves and their books, the general disarray of his desk, the two American Southwest prints. They came to rest on the room's single photograph, and Lynley waited for the other man to comment upon its solitary subject. Corntel and Lynley had both been at Eton with Simon Allcourt-St. James, and since the photograph of him was more than thirteen years old, Corntel would no doubt recognise the jubilant face of that wild-haired young cricket player who was frozen in time, captured in that pure, exhilarating joy of youth with trousers ripped and stained, a sweater pushed above the elbows, and a streak of dirt on his arm. He was leaning against a cricket bat, laughing in sheer delight. Three years before Lynley crippled him.

"St. James." Corntel nodded. "I've not thought of him in ages. Lord. Time does go, doesn't it?"

"It does." Lynley continued to study his old schoolmate curiously, noting the manner in which his smile flashed and disappeared, noting how his hands drifted to his jacket pockets and patted them down as if reassuring himself of the presence of some item he intended to produce.

Sergeant Havers flipped on the lights to dispel the gloom of the late afternoon. She looked at Lynley. *Stay or go?* her eyes asked. He nodded her towards one of the office chairs. She sat, reached in her trouser pocket, brought out a packet of cigarettes, and shook out several.

"Have one?" she offered Corntel. "The Inspector here's decided to give up yet another vice—curse him for his sanctimonious desire to stop polluting the air—and I hate to smoke alone."

Corntel seemed surprised that Havers was still in the room, but he accepted her offer and produced a lighter.

"Yes. I will. Thank you." His eyes danced to Lynley and then away. His right hand rolled the cigarette against his left palm. His teeth gnawed momentarily at his lower lip. "I've come for your help," he said in a rush. "I pray you'll do something, Tommy. I'm in serious trouble."

2

"A boy's gone missing from the school, and as I'm his housemaster, I'm responsible for what's happened to him. God, if something *has* . . ."

Corntel explained himself tersely, smoking between scattered phrases. He was housemaster and head of English at Bredgar Chambers, an independent school tucked into a roll of land between Crawley and Horsham in West Sussex, little more than an hour's drive from London. The boy in question—thirteen years old, a third former, and hence new to the school this year—was a Hammersmith child. The entire situation appeared to be an elaborate ruse orchestrated by the boy to allow him a weekend of perfect freedom. Except that something had gone wrong, somehow, somewhere, and now the boy was missing, had been missing for more than forty-eight hours.

"I think he may be a runaway." Corntel rubbed his eyes. "Tommy, I should have *seen* that something was bothering the boy. I should have known. That's part of my job. Obviously, if he was determined to leave the school, if he's been that unhappy all these months and I've failed to see it . . . God in heaven, the parents arrived at the school in a state of hysteria, one of the board of governors just happened by at the time, and the Headmaster has spent all afternoon trying to keep everything out of the hands of the local police, trying to keep the parents calm, and trying to find out who saw the boy last, and why, most of all *why*, he ran off without a word. I don't know what to tell anyone, how to excuse . . . how to make reparation or find some sort of resolution." He ran a hand back over his short hair, tried and failed to force a smile. "I didn't know where to turn at first. Then I thought of you. It seemed an inspired solution. After all, we were mates back at Eton, you and I. And . . . Christ, I sound like an idiot. I can't even think straight any longer."

"This is a matter for the West Sussex police," Lynley replied. "If indeed it's a police matter at all. Why haven't they been called in, John?"

"We've a group on the campus—called the Bredgar Volunteers. Isn't that an absurd name?—and they're out looking for him now, assuming that he's not got that far. Or assuming that something happened to him nearby. It was the Headmaster's decision not to send for the police. He and I spoke. I told him I had a contact here at the Yard."

Lynley could colour in the details of Corntel's situation well enough. Beyond his legitimate concern for the boy, John Corntel's job—perhaps his entire career—rested upon finding him quickly and finding him well. It was one thing for a child to be homesick, perhaps to make an attempt to go to his parents or his old friends, only to be stopped a short distance—and a short time—away from the school. But this was serious indeed. According to the halting details Corntel had given them, the boy had last been seen on Friday afternoon, with no one giving a thought as to his whereabouts since then. As to the distance he had probably managed to travel since that time . . . The situation was more than grave for Corntel. It was a prelude to professional disaster. No wonder he was assuring the Headmaster that he could handle it himself, discreetly, quickly, and well.

Unfortunately, there was nothing that Lynley could do. Scotland Yard did not take on cases in this manner, and the force certainly did not step into the jurisdiction of the county police without a formal request from the regional constabulary. So Corntel's trip into London was a waste of time and the sooner he got back to the school and got the case into the hands of the appropriate authorities, the better it would be. Lynley sought to convince him of this, gathering what disjointed facts he could, determined to use them to lead Corntel to the inescapable conclusion that the local police had to be involved.

"What exactly happened?" he asked. Sergeant Havers, in rote reaction to her superior's question, reached for a spiral notebook on Lynley's desk and began jotting down questions and responses in her usual competent fashion. She squinted against the smoke from her cigarette, coughed, stubbed it out on the sole of her shoe, and tossed it into the rubbish.

"The boy—Matthew Whateley—had an exeat this weekend to go to the home of another student, Harry Morant. Morant's family has a country house in Lower Slaughter, and they'd arranged a gathering there for Harry's birthday. Five of the boys were going, six including Harry. They had parents' permission. Everything was in order. Matthew was one of them."

"Who are the Morants?"

"Top drawer sort of family," Corntel said. "Three older sons have gone through Bredgar Chambers. A sister's in the lower sixth there now. We take girls in their last two years," he added uselessly. "Lower and upper sixth girls. I think what happened is that Matthew got cold feet about the business because of that. I mean, because of the family—the Morants—not because we take girls at the school."

"I don't see why. What's the family got to do with it?"

Corntel shifted in his seat with a look at Sergeant Havers. Lynley saw in that nervous sweep of the eyes what would be said next. Corntel had heard Havers' distinct working class accent. If the Morants were being brought forward as the source of the problem—and were, as Corntel said, a top drawer family—then Matthew was no doubt, like Havers, from a distinctly different part of the chest.

"I think Matthew got cold feet," Corntel explained. "He's a city boy, this is his first year in an independent school. He's always been in the state schools before. He's always lived at home. Now that he's mixing with a different sort of people . . . it takes time. It's difficult to adjust." His hand moved out, open-palmed, in an appeal for mutual understanding. "You know what I mean."

Lynley saw Havers' head come up, saw her eyes narrow at the implication behind Corntel's words. She had, he well knew, always worn her working class background like a suit of armour. "And when Matthew failed to show up for the journey on Friday? There must have been some meeting place where the boys gathered before they set off for their weekend together. Didn't they wonder where he was? Didn't they report to you when he didn't show up?"

"They thought they knew where he was. We had games Friday afternoon, and the trip to Lower Slaughter was scheduled afterwards. The boys are all on the same hockey team. Matthew didn't show up for the game, but everyone thought it was in perfect order because the third form hockey master—Cowfrey Pitt, one of our teachers—had received a note from the Sanatorium, saying that Matthew had become ill and wouldn't be there for the game. When they heard this, the boys assumed that he wouldn't be going on the weekend either. It seemed logical enough at the time."

"What sort of note was it?"

"An off-games chit. Just a standard form from the Sanatorium with Matthew's name on it. Frankly, it looks to me as if Matthew set the entire situation up in advance. He would get permission from home to leave campus and arrange it to look as if he were going to the Morants'. At the same time, he would have in his possession an off-games chit indicating that he was ill in the Sanatorium. But because the chit wasn't legitimate, I would get no copy of it from the San. So I would think Matthew left with the Morants. The Morants, in the meantime, would think he was still at the school. Then the weekend would be his own to do as he liked. Which is exactly what he did, the little beggar!"

"You didn't check up on his whereabouts?"

Corntel leaned forward and crushed out his cigarette. The movement was unsteady. Ashes spilled onto Lynley's desk. "I thought I *knew* his whereabouts. I thought he was with the Morants."

"And the hockey master—was it Cowfrey Pitt?—didn't inform you that he'd gone to the Sanatorium?"

"Cowfrey assumed the San would let me know. That's how it's usually done. And if I'd been told Matthew was ill, I *would* have gone to the San to see him. Of course I would have." The strength of Corntel's protestations was curious. With each of them, the man spoke more intently.

"You've a head of house as well, don't you? What was he doing all this time? Was he in school this weekend?"

"Brian Byrne. Yes. A senior boy. A prefect. Most of the seniors were off on exeats—at least those who hadn't gone to a hockey tournament in the North—but he was there. Right in the house. As far as he knew, Matthew was with the Morants. He didn't check into that any more than I did. Why should he have done so? If any checking was to be done, it was my responsibility, not Brian's. I'll not foist it off onto my prefect. I won't."

Like the earlier protestations, there was peculiar force behind Corntel's declaration, child of a need to take all blame upon himself. Lynley knew that there was usually only one reason for the existence of such a need. If Corntel wanted the blame, no doubt he deserved it.

"He must have known that he'd be out of his depth with the Morants. He must have felt it," Corntel said.

"You seem certain of that."

"He was a scholarship student." Corntel seemed to feel that statement explained everything. Nonetheless, he went on to say, "Good boy. Hard worker."

"Liked by the other students?" When Corntel hesitated, Lynley said, "After all, if he'd been invited for a weekend at one of their homes, it seems reasonable to conclude he was liked."

"Yes, yes. He must have been. It's just that . . . Do you see how I've failed the boy? I don't *know*. He was so quiet. All he ever seemed to do was his schoolwork. He never had a problem. He never even spoke of one. And his parents were so keen to have him go on this weekend. His father said as much to me when he wrote his permission. Something like 'Nice to have Mattie move into the world a bit.' Mattie. That's what they called him."

"Where are the parents now?"

Corntel's face pinched with misery. "I don't know. At the school perhaps. Or at home waiting for word. If the Headmaster hasn't managed to stop them, they may have gone directly to the police themselves."

"Has Bredgar Chambers access to a local police force?"

"There's a constable in Cissbury—that's the nearest village. Otherwise, we're under the jurisdiction of the Horsham force." He smiled grimly. "Part of their patch, you'd call it, wouldn't you?"

"Yes. And I'm afraid it's not part of mine."

Corntel's shoulders caved in further at this admission. "Surely you can do something, Tommy. Put some sort of wheels in motion."

"Discreet wheels?"

"Yes. All right. Whatever you want to call them. It's a personal favour, I know. I've no rights here. But for God's sake, we have Eton."

It was a draw upon loyalties. The old school tie. That assumption of devotion to the calls of the past. Lynley wanted to cut beyond it as ruthlessly as he could. The policeman in him insisted that he do so. But the boy who had once shared school days with Corntel was not quite as dead as Lynley wanted him to be. So he asked:

"If he had run off, perhaps with the intention of coming up to London, he'd need transportation, wouldn't he? How close are you to the trains? To the motorway? To one of the larger roads?"

Corntel seemed to take this as the extending hand of help he wanted. He answered definitively, eager to be of assistance.

"We're not very near anything useful, Tommy, which is why parents feel secure in sending their children to the school. It's isolated. There's no trouble to get into. There's nothing around to distract. Matthew would have had quite a hike to get safely away. He couldn't afford to hitch a ride too near the school because if he did, the chance would have been very good that someone from the school—one of the instructors, perhaps, or a workman or the porter— might have gone driving by, seen him, and packed him right back where he belongs."

"So he probably wouldn't have kept to the road at all."

"I don't think he would. I think he'd have had to go through the fields, through St. Leonard's Forest, up to Crawley and the M23. He'd have been safe at that point. He would have been seen as just any child. No one would suspect that he was from Bredgar Chambers."

"St. Leonard's Forest," Lynley said reflectively. "The likeliest possibility is that he's still there, isn't it? Lost perhaps. Hungry."

"And two nights without shelter in March. Exposure. Hypothermia. Starvation. A broken leg. A bad fall. A broken neck." Corntel compiled the list bitterly.

"Starvation's unlikely after only three days," Lynley responded. He did not add the more damning remark that any of the others were distinctly possible. "Is he a big child? Hefty?"

Corntel shook his head. "Not at all. He's very small for his age. Delicate bones. Extremely fragile. Good structure in the face." He paused, his eyes focusing on an image the others could not see. "Dark hair. Dark eyes. Long-fingered hands. Perfect skin. Lovely skin."

Havers tapped a pencil against her notebook. She looked at Lynley. Seeing her do so, Corntel stopped speaking. Colour dashed across his face in great bruising patches.

Lynley pushed his chair away from his desk and let his eyes rest on one of the two prints on his wall in which an Indian woman dumped a basket of peppers onto a blanket. It was a compilation of vibrant colours. Her veil of black hair, the living red of the vegetables, the tawny velvet of her skin, her purple gown, the blend of rose and blue background that called the time of day *sunset.* Beauty, he knew, always offered its own form of seduction.

"Have you brought a picture of the boy?" Lynley asked. "Can you write out an accurate description of him?" The last question, he thought, would probably be unnecessary.

"Yes. Of course. Both." Never before had Lynley heard such relief.

"Then if you'll leave them with the sergeant, we'll see if there's anything we can do from this end. Perhaps he's already been picked up in Crawley and is too afraid to give his name. Or even closer to London. One can never tell."

"I thought . . . I *hoped* you'd help. I've already . . ." Corntel reached into the breast pocket of his coat, bringing out a photograph and a folded page of typescript. He had the grace to look faintly abashed by the assumption of Lynley's cooperation that was implied by his possession of both.

Lynley took them wearily. Corntel had been confident of his man indeed. The old Viscount of Vacillation would hardly desert one of his former schoolmates now.

Barbara Havers read the description that Corntel had left with them. She studied the photograph of the boy as Lynley dumped out the ashtray that she and Corntel had managed to fill during the interview. He wiped it carefully with a tissue.

"God, you're getting to be an unbearable prig over this smoking business, Inspector," Barbara complained. "Should I start wearing a scarlet S on my chest?"

"Not at all. But either I clean the ashtray or find myself licking it in desperation. Somehow, cleaning seems closer to a behaviour I can live with. But only just, I'm afraid." He looked up, smiled.

She laughed even through her exasperation. "Why did you give up smoking? Why not march right into an early grave with the rest of us? The more the merrier. You know the sort of thing."

He didn't answer. Instead, his eyes went to the postcard propped up against a coffee cup on his desk. So Barbara knew. Lady Helen Clyde did not smoke. Perhaps she would find more acceptable upon her return a man who had given up smoking as well.

"Do you really think that's going to make a difference, Inspector?"

His reply was as good as ignoring her altogether. "If the boy's run away, I shouldn't be surprised if he turns up in a few days. Perhaps in Crawley. Perhaps in the city. But if he doesn't turn up, as callous as it sounds, his body may. Are they prepared for that, I wonder."

Barbara skilfully turned the statement to her own use. "Is anyone ever really prepared for the worst, Inspector?"

Send my roots rain. Send my roots rain.

With those four words pressing into her brain like a persistent melody, Deborah St. James sat in her Austin, eyes fixed on the lych gate of St. Giles' Church outside the town of Stoke Poges. She scrutinised nothing in particular. Instead, she tried to count how many times over the last month she had recited not just those final words but Hopkins' entire sonnet. She had started every day with it, had made it the force that propelled her from beds and hotel rooms, into her car, and through site after site where she took photographs like an automaton. But beyond every morning's determined recitation of those fourteen lines of supplication, she could not have said how many times during each day she had returned to it, when some unexpected sight or sound she was unprepared for broke through her defences and attacked her calm.

She understood why the lines came to her now. St. Giles' Church was the last stop in her four-week photographic odyssey. At the end of this afternoon she would return to London, avoiding the M4, which would take her there quickly, and choosing instead the A4 with its traffic signals, its congestion round Heathrow, its infinite stream of suburbs grimy with soot and the grey end of winter. And its additional blessing of extending the journey. That was the crucial part. She didn't yet see how she could face the end of it. She didn't yet see how she could face Simon.

Ages ago when she had accepted this assignment to photograph a selection of the literary landmarks of the country, she had planned it so that Stoke Poges, where Thomas Gray composed "Elegy Written in a Country Churchyard," would fall directly after Tintagel and Glastonbury, and thus bring her month of work to a conclusion only a few miles from her doorstep. But Tintagel and Glastonbury, rich with ineluctable reminders of King Arthur and Guinevere, of their ill-fated and ultimately barren love, had only given teeth to the despondency with which she had begun the trip. Those teeth bit; today on this final afternoon, they tore, working upon her heart, laying bare its worst wound. . . .

She *wouldn't* think of it. She opened the car door, took up her camera case and tripod, and walked across the car park to the lych gate. Beyond it she could see that the graveyard was divided into two sections and that midway down a curved concrete path, a second lych gate and second graveyard stood.

The air was cold for late March, as if deliberately withholding the promise of spring. Birds tittered sporadically in the trees, but other than the occasional muffled roar of a jet from Heathrow, the graveyard itself was quiet. It seemed a suitable spot for Thomas Gray to have created his poem, to have chosen as his own resting place.

Closing the first lych gate behind her, Deborah walked along the path between two lines of tree roses. New growth sprouted from them—tight buds, slim branches, tender young leaves—but this springtime regeneration contrasted sharply with the area in which the trees themselves grew. This outer graveyard was not maintained. The grass was uncut, the stones left to lurch at odd angles with haphazard disregard.

Deborah went under the second lych gate. It was more ornate than the first and, perhaps in the hope of keeping vandals away from the delicate oak fretwork along the line of its roof—or perhaps from the graveyard and the church itself—a floodlight was secured to a beam. But this was a useless safeguard, for the light was shattered and shards of glass lay here and there on the ground.

Once inside the interior churchyard, Deborah looked for Thomas Gray's tomb, her final photographic responsibility. Almost immediately, however, as she made a fleeting survey of the monuments and markers, she saw instead a trail of feathers.

They lay like the result of an augur's handiwork, a rebarbative collection of ash-coloured down. Against the manicured lawn, they looked like small puffs of smoke that had taken on substance rather than drifting off to be absorbed into the sky. But the number of feathers and the unmistakably violent way in which they were strewn about suggested a vicious battle for life, and Deborah followed them the short distance to where the defeated party lay.

The bird's body was about two feet from the yew hedge that separated inner and outer graveyards. Deborah stiffened at the sight of it. Even though she had known what she would find, the brutality of the poor creature's death evoked in her an answering rush of pity so intense—so utterly absurd, she told herself—that she found her vision momentarily obscured by tears. All that remained of the bird was a frail blood-imbued rib cage covered by an insubstantial and inadequate cuirass of stained down. There was no head. Frail legs and claws had been torn off. The creature could have once been a pigeon or a dove, but now it was a shell in which life had once existed, all too briefly.

How fleeting it was. How quickly it could be extinguished.

"No!" Deborah felt the anguish well within her and knew she lacked the will to defeat it. She forced herself to think of something else—of burying the bird, of brushing the scurrying ants from the serrated ridge of one cracked rib—but the effort was useless. Hopkins' sonnet, whispered in a rush against a rising onslaught of sorrow, was insufficient armour. So she wept, watching the dead bird's image blur, praying that a time would soon come when she could put an end to grief.

For the last four weeks, work had been an anodyne. She turned to it now, backing away from the bird, clutching her equipment in hands that were cold.

The job called for a set of photographs which reflected the piece of literature that had inspired them. Since late February, Deborah had explored the Brontës' Yorkshire and given herself over to Ponden Hall and High Withens; she had set up camera and tripod for a moonlit examination of Tintern Abbey; she had photographed the Cobb and most particularly Granny's Teeth from which Louisa Musgrove took her fatal fall; she had wandered the tournament field in Ashby de la Zouch, sat on the sidelines and watched the comings and goings in the pump room in Bath, walked the streets of Dorchester looking for the slow hand of destiny that destroyed Michael Henchard, and felt the enchantment of Hill Top Farm.

In each case, the site itself—and her research into the literature that had grown from it—inspired her camera. But as she looked round this final location and caught sight of the two structures that, from their proximity to the church, had to be the tombs she had come to inspect, she felt the pricking of irritation. How on earth, she thought, was she ever going to make something so inordinately mundane look attractive?

The tombs were identical, constructed of brick, slabbed across the top with lichened stone. The only decorative detail that had been supplied them had been done so by two hundred years of visitors who had obligingly carved their names into the bricks. Deborah sighed, stepped back, and examined the church.

Even here there was little scope for artistry. The building fought with itself, two different periods of architecture moulded together to form a whole. Plain fifteenth-century Tudor windows set into a faded redbrick wall existed hand-in-glove with the perpendicular structure of a lancet window nearby, this set into the older chalk and flint of the Norman Chancel. The effect could hardly be called picturesque.

Deborah frowned. "A disaster," she murmured. From her camera case she took the rough manuscript of the book which her pictures would illustrate and, spreading several pages across the top of Thomas Gray's tomb, she spent a few minutes reading not only "Elegy Written in a Country Churchyard" but also the interpretation of the poem supplied by the Cambridge don whose manuscript this was. Her eyes stopped thoughtfully, with growing understanding, upon the poem's eleventh stanza. She dwelt upon it.

> Can storied urn or animated bust,
> Back to its mansion call the fleeting breath?
> Can honour's voice provoke the silent dust,
> Or flatt'ry soothe the dull cold ear of death?

She looked up, seeing the graveyard as Gray had intended her to see it, knowing that her photographs had to reflect the simplicity of life that the poet had sought to celebrate with his words. She cleared her papers from the tomb and set up her tripod.

It would be nothing lush, nothing clever, just photographs that used light and dark, angle and depth to depict the innocence and beauty of a country evening at dusk. She worked to capture the humble quality of the environment in which Gray's rude forefathers of the hamlet were sleeping, completing her catalogue of impressions with a photograph of the yew tree under which the poet ostensibly wrote his verse.

That done, she stepped away from her equipment and gazed towards the east, towards London. There was, she knew, no more putting it off. There was no further excuse to keep her from home. But she needed preparation prior to facing her husband. She sought it by going into the church.

Her curse, she saw, would be the centrepiece of the nave, that object upon which her eyes fell when the door closed behind her. It was an octagonal marble baptismal font, dwarfed beneath the arched timber ceiling. Each side of the font bore intricate carving, and two tall pewter candlesticks stood behind it, waiting to be lit for the ceremony that brought another child to Christianity.

Deborah walked to the font and touched the smooth oak that covered it. Just for a moment, she let herself imagine the infant in her arms, the tender pressure of its head against her breast. She let herself hear its cry of indignation as the water poured over its sweet, defenceless brow. She let herself feel the tiny, fragile hand curve over her finger. She let herself believe that she had not—this fourth time in eighteen months—miscarried Simon's child. She let herself pretend that she had not been in hospital, that the last conversation with her doctor had never occurred. But his words intruded. She could not escape.

"An abortion doesn't necessarily preclude the possibility of future successful pregnancies, Deborah. But in some cases it might. You said it was more than six years ago. There might have been complications. Scarring, that sort of thing. We won't know that for a certainty until we do some thorough tests. So if you and your husband really want—"

"No!"

The doctor's face had shown immediate comprehension. "Then Simon doesn't know?"

"I was only eighteen. I was in America. He doesn't ... he *can't* ..."

Even now she reeled from the thought of that. She felt in panic for the edge of a pew and, jerking open its small door, she stumbled inside and dropped onto the seat.

You will, she told herself with a ruthless desire to inflict as much pain as possible, never have another child. You might have had one once. You might have felt that frail life take shape within your body. But you destroyed it, discarded it, threw it away. Now you pay. Now you are punished in the only coin you can understand. You will never have Simon's child. Another woman might. Another woman could. But the mingling of your body and your love with Simon's will not produce a child. That will never happen. You will not do this.

She stared at the needlepoint kneelers that hung against the back of the pew, each one centred with a cross, each one directing her to turn to the Lord to assuage a despair that was without limit. Musty-smelling blue and red hymnals offered her songs of praise and thanksgiving. Dusty silk poppy wreaths hung against the far walls, and even at this distance Deborah could read the signs beneath them. *Brownies, Girl Guides, Rangers of Stoke Poges.* There was no comfort here.

She left the pew, walked to the altar rail. This too had its message, lettered in yellow onto a faded blue pad that covered the stones: "Come unto me all ye that travail and are heavy laden and I will refresh you."

Refresh, she thought bitterly, *but not change, not cure, and not forgive. There is no miracle here for me, no Lourdes to bathe in, no laying-on of hands, no absolution.* She left the church.

Outside, the sun was beginning to set. Deborah retrieved her equipment and retraced her steps down the path towards her car. At the interior lych gate, she turned for a last look at the church, as if it might give her the peace of mind she sought. The setting sun was shooting up final rays of dying light, like an aureole that backdropped the trees behind the church and the crenellated Norman tower that housed its bells.

At another time and without a thought, she would have taken a photograph, capturing the slow change in the sky's hue as the day's death intensified the sunset. But at this moment she could only watch the light's beauty fade and fail, and she knew she could no longer avoid the homecoming and Simon's unsuspecting, unconditional love.

Across her path just inches from her feet, two squirrels scampered, chattering angrily. They were spoiling with one another over a tidbit of food, each determined to be victor in the fray. They raced round the side of an elaborate marble tomb at the graveyard's edge and scrambled onto the waist-high flintstone wall that separated the church property from the back field of a local farm, screened off by several heavy-limbed conifers. Back and forth they flew along the top of the wall, first one then the other surging into the attack. Paws, teeth, tiny legs all embroiled in a fight as the cherished food dropped onto the ground below.

It was the diversion Deborah needed. "Here, no!" she said. "Don't fight. Stop it! Now!"

She approached the two animals and, seeing her coming, they fled over the side of the wall and up into the trees.

"Well, at least that's better than fighting, isn't it?" she said, looking up into the branches that overhung the graveyard. "Behave yourselves now. It's not polite to quarrel. It's not even the place."

One of the squirrels was tucked into the joint of a branch and the tree trunk. The other had disappeared. But the one that remained watched her with bright eyes from his position of safety. After a moment, feeling secure, he began to groom himself, rubbing paws sleepily over his face as if he intended to nap.

"I wouldn't be so sure of myself if I were you," Deborah warned. "That little bully is probably waiting for just this sort of opportunity to pounce again. Where do you suppose he's gone?"

She started to look for the other squirrel, moving her eyes along the branches fruitlessly and then dropping them after a time to the ground.

"You don't think he's clever enough to—"

Her voice died. Her mouth was instantly dry. Words fled. Thoughts dissolved.

A child's naked body was lying beneath the tree.

3

Horror immobilised her. It was a shaft of ice driven down the length of her spine, rooting her to the spot. Details intensified, impelled into her brain by the force of shock.

Deborah felt her lips part, felt the rush of air distend her lungs with an unnatural force. Only a terrified shriek could dispel the air fast enough, before her lungs burst and left her helpless.

Yet she couldn't cry out and even if she did so, there was no one nearby to hear her. So she only whispered, "Oh God." Then uselessly, "Simon." And then, although she didn't want to do so, she stared, hands drawn into fists and muscles coiled, ready to run if she had to, when she could.

The child was lying partially on its stomach just beyond the flintstone wall in a bed of bloomless creeping jenny. By the length and the cut of hair it appeared to be a boy. He was very dead.

Even if Deborah had been silly enough or hysterical enough to convince herself that he was merely asleep, explaining why he would be sleeping completely naked in a late afternoon growing colder by the minute was an impossibility. And why under a tree in a copse of pines where the temperature was even lower than it would be had he sought out the last rays of the afternoon sun? And why would he sleep in that unusual position, with his right hip taking the burden of his weight and his legs splayed out, and his right arm twisted awkwardly so that it was doubled up beneath itself, and his head turned to the left with three quarters of it pressed into the ground, into the creeping jenny? Yet his skin was quite flushed—very nearly red—and surely that indicated warmth, life, the pulse and flow of blood. . . .

The squirrels resumed their bickering, racing down the tree that had sheltered them, scampering over the inert form near the trunk. The tiny claw of the lead squirrel caught at the flesh of the child's left thigh, held, and made the animal a prisoner. Wild chattering erupted, companion to a frantic scramble for freedom. The proximity of his pursuer gave fire to the squirrel's need to escape. The child's flesh tore. The animal vanished.

Deborah saw that no blood seeped from the wound the claw had made, small though it was. That seemed momentarily odd until she remembered that the dead do not bleed. Only the living have that pleasure.

At last she cried out, spinning away. But every impression stayed so vividly before her that she knew she might as well have gone on staring forever. A leaf caught in hair the colour of walnuts; a crescent scar cradling the left kneecap; a pear-shaped birthmark at the base of the spine; and running along the length of the visible parts of the left side of the body, an odd bruising of the flesh, as if the child had been hurled down on his side sometime in the past.

He could have been asleep. He *should* have been asleep. But even Deborah's brief viewing of him from a distance of two yards had allowed her to see the telling abrasions at his wrists and ankles: stark white flecks of dead skin against a background that was red and inflamed. She knew what that meant. She guessed what the uniform circular burns along the tender flesh of his inner arm meant as well.

He wasn't asleep. Death had not come to him as a friend.

"God, *God*," she cried out.

Her words gave her sudden, unexpected strength. She ran towards the car park.

Simon Allcourt-St. James pulled his old MG next to the police line that had been set up at the entrance to the car park of St. Giles' Church. Briefly his headlamps shone upon the white face of a young, very gawky police constable who maintained a duty post there. He seemed an unnecessary appurtenance, for although the church did not stand in complete isolation, the houses in the surrounding neighbourhood were not closely situated to it, and no curious crowd had gathered upon the road.

But it was Sunday, St. James recalled. Evensong was due to be celebrated within the hour. Someone would have to be present to turn the faithful away.

Down the narrow lane that led into the car park, he could see an arc of lights where the incidents room had been set up by the police. A stark blue flashing broke into the white illumination there with a steady, pulsating rhythm. Someone had allowed a police car's light to continue to whirl, disregarded, on its roof.

St. James switched off the MG's ignition and released the hand grip that operated the clutch. He got out of the car awkwardly, his braced left leg landing at an irritating angle that put him off balance for a moment. The young constable watched him right himself, his face wearing an expression that said he was unsure whether to go to the other man's assistance or warn him off the grounds. He chose the latter. It was more within his purview.

"Can't stop here, sir," he barked. "Police investigation in progress."

"I know, Constable. I've come for my wife. Your DI phoned me. She found the body."

"You'll be Mr. St. James, then. Sorry, sir." The constable unabashedly examined the other man as if this would allow him to verify his identity. "I didn't recognise you." When St. James did not make an immediate reply, the young man seemed to feel compelled to continue. "I did see you on the news last week, but you didn't—"

St. James interrupted. "Of course." He anticipated the rest of the embarrassed words that halted from the constable's mouth. *On the news, you didn't look crippled.* Certainly not. Why ever should he? Standing on the steps of the Old Bailey, submitting to an interview about the recent use of genetic fingerprinting in a court of law, why should he look crippled? The camera was kept on his face. It didn't make a study of the worst that fate had done to his body.

"Is my wife in the incidents room?" he asked.

The constable waved in the direction of a driveway across the road. "They've kept her in the house over there. That's where she made the call to us."

St. James nodded his thanks and crossed the road. The house in question stood a short distance behind two wrought-iron gates that hung open from a brick wall. It was a nondescript building with a pantiled roof, a three-car garage, and white curtains—all of identical pattern—at the windows. There was no front garden, only a wide expanse of driveway edging a hillock that, along with the wall, shielded the house from the road. The front door was a single sheet of opaque glass framed in white wood.

When St. James rang the bell, the door was opened by another constable, this one a woman. She directed him to the sitting room at the back of the house, where four people sat on chintz-covered chairs and a sofa surrounding a coffee table.

St. James paused in the doorway. The scene before him was like a tableau consisting of two men and two women who posed in a study of gently probing confrontation. The men wore their police identities like suits of clothes even though neither was in uniform. They leaned forward in their chairs, one with a notebook and the other with a hand extended as if to emphasise some remark. The women sat without speaking or looking at one another, perhaps in the expectation of further questions.

One of the women was a girl of not more than seventeen. She wore a shapeless terry robe stained with chocolate on one of its cuffs and a pair of thick woollen socks that were overlarge and dusty-bottomed. She was small, excessively pallid, and her lips were cracked as if from exposure to harsh wind or sun. She was not unattractive; rather she was sweet-looking in a wispy sort of way. But it was clear that she was unwell. Next to her fleeting prettiness, Deborah was like fire with her mass of flaming hair and ivory skin.

Although St. James had wanted to go to his wife several times during her trip, Deborah had refused his offers to meet her both in Yorkshire and in Bath, so he had not seen her for a month. Instead, he had only spoken to her on the telephone, in conversations that, with the passing weeks, had grown more and more strained and difficult to complete. Each time her hesitant speech revealed to him the extent to which she continued to mourn the child they had lost, but she would not allow him to speak of it to her, saying only, "Please, no," when he tried. As he saw her now, absorbing her presence as if presence alone could bind her to him once again, he realised that he had never understood until this moment the terrible risk attendant to giving his love to Deborah.

She looked up and saw him. She smiled, but he read the heart-ache in her eyes. They had never been able to lie to him. "Simon."

The others looked in his direction and he came into the room, crossed to his wife's chair, touched her bright hair. He wanted to kiss her, to hold her, to infuse her with strength. But he only said, "You're all right?"

"Of course. I don't know why they phoned you at all. I can certainly get back to London on my own."

"The DI said you weren't looking very well when he got out here."

"The shock, I suppose. But I'm well enough now." Her appearance belied the words. There were dark circles under her eyes, and her clothes hung upon her loosely, testament to the amount of weight she had lost in the last four weeks. Seeing this, St. James felt a prickling of fear.

"Just a minute more, Mrs. St. James, and you can be on your way." The older policeman, probably a sergeant who'd been assigned the duty of preliminary enquiries, turned his attention to the girl. "Miss Feld," he said. "Cecilia, if I may?"

The girl nodded, her face chary, as if the request to use her given name were the kind of liberty that led to a trap.

"You've been ill, I take it?"

"Ill?" The girl seemed oblivious of the fact that her choice of clothing at six o'clock in the evening was hardly apt to suggest anything other than ill health. "I . . . no, I'm not ill. I've not been ill. Perhaps a bit of flu, but not ill. Not really."

"Then we can take you one last time through everything," the policeman said. "Just to make certain we've the facts straight and proper?" He phrased it as a question, but no one thought it was anything other than an indication of what would happen next.

Cecilia's overall appearance suggested that going through another round of parry and thrust with the police was the last thing she could bear at the moment. She looked sapped and worn. She crossed her arms in front of her, and lowered her head to examine them as if she were surprised by their presence. Her right hand began to move on her left elbow: up, down, and around in what could have been mistaken for a caress.

"I don't think I can be any more helpful than I've been already." She attempted patience, but the effort sounded strained. "The house is well off the road. You can see that for yourself. I didn't hear a thing. I've not heard a thing for days. And I've certainly not seen anything. Not anything suspicious. Not anything to suggest a little boy . . . a little boy . . ." She stumbled on the words. Her hand stopped its caress of her elbow for a moment. Then it resumed.

The second policeman wrote laboriously with the stub of a pencil. If he had taken all this down earlier in the evening, he was not giving any sign of having heard it before.

"You understand why we need to ask you this, though," the sergeant said. "Your house is closest to the church. If anyone had the opportunity to see or hear the killer's movements, it would have been you. Or your parents. You say they're not here at the moment?"

"They're my foster parents," the girl corrected. "Mr. and Mrs. Streader. They're in London. They'll be back sometime this evening."

"Were they here this weekend? On Friday and Saturday?"

The girl glanced towards the fireplace and the overmantel, on which a set of photographs were displayed. Three of them were of young adults, perhaps grown children of the Streaders'. "They went into London yesterday morning. They're spending the weekend helping their daughter settle into her new flat."

"Here alone quite a bit, are you, then?"

"No more than I like to be, Sergeant," she responded. It was a strangely adult reply, spoken not so much with assurance as with a listless acceptance of an immutable fact.

The despondency in her answer prompted St. James to question the girl's presence in this place. It was comfortable enough and bore the appointments one would expect in a home deemed lived-in rather than fashionable. Good furniture filled the room; a nubby wool carpet covered the floor; watercolours decorated the wall; a stone fireplace held a basket of silk flowers arranged with more enthusiasm than artistic technique. There was a large television with a video recorder on a shelf beneath it. Plenty of books and magazines lay about, offering to occupy one's idle time. But by her own admission the girl was an outsider, even if the mantel photographs had not identified her as such, and the emptiness with which she spoke suggested that she was an outsider everywhere else as well.

"But you can hear noise from the road, can't you?" the sergeant insisted. "Even as we sit here, cars go by. One can tell."

They all listened for a demonstration of this fact. As if on cue, a lorry rumbled past.

"It's not something one remembers, is it?" the girl replied. "Cars go by on streets all the time."

The sergeant smiled. "Indeed they do."

"You seem to be suggesting that a car was involved. But how can you know that? You've said this boy's body was in the field behind the church. It seems to me that it could have got there several other ways, none of which I would have noticed even if I—or the Streaders or any of our neighbours—had been sitting on the verge the weekend through."

"Several other ways?" the sergeant said amiably, his interest aroused by this admission of knowledge.

The girl replied, "Through the back field itself by means of the farm. Through Gray's field, for that matter, next to the church."

"Did you notice anything to indicate that, Mrs. St. James?" the sergeant asked.

"I?" Deborah looked flustered. "No. But I didn't look for anything. I wasn't thinking. I'd come to photograph the graveyard and I was preoccupied. All I remember is the body. And the position. As if he'd been dumped like a sack of flour."

"Yes. Dumped." The sergeant examined his hands. He said nothing more. Someone's stomach growled loudly, and although the other policeman did not raise his head, he looked abashed. As if the sound had reminded him of where they were and what they were doing and how long they'd been at it, the sergeant got to his feet. The others did likewise.

"We'll have statements for the both of you to sign tomorrow," the sergeant said to the women. He nodded and left them. His companion followed. In a moment, the front door closed.

St. James turned to his wife and could see Deborah's reluctance to leave Cecilia alone, as if the past hour had drawn them together in some obscure way.

"I . . . Thank you," Deborah said to her. She reached impulsively for the girl's hand, but Cecilia jerked away in a reflex reaction. She looked instantly apologetic. Deborah spoke again. "I've caused you no end of trouble by coming to use your phone, it seems."

"We're the closest house," Cecilia replied. "We'd be questioned anyway. As will most of the neighbours, I dare say. You had nothing to do with it."

"Quite. Yes. Well, thank you at any rate. Perhaps now you can get a bit of rest."

St. James saw the girl swallow. Her arms cradled her body. "Rest," she repeated, as if the idea were entirely new to her.

They left the house, crossed the driveway, and made for the road. St. James did not fail to notice that his wife walked more than a yard away from him. Her long hair shielded her face from his view. He sought something to say. For the first time in their marriage, he felt cut off from her. It was as if the month of her absence had created an unbreachable barrier between them.

"Deborah. My love." His words stopped her by the wrought-iron gate. He saw her reach out and grasp one of its bars. "You must stop trying to bear everything alone."

"It was finding him like that. One doesn't expect to see a little naked boy lying dead beneath a tree."

"I'm not talking about the graveyard. You know that very well." She averted her face. Her hand raised as if to stop him, then fell to her side. The movement was weak, and St. James berated himself for having allowed her to go off on her own so soon after she had lost the baby. No matter that she had been adamant about meeting her commitment to the photographic contract. He should have insisted upon more time for her to convalesce. He touched her shoulder, brushing his hand against her hair. "My love, you're only twenty-four. There's plenty of time. We've years ahead of us. Surely the doctor—"

"I don't *want* . . ." She released the bar of wrought iron and quickly crossed the street. He caught her up at his car. "Please, Simon. Please. I can't. Don't insist."

"Don't you know I can see what it's done to you, Deborah? What it's continuing to do?"

"Please."

He could hear her tears. They destroyed his own need, as they always would. "Then let me drive you home. We'll come back for your car tomorrow."

"No." She stood taller, offered a tremulous smile. "I'm fine. If we can just persuade the police to let me get at the Austin. We'll both be far too busy tomorrow to want to make another drive out here."

"I don't like the idea—"

"I'm fine. Truly."

He could see how much she wanted to be away from him. After a month's separation from her, he felt her continued need for isolation like the worst kind of blow. "If you're sure." It was a mere formality on his part.

"I am. Completely."

The constable, who had disregarded their conversation by looking in the direction of the church, now turned and nodded them cooperatively across the police line. They walked down the lane, guided in the darkness by the lights set up near the incidents room, a police caravan round which a knot of scenes-of-crime men were packing evidence bags into their cases. A heavy-set man was just coming out of the police caravan as St. James and his wife reached Deborah's car. He saw them, raised a hand in recognition, and joined them.

"Inspector Canerone," he said to St. James by way of introduction. "We met at Bramshill some eight months ago. You were giving a lecture on the recovery of accelerant residues."

"Dry forensic stuff, that," St. James replied, offering the other man his hand. "Did you manage to stay awake?"

Canerone grinned. "Only just. We've not a lot of arson to contend with round here."

"Just this mess." St. James nodded towards the graveyard.

The inspector sighed. The skin under his eyes looked permanently blue-black with fatigue, and his weight of flesh seemed too much for his body. "Little bloke," he responded. "I've never made strides in getting used to the murder of a child."

"It *is* murder, then?"

"Seems to be. Although there are some distinct incongruities. They've just gone out to bag him. Want to have a quick look?"

With Deborah finally near, the last thing St. James wanted was to have any sort of look—quick or scrutinising or indifferent—at the body she had found. But forensic science was his field. He was a national authority. He could hardly shrug off the invitation with the excuse of having better things to do on a Sunday night, no matter how true an excuse it was at the moment.

"Do go, Simon," Deborah was saying. "I'll just head on home. It's been dreadful. I'd very much like to be on my way."

He felt the requisite answer rise. "I'll see you in a bit, then, shall I?"

"Dinner?" She made a little self-deprecatory gesture and added, "Except that I don't imagine either of us shall want much to eat after this. Shall I arrange for something light?"

"Something light. Yes. Fine." He was beginning to feel like stone. He watched her get into the car, noticing how the interior light shone against her hair like gold upon copper, against her skin like the sheen of sunlight on cream. Then she closed the door, switched on the ignition, and was gone. He tore his eyes from the Austin's path of departure. "Where's the body?" he asked Canerone.

"This way."

St. James followed the inspector not into the graveyard, but rather into Gray's field which adjoined it. At one end, a monument to the poet loomed in the darkness. The ground was fallow with the end of winter; the earth gave off a rich, heady scent of humus. In another month it would be burgeoning with life.

"No footprints here," Canerone explained as they walked towards a wire fence overgrown by a hedge at the far end of the field. A hole had been cut through this, giving the police access to the second field beyond in which the body lay. "Looks as if the killer carried the body directly through the graveyard and dumped it over the wall. No other access."

"From the farm?" St. James indicated the lights of a house some distance across the field.

"Again, no footprints. And three dogs on the premises who'd raise the devil if anyone came that way."

St. James appraised the copse of trees they were approaching.

Lights bobbed beneath them. He could hear the quiet conversation of the police still there. Someone laughed. Like so many professionals, the Slough police had long ago become immune to the presence of violent death.

Apparently, however, Canerone's skin was thin when it came to that sort of thing. He said, "Excuse me, Mr. St. James," and walked into the group of men under the tree. He spoke hotly for a moment. His arm swung out. Then he returned, his face impassive. Too close to the job, St. James thought. "Right. Come this way, if you will."

The men on the scene stood back to give St. James access to the body. Nearby, the police photographer was unloading his camera. He stopped, watched, lowered his equipment into the case at his feet.

St. James wondered what they expected him to do. They could see the obvious as well as he, and anything beyond that would have to wait for the autopsy. He was no mystic, no magician. He had no special powers outside of his lab. Besides, he didn't even want to be here at the moment in this dark, cold field with a night's wind tossing its way through his hair as he stared down at the corpse of a child he didn't know. It was hardly rational to assume that his personal perusal of this grim little scene would unveil the truth behind the child's life and his death. Beyond that, at the moment, there was Deborah to consider, Deborah who had been gone for a month, who had left as his wife and returned a stranger. And worse, there was the condition of his heart, which felt torn with worry and completely alone.

Still, he gazed upon the corpse. The colour of the skin suggested some sort of contaminant in the blood, possibly even an accidental death. But the condition of the body contravened this conclusion. As Canerone had said, there were incongruities that only an autopsy could explain. Because of this, St. James settled upon saying the obvious, something any probationary DC could have said himself. He could tell it easily enough from the bruiselike stain that ran the length of the child's left leg.

"The body's been moved. Sometime after death."

Next to him Canerone nodded. "What went on before death concerns me more, Mr. St. James. He was tortured."

4

Lynley flipped open his ancient, dented pocket watch, saw that it was a quarter to eight, and admitted that he could hardly stretch his day very much longer. Sergeant Havers had already departed, their report was assembled and ready for presentation to Superintendent Webberly, and unless something happened to forestall his departure, he was going to have to go home.

That he wanted to avoid this was something he freely admitted to himself. Home had provided neither escape nor sanctuary in the last two months. Rather, it had become an insidious adversary, throwing down the gauntlet of memory every time he walked in the door.

For so many years he had lived without bothering to evaluate what Lady Helen Clyde actually meant in his life. She had simply always been there, breezing into his library with a shopping sack of detective novels which she insisted he read; appearing on his doorstep at half-past seven in the morning and browsing through his breakfast dishes as she chatted about her plans for the day; amusing him with mad anecdotes about her work in St. James' forensic laboratory ("My God, Tommy darling, today the little beast was actually cutting up a *liver* while we were having our tea!"); travelling with him to his family home in Cornwall and riding across the fields and making life worthwhile.

Every room in his house reminded him in some way of Helen. Save his bedroom. For Helen had been his friend, not his lover, and when she saw how intent he was to have her come to be more in his life than mere confidante and companion, she had left him.

It would have been so convenient to have learned to despise her for running away. It would have been so much easier to take up with another woman and bury himself in the diversion of an affair. It wasn't as if there were no women available for this sort of short-lived but engrossing encounter. Yet he found he wanted only Helen, with a longing that went beyond the desire to taste the fine warmth of her skin, to tangle his fingers in her hair, to feel the length of her body arch with pleasure against his own. He wanted a union to exist between them, one brought about through more than merely the momentary possession of her in his bed. While that union continued to be denied him, he stayed away from his home, engulfed in work, driven to fill up the hours with anything to keep himself from thinking of Helen Clyde.

Still, in moments like this when the day's conclusion caught him with his defences ill-placed, his thoughts turned to her instinctively, like wild birds seeking a familiar resting place to shelter them through the night. Yet the memory of Helen offered him no protection. Instead, it had become a tool that only served to gauge the depth of his loss.

He picked up her postcard, read once more the cheerful words that he already had memorised, and tried to believe that they contained an underlying expression of love and commitment that a few minutes' pondering would finally reveal. But he could not lie to himself. Her message was clear enough. She wanted time. She wanted distance. He upset the delicate balance of her equilibrium.

Dispiritedly he shoved the postcard into his jacket pocket and accepted the inevitable reality of having to go home. As he rose, his eyes fell on the photograph of Matthew Whateley that John Corntel had left. Lynley picked up the picture.

He was a distinctly attractive child, dark-haired, with skin the colour of blanched almonds and eyes so dark that they could have been called black. Corntel had said that the boy was thirteen, in the third form at Bredgar Chambers. He looked far younger, and his features were as sweetly defined as a girl's.

Lynley felt a stirring of discomfort as he studied the picture. He had been on the police force long enough to know what the disappearance of a child this lovely might mean.

It would take only a moment to check the PNC. Since every police force in England and Wales was hooked into it, if Matthew had been found somewhere—either dead or alive and unwilling to identify himself—the computer would be carrying a full description in the hope that another police force might be able to identify the boy. It was worth a try.

The computer room was manned at this hour by only one person, a detective constable whom Lynley recognised as a member of the robbery squad. He couldn't recall his name at the moment. They nodded at one another casually but did not speak. Lynley went to one of the consoles.

Because he wasn't expecting to find anything that applied to the boy from Bredgar Chambers so soon after his disappearance, once he typed in the appropriate information, he watched the screen idly and thus almost missed the report that had been supplied from the Slough police: the body of a male child, brown hair, brown eyes, roughly nine to twelve years of age, in the vicinity of St. Giles' Church, Stoke Poges. Cause of death presently unknown. Identity unknown. Noticeable scar four inches on left kneecap. Birthmark lower spine. Height four feet, six inches. Weight approximately six stone. Found at 5:05 P.M.

His mind on other matters, all this actually rolled past Lynley, and the only reason he noticed it at all was that the name of the person who had discovered the body fairly leapt out at him at the end of the report. He caught his breath in sheer amazement as *Deborah St. James, Cheyne Row, Chelsea* appeared on the monitor.

In the incidents room at St. Giles' Church, Inspector Canerone checked the time. It was more than three hours since the body had been found. He tried not to think of it.

He believed that, after eighteen years on the force, he ought to have become more immune to death. He ought to be able to look upon a corpse with some degree of impassivity, taking it not as a human being who had met a violent end but merely as a job to be done.

After his last case, he thought that he had managed to find the balance he was seeking between professional detachment and human outrage. It had been simple enough to convince himself of that at the time. The body of a notorious pimp sprawled at the foot of a filthy staircase in a half-burnt tenement was hardly likely to inspire him to dwell very long on man's inhumanity to man. Especially when part of him—the sententious Puritan within—believed that the pimp had got what he'd long deserved. When he first squatted by the body, saw the garrote round the neck, and felt unmoved by the sight, he even managed to convince himself that he'd arrived at that fine objectivity he had sought so long.

Objectivity had disintegrated fast enough tonight, however. Canerone knew why. The child looked remarkably like his own son. There had even been a ghastly moment when he thought it *was* Gerald, when his mind swept through a swift series of impossible events beginning with Gerald's decision that he could no longer live with his mother and her new husband in Bristol and ending with his death. The pieces fit together so neatly in Canerone's imagination. His son would telephone the flat and, getting no answer, would run off to seek his father in Slough. He would be picked up on the roadside, held prisoner somewhere, and tortured to give someone a few minutes' sadistic pleasure. When the torture was over—or perhaps before—he would die alone, afraid, abandoned. Naturally, once Canerone had got a good, clear look at the corpse, he could see that it wasn't Gerald at all. But for a moment the terrifying possibility that it could be his son vanquished the indifference with which he believed he had to do his job. Now he was faced with the aftermath of that moment in which he had left himself unguarded.

He saw his son rarely, telling himself that an occasional weekend was all that he could reasonably manage away from work. But that was a lie and he faced it now, with the scenes-of-crime men gone and the police surgeon escorting the corpse to the hospital and a solitary female probationary constable at a nearby desk, waiting for the word from him that she could pack up and go for the night. The truth was that he saw his son rarely because he could no longer endure seeing him at all. Seeing him even in the most nonthreatening environment, he had to admit what he had lost, and admitting this, he came face to face with the emptiness that dominated his life now that his family had left him.

He'd seen many police marriages dissolve through the years, but he had never once thought that his own might fall victim to the irregular hours, the load of work, and the sleepless nights intrinsic to a detective's life. When he first noticed his wife's unhappiness, he chose not to confront it, telling himself that she was a difficult woman, that if he was patient, it would all blow over, that she had it damned good being married to him at all, and with a temper like hers, who else would ever put up with her? Several men, it turned out, and one who married her, taking her to Bristol, taking Gerald as well.

Canerone poured himself a cup of coffee. It looked too strong. He knew he would be up half the night if he drank it. He took a swift gulp, grimacing at the bitter flavour. His mind and his heart were filled to capacity with this little boy in the graveyard. The child's wrists and ankles had been tightly bound; his body had been burned; he had been discarded like rubbish. He was so like Gerald.

Canerone felt shaken. He couldn't even have said what ought to be done first to bring about justice in the death of this boy. Such professional torpidity told him that he ought to give the case over to another DI. But he didn't see how he could. He didn't have the manpower.

The telephone rang. From his position near the doorway, he listened to his police constable's side of the conversation.

"Yes, a little boy. . . . No, there's no indication where he's come from. It looks like a body dump at the moment. . . . It doesn't appear to be exposure, sir. He'd been tied up, you see. . . . No, we've absolutely no idea at the moment who—" She hesitated, listening, her shapely eyebrows drawn together. Then she said only, "Let me put you through to the Inspector. He's here."

Canerone turned. The constable extended the phone to him. Salvation came with it.

"Inspector Lynley," she said. "New Scotland Yard."

Queen Caroline Street was as close as Lynley could get to the Whateleys' cottage on the river. He parked his car illegally in the only space available, blocking off half the driveway of an apartment building, and propped his police identification against the steering wheel. On either side of the street stood a grim collection of postwar housing where institutional buildings of mushroom-coloured concrete squared off against other buildings of dirty brown brick. Both were devoid of architectural decoration, bleak and overcrowded and inhospitable.

Even at ten o'clock on a Sunday night, the neighbourhood was alive with noise that rocketed through the street and reverberated against the buildings. Cars and lorries roared along the flyover. Additional traffic fired across Hammersmith Bridge. Shouts echoed in apartment courtyards, followed by the antiphonal barking of dogs.

Lynley walked to the end of the street and descended to the embankment. The tide was up, the water shimmered in the darkness like cool black satin, but what vague, life-giving smell rose from the river was overpowered by the exhaust fumes that drifted down from the bridge above him.

Lynley found the Whateleys' cottage a few hundred yards along the Lower Mall, an obdurate reminder of Hammersmith's past. It was an old unrestored fishing cottage, with whitewashed walls, thin strips of black woodwork, and dormer windows rising from its roof.

Access to the cottage interior was gained by means of a tunnel that served as boundary between the Whateleys' home and a pub next door. The passage was narrow, unevenly paved, and redolent of the yeasty smell of lager and ale. As he made his way to the door the top of Lynley's head grazed the rough timbers that crisscrossed the tunnel's low ceiling.

So far, everything had followed the usual roll of policework. Lynley's phone call to the incidents room in Stoke Poges had resulted in Kevin Whateley's identification of his son's body less than an hour later. This led to Lynley's suggestion that Scotland Yard coordinate the investigation into the death of the boy, since more than one police organisation was involved: the constabulary of West Sussex where Matthew Whateley was last seen alive at Bredgar Chambers and that of Buckinghamshire where his body had been found near St. Giles' Church. Once Inspector Canerone had given his approval to this plan of action—with rather more relief than was usual when someone from the Met proposed an invasion into another police force's territory—all that had been left to ensure another case keeping Lynley occupied for the days or weeks it would take to see it to its completion was to secure approval from his own superior, Superintendent Webberly. Summoned away from his favourite Sunday night television show, Webberly had listened to Lynley's quick recitation of the facts, agreed to his proposed involvement, and returned happily to BBC-1.

Sergeant Havers was the only person who promised not to be relieved by their involvement in yet another new case. But her displeasure could not be helped at the moment.

Lynley knocked on the discoloured door. It was recessed into the wall, and its lintel sagged as if it carried the weight of the entire building. When no one opened it, he looked for a bell, failed to find one, and rapped against the wood again, more forcefully. He heard a key being turned and bolts being drawn. Then he found himself face to face with the father of the boy.

Until that moment, the death of Matthew Whateley had represented to Lynley a means by which he might escape his own troubles and stave off the void. Confronted now with the kind of suffering incised onto Kevin Whateley's face, Lynley felt only shame at the base selfishness of his own motivation. Here was the real void. Whatever loneliness or loss he felt was risible by comparison.

"Mr. Whateley?" He offered his police identification. "Thomas Lynley. Scotland Yard CID."

Whateley's eyes made no move to study the warrant card. He gave no immediate indication that he had heard Lynley. Looking at him, Lynley saw that he'd probably only just returned from identifying his son's body, for he was wearing a threadbare peaked wool cap, and under his thinning tweed overcoat a brown suit gaped round his neck and sagged at his knees.

His face told Lynley that he would deal with loss through the means of denial. Every muscle was held in rigid control. His grey eyes looked dull, like unpolished stones.

"May I come in, Mr. Whateley? I need to ask you some questions. I realise how late it is, but the sooner I can get information—"

"No good, is it? Information won't bring Mattie back."

"You're right. It won't. It'll only bring justice. And I know that justice is a meagre replacement for your son. Believe me. I do know that."

"Kev?" a woman's voice called from the upper floor. It sounded weak, perhaps sedated. Whateley's eyes shifted in the direction of the sound, but it was the only indication he gave that he had heard it. He did not move from the doorway.

"Have you anyone to stay the night with you?" Lynley asked.

"We don't want no one," Whateley replied. "Pats and me will cope. Just us."

"Kev?" The woman's voice was closer now, and steps sounded upon uncarpeted stairs somewhere behind the door. "Who is it?"

Whateley looked over his shoulder at the woman who was out of Lynley's line of vision. "Police. Some bloke from Scotland Yard."

"Let him in." Whateley still did not move. "Kev, let him in."

Her hand came round the side of the door, pulling it completely open and giving Lynley a chance to see Patsy Whateley for the first time. The mother of the dead boy was, he guessed, in her late forties, an ordinary woman who, even in grieving, would fade into faceless anonymity within a crowd. On the street she probably would not garner a moment's attention from anyone at this time in her life, no matter the transitory beauties that might have graced her youth. Her womanly figure had thickened through time, making her appear more solid than she probably was. Her hair was very dark, that sort of uncompromising black which comes from a hasty application of inexpensive dye rather than from nature, and it lay unevenly against her skull. Her nylon dressing gown was wrinkled, printed with Chinese dragons that snarled across her bosom and down her hips. That the dressing gown, for all its garish design, was a possession holding meaning for Patsy Whateley was attested to by the fact that her green slippers had obviously been chosen in an unsuccessful attempt to match the dragons on the gown itself.

"Come in." She reached for the sash of her dressing gown. "I look like . . . Not done much, you see . . . since . . ."

"Please. It's fine, Mrs. Whateley." Lynley sought to brush her words away. What did the poor woman think he expected from the mother of a child who'd just been found murdered? he asked himself. Haute couture? The idea was absurd, yet still, with one hand smoothing down a rucked seam, she seemed to be comparing her appearance with his, as if his tailored presence was somehow a derogation of her own. He felt distinctly uncomfortable and wished for the first time that he had thought far enough ahead to bring Sergeant Havers. Her working class background and sartorial nonchalance would have eased them through the superficial difficulties created by his own blasted upper-crust accent and his Savile Row clothes.

The door admitted him directly into the cottage sitting room. It was sparsely furnished with a three-piece suite, a sideboard constructed of Formica-topped pressed wood, a single armless chair upholstered in brown and yellow plaid, and one long shelf running beneath the front windows. Two disparate collections sat upon this, one of stone sculptures and the other of teacups, both equally revealing.

Like any collection of art, the stone sculptures acted as a disclosure of someone's taste. Nude women sprawled in unusual positions, their pointed breasts jutting into the air; couples entwined and arched in mock passion; nude men explored the bodies of nude women who received this attention with heads flung back in rapture. Rape of the Sabine women, Lynley thought, with the women apparently begging for abduction.

Sharing this shelf, the teacups bore inscriptions that identified them as souvenirs. Gathered from holiday spots across the country, each sported a scene to identify its location and gold letters lest the image not be enough stimulus to the memory. Some of them Lynley could read from where he stood by the door. *Blackpool, Weston-Super-Mare, Ilfracombe, Skegness.* Others were turned from him, but he could guess their origins from the scenes painted upon them. Tower Bridge, Edinburgh Castle, Salisbury, Stonehenge. They represented places, no doubt, that the Whateleys had taken their son, places whose association would pain them treacherously—when they least expected—for years to come. That was the nature of sudden death.

"Please sit . . . Inspector, is it?" Patsy nodded towards the couch. "Yes. Thomas Lynley."

The sofa—blue vinyl—was covered with an old pink counterpane to protect it. Patsy Whateley removed this and folded it slowly, giving care to matching the corners and smoothing the lumps. Lynley sat.

Patsy Whateley did likewise, choosing the plaid chair and making sure that her dressing gown did not become disarranged. Her husband remained standing next to the stone fireplace. This held an electric fire, but he made no move to light it, even though the room was uncomfortably cold.

"I can return in the morning," Lynley told them. "But it seemed wisest to me to begin working at once."

Patsy said, "Yes. At once. Mattie . . . I want to know. I must know." Her husband said nothing. His bleak eyes were on a picture of the boy that had pride of place on the sideboard. Grinning like any brand new third former, Matthew had been photographed wearing his school uniform—yellow pullover, blue blazer, grey trousers, black shoes. "Kev . . ." Patsy sounded uncertain. It was clear that she wanted her husband to join them, clearer still that he had no intention of doing so.

"Scotland Yard will handle most of the case," Lynley explained. "I've already spoken to John Corntel, Matthew's housemaster."

"Bastard," Kevin Whateley said on a breath.

Patsy straightened in her chair. She kept her eyes on Lynley. Her hand, however, drew a fold of her dressing gown into her fist. "Mr. Corntel. Mattie lived in Erebus House. Mr. Corntel's housemaster there. At Bredgar Chambers. Yes."

"From what I've been able to gather from Mr. Corntel," Lynley went on, "it appears that Matthew may have had the idea to seek some freedom this past weekend."

"No," Patsy replied.

Lynley had expected the automatic denial. He continued as if she had not said it. "It appears that he'd got hold of an off-games chit, a paper from the Sanatorium saying that he was unfit for Friday afternoon's hockey game. The school seems to think that perhaps he was feeling out of place and he wanted to use the opportunity of his proposed visit to the Morant family and the off-games chit to get away, perhaps to come back to London with no one being the wiser. They think he was trying to hitchhike and was picked up by someone on the road."

Patsy looked at her husband as if hoping that he would intervene. His lips moved convulsively, but he said nothing.

"Can't be, Inspector," Patsy said. "That's not our Mattie."

"How did he get on in school?"

Again Patsy's eyes went to her husband. This time, his own met hers momentarily before they slid away. He removed his peaked cap and twisted it once in his hands. They were strong labourer's hands, Lynley saw, nicked in several places.

"Mattie got on well in school," Patsy said.

"He was happy there?"

"Quite happy. He'd won a scholarship. The Board of Governors Scholarship. He knew what it meant to go to a proper school."

"Prior to this year, he'd gone to school here locally, hadn't he? If so, he could have been missing his mates."

"Not a bit of that. Mattie loved Bredgar Chambers. He knew how important it was to be educated right. This was his chance. He'd not have thrown it away because he missed some mate of his here at home. He could see his mates at half term, couldn't he?"

"But perhaps someone special in the neighbourhood?"

Lynley saw Kevin Whateley's reaction to the question, a quick uncontrolled movement of his head towards the windows.

"Mr. Whateley?"

The man said nothing. Lynley waited. Patsy Whateley spoke.

"You're thinking of Yvonnen, Kev, aren't you?" she said and explained to Lynley. "Yvonnen Livesley. From Queen Caroline Street. She and Mattie were mates in primary school. They played together. But it was just children playing, Inspector. Yvonnen wasn't more to Matthew than that. And besides . . ." She blinked and said nothing more.

"Black," her husband finished.

"Yvonnen Livesley's a black?" Lynley clarified.

Kevin Whateley nodded, as if the colour of Yvonnen's skin were adequate evidence to support their contention that Matthew would not have left the school illegally. It was a weak position, especially if they had grown up together, especially if they were—as the boy's mother claimed—mates.

"Was there anything at all that might have given you the impression that Matthew was recently unhappy at school? Not unhappy throughout the year, but unhappy within the past few weeks. Arising perhaps from a cause you know nothing about. Sometimes children go through things and don't feel quite up to admitting it to their parents. It was nothing to do with the relationship that exists between parent and child. It's just something that happens." He thought of his own school days and the pretence of getting on.

He had never spoken of it to a single soul, least of all to his parents.

Neither of them replied. Kevin examined the lining of his cap. Patsy frowned down at her lap. Lynley saw that she had started trembling, so he addressed his words to her.

"It's not your fault if Matthew ran off from the school, Mrs. Whateley. You're not responsible. If he felt a need to run away—"

"He *had* to go there. We did swear . . . Oh, Kev, he's dead and we did it. You know we did it!"

Her husband's face worked in reaction to her words, but he didn't go to her. Instead, he looked at Lynley.

"The boy went dead quiet within the last four or five months." He spoke tautly. "Last holiday I come on him three or four times just staring out his bedroom window at the river. Like he was in a trance. But he wouldn't talk about it. Wasn't his way." Kevin looked at his wife. She was attempting to maintain that shell of bland civility that she seemed to feel was appropriate. "We did it to him, Pats. We did."

Barbara Havers stared up at the facade of her family's home in Acton and made a mental note of everything that needed to be done to the building to make it more habitable. It was an exercise she engaged in nightly. Always, she dwelt on the easiest items first. The windows were filthy. God alone knew when they had last been washed. But it wouldn't take too much trouble to see to them if she had enough time off, a ladder to use, and sufficient energy to do the job right. The bricks needed scrubbing. Fifty years or more of soot and grime permeated their porous surfaces, leaving an unpalatable patina in every variation of the colour black. The woodwork at the windows, along the roofline, and on the door had long since lost its last flake of paint. She shuddered to think how long it would take to return that innocent decorative carving to its original condition. Drainpipes down the side of the house were rusted through, spouting like sieves whenever it rained. They would have to be replaced entirely. As would the front garden, which was not a garden at all but a square of concrete-hard dirt upon which she parked her Mini, its rusting condition a suitable complement to the environment in general.

Her survey complete, she got out of the car and went into the house. Noise and odours assaulted her. The television blared from the sitting room, while poorly cooked food, mildew, woodrot, unwashed bodies, and old age all battled to be the ascendant smell.

Barbara laid her shoulder bag on the wobbly rattan table by the door. She hung her coat with the others on the line of pegs beneath the staircase and walked towards the sitting room at the back of the house.

"Lovey?" Querulously, her mother spoke from above. Barbara stopped, looked up.

Mrs. Havers was standing on the top stair, clad only in a thin cotton nightdress, her feet bare and her hair uncombed. The light behind her, shining from her bedroom, served to emphasise each angular detail of her skeletal body through the insubstantial material. Barbara's eyes widened at the sight of her.

"You've not dressed, Mum," she said. "You've not dressed today at all." She felt a great weight of depression settle upon her as she said the words. How much longer, she asked herself, would she be able to hold down a job and still care for two parents who had become like children?

Mrs. Havers smiled vaguely. Her hands slid over the nightdress as if for confirmation. Her teeth caught at her lip. "Forgot," she said. "I was looking at my albums—oh, lovey, I did so want to spend more time in Switzerland, didn't you?—and I must not have realised . . . Shall I dress now, lovey?"

Considering the time, it seemed a rather useless expenditure of energy. Barbara sighed, pressed her knuckles to her temples to stave off a headache. "No, I don't think so, Mum. It's almost time for you to be in bed, isn't it?"

"I *could* dress for you. You could watch me and see if I do it proper."

"You'd do it proper, Mum. Why don't you run yourself a bath?"

Mrs. Havers' face wrinkled at this new idea. "Bath?"

"Yes. But stay with the water. Don't let it overflow this time. I'll be up in a moment."

"Will you help me then, lovey? If you will, I can tell you my ideas about Argentina. That's where we'll go next. Do they speak Spanish there? I think we'll have to learn more Spanish before we go. One so likes to be able to communicate with the natives. *Buenos días, señorita. ¿Como se llama?* I remember that from the telly. I know it's not nearly enough. But it's a start. If they speak Spanish in Argentina. It could be Portuguese. Somewhere they speak Portuguese."

Barbara knew her mother might go on in this disjointed fashion for an hour or more. She had often done so, sometimes coming into her bedroom at two or three in the morning to chat aimlessly, unmindful of Barbara's entreaties that she return to her bed.

"The bath," Barbara reminded her. "I'm going to check on Dad."

"Dad's well today, lovey. Such a man. *So* well. See for yourself."

That said, Mrs. Havers flitted back out of the light. In a moment water began to splash noisily into the bath. Barbara waited to see if her mother would leave the tub unattended, but apparently the idea of watching the water had been planted well enough in her mind to ensure her staying put for at least a few minutes. Barbara went to the sitting room.

Her father was in his usual chair, watching his usual Sunday night programme. Newspapers covered most of the floor where he had dropped them once he'd given them his usual cursory read. He, at least, was more predictable than her mother. He lived by routine.

Barbara watched him from the doorway, tuning out the raucous roar of a commercial for Cadbury chocolates on the television, concentrating instead on the aqueous sound of his breathing. It had become more laboured within the last two weeks. The oxygen fed to him through the omnipresent tubes no longer seemed sufficient.

Perhaps feeling his daughter's presence, Jimmy Havers pushed himself to one side in his old wing-backed chair.

"Barbie." As always, he smiled a greeting, showing teeth that were cracked and blackened. But for once Barbara noticed neither this nor the fact that his hair was unwashed and greasily malodorous. Rather, she saw that his colour was bad. There was no pink to his cheeks; his fingernails were turning a misty grey-blue. She didn't have to cross the room to see that the veins in his arms looked shrunk to nothing.

She walked to the tank on its trolley by his chair and adjusted the oxygen flow. "We've the doctor tomorrow morning, haven't we, Dad?"

He nodded. "Tomorrow. Half-nine. Got to be up and about with the birds, Barbie."

"Yes. With the birds." Fleetingly Barbara mulled over how she would manage this scheduled trip to the doctor with both her parents. She'd been dreading it for weeks. It was inconceivable that her mother should be left alone in the house while she took her father to the doctor. Anything could happen if Mrs. Havers found herself unsupervised for more than ten minutes at a time. Yet the idea of having them both to contend with was overwhelming—her father's oxygen supply, his virtual immobility thrown against her mother's tendency to wander off and lose herself blissfully in the crystal cave of her dementia. How was she going to do it?

Barbara knew it was time for some sort of help. Not a well-meaning social worker who'd stop by to make sure the house was still standing, but a permanent live-in. Someone reliable. Someone who would take an interest in her parents.

It was impossible. It couldn't be managed. There was nothing to be done save muddling on. The thought was suffocating, a nightmare glimpse into a future with neither hope nor end.

When the telephone rang, she trudged into the kitchen to answer it, doing her best not to let her heart sink any lower when she saw the unwashed breakfast dishes with their smears of dried egg still cluttered on the table. The caller was Lynley.

"We've a murder, Sergeant," he announced. "I'll need you to meet me at the St. James house at half-past seven tomorrow."

Barbara knew that a brief request on her part for time off would be met with Lynley's immediate acquiescence. While she'd been careful never to reveal the truth of her living circumstances to him, the number of hours that she'd spent on the job in the last few weeks had certainly garnered her several days of freedom. He knew that. He would not even stop to question such a request. She wondered what was preventing her from making it, but even in the act of wondering, she recognised her self-deception. A new case tomorrow promised at least a moment's reprieve from the inevitable struggle with her parents in the morning, from the endless trip to the doctor, from the anxious wait to be called into his office while all the time she kept her mother in rein like a fractious two-year-old. A new case obviated the necessity of going through all that. It was licence to avoid, permission to procrastinate.

"Havers?" Lynley was saying. "Did you get that?"

Now was the time to make the request, to explain the situation, to say that she needed a few hours—perhaps a day—to take care of some personal business at home. He would understand. All she need say was *I need some time off.* But she couldn't do it.

"The St. James house at half-past seven," she repeated. "Got it, sir."

He rang off. Barbara hung up. She tried to plumb the depths of her feelings, to put a name to what was slowly washing through her veins. She wanted to call it shame. She knew it was liberation.

She went to tell her father that they would need to reschedule his doctor's appointment for another day.

Kevin Whateley had not gone to the Royal Plantagenet, which was the pub next door to his cottage. Rather, he had walked along the embankment, past the triangular green where he and Matthew had once learned to operate their pair of remote-control planes, and had instead entered an older pub that stood on a spit of land reaching like a curled finger into the Thames.

He'd chosen the Blue Dove deliberately. In the Royal Plantagenet—despite its proximity to his house—he might have forgotten for five minutes or so. But the Blue Dove would not allow him to do so.

He sat at a table that overlooked the water. In spite of the night's falling temperature, someone was out, night fishing from a boat, and lights bobbed periodically with the river's movement. Kevin watched this, allowing his memory to fill with the image of Matthew running along that same dock, falling, damaging a knee, righting himself but not crying at all, even when the blood began to seep from the cut, even when the stitches were later put in. He was a brave little bloke, always had been.

Kevin forced his eyes from the dock and fastened them on the mahogany table. Beer mats covered it, advertising Watney's, Guinness, and Smith's. Carefully, Kevin stacked them, restacked them, spread them out like cards, restacked them again. He felt how shallow his breathing was and knew that he needed to take in more air. But to breathe deeply was to lose his grip for an instant. He wouldn't do that. For if he lost control, he didn't know how he would get it back. So he did without air. He waited.

He didn't know if the man he sought would come into the pub this late on a Sunday night, mere minutes before closing. In fact, he didn't even know if the man came here at all any longer. But years ago he'd been a regular customer, when Patsy worked long hours behind the bar, before she'd got her job in a South Kensington hotel. *For Matthew's sake,* she had said when she'd taken on the job, in spite of the fact that the pay was lower than what she'd received for years at the Blue Dove. *No boy wants to tell his mates that his mum's a barmaid.*

No indeed, Kevin had agreed.

They'd bring their son up proper, they decided. He'd have more opportunity than they'd had. He'd have a solid education and a chance to make something grand of his life. They owed it to him, after all, and they knew it. He was their miracle baby. He was their dear little chap. He was the bond between them. He was the living fulfillment of all their dreams, dreams brought to nothing on that stainless steel cart in the hushed postmortem room where Kevin had been taken to identify the body.

Matthew had been covered by some sort of regulation green

cloth, the incongruous words LEWISTON LAUNDRY AND CLEANING stamped across the front, as if he were waiting to be bundled into a washing machine. Although the quietly sympathetic police sergeant had uncovered the face, there had been no real need for him to do so. Sometime in the process of moving the body from one location to another, the left foot had become loosened from the material that enshrouded it, and Kevin knew at once that he was looking at his son.

It was odd to think that one could know a child's body so well, that merely the glimpse of a foot could wreak such horrible devastation. But that had been enough. Still, he had done his duty and made a formal observation of the rest of the body.

Kevin thought of the sight of Matthew's face, the glow wiped from it by the impartial hand of death. He had heard once that people's faces reflected the manner in which they died. But he knew now that old tale wasn't true. Matthew's body bore evidence of brutality and violence, but his face was serene. He might have been asleep.

Kevin had heard himself asking the impossible, the ridiculous, the unutterably laughable. "The boy's dead? You're sure of it?"

The sergeant had lowered the cloth to cover Matthew's face. "Quite sure. I'm sorry."

Sorry. What did *he* know of Matthew to be sorry at his death? What did he know of the railway they'd built together in the cellar, or the buildings they'd constructed to comprise the three villages through which their trains rolled? How could he know that Matthew had insisted each building be accurately designed to scale, be built of authentic materials, not of plastic? How could he know of the years it had taken them to complete it? Or the hours of pleasure they had got from the work? He didn't know. He couldn't know. All he could do was mutter words of sympathy that would be forgotten as soon as Mattie was lowered into the ground.

That little body on the stainless steel cart. Waiting for the knife that would cut through muscle and tissue, that would remove organs for examination, that would seek and probe and relentlessly investigate until a cause of death was found. What did it matter? Putting a name to his death would not give him life. Matthew Whateley. Thirteen years old. Quite dead.

Kevin felt the sob like a constriction in his chest. He fought it down. Dimly he heard time called in the pub, and it was in a fugue that he made his way outside into the night.

He turned towards his home. Ahead of him by the embankment wall stood a green rubbish bin, and he approached this dully.

Sunday-afternoon strollers had filled it with an assortment of wrappers and bottles, empty tins and newspapers, a bedraggled kite.

Here, Dad, let me! Let me fly it! Let me!

"Matt!"

The word rent Kevin's body, as if part of his spirit were clawing to be free. He bent, felt the rim of the rubbish bin beneath his hands.

Let me fly it! I can! Dad, I can! I can!

Kevin broke. His fingers dug and scratched at the bin. He picked it up, hurled it down onto the pavement, and fell upon it, beating it with his fists, kicking at it with his feet, driving his head into its metal sides.

He felt his knuckles split. His feet became entangled in foul-smelling rubbish. Blood from his forehead began to drip into his eyes.

But he did not cry.

5

Deborah St. James had fallen into a fitful sleep sometime after three-fifteen. She awoke shortly before half past six to find that her body ached with the rigid tension that had kept her from instinctively seeking her husband during the night.

Behind the curtains the morning sun created a dusky glow in the room. It settled upon furniture, transforming drawer pulls from base brass and enamel into russet gold. It washed over photographs, creating round each a visible aura of light. It drove out shadows and gave full definition to night-amorphous shapes.

This same light cast a thin diagonal beam across Simon's form, illuminating his right hand, which lay, unmoving, on the bed between them. As Deborah watched, his fingers curled into his palm and then extended. He was awake.

Only six weeks ago at this first waking, she would have slid across the bed and into his arms. She would have felt his hands knowing all of her body and his mouth tasting the dawn on her skin. She would have heard him murmur *my love* as she bent over him and let her hair sweep a skeinlike pattern across his chest. She would have seen his smile as he touched her abdomen and whispered a good morning to their growing child. And their lovemaking at this early hour would have been not so much passion as affirmation and joy.

Her body yearned for him, her nerves glass-edged and longing to be soothed by his touch. She turned to look at him, only to find that he was already looking at her. How long he had been doing so she could not have said. But as they gazed at one another across the expanse of their bed, Deborah took the full measure of how completely her past was obliterating whatever future was possible with her husband.

She had not thought of it in those terms at the time. Eighteen years old, pregnant, a student alone in a foreign country. Having a baby under those circumstances would have been more than an irritating inconvenience to which one learns to adjust. It would have been an impossibility, a complete disaster. More, it would have ended her professional life before it had begun. At the time, the promise of her profession had been paramount to her. She and her father had saved for years so that she might attend school in America and emerge from her three years there as the master of photography she longed to be. To let all that go in order to have a baby had been inconceivable. She had not even contemplated it. Nor, however, had she contemplated how an abortion might ricochet against the walls of the rest of her life.

It was with her now, daily. The memory of the harsh lights, the prick of the needle, the explanation of the scraping and suction that would follow, the residual bleeding, the attempt to forget. She had done so, very successfully, for years. But now the recollection dominated her every waking moment, for although she tried to tell herself that her continued, failed pregnancies had nothing whatsoever to do with that hastily terminated pregnancy of six years ago, she could not bring herself to believe that there was no connection. God sometimes stayed the hand of punishment, but it was only a stay. Retribution always fell upon the sinner in the end.

That non-child would have had his fifth birthday sometime this next September. He would have been running about the house, raising a ruckus in the way of small boys. He would have played in the garden, teased the cat, pulled the dog's ears. He would have scraped his knees and asked for stories to be read. He could have existed. He could have been hers.

But beyond any concerns about her schooling and career, his birth would have meant the end of her relationship with Simon. And the mere knowledge of that short-lived pregnancy would crush her husband now. He had been able to accept everything else about her past, but he would not accept that. He could not do so.

He stirred, raised himself on one elbow. He reached out to trace her eyebrows, her jaw. "Feeling better?" His words were gentle, his touch a source of unbearable pain.

"Yes. Much." The lie seemed inconsequential, set against the rest.

"I missed you, my love." His fingers touched her cheek, her shoulders, her throat. They brushed softly against her lips before he bent to kiss her.

She would have drawn him to her. She would have parted her lips. She would have caressed and aroused him. She ached to do so.

Tears stung her eyes. She turned her head away that he might not see them, but she wasn't quick enough.

"Deborah." He sounded stricken.

She shook her head wordlessly.

"Oh God, it's too soon. I'm sorry. Forgive me, Deborah. Please." He touched her a last time before moving away from her, reaching for his crutches that leaned against the wall next to the bed. He swung himself to his feet and picked up his dressing gown, shrugging into it clumsily, hindered by his disability.

Under different circumstances, she would have helped him put it on, but now such an act seemed to Deborah a declaration of devotion that he would surely find spurious. So she remained where she was and watched his halting progress towards the bathroom. His knuckles were white where he grasped the crutches. His face was a study in desolation.

When the door closed behind him, Deborah began to weep, tears that provided the only sort of rain that had been sent to her roots for the last six weeks.

Their days together had always possessed a sameness to them that Deborah had treasured. When she was not out completing a photographic assignment, she would be busy in her darkroom, readying a portfolio for presentation. Simon's extensive forensic laboratory adjoined Deborah's smaller workspace, sprawling through most of the upper floor of the house. When he was not in court or delivering a lecture or meeting with solicitors and their clients, he would be in the lab, as he was now. Just as she was in the darkroom with the door propped open, trying to summon up the interest to get to work on her month's collection of photographs. The only difference from any other workday was the distance she had created between them and everything that was waiting to be said.

The house was so hushed that the front doorbell sounded like splintering glass.

"Who on earth . . . ?" Deborah murmured. Then she heard the easy, familiar voice, followed by brisk footsteps on the stairs.

"I couldn't believe it when I saw Deb's name come across that computer screen last night," Lynley was saying to Deborah's father. "What a homecoming that must have been."

"Upset the girl a bit," was Cotter's polite response.

Hearing it, Deborah found herself grateful for once that her father habitually slipped into the role of servant whenever someone came to the house. *Upset the girl a bit* was sufficient information to answer a casual remark of Lynley's. It hid reality while it served as reply.

As he entered the lab with the role of servant pulled out of his repertoire, Cotter said, "Lord Asherton's here to see you, Mr. St. James."

"To see Deb, more accurately, if she's about this morning," Lynley added.

"She is," Cotter replied.

Deborah rued the fact that she had not shut herself in the darkroom with the warning light burning to indicate she was not to be disturbed. Seeing anyone at the moment for friendly conversation seemed an unendurable pretence to have to live through. Seeing Lynley and being exposed for even an instant to his intuitive ability to read moods was excruciatingly worse. But she could hardly escape. Her father had nodded in her direction before leaving them, and Lynley had already come far enough into the lab to see that the darkroom door stood open. Simon, she saw, was studying a set of fingerprints in a far corner of the lab.

"You're up early enough," he said by way of greeting his friend.

Lynley's eyes swept the room and came to rest on the wall clock. "Havers isn't here yet?" he enquired. "It's not like her to be late."

"Late for what, Tommy?"

"A new case. I need to talk to Deb about last evening. You as well if you had a chance to see the body."

Deborah realised that it could not be avoided. She left the darkroom. She knew she looked terrible with her hair shoved back haphazardly, her complexion dull, her eyes without life. But she was not prepared for how quickly Lynley made his assessment, looking from her to Simon, then back again. He started to speak. She deflected his words quickly by crossing to him and greeting him in her usual manner, brushing a kiss against his cheek.

"Hello, Tommy." She smiled. "Look at what a dreadful sight I am. Find a body, fall apart. I don't think I could survive a day in your job."

He accepted the lie although his eyes told her that he didn't believe it. He knew, after all, that she had been in hospital less than two weeks prior to leaving for her trip. "I've been asked to head up the investigation," he explained. "Will you tell me about finding the body last evening?"

The three of them sat at one of the worktables, perching on tall stools, leaning their arms among the comparison microscopes, the vials, and the slides. Deborah recounted her finding of the body much the same way as she had the night before for the Slough police: taking the photographs, going into the church, seeing the fighting squirrels, finding the child.

"And you noticed nothing out of the ordinary in the graveyard?" Lynley asked. "Even something that might appear to be unrelated to all this?"

The bird. Of course, there was the bird. It seemed so silly to tell him about it, let alone run the risk of confronting the upheaval of emotion that had struck her yesterday.

Typical of him, the gift he brought to policework, Lynley saw it in her face. "Tell me," he said.

Deborah looked towards her husband. He was watching her gravely.

"It's ridiculous, Tommy." She attempted to keep her words light, an endeavour that was only marginally successful. "Just a dead bird."

"What sort of bird?"

"I really couldn't tell. Its head . . . you see, it had no head. And the claws were torn off. There were bits of feathers everywhere. I felt sorry for the little thing. I ought to have buried it." Again she felt the emotion of the day before, hating herself for allowing it any degree of rein. "I could see its ribs. They were bloody and broken and . . . it's not even as if a larger animal were after it for food. It looked like sport. *Sport,* can you imagine? And . . . oh, this is so ridiculous. It was probably nothing of the kind. Just some tomcat playing the way cats do when they catch a smaller creature. It was just inside that second lych gate, so that when I walked in . . ." She hesitated, struck by something she had not remembered until this moment.

"You saw something else?"

She nodded. "No doubt the Slough police have already told you because they could hardly have failed to notice, but there's a security light just on the inside of the second lych gate. It was broken. It must have happened recently because there was glass here and there, brushed to one side."

"That would be how the killer brought the body into the graveyard in the first place," Lynley said.

"Drive into the car park, black out the security lights, carry the body to the wall, and dump him under the trees," St. James noted.

"But why go to that much trouble?" Deborah asked. "And why choose that, of all locations?"

"If, indeed, it was a matter of choice."

"What else could it be? The church is virtually in the middle of nowhere. Down a little lane that veers off from a country road. One wouldn't exactly come upon it by chance."

"If the boy was a local child, the killer might well be a local man as well," St. James suggested. "He'd know about the church."

Lynley shook his head. "The boy's from Hammersmith. He was at school in West Sussex. Bredgar Chambers."

"A runaway?"

"Perhaps. Whatever the case, the body was apparently moved sometime after death."

"Yes, I did see that."

"And the rest?" Lynley asked. "How close a look did you get at the body, St. James?"

"Only a superficial one at best."

"But you did see . . ." Lynley hesitated, glancing at Deborah. "I spoke to Canerone on the phone last night."

"He told you about the burns, I take it. Yes, I saw them as well."

Lynley frowned. Restlessly he twirled an empty test tube. "They've a backlog of work at Slough, so Canerone said they won't have the autopsy results for a day or so, but the preliminary examination showed the extent of the burns."

"Made by cigarettes, I should guess. That's what they looked like to me."

"On the inside of his arms, on his upper thighs, on his testicles, inside his nose."

"Good God," Deborah murmured. She felt weak and faint.

"There's a perverted sexuality here, St. James. More evidently so when one considers how lovely a child Matthew Whateley was." He shoved the entire rack of test tubes away from him and got to his feet. "I can never understand a child's death, you know. With millions of people desperate to have a child of their own, it always seems . . ." He stopped abruptly. His face drained of colour. "Christ. I'm sorry. What a *bloody* stupid thing—"

Deborah halted his words. Her own were rapid, spoken without thought, heedless of answer. "Where will you start with a case like this, Tommy?"

Lynley looked grateful that she had got them through the moment. "At Bredgar Chambers. As soon as Havers shows up."

As if in reply, the doorbell shrilled a second time that morning.

*　　*　　*

Set into two hundred acres partially hewn from St. Leonard's Forest in West Sussex, Bredgar Chambers appeared to provide the ideal environment for serious students. There were absolutely no external distractions. Cissbury, the nearest village, was three quarters of a mile away, and it boasted nothing more than a cluster of houses, a post office, and a pub; there was no major thoroughfare within five miles of the campus, and the country lanes that surrounded it were largely untravelled; although there were several isolated cottages in the vicinity, they were inhabited almost entirely by retired people who had no especial interest in the life of the school. Nearby were vast fields, rolling hills, several farms, and extensive woodland. But beyond the combined stimulation of eternally fresh air and generally blue sky, there was nothing. Thus the school could in good faith promise hopeful parents that their children would be exposed to a monastic existence in which education, manners, moral fibre, and religious training were inculcated into them.

Bredgar Chambers was not in itself, however, an inherently ascetic environment. A surfeit of beauty prevented this. Access to the school was gained by means of a long serpentine drive that passed a neat porter's lodge and curved beneath ancient beech and ash trees whose spring growth furled in tight specks of green. On either side of this drive, manicured lawns, broken by scattered copses of fir, pine, and spruce, swept to the flintstone walls that served as the school's formal boundaries. The buildings themselves were not typical to a district of the country in which knapped flint was generally used for construction. Rather, they were made of honey-coloured Ham stones, named for the village in Somerset near which they had been quarried, and they were roofed in slate. No vines grew upon them, and in the morning sun, palpable warmth seemed to exude from their ashlar walls.

Lynley had felt Sergeant Havers' disapproval the moment they passed the porter's lodge. She didn't wait long to voice it.

"Lovely," she remarked, stubbing out her cigarette. She'd been smoking like a fiend ever since they'd left the city. The interior of his Bentley smelled like the aftermath of a conflagration. "I always did want to see where rich nits send their little buggers to learn how to say *pater.* La-di-da."

"I imagine it's a bit more Spartan on the inside, Havers," he replied. "These places usually are."

"Quite. Oh, yes."

Lynley parked in front of the main school building. Its front door stood open, acting as frame for the lovely picture of a grassy quad beyond it and more importantly, no doubt, for the statue that stood at the quad's centre. Even from a distance, Lynley recognised the regal profile of Henry Tudor, Earl of Richmond, later Henry VII and the putative founder of Bredgar Chambers.

Although it was nearly nine, no one appeared to be out on the grounds, an odd circumstance in a school claiming an enrollment of six hundred. But as they got out of the car, they heard the swelling notes of an organ, followed by the opening of "A Mighty Fortress Is Our God," sung by a well-practised congregation.

"Chapel," Lynley said in explanation.

"It's not even Sunday," Havers muttered.

"I'm sure an exposure to prayer won't corrupt our secular sensibilities, Sergeant. Come along. Try to look suitably devout, will you?"

"Right, Inspector. It's one of my better acts."

They followed the sounds of organ and singing through the school's main door, where they found themselves in a cobbled vestibule off which the chapel opened, taking up half the eastern quarter of the quad. They entered quietly. The singing continued.

Lynley saw that the chapel was typical of those found in independent schools throughout the country, with pews facing into the centre aisle after the fashion of King's College, Cambridge. He and Havers stood at the south end of the building, between two minor chapels set aside for other use.

On their left was the War Memorial Chapel, sombrely panelled in walnut upon which was carved the grim accounting of what Bredgar Chambers had lost to two brutal world wars. Above these names of boys fallen in battle scrolled the epigraph: *Per mortes eorum vivimus.* Lynley read the words, dismissing the pitiful solace that was supposed to arise from such a simplistic resolution to loss. How could anyone shrug off death by concluding that if others benefitted from it—no matter how violent or disgusting it had been—it perpetuated an intrinsic good? He had never been able to do so. Nor had he ever quite come to terms with his country's love affair with the nobility of such sacrificial offerings. He turned away.

The second chapel, however, had much the same theme. On their immediate right, this small chamber was equally dedicated to the passing of students. But Lynley saw that war had not caused their untimely deaths, for memorial plaques recorded the length of their short lives, and all of them had been far too young to be soldiers.

He entered. Candles flickered upon a linen-covered altar, surrounding a tender-faced stone angel atop it. Seeing this, he was struck all at once by a powerful image, one which he had not suffered in years. In it, once again he was that sixteen-year-old boy who knelt in the tiny Catholic chapel at Eton, tucked to the left of the main altar. He had prayed for his father there, comforted by the presence of four towering, gilded archangels that guarded each corner of the room. Although he himself was not a Catholic, somehow those fierce angels, the candles, the altar had made him feel as if he were closer to a god who might listen. So he prayed there daily. And his prayer was granted. Indeed, how it was. The memory felt like a wound. He sought a distraction and found it in the largest memorial in the room. He began to study it with unnecessary intensity.

Edward Hsu—beloved student—1957–1975. Unlike the other memorials which named boys—and two girls—who were entirely faceless, this memorial had been fashioned in such a way to include a photograph of the dead boy, a handsome Chinese. The words *beloved student* held a fascination for Lynley, since they suggested that one of the boy's teachers was responsible for creating this fond tribute to him. Lynley thought immediately of John Corntel but pushed the thought aside. It wasn't possible. Corntel would not have been teaching here in 1975.

"You must be Scotland Yard."

Lynley swung round at the hushed voice. A black-gowned man stood at the smaller chapel door.

"Alan Lockwood," he said. "I'm Bredgar's Headmaster." He came forward and extended his hand.

Handshakes were the sort of detail Lynley always took note of. Lockwood's was firm. His eyes darted to Sergeant Havers, but if he was surprised that Lynley's partner was a woman, he was careful not to show it. Lynley made the introductions.

Havers, he saw, had flopped into a small pew at the rear of the chapel where she was awaiting direction. Without bothering to camouflage what she was doing, she made a concerted study of Bredgar Chambers' Headmaster.

Lynley himself recognised the details that his sergeant would memorise and deem worthy of later comment. Lockwood appeared to be in his mid-forties, and although his height was average, he positioned his body on a subtle angle so that he seemed not to stand but to tower. His elaborate clothing served to emphasise the sense of domination he wished to project, for his academic gown was edged in red crimson and he carried a mortarboard under his arm.

His suit was impeccably cut, his shirt pristinely white, his tie perfectly knotted. Everything about him suggested a man who gave orders without expecting to be questioned. Yet the entire effect—including the man's handshake—seemed cultivated somehow, as if Lockwood had done research in the area of "headmaster grooming" and had sculptured himself to fit an image not quite in keeping with his character.

At the back of the chapel, Havers reached into the side pocket of her green wool jacket and pulled out her notebook, flipping it open. She smiled with perfect insincerity.

Lockwood turned back to Lynley. "A bad business, this is," he said soberly. "I can't tell you how relieved I am to have Scotland Yard take it on. You'll want to talk to the boy's teachers, no doubt, to John Corntel again, to Cowfrey Pitt—he's our third form hockey master. Perhaps to Judith Laughland, our San sister. And the children. Harry Morant as well. He's the boy Matthew was supposed to be visiting this past weekend. I should think Morant would know Matthew the best. They were rather special chums, as I gather."

"I'd like to start in Matthew's dormitory," Lynley said.

Lockwood adjusted the collar of his shirt. It rode high on his neck, which was puckered with a rash from shaving. "His room. Yes. That makes proper sense."

"Alan?" a woman murmured hesitantly from just outside the small chapel. "The service's just ending. Do you want—"

Lockwood excused himself and disappeared in the direction of the main chapel. After a moment, they heard his voice—strangely distorted without a microphone—dismissing the students to their classes. There was a general shuffling of feet but no talking as the students began filing out to start the school day.

Lockwood returned. With him was a woman, simply dressed in a serviceable skirt, blouse, and jacket. She was scrubbed and clean-looking, with pretty features and attractively styled iron-grey hair.

"My wife, Kathleen." Lockwood picked a speck of lint from her shoulder, and before she had time to respond to the introduction, he continued speaking, with a quick examination of his watch to illustrate his point. "I've an appointment with a parent in just a quarter-hour. Kathleen will give you over to Chas Quilter. He's our senior prefect this year. Son of Sir Francis Quilter. You've no doubt heard of him."

"Sorry. No."

Kathleen Lockwood smiled. It was lovely, but tired-looking, drawing energy from her face. "Dr. Quilter," she explained. "He's a plastic surgeon. In London."

"Ah." With, no doubt, a Harley Street address and the better secrets of two dozen or more society women under his scalpel.

"Yes," Alan Lockwood said, in agreement with nothing in particular. "I've spoken to Chas. He'll make himself available for as long as you need him. Kathleen will take you to him now. He's just gone into the vestry with the rest of the choir. When he's shown you round the school, perhaps you and I—and the sergeant, of course—can have a chat. Later in the day."

Lynley saw no need to establish dominance over the Headmaster at this juncture. If it was important to the man to seem in control of the investigation, he was more than willing to let him harbour that illusion.

"Certainly," he replied. "You're being more than helpful."

"Whatever we can do." Lockwood gave his wife momentary attention. "You'll see to the *hors d'oeuvres* this afternoon, Kate. Make certain they're better than the last lot you served, will you?" With that, Lockwood lifted a hand—farewell or blessing, it was hard to tell—and was gone.

In her husband's absence, Kathleen Lockwood murmured, "I had no real chance to speak to the poor boy's parents yesterday. They were here in the afternoon when we thought Matthew had run off. Then they left. And once we'd had the word that the boy's body had been found . . ." She rubbed her knuckles along the line of her jaw, her eyes cast down. "Let me take you to Chas. Please come this way. It's just through the chapel."

She led them to the main aisle from which the chapel's ethereal beauty was demonstrated to high effect. Since the aisle ran from north to south, its windows faced east so that the morning sun shone upon the medieval stained glass and cast pools of colour across the pews and the worn stone floor. Smoky-looking panelling covered the walls to the height of the windows, and high above them a fan-vaulted ceiling displayed a series of intricately detailed bosses. Candles had been lit during the service and recently extinguished, so their scent still hung heavily in the air, mixing with the perfume of flowers that stood at intervals along the aisle.

Kathleen Lockwood walked towards the altar. Behind it, a carved marble reredos formed a bas-relief triptych whose three panels displayed Abraham stopped in the act of obediently slaying Isaac, Adam and Eve cast out of Eden by an unforgiving archangel, and in the centre Mary weeping at the foot of the crucified Christ. More flowers decked the altar in front of this, along with six candles and a crucifix. All of it seemed excessive, too much of a display of religious fervour to be in good taste.

"I do the flowers myself," Kathleen told them. "We've a conservatory of our own, so I can have flowers on the altar all year long."

It seemed a dubious blessing.

The vestry opened directly off the chancel. At the moment it was crowded with the members of the choir, some forty boys all in the process of removing cassocks and surplices, which they hung on numbered hooks in the wall.

None of the students seemed surprised when Mrs. Lockwood ushered Lynley and Havers into the room. Conversation went on, the happy sort of noise that young people make when they are particularly pleased with themselves. Activity appeared to be conducted as it normally was. The only indication of interest or concern that any student gave at the presence of the strangers was a voice coming from nowhere that said a single name monitorially:

"Chas."

At that, talk slowly died. Students stole furtive glimpses of one another. Lynley saw that they spanned the entire range of age at the school, from the youngest third formers at twelve and thirteen to the oldest upper sixth boys approaching or beyond their eighteenth birthdays. There were no girls. Nor was a teacher present at the moment.

"Chas Quilter," Kathleen said tentatively.

"I'm here, Mrs. Lockwood."

A boy with a face to die for stepped forward.

6

Lynley's first reaction to the boy's appearance was the thought that he deserved a more exalted name than Chas. Raphael or Gabriel came to mind immediately, or, carried to an extreme, Michelangelo would have done well enough, for Chas Quilter looked like an eighteen-year-old angel.

Nearly everything about him suggested celestial perfection. His hair was blond, and although it was cut short, it capped his head with the sort of ringlets one sees upon cherubim in Renaissance paintings. His features, however, had none of that amorphous lack of character inherent to those angelic creatures on sixteenth-century canvas. Instead, they could have come off a sculpture, so pure of definition were they: wide brow, firm jaw, finely shaped nose, square chin, and an unblemished complexion carrying a faint colour in his cheeks. He was six feet tall with the body of an athlete and the grace of a dancer. The only human imperfection he seemed to possess was a need to wear spectacles, which he knuckled into place as they slipped down his nose.

"You must be the police." He was pulling on his blue school blazer. On its left breast pocket the ensign of Bredgar Chambers, a tripartite escutcheon, bore a small portcullis, a crown hovering above a sprig of hawthorn, and two roses twined together, one red and one white, all symbols close to the heart of the school's founder. "The Headmaster asked me to show you round. I'm glad to be whatever help I can." Chas smiled and continued with disarming honesty, "Gets me out of lessons for the morning, doesn't it?"

Around them, the other boys resumed donning their own jackets, as if they had been waiting to see how the senior prefect would manage his greeting of the police. Apparently satisfied that Chas had done it well, they seemed prepared to carry on themselves. They gathered schoolbooks from the benches that lined the vestry walls and within moments had exited the room, not back through the chapel but through another door that led into an adjoining room. Their voices echoed, a third door opened, and sound faded altogether.

Alone with the adults, Chas Quilter seemed perfectly comfortable. There was no adolescent anxiety in his behaviour, no shifting of weight, no awkward posture, no hunt for conversation.

"I expect you'd like to see some of the school first. It's easiest if we go out this way." That said, with a nod of farewell to Mrs. Lockwood, Chas directed them towards the door which the other students had used.

This opened into an empty rehearsal hall, disused by the look of it, and by the smell, which was fusty and heavy with dust that clung to the patchy velvet curtains which hung from the proscenium of a small stage. They walked across a scratched parquet floor and through another door which took them out into the cloister, the oldest part of the school. Here, unpaned lancet windows gave them an ample view of the quad with its four matched squares of grass, its four intersecting cobbled paths with Henry Tudor's statue at their centre, and in the corner closest to the chapel, a bell tower with a crusty steeple.

"This is the humanities section," Chas said as they walked. He raised a hand in greeting to three boys and a girl who dashed past, shoes clattering against the stone floor. "Late for a fifth time and you're gated for two weeks, aren't you?" he called out to them.

"Sod you, Quilter," was the reply.

He smiled, unoffended. "Senior prefect gets no respect from other seniors," he explained to Lynley. He seemed to expect no response to this gentle self-denigration. He merely continued on his way, pausing at one of the windows to explain the layout of the quad.

Four buildings comprised it. Chas indicated each one as he identified its purpose. The entire eastern structure, he explained, contained the chapel on one side of the main entry to the school and on the other side the administrative offices of the bursar, the porter, and the secretaries, along with the Headmaster's study, and the council room shared by the Board of Governors and the school prefects. The south building held the library, the original big school-room used in the days when Bredgar Chambers had admitted its first forty-four pupils, the masters' common room where the staff took their meals and received their mail, and the kitchen. The west building held the pupils' dining hall and a string of humanities classrooms, and the north building through which they were walking was the home of the music department. Above them, on the first floor of all four buildings—which were joined by a series of corridors and doorways—were the classrooms devoted specifically to English, social science, art, and languages.

"Everything else is away from the main quad," Chas explained. "Theatre and dance classrooms, technical centre, maths building, science building, sports hall, and the Sanatorium."

"What about the boys' and girls' houses?"

Chas made a quirky face and rubbed the back of his wrist against his right temple as if in the need to discipline his hair. "Separated by the quad. Girls on south grounds, boys on north."

"And if the twain should meet?" Lynley enquired, interested to discover how the modern independent schools—seeking to keep their doors open through a more liberal admissions policy—were dealing with the treacherous waters of male and female boarders.

Chas blinked behind his gold-rimmed spectacles and replied, "I expect you know, sir. Or you can probably guess. Expulsion. Generally with no questions asked."

"Rather stiff sentence, that," Havers noted.

"It does get the message across, though, doesn't it?" Chas quoted solemnly. " 'The true-spirited Bredgardian does not engage in sexual misconduct of any kind.' Page twenty-three of the code book. The first page everyone turns to *and* dribbles over. Wishful thinking." He grinned, opened a door, and motioned them into a short corridor, newer-looking than the rest of the building. "We'll go through the sports hall. It's a short cut to Erebus House. That's where Matthew Whateley's dormitory is."

Their entrance to the sports hall—an obviously recent addition to the school—produced an awkward suspension of a gymnastics lesson that was going on at a trampoline in the west end of the building. The small collection of pupils—all young boys—turned as a body and stared without speaking. It was decidedly odd. One would expect them at least to murmur to one another, to poke, to jab. They were children, after all. Not one appeared to be more than thirteen years old. But if any of them possessed that energetic restlessness so typical to the age, they did not show it. Instead, they fixed their eyes on Lynley. Their teacher, a young man in gym shorts and a jersey, said, "Boys. *Boys,*" but they did not attend. Lynley could almost imagine them heaving a collective sigh of relief when he and Havers followed Chas Quilter out of the sports hall and into the north section of the school.

A pebbled path led them past the maths building, winding along the lawn through a small but lovely grove of birches, and delivered them to the pupils' entrance to Erebus House. Like the other school buildings, Erebus was constructed of honey-hued Ham stones. Like the others, it too was roofed in slate and devoid of climbing plants save for a single clematis that hung over a closed door at the east end of the building.

"Those are the private quarters," Chas said, following the direction of Lynley's gaze. "Mr. Cornel's rooms. The third formers' digs are just this way." He opened the door and went inside.

For Lynley, it was unavoidable, this stepping back into the past. They stood in a different sort of entry hall than had been in his own house at Eton. But the smells were just the same. Spoiled milk gone sour and never mopped up, burnt toast disregarded on someone's private cooker, clothes stiff with dirt and exuding a foul miasma of sweat, and heat from the radiator bubbling away, cooking all these odours permanently into the woodwork and the floors and the ceiling. Even when the house was empty of boys on weekends or during their holidays, the smell would linger stubbornly on.

That Erebus was one of the older houses was evidenced by the fact that the entry was panelled from floor to ceiling in what once had been lustrous golden oak. Through the years this golden hue had darkened, and generations of schoolboys, who found it impossible to attach sentiment to something merely because of its age, had gone to great lengths to finish off its lustre. The panelling was banged, battered, and brutalised.

The furniture in the entry was not in much better condition, what little there was of it. A long, narrow refectory table against one wall—the repository for mail, it seemed—bore the battle scars of generations of trunks, suitcases, tuck boxes, schoolbooks, and packages from home having been dumped carelessly upon it. There were two overstuffed chairs not far from this, both stained, both with their cushions missing. Between them on the wall hung a pay telephone with countless names and numbers scratched into the panelling surrounding it. The only item in the entry that could have remotely been called decorative was the house banner which someone had sensibly encased in glass on the wall. Even it had seen better days, for it was worn thin almost to transparency, and its image was indistinguishable.

"It's supposed to represent Erebus," Chas explained as Lynley and Havers inspected the banner in its place of honour, "the primeval darkness that emerged from Chaos. The brother of night. The father of day and sky. You can't tell from the banner, any longer, I'm afraid. It's awfully faded."

"You're studying classics?" Lynley asked.

"Chemistry, biology, and English," Chas replied. "We all have to know the meanings behind the houses' names. It's part of the tradition."

"What are the other houses?"

"Mopsus, Ion, Calchus, Eirene, and Galatea."

"Interesting selection, considering the array of mythological allusions one has to choose from. The last two are for the girls, I suppose."

"Yes. I'm in Ion myself."

"The son of Creusa and Apollo. An interesting story."

Chas' spectacles slipped on his nose. He pushed them up, smiled, and said, "Third formers are up above. The stairs are this way." He continued on his way, leaving Lynley and Havers to follow.

On the first floor of the building, no one was about. They walked down a narrow corridor floored in worn brown linoleum with walls painted a dirt-covering institutional green. It smelled exclusively of sweat and damp. At ceiling height, water pipes ran the length of the hall, curved down the wall, and disappeared through a hole in the floor. Doors lined both sides of the hall. None bore locks, but all were closed.

At the third door on the left, Chas paused, knocked once, announced "Quilter," and shouldered it open a bit. He gave a quick look inside, said, *"Jesus,"* and turned back to Lynley and Havers. His expression told them that something was wrong. He did his best to cover the momentary rupture in his facade by holding out his hand with an apologetic flourish. "Here it is. Pretty bad. It's hard to believe four boys could . . . well, see for yourself."

Lynley and Havers entered. Chas remained by the door.

The room was mayhem, with magazines and books thrown here and there, papers underfoot, rubbish unemptied, unmade beds, cupboards gaping open, drawers crammed too full and overflowing, clothing strewn about in three of the four cubicles. Either a hasty search had been conducted in the room recently or the house prefect—whose job it was to see to it that the boys kept themselves in order—was not doing anything to make them toe the line.

Lynley considered the likelihood of both possibilities. As he did so, he saw Chas leave the dormitory, heard him opening and closing doors all down the hall, heard his voice murmuring in disbelief. Lynley had his answer.

"The house prefect, Sergeant. Do we have his name?"

Havers flipped back through her notebook, read, continued turning pages. "John Corntel said it was . . . Here. Brian Byrne. Is this his doing, sir?"

"More likely his undoing," Lynley replied. "Let's see what we have."

The dormitory was divided into cubicles, each cubicle defined by white painted pressed-wood boards which rose about five feet from the floor and provided a small degree of privacy. Contained within the cubicle's extremely limited space were a bed with two drawers built into its lower frame, a cupboard with the name of the cubicle's inhabitant fixed to it with tape, and whatever wall decoration the boy himself chose as his personal statement of ownership.

It was intriguing to see the difference between what Matthew Whateley had put upon his walls and what the other boys had chosen. In the cubicle identified as belonging to someone named Wedge hung a collection of rock and roll posters, revealing a rather eclectic taste in music. U2, the Eurythmics, Pink Floyd's *The Wall*, Prince, mixed with vintage photographs of the Beatles, the Byrds, as well as Peter, Paul, and Mary. In Arlens' cubicle, bathing beauties posed languidly, their bodies well-oiled and clothed in fantasy-producing swimming apparel, surrounded by sand, striding Amazon-like across the dunes, arching hard-nippled and with Freudian explicitness into the foaming brine. Smythe-Andrews, the inhabitant of the dormitory's third little niche, had devoted himself to a collection of photographs comprising a memorial to some of the more grisly scenes from the motion picture *Alien*. Anyone who had met a violent end was depicted in ghastly, stomach-turning detail. As was the alien himself, looking like a combination of chain saw, praying mantis, and what came out of the scientist's machine in *The Fly*.

The fourth cubicle, by the window, belonged to Matthew Whateley. His choice of decoration was photographs of locomotives—steam, diesel, and electric—from an assortment of countries. Lynley looked at them curiously. They were arranged neatly in rows on the wall above his bed. Across one had been written "choo-choo, little poof," a strange derogation for a young boy to leave hanging.

From the middle of the room, Havers said, "Less mature than the other boys. Everything else seems fairly typical to the normal thirteen-year-old."

"If thirteen-year-olds can ever be said to be normal," Lynley replied.

"True. What was up in your room at thirteen, Inspector?"

Lynley put on his spectacles to look at Matthew's clothing. "Reproductions of early Renaissance art," he replied absently. "I had a youthful devotion to Fra Angelico."

She laughed. "Sod you."

"You doubt me, Sergeant?"

"Completely."

"Ah. Well, come and see what you make of this."

She joined him in the cramped confines of Matthew's cubicle where he had opened the cupboard. Like everything else, it was made of pressed wood, painted white, and, in keeping with the monastic atmosphere of Bredgar Chambers, it contained only two shelves and eight pegs for clothes. On the former were three clean white shirts, four pullovers in assorted colours, three jerseys, and a stack of T-shirts. On the latter hung trousers for both school and leisure wear. On the floor were dress shoes, gym shoes, and scuffed-up casual shoes. Into a ball had been tossed his games clothes.

Havers, Lynley saw, assessed the facts and drew her conclusion. "No school uniform here. Which means if he ran off, he did it in his school clothes."

"A bit unusual, wouldn't you say?" Lynley noted. "He'd be running off—clearly in defiance of school rules—wearing something that would immediately identify him as a pupil of Bredgar Chambers. Why do you suppose he might do that?"

Havers frowned, sucked at her lower lip. "Got some sort of message that he didn't expect—we saw the telephone down in the entry, didn't we? Anyone could have phoned him. He felt he needed to be off at once. No time to delay."

"A possibility," Lynley admitted, "except that his possession of an off-games chit to get him out of playing hockey that afternoon seems to suggest he had this planned."

"Yes, there's that." She drew a pair of trousers from the cupboard and examined them absently. "Then I should think he wanted to be seen. He wanted to be picked up. Perhaps he wore his uniform as a means of identifying himself."

"So someone he was meeting would know who he was?"

"That works, doesn't it?"

Lynley was going through the drawers beneath the bed. As he did so, he saw Chas Quilter return to the dormitory where he stood, watchful, hands in his pockets, inside the door. Lynley ignored him for the moment, fascinated at what the drawers revealed about Matthew Whateley, and, even more, about his mother.

"Havers," Lynley said, "hand me trousers and a pullover, will you? Any will do."

She did so and Lynley laid them across the bed, took a matching pair of socks from the drawer, and stood back, looking down at the outfit he'd created.

"She's put his name on everything," he said to Havers, "which is no doubt required by the school. But look at what else she's done for the boy." He turned a sock down to reveal the numbers *3, 4,* and *7* fixed to tape. He reached for the trousers, and on the inner waistband alongside the boy's name was the single number *3.* On the collar of the pullover again they saw *3.* Another pair of trousers was marked with a *7.*

"Match the numbers so he knew how to dress himself?" Havers asked in disgust. "Gives me the flipping chills, that does, sir. Choo-choo trains on the walls and Mummy's dress-by-numbers in his clothes?"

"It tells us something, doesn't it?"

"It tells me Matthew Whateley was probably as good as suffocating. If he had any sense, that is. Was it his parents' idea that he come to this place, Inspector?"

"It appears to have been."

"So they wanted little Matt to fit in with the swells he'd be meeting in his new school. No slip-ups would do if he was to climb the ladder of social success. Starting at thirteen with his clothes all numbered so he put them on right. No wonder he ran off."

Lynley was thoughtful, pondering the numbers. He replaced the clothes and asked the senior prefect to verify whether the requisite clothing allowed by the school was present in Matthew Whateley's cupboard. Chas came to look it over and indicated that, aside from the school uniform, everything was there. Lynley closed the cupboard and drawers and said to the boy, "There's no study area in here. Is there a day room in the building where the boys do their prep?"

Chas nodded. He seemed uncomfortable, and perhaps, as the chief representative of the school, anxious to make an excuse for the chaotic condition in which they'd found the dormitory. Like other people Lynley had encountered in his years of policework, Chas alleviated the pressure of discomfort through a momentary garrulity, giving out information that wasn't asked for but was, by its nature, revealing.

"There's a day room down the hall if you'd like to see it, sir. Every floor in the house has at least three to five senior boys living on it. They're upper sixth boys, so they're *supposed* to understand what order is all about and see that the younger boys hold to it. The house prefect is supposed to see that the senior boys under him keep tabs on the dormitories assigned to them. *And* to the day rooms." He smiled rather dismally, but said no more than, "God knows what condition we'll find the day room in."

"Sounds as if the system has broken down a bit in Erebus House," Lynley concluded. As they followed Chas Quilter down the hallway, through a door, and into a second corridor, Lynley recognised the only conclusion possible to reach, based on the information Chas had just given them. Indeed, the senior boys were responsible for seeing to it that the younger boys were disciplined. Indeed, the house prefect was responsible for seeing to it that the senior boys did exactly that job. But the senior prefect—Chas Quilter himself—was responsible for the smooth working of the entire scheme. If the scheme didn't work, chances were very good that Chas Quilter himself was at the root of the problem.

Ahead of them, Chas was opening a door. "The third form Erebus boys do their prep in here," he was saying. "Each one has his own desk and shelf. We call them barn stalls."

The day room was in only slightly better condition than the dormitory had been, and like the entry to Erebus House, it showed its age. Vague odours lingered in the air: a piece of forgotten, moulding food; a pot of glue left open; hastily discarded clothing that needed to be washed. An uncarpeted hardwood floor was stained with ink and splodged with grease spots where contraband food had been dropped. Dark knotty pine panelled the walls, and where it was not covered with assorted posters, it was heavily gouged. As were the study areas themselves—the barn stalls, as Chas had called them. Lined up along the four walls of the room, these showed the most severe signs of age.

They looked very much like a series of tall-backed pews with unpadded wooden seats perhaps three feet long. These seats faced a large shelf with a single drawer beneath it to serve as a desk. Above this were two narrower shelves for schoolbooks. As in the dormitory, each barn stall had been given the stamp of the personality of the boy who used it. Postcards and photographs and wildly coloured transfers had been stuck onto every surface of every stall, and where a previous occupant had left his mark a bit too permanently, the current owner had merely ripped it off, leaving traces of glue and paper behind, showing a disembodied hand here, part of a face there, a few letters from a word, the wheel of a vehicle. Everywhere restless thirteen-year-old fingers had picked at wood that was centuries old. Everywhere young bodies had worn away the varnish so that great pale patches showed through the dark, protective lacquer.

Like his cubicle in the dormitory, Matthew Whateley's barn stall was not decorated in the fashion of the other boys'. No rock and roll posters, no film stars, no nubile young ladies in suggestive dress, no longed-for automobiles, no photographs depicting athletic prowess. Nothing at all, in fact, save a snapshot of two children squatting, mud-splattered, on the tide-receding bank of the Thames, with Hammersmith Bridge in the background. One of the children was a grinning Matthew, poking at the mud with a long, curved switch. The other was a laughing black girl whose feet were bare and whose hair fell to her shoulders in dozens of beautiful beaded plaits. Yvonnen Livesley, Lynley thought, Matthew's friend from home. He examined the picture and once again doubted Kevin Whateley's assertion that Matthew would not have been running home for an opportunity to see this girl. She was lovely.

He handed the photograph to Sergeant Havers, who slipped it into her notebook wordlessly. While she watched, he put on his spectacles and looked over Matthew's textbooks. They were fairly standard academic material, representing English, maths, geography, history, biology, chemistry, and, in keeping with the spirit of the school, religious studies. On the desktop was an incomplete maths assignment. Next to it lay a stack of three spiral notebooks. Lynley divided it all, giving half to Havers and taking half himself. He sat in Matthew's barn stall—a tight fit for a man of his height—while Havers disappeared into the stall in front of him. Chas walked to the window, opened it, and looked out on the grounds.

A voice called from outside, another answered. Several boys laughed. But in the day room there was only the sound of books being opened, pages being thumbed through, notebooks being checked. Tedious, painstaking, absolutely necessary.

Havers spoke. "Something here, sir." Over the top of the barn stall, she handed him a spiral notebook. It contained a letter of some sort, obviously a rough draft, for several words had been scratched out and replaced by others more suitable.

Lynley read it.

Dear Jeanne [crossed out] Jean:

    I would like to thank you very much for the dinner Tues-
day last. You're not to worry about how late I got back because
I know the boy who saw me won't say anything. I still feel
[crossed out] think I could beat your father at chess if he'd only
give me some proper time to think out the moves! I can't see
how he manages to think so far ahead. But next time I shall do
better. Thanks awfully again.

Lynley removed his spectacles and looked towards the window
where Chas Quilter still maintained his distance.

"Matthew has written a letter to someone named Jean," he said.
"Someone with whom he had dinner. On a Tuesday, evidently, but
there's no telling which Tuesday since he hasn't dated the letter.
Have you any idea who Jean might be?"

Chas' brow furrowed. He took his time about replying, and when
he finally did so, he excused the delay by saying, "I was trying to
think of the names of the masters' wives. It seems likeliest that it
might be one of them."

"It doesn't seem likely he'd be on a first-name basis with one of
the wives, does it? Or is that generally the accepted manner of
address?"

Chas admitted that it wasn't and shrugged in apology.

"He also says that he got back late, that one of the boys saw him
but won't say anything. What do you take that to mean?"

"That he was out after curfew."

"Isn't that something his house prefect should have known?"

Chas looked uncomfortable. He studied his shoe tops before
replying. "Should have. Yes. Bed checks are generally done every
night."

"Generally?"

"Always. Nightly."

"So someone—one of the senior boys or the house prefect—
should have reported Matthew missing if he wasn't in his dormitory
after curfew. Is that correct?"

The hesitation was marked. "Yes, someone should have seen he
wasn't in Erebus."

He didn't mention the person at fault. But Lynley did not miss the
fact that both John Corntel and now Chas Quilter seemed determined to protect the Erebus House prefect, Brian Byrne.

*   *   *

John Corntel knew that the police were at the school. Everyone did. Even if he hadn't seen Thomas Lynley walk into the chapel that morning, he would have noticed the silver Bentley on the front drive and, noticing it, he would have put two and two together. The police did not usually arrive in such automotive splendour, to be sure. But most of the police did not also lead secondary lives as belted earls.

In the masters' common room on the south side of the quad, Corntel watched the last of the morning coffee trickle out of the urn and into his cup. He tried to blot from his mind every image that threatened to crack the fragile composure he had developed to get him through the day. His mind swarmed with *if onlys.* If only he had phoned the Morants to see if Matthew was among their son's guests; if only he had thought to see the boy off personally in the first place; if only he had spoken to Brian Byrne and made certain that Brian had kept account of all the boys; if only he had visited the dormitories more frequently instead of leaving it to the senior boys; if only he had not been preoccupied . . . had not been mortified . . . had had not felt trapped and naked and utterly humiliated.

On the table with the coffee urn lay the remains of the masters' breakfast. Three racks of cold toast sat among a silver tray of gelatinous eggs, five strips of bacon glistening iridescently with fat, corn flakes, a bowl of tinned grapefruit sections, and a platter of bananas. Corntel shut his eyes at the sight of all this, felt his stomach churn, and demanded cooperation from his body. He couldn't remember for a certainty when he had last eaten anything substantial. He vaguely recalled looking at a meal Friday night, but nothing since then. It had been impossible.

He lifted his head to gaze out the window. Across an expanse of lawn, he could see the pupils at work in a classroom inside the technical centre, drilling and pounding and chiselling away in affirmation of Bredgar Chambers' philosophy that the creative urge within each child had to be stimulated rigorously. Not ten years old, the centre had long been a source of controversy on the campus, with staff members divided on its propriety at a school such as Bredgar Chambers. Some argued that it gave the pupils a necessary outlet for energies often stifled in a purely academic environment. Others claimed that afternoon games and societies provided that outlet, while a technical centre would do nothing more than ultimately encourage "the wrong element" to seek application to the school. Corntel smiled sardonically at this latter thought. The mere presence of a building in which pupils played with wood and fibreglass and metal and electronics had hardly altered an unspoken policy of admissions that had been in effect for five hundred years and supported by every headmaster. The school's prospectus might well give lip service to an egalitarian approach to education. The reality was much different. Or at least it had been until Matthew Whateley had come along.

Corntel didn't want to think of the boy. He pushed him from his mind. But in Matthew's place—as if he were there to shake an admonishing finger at Corntel's failures—came his own father, headmaster of one of the country's most prestigious independent schools, one entrenched in tradition and fully committed to defining boundaries. No technical centres there.

"Housemaster!" Patrick Corntel had roared his approval over the telephone line as if they were speaking to one another from foreign countries and not at a distance of less than one hundred miles. "That's the stuff, Johnny! Housemaster *and* head of English! By God! Your next move is deputy headmaster, lad. Give yourself two years. Don't rot in one place!"

Don't rot in one place was the credo that had defined his father's career, driving him ruthlessly from one school to another for twenty years until he had what he wanted, the title of headmaster, the title he wanted his own son to possess.

"Keep on the ladder, Johnny-lad. When I'm ready to retire, I'll want *you* to step into my shoes here at Summerston. But you've got to be ready, lad. You've got to have the background. So start looking. Start sniffing. Deputy head comes next. You hear me? Deputy head. I'll keep an ear to the ground and if I hear of anything . . ."

Corntel would reply obediently. Yes, Father. Deputy head. Whatever you say. It was easier than arguing, and certainly far easier than telling the truth. Housemaster of Erebus was as far as he was going. Head of English was the pinnacle of his career. He didn't burn with the need to prove himself to himself or to anyone else. He burned with other needs. They were not the same.

"Calling in debts, are we, John?"

Corntel started at the unexpected voice so near his shoulder and turned to see that he had been joined at the coffee urn by Cowfrey Pitt, the German master and head of languages. Pitt was looking particularly unkempt this morning. His fringe of hair was scaly with dandruff. His craggy face had not been shaven well enough and he had done nothing to trim the hair that sprouted like a weed from his right nostril. One sleeve of his gown had a rent along the seam, and chalk marks on his grey suit beneath it had not been removed.

"I beg your pardon?" Corntel went about the business of adding milk and sugar to the coffee he had poured.

Pitt leaned closer. He spoke in a low, chummy fashion, as if they shared a secret. "I said, calling in old debts? This Scotland Yard bloke's an old school friend, isn't he?"

Corntel moved a step away, giving his attention to the tray of eggs as if with the intention of taking one of them. "Word gets around quickly enough," he replied.

"You scampered off to London yesterday. I asked why. But your secret's safe with me." Pitt took up a piece of toast and munched upon it. He leaned against the table, smiling at his colleague.

"Safe with you?" Corntel replied. "I'm not sure I understand."

"Come now, John. No need to play the astounded innocent with me. The boy was your responsibility, wasn't he?"

"Just as the girls in Galatea House are your responsibility," Corntel said. "But I should guess you absolve yourself of guilt fast enough when one of them gets into trouble, don't you?"

Pitt smiled. "The cat has claws, I see." He brushed his fingers on his gown and selected another slice of toast and a piece of bacon. His eyes lingered hungrily upon the eggs. Corntel saw this and, in spite of his natural dislike of the German master, he felt touched by a momentary, unwanted pity. He knew that Pitt would never come into the masters' common room when breakfast was first being served, when his meal would be hot. It was a matter of pride. To come into the masters' common room for hot food would be an open admission that life in the private quarters of Galatea House was too unpleasant for Pitt to take his breakfast there. And Pitt would not admit to that any more than he would admit to the fact that his wife was in bed at the moment, soundly sleeping off her regular Sunday evening's binge.

Whatever pity Corntel felt for the other man died, however, as Pitt continued to speak. "I suppose this really screws it up for you, doesn't it, John? You have my complete sympathy, of course, but after all, didn't you think to check with the Morant family to see that all six boys actually went with them for the weekend? That's fairly standard procedure. At least it is for me."

"I didn't think—"

"What about checking the Sanatorium? A boy gets sick and you don't even think to pop by and put your hand on his forehead? Or"—Pitt smiled—"was your hand somewhere else at the time?"

Quick fury damaged Corntel's forced calm. "You know very well that I had no word from the San. But *you* did, didn't you? What did you do when you found Matthew Whateley's off-games chit sitting in your pigeonhole last Friday? You were running that hockey game in the afternoon, weren't you? Did you dash over to see what was wrong with him, Cowfrey? Or did you just go on your way, satisfied that the chit was what it seemed?"

Pitt was deliberately unperturbed. "Don't tell me you feel a need to push that off on to me." His eyes—grey-green and reptilian—slid away from Corntel's to make a quick assessment of who was in the room. There was no one, but in spite of this, his voice lowered confidentially. "We both know who was responsible for Matthew, don't we, John? You can point out to the police that I saw an off-games chit and did nothing to verify its validity. Please feel free to do so, in fact. But I'm not so sure there's a crime involved in that. Are you?"

"Are you even *suggesting*—"

Pitt's face broke into a smile as he looked beyond Corntel's left shoulder. "Headmaster. Good morning," he said.

Corntel turned to see Alan Lockwood watching their exchange from the doorway. He took their measure from head to toe before he crossed the room, his gown flowing round him.

"Do something about your appearance, Mr. Pitt," Lockwood said and consulted a schedule which he pulled from his jacket pocket. "You've a lesson in a half-hour. That should give you time to clean yourself up. You look like a tramp, or weren't you even aware of that? We've the police on campus. The Board of Governors may show up before the morning's over, and I have enough on my mind already without having to worry about my teachers' lack of interest in their personal grooming. Do something about it. Now. Is that clear?"

Pitt's features hardened. "Perfectly," he replied.

Alan Lockwood nodded and walked away.

"Little bum-boy," Pitt murmured. "What a show of Headmaster our Alan puts on. What a lovely show of power. What a man. What a god. But just scratch the surface and you'll see who's in control. Little Matt Whateley proved that."

"What are you talking about, Cowfrey?" Corntel's anger was fading, giving place to irritation. Yet he saw that again he had foolishly played into Pitt's hands.

"Talking about?" Pitt repeated with factitious surprise. "My, you *are* out of touch, aren't you, Johnny? What's been keeping you so busy that you've even lost sight of the latest school gossip? Hmm? Is there something I should know about your personal life? Or perhaps I ought to guess?"

Anger returned. Corntel walked away.

7

Lynley decided to meet with Matthew Whateley's three roommates in the dormitory they had shared. When Chas Quilter delivered them to the room, each boy went immediately to his own cubicle, like an animal scurrying for safety. They seemed to take care not to look at one another, but two of them cast their eyes quickly upon the senior prefect, who followed them into the room and stood, as he had before, by the door.

Seeing the contrast between Chas and these boys, Lynley realised that he had forgotten how great are the changes that occur between the ages of thirteen and eighteen. Chas was developed, fully formed, a man, while the boys still possessed all the softness of childhood—round cheeks, silky skin, indefinite jaws. There was a wariness to them as they perched each one upon the edge of his bed, and Lynley wagered that it had more to do with the presence of the senior prefect than it did with the police. Chas' physical presence alone would probably be more than enough to intimidate a boy five years younger than he. His position of importance at the school did not help matters.

"Sergeant," Lynley said to Havers, who had automatically opened her notebook in preparation for the interview, "will you take stock of the school for me? Interior and exterior." He saw her mouth begin to open with the automatic reference to police procedure and Judge's Rules, and stopped her by saying, "Have Chas show you everything, if you will."

Havers was quick enough to understand, wise enough to keep the comprehension from showing upon her face. She nodded and escorted the senior prefect from the room, leaving Lynley alone with Wedge, Arlens, and Smythe-Andrews. He took stock of them. They were nice-looking boys, neatly dressed in grey trousers, crisp white shirts, yellow pullovers, and blue and yellow striped ties. Of the three, Wedge seemed the most self-possessed. Once the senior prefect was gone, he looked up from his examination of the faded linoleum floor. Backed by his collection of rock and roll posters, he appeared confident and ready to engage in conversation. The other two seemed less so. Arlens was giving his full attention to the bathing beauty arched into the surf while Smythe-Andrews squirmed restlessly on his bed, poking at the heel of his shoe with the stub of a pencil.

"Matthew Whateley appears to have run away from the school," Lynley said, going to sit on the end of Matthew's bed. He leaned towards them, his arms on his legs, his hands clasped loosely in front of him, a model of relaxation. "Have you any idea why?"

The boys exchanged furtive looks.

"What was he like?" Lynley queried. "Wedge?"

"Nice bloke," Wedge responded, fastening his gaze on Lynley's face as if this act might serve as verification of complete truth. "Decent bloke, Matt was."

"So you know he's dead."

"Whole school knows he's dead, sir."

"How did you find out?"

"Heard about it this morning at breakfast, sir."

"From whom?"

Wedge picked at his palm. "Don't know. It just came down the side of the table. Matt's dead. Whateley's dead. Some boy from Erebus House is dead. Don't know who started it."

"Were you surprised?"

"I thought it was a joke."

Lynley looked at the other two boys. "And you?" he asked them. "Did you think it was a joke?"

They took their lead from Wedge, both of them nodding solemnly. Wedge spoke again.

"One doesn't expect that sort of thing."

"But Matthew had been missing since Friday. Something had to have happened to him. It couldn't have come as a complete surprise."

Arlens bit at the nail of his index finger. "He was to go with Harry Morant for the weekend, sir. With some boys from Calchus House— that's where Harry has his digs. We thought Matt had gone with them to the Cotswolds. He had an exeat. Everyone knew . . ." Arlens hesitated, as if he'd said too much, dropped his head, went back to chewing his nail again.

"Everyone knew what?" Lynley asked.

Wedge took the initiative. He spoke with surprising patience. "Everyone knew that Harry Morant was taking five boys home for the weekend. Harry made a big thing of it to everyone. Like it was something special and only the select would be invited. Harry's like that." Wedge concluded sagaciously, "Makes him feel important."

Lynley watched Smythe-Andrews repeatedly stab at his shoe. His face was sullen.

"All the other boys going on the weekend were from Calchus House? How did Matthew come to know them that well?"

None of the boys replied at first. But none of them were successful in hiding the fact that there was a simple and direct answer to the question which all of them knew and were reluctant to give. Lynley thought about his interview with Matthew's parents, thought about their persistent assertions of their son's contentment at Bredgar Chambers.

"Was Matthew happy here?" He noticed the momentary cessation of Smythe-Andrews' pencil.

"Who's really happy here?" the boy replied. "We're here because our parents sent us. Matt was no different."

"But he was, wasn't he?" Lynley asked. Again, they didn't reply, but this time he saw Arlens and Wedge regard one another briefly. "Just look at what he hung on his walls."

"He was a decent chap." This from Wedge, like a protest.

"Who ran away?"

"Kept to himself," Arlens said.

"He was different," Lynley countered.

The boys didn't respond. Their determined reserve was its own affirmation. Matthew Whateley had indeed been different, but Lynley guessed that the difference had gone far beyond the pictures on his walls. It sprang from his background, from the neighbourhood in which he had spent his childhood, from his accent, from his values, from his choice of friends. The boy had been out of place in this environment, and all of them knew it.

He gave his attention to Arlens. "What do you mean when you say he kept to himself?"

"Just that . . . well, he ignored traditions."

"What sort of traditions?"

"Things that we do. You know. Just things. School things."

"School things?"

Wedge looked exasperated, frowned at Arlens. "Stupid stuff, sir. Like everyone carves his name in the bell tower. It's supposed to be locked, but the lock's been broken for ages, and everyone—the boys, not the girls—climbs up and carves his name somewhere on the wall inside. And has a smoke there as well, if he wants."

Wedge's information seemed to loosen Arlens' tongue. "And hunting for magic mushrooms," he added with a smile.

"There are drugs in the school?"

Arlens shrugged, subdued perhaps by his own inadvertent admission. Lynley interpreted the shrug as negation and went on.

"But you've said magic mushrooms."

Wedge again took the initiative. "It's a lark. Going out at night with a torch and a blanket over one's head and picking magic mushrooms. We never eat any. I don't think anyone actually eats them. But blokes like to have them about. That was the sort of thing Matt wasn't interested in."

"Was he above it all?"

"He just wasn't interested."

"He was interested in the Model Railway Society," Arlens offered.

The other boys rolled their eyes at this. Obviously, an interest in model railways was a little childish in the eyes of this lot.

"And in doing his lessons," Wedge put in. "He was serious about that. About school."

"And about his trains," Arlens reaffirmed.

"Did you ever meet his parents?" Lynley asked.

A shuffling of feet, a fidgeting on the beds, quite telling at that particular question.

"There was a parents' day, wasn't there? Did you meet them?"

Smythe-Andrews spoke, but he did not look up from his shoe as he did so. "Matt's mum used to work in a pub. His dad carves tombstones outside of London. And Matt didn't hide that from anyone the way some boys might. He didn't care. It's like he wanted people to know."

Hearing the words, seeing the boys' reactions, Lynley wondered if schools had changed at all. He wondered if, in fact, their society had changed. In this age of enlightenment, they all gave lip service to the end of class barriers, but how honest were those declarations of equality in a culture that had for generations judged a man's worth by his accent, by his chance of birth, by the age of his money, by the clubs he belonged to and the people who called him *friend*? What had Matthew Whateley's parents been thinking of in sending their son to a school like Bredgar Chambers, even on a scholarship?

"Matthew was writing a letter to someone called Jean. Do you know who that is? It was someone he had dinner with."

The boys shook their heads in unison at this. Their confusion looked genuine. Lynley took out his pocket watch, checked the time, and asked them a final question.

"Matthew's parents don't believe that he ran away from the school. Do you believe he did?"

It was Smythe-Andrews who replied for them all. He laughed once—it sounded like something between a yelp and a sob—and said bitterly, "We'd all run off from this place if we only had the nerve. Or somewhere to go."

"Matthew had somewhere to go?"

"Looks like he did."

"Perhaps he only thought he had that. Perhaps he only thought that he was running to safety when in reality he was running to his death. He'd been tied up. He'd been tortured as well. So whatever he saw as safety was in reality—"

A loud thump issued from one of the cubicles. Arlens had fainted and fallen to the floor.

It was time for history. Harry Morant knew he should have gone to the lesson, since he was part of a panel giving a report to the class this very morning. He would be missed. The cry would be sent out to find him. Harry didn't care. He didn't care about anything any longer. Matthew Whateley was dead. Things were changed. The weight of power had shifted. He had lost all.

For a time he had been deliriously safe after months of terror. For three short weeks he had known what it was to fall asleep without the fear of being roughly awakened, of being dragged from his bed and thrown to the floor, of that terse voice grunting *want a grind, nancy boy? want a grind? want a grind?*, of quick slaps to the face—never enough to leave a mark—and hands grabbing and squeezing and poking his body, of being led through a dark corridor and into the lavatory, where a candle was lit and an unflushed toilet brimmed with excrement and urine and the voice said *bog-washing tonight ... still want to be cheeky?* And then being dunked into the foul mess and trying not to cry, trying not to vomit, and failing at both.

Harry couldn't understand why he had been chosen, for he'd done everything just as he was supposed to do at Bredgar Chambers. His older brothers had attended the school, and far in advance they'd let Harry know exactly what would be expected of him if he wanted to fit in. He'd done it all. He'd climbed to the highest part of the bell tower—up that claustrophobic, winding stone staircase—and carved his name deeply into the wall. He'd learned to smoke—although he didn't like it much—and had jumped to the bidding of every prefect who ever spoke to him. He'd followed the rules, tried to remain anonymous, never sneaked on another pupil no matter what the offence. Yet it hadn't worked. He'd been singled out anyway. Now it would all begin again. At the thought, a cry caught in his throat. He fought against tears.

In the late morning, the air was still cool. The sun was out but it didn't do very much to cut through the chill. Where Harry sat on a concrete bench in a corner of the walled sculpture garden that was the midway point between the school and the Headmaster's house, it seemed particularly cold, as if the marble and bronze statues that stood among the rose bushes were themselves contributing to the glacial air. He shivered, hugging himself tighter until he was bent double.

He had seen the arrival of the police, had been in the vestry with the rest of the choir when Mrs. Lockwood brought them in and gave them over to Chas Quilter. At first he hadn't thought they were police at all, for they didn't look like what he'd been expecting ever since breakfast when the word filtered through the dining hall that Matthew Whateley was dead and that New Scotland Yard would be coming to the school. Harry had never seen detectives before, had never been exposed to the mysteries and rituals associated with those three words *New Scotland Yard.* So he'd developed an elaborate idea of what the metropolitan police would look like and how they would act, based largely upon what he had seen on television and read in books. But these detectives did not fit into the mould he had created for them.

For one thing, the man was too tall, too handsome, too well-groomed, and too splendidly dressed. His voice was too patrician, and the cut of his suit did not suggest that he carried any sort of weapon. The woman who accompanied him was not much better. She was far too short, too unattractive, too plump, and too frumpy. Harry could not imagine confiding what he knew to either one of them. Not for a moment. Not at all. The man would listen from his icy great height and the woman would watch through her little pig eyes and he would talk and talk and try to make them understand what he knew and how he knew it and why it had all happened and who was responsible and . . .

It was all an excuse. He was looking for excuses. He was wild for excuses. He needed a reason not to speak at all. Deciding that they weren't *proper* detectives was about as good a reason as he was going to be able to come up with. So he would cling to it. They couldn't help him anyway. They wouldn't even believe him. They didn't carry guns. They would listen, take notes, go on their way, and leave him behind to face the consequences. All alone. Without Matthew any longer.

Stubbornly, he refused to dwell upon Matthew. To think of Matthew was to think of what he owed him. To think of what he owed him was to think of what was right and honourable and required of him now. To think of that was to head directly into the realm of terror. For what was required of him was the truth, and Harry knew what he faced if he told it. The choice was simple. To die or say nothing. He was only thirteen. There was no choice at all.

". . . sculptures and roses mostly. It's only a few years old, if you'd like to see it."

"Yes, let's have a go at that as well."

Harry cringed at the sound of approaching voices, shrivelled at the noise of the wooden gate opening in the flintstone wall. Panicked, he looked for a place to hide. But there was nothing to protect him from discovery. He felt tears of futility burn his eyes as the female detective and Chas Quilter came into the sculpture garden. They stopped dead when they saw him.

Lynley met Sergeant Havers in the centre of the quad where, in blatant defiance of the propriety which said that adults should not set a bad example for pupils in an academic setting, she was smoking a cigarette as she scowled down at her notes. Towering above her, Henry VII managed to look disapproving about it.

"Have you noticed our Henry's facing north?" Lynley asked as he joined her on the steps beneath the statue. "The school's main entry is east, but he's not even looking in that direction."

Havers made a quick observation of the statue and said, "Perhaps he means to give the entrance the benefit of his profile."

Lynley shook his head. "He wants us to remember his moment of glory. So he looks to the north, in the direction of Bosworth Field."

"Ah. Death and treachery. The end of Richard III. Why does it always slip my mind that you're a Yorkist, Inspector? You never give me a real fighting chance to forget it. Do you spit on Henry's tomb whenever you get the chance to slip down to the Abbey?"

He smiled. "Religiously. It's one of my rare pleasures."

She nodded thoughtfully. "A man must take his pleasures where he can."

"Did you learn anything useful in your time with Chas?"

She stubbed out her cigarette on the base of the statue. "As much as I hate to admit to it, you were right about most of the condition of the school. From the outside, it's fine. Green grass, trimmed bushes, beautiful trees, clean buildings, scrubbed windows. The whole lot. But most of the interiors look like Erebus House did. Worn and ill-used. Except for the newer buildings—theatre, technical centre, and girls' houses—on the south side of the school, everything is ancient, Inspector. Classrooms as well. And the science building looks as if it hasn't changed much since Darwin's time." She swung her hand around to encompass the quad. "So why do fancy nobs send their kids here? My comprehensive school was in better shape than this. At least it was more up-to-date."

"The mystique, Havers."

"The old school tie?"

"That as well. Like father, like son."

"I suffered, you suffer?"

He smiled bleakly. "Something like that."

"Did you like Eton, sir?" she asked him shrewdly.

The question caught him off guard. It hadn't been Eton. It could never have been Eton with its beautiful buildings and its rich traditions. The place itself had no power to wound. It merely had been the wrong time in his life to be sent away from home. It wasn't a time to be cut off from a family in crisis and a father who was wasting away under the onslaught of disease.

"As well as anyone liked it," he replied. "What else have you besides the condition of the school?"

Havers looked as if she were about to say more about Eton. But instead she went on with, "They've something called a sixth form social club here. The seniors belong. It's in a building attached to Ion House—where Chas Quilter lives—and the students go there to do their drinking on weekends."

"Which students?"

"It's only for the upper sixth formers, but I got the impression that there's some sort of initiation rite involved because Chas said that some students choose not to belong. He called it 'not going through the steps for membership.' "

"He's in the club?"

"I suppose that's rather expected of him, isn't it, since he's senior prefect. Sort of shoring up the school's great traditions."

"The initiation rite is one of the traditions?"

"Apparently. I asked him how one became a member and he blushed and said that one did 'all sorts of rot' in front of one's mates. At any rate, there appears to be some heavy drinking going on. The students are supposed to be limited to two drink chits a week, but since other students are in charge of handing out the chits and of keeping account of how many drinks are taken by a single individual, things have got out of hand. It sounds as if their Friday night parties get a bit wild."

"Chas does nothing to control the wildness?"

"I don't understand it, to tell you the truth. It's his job, isn't it? Why even be senior prefect if he's not going to do it?"

"That's easy enough to answer, Havers. Any prefectship looks good on a student's academic record. I dare say universities don't actually check to see what kind of prefect the student was. They just see that he was one and make assumptions about him from there."

"But how did he get to be senior prefect in the first place? If he had no leadership skills to begin with, wouldn't the Headmaster have known that?"

"Showing leadership skills when you're not senior prefect is far easier than showing them when you are. It's a pressured situation. People change under pressure. Perhaps that happened with Chas."

"Or perhaps the Headmaster found Chas too attractive to hide him away," Havers commented in her usual acerbic fashion. "I imagine they spend lots of time alone together, don't you?" Lynley shot her a look. She defended herself with, "I'm not blind, Inspector. He's a beautiful boy. Lockwood wouldn't be the first to cave in to a pretty face."

"Indeed. What else did you discover?"

"I spoke with Judith Laughland, the nurse in charge of the Sanatorium."

"Ah. The San sister. Tell me about her."

Havers had worked with him long enough to know his fondness for details, so she described the San sister first: perhaps thirty-five years old, brown hair, grey eyes, a large birthmark on her neck beneath her right ear which she kept attempting to hide by swinging her hair forward to cover it and finally by raising up the collar of her blouse and holding it together. She smiled a great deal and unconsciously groomed herself as she spoke, patting her hair, playing with the buttons of her blouse, smoothing her hand down her leg to make sure her stockings fit well.

Lynley focused on these last points of interest. "As if she were preening? For whom? Were you with Chas?"

"I got the impression it's how she would act round any male, sir, not only Chas, because while we were there, one other of the older boys came in, complaining of a sore throat, and she laughed about it and teased him and said something like, 'Just can't stay away from me, can you?' and when she popped a thermometer into his mouth, she touched his hair and patted his cheek."

"Your conclusion?"

Havers looked thoughtful. "Not that she would get herself involved with any of the boys—she must be nearly twenty years older than they are, after all—but I think she needs their flattery and admiration."

"Married?"

"The boys called her Mrs. Laughland, but she's not wearing a wedding ring. Divorced is my guess. She's been here three years, and I'll wager that she arrived right after the divorce. So she's got herself concerned with starting a new life, and she needs a bit of reassurance that she can still attract men. You know the sort of thing."

This would not be the first time they had come into contact with those by-products of separation and dissolution. Both of them had witnessed the initial loneliness, the panic caused by the thought of spending the rest of one's life without a partner, the rising fear and the need to cover it with a facade of gaiety, the subsequent rush into activity and involvement. These reactions to loss were not solely appended to the world of women.

"What about the off-games chits?" Lynley asked the sergeant.

"They're kept in her desk drawer. But it isn't locked. And the San's not policed."

"Could Matthew have got to them?"

"As far as I could tell. Especially if she were distracted at the moment. If an upper sixth boy were in the room when Matthew popped by to nick the chit, I dare say she'd be distracted well enough if her behaviour today is any indication."

"Did you broach that with her?"

"I asked her how the system worked. Apparently, when a student is feeling unwell and unable to join the games in the afternoon, he goes to the San where Judith Laughland examines him—takes his temperature or whatever else is required—and if he's really ill, she gives him the off-games chit. If he needs to be admitted into the San, she sends the off-games chit with another student to give to the master in charge of the games or to put it into his pigeonhole. Otherwise, the sick student himself takes the chit and gives it to the master and goes on to his dormitory where he goes to bed."

"Does she keep a record of who is requesting to be let off games?"

Havers nodded. "Matthew hadn't got one on Friday, sir. There was no record of it. But he'd got one on two other occasions earlier in the year. It seems to me that he could have saved the last chit he got—it was about three weeks ago—and just bided his time, waiting for a chance to run off. Which reminds me. Harry Morant. Chas and I ran into him doing a bit of a scarper in the sculpture garden a few minutes ago."

"Did you speak to him?"

"As much as I could. No eye contact. Monosyllabic responses."

"And?"

"Matthew and he were in the Model Railway Society. That's how they'd become mates in the first place."

"Close friend?"

"That was hard to tell. But I did get the impression that Harry admired Matthew a great deal." She hesitated, frowned, appeared to be searching for the right words.

"Sergeant?"

"I think he knows why Matthew ran off. And wishes like hell he could join him."

Lynley raised an eyebrow. "That changes things a bit."

"Why?"

"It takes away any issue of class. If Harry was unhappy, and Matthew was unhappy, and Smythe-Andrews was unhappy . . ." His eyes lifted to Henry VII, so sure of himself, so completely confident that he could change the course of a country's history.

"Sir?"

"I think it's time we kept our engagement with the Headmaster."

Like the chapel, Alan Lockwood's study faced the east, and like the chapel, it contained elements designed to impress. A wide bay window, its side panels open to the cold, allowed enough space to accommodate a large satinwood conference table, six velvet-covered chairs, and a rococo silver candelabrum that shone against the highly polished wood. Directly across from this, a fireplace decorated with blue and white delft tiles held not the expected electric fire but the luxury of a real one. Above this hung what appeared to be a Holbein portrait of an unidentifiable Renaissance youth, and near it on the wall hung a second portrait—extremely unflattering—of Henry VII. Glass-fronted bookshelves took up two walls of the room and a third held photographs that spanned the school's recent history. A richly hued blue and gold Wilton carpet covered the floor, and as Lynley and Havers entered the room, Alan Lockwood crossed this carpet from his desk to greet them. He had removed his gown, which now hung on the back of the door. He looked strangely unfinished without it.

"Everyone's been cooperative, I take it?" he asked, motioning them to the conference table and choosing for himself a seat that would put his back to the window and allow the strong light behind him to obscure his face. He seemed oblivious of the low temperature in that part of the room, and he made no effort to close the windows.

"Extremely," Lynley replied. "Your senior prefect especially. Thank you for the loan of him."

Lockwood smiled with genuine warmth. "Chas. Superb boy, isn't he? One of a kind. Unanimously liked by one and all."

"Respected?"

"Not only by students but also by staff. It was the easiest choice I've ever had to make for senior prefect. Chas was nominated by every one of his teachers at the end of last year."

"He seems a nice boy."

"A bit of an overachiever, but after the disaster that his older brother made of his time here, I think Chas is bent upon rescuing the family name. That would be like him, making amends for everything Preston did."

"Black sheep of the family?"

Lockwood reached towards his neck but dropped his hand before it made contact with his skin. "A rotter, I'm afraid. Disgrace and disappointment. He was expelled early last year for stealing. He had the option to withdraw from the school—after all, his father is Sir Francis Quilter and one must make allowances for that. But he refused to withdraw and insisted that the charges against him be proved." Lockwood adjusted his tie, sounding regretful as he continued. "Preston was a kleptomaniac, Inspector. It wasn't at all difficult to prove the charges. At any rate, once he left us, he went off to Scotland to stay with relations. Now I understand he's taken to harvesting peat. So the family hopes—and pride, I expect—rest on Chas' shoulders."

"That's a hefty burden."

"Not for a boy of his talents. Chas will be a surgeon like his father. As would have Preston had he been able to keep his hands off other boys' belongings. He was my most trying expulsion from Bredgar Chambers. There have been others, of course. But that one was the worst."

"And you've been here—?"

"This is my fourth year."

"Before that?"

Lockwood opened his mouth, then closed it. His eyes narrowed in speculation at the smooth change Lynley had effected in the direction of the questions. "I was in the state school system. May I ask what that has to do with your investigation, Inspector?"

Lynley shrugged. "I like to get to know the people I'm working with," he replied. But he knew even as he spoke that Lockwood neither trusted nor accepted the bland answer. How could he, with Sergeant Havers sitting stoically at the table, writing down his every word?

"I see. Now you have that information, perhaps you'll allow me to ask for some in return."

"If I can give it to you, I'll certainly do so."

"Fine. You've been here all morning. You've spoken to students. You've seen the school. I understand your sergeant has been to the San to question Mrs. Laughland. Is there any reason, in all this time, why no one has initiated the process of striking out on the roads to look for the driver who picked up a small boy and murdered him?"

"A fair question," Lynley conceded affably. At her end of the table, Sergeant Havers continued to write. Together they played the roles of concession and contradiction, an orchestrated game to keep the suspect just slightly off balance. They had operated in this manner hundreds of times in the last eighteen months of their partnership. At this point, they did it without thinking. "The problem as I see it is that Bredgar Chambers is in a rather secluded area. So I question how likely it was that a thirteen-year-old boy would have been successful in getting a ride at all."

"He had to have got a ride, Inspector. You're not suggesting he walked all the way to Stoke Poges, are you?"

"I'm merely suggesting that there's a possibility that Matthew didn't attempt to hitchhike anywhere. That, in fact, he had his ride arranged. That he knew his driver. If that's the case, I should imagine we'd be spending our time more profitably here than in any other place."

Lockwood's face mottled. "Are you implying that someone from the *school* . . . You know as well as I that the death of that child, while indeed unfortunate, has nothing to do with this school directly."

"I'm afraid I haven't been able to reach that conclusion."

"He ran off, Inspector. He cleverly arranged it to look as if he was in two places at once. Then he ran off to be with his chums in London. It's unfortunate that it happened. But it did. He broke the school rules, and nothing can be done about that fact now. It's not the school's fault, and I have no intention of assuming blame."

"The staff have their cars here. And there are school vehicles, aren't there, for transporting students?"

"The *staff*?" Lockwood exploded. "One of the boy's *teachers*?"

Lynley was unruffled. "Not necessarily," he replied and waited for the Headmaster to read his meaning. When he saw that Lockwood had done so, he went on as if in the need to clarify his statement. "You've groundsmen here, nonteaching staff—matrons and porters and kitchen workers—not to mention the spouses of all the faculty who live on the campus. There are the pupils themselves . . ."

"You're mad," Lockwood said numbly. "The child's body was found on Sunday night. He'd been missing since Friday. It only stands to reason that he walked a hell of a long way before he got a ride in the first place."

"Perhaps. However, he was wearing his school uniform when he left. That certainly indicates he wasn't frightened that he might be recognised and returned to the school."

"He might have stuck to the fields and the ditches—and to the forest—until he was well away. This boy was nobody's fool. He was here on a scholarship. We're not talking about a child with no brains, Inspector."

"That scholarship interests me. When exactly did Matthew come to the attention of the school?"

Lockwood pushed back from the table, went to his desk, and returned with a file which he riffled through for a moment before he replied. "His parents reserved a place for him when he was eight months old." The Headmaster looked up, as if he expected some conclusion from Lynley that would further blacken the reputation of the school. "That's how it's usually done in independent schools, Inspector. But you already know that. Eton, wasn't it?"

Lynley ignored the question. "And the scholarship?"

"All prospective third form pupils get information about the scholarships we offer. This particular scholarship goes to a child who shows academic promise as well as financial need."

"How is the pupil selected?"

"He applies through a member of the Board of Governors. I make the final selection based upon the recommendation of the board."

"I see. Who put Matthew Whateley's name forward?"

Lockwood hesitated. "Inspector, some things are privileged— "

Lynley lifted a hand. "Not in a murder investigation, I'm afraid."

They were at impasse for a moment. At her end of the table, Sergeant Havers stopped writing and looked up, pencil poised.

The Headmaster's eyes locked with Lynley's, held for ten seconds, finally dropped. "Giles Byrne put up Matthew's name for the scholarship," Lockwood said. "You've heard of him, no doubt."

He had. Giles Byrne, the brilliant analyst of the political, social, and economic ills of the country. He of the rapier tongue and acid wit. A graduate of the London School of Economics with a BBC radio programme on which he regularly tore apart anyone who submitted to an interview. This was interesting news. But far more interesting was the connection Lynley made when he heard the name.

"Byrne. So the prefect of Erebus House—Brian Byrne . . ."

"Yes. He's Giles Byrne's son."

8

Emilia Bond had never cared for the days on which she had to give instruction to her upper sixth chemistry pupils immediately after lunch. In her two years at Bredgar Chambers, she had often argued with the Headmaster about rearranging her schedule so that the upper sixth pupils could meet with her at one time or another in the morning. After lunch, she would patiently explain, they can't concentrate well. Their bodies are concerned with digestion. There is insufficient flow of blood to the brain. How can they devote themselves to formulae and experiments when a basic biological function of the body makes it impossible for them to do so?

The Headmaster always listened with a clearly specious effort at sympathy, always declared that he would look into it, and always left things exactly as they were. It was exasperating. As was his insincere, paternal smile. It barely hid the fact that he disapproved of her presence at Bredgar Chambers altogether. At twenty-five years old, she was the only female teacher on the staff, and the Headmaster generally acted as if he expected her presence to be a corrupting influence on the boys with whom she dealt. No matter to him that there were ninety lower and upper sixth girls on the campus to act as considerable distractions in their own right. The fact that Emilia was a member of staff seemed to make her a more dangerous breed of female.

It was hardly a credible idea. Emilia knew quite well that she was unlikely to become the object of any eighteen-year-old's fantasy. She was attractive enough in a wholesome, dairy-product sort of way, perhaps a bit too full-bodied for her height, but not at all fat. She got far too much exercise for fat to be a problem, although she knew that the moment she stopped playing tennis, hiking, swimming, golfing, running, and riding her bicycle, her body would respond to the lack of attention by swelling up like a suckling pig's. Yet that same exercise which saved her body wreaked havoc on the rest of her personal appearance. She was very fair. Constant exposure to the sun had produced a heavy splattering of freckles across her nose. Constant exposure to the wind, while whipping natural colour into her cheeks, necessitated a hairstyle which was childlike and, to her way of thinking, less than absolutely flattering—very short and wispy, and so blonde that it was very nearly white. Indeed, it was unlikely that any boy at the school ever looked upon her in any way other than with fraternal affection. For it was her curse to be the universal big sister, always there with a bit of advice and a friendly pat on the shoulder. She hated that role even as she continued to play it with everyone.

She had not, however, played it with John Corntel. Emilia felt the sickness swell within her at the thought of John, and she tried to concentrate on something else. The effort was useless. Stubbornly, he intruded, forcing himself upon her, forcing her to dwell upon the distance they had travelled from colleagues and acquaintances nineteen months ago to what they were now. And what was that? she wondered. Friends? Lovers? Two individuals without any other connection, who gave in to a moment of physical weakness? Or perhaps, what was more likely, a cosmic joke, a monumental jest of a laughing God?

She liked to believe it had all started out innocently between them, with nothing more on her part than a desire to befriend a man who was painfully shy. But the reality was that from the beginning she had seen in John Corntel the possibility of coming home to rest with what she truly wanted. Her friendship with him represented a first link in the chain of husband, family, and security. So although she had told herself initially that she only wanted to help him feel less ill at ease round women, the truth of the matter was that she had only wanted him to feel less ill at ease round her. That newly found comfort in a woman's presence would lead, she believed, to a more permanent relationship.

What she had not expected, setting forth so cold-bloodedly to capture the man and secure her own future, was that she would fall in love with him as well, that she would come to care so much about his every thought, about his pain, about his turmoil, about his past, about his future. It had been such a seductive act, this falling in love with him. Until she was in the midst of it, she hadn't even realised it had happened to her. Once she had come to understand how strong her feelings for John really were, once she had decided to act upon those feelings in the forthright manner that was characteristic of her, everything had fallen apart in the most horrible and irreparable fashion.

Not the man I thought he was. She laughed inwardly at the ease with which she drew the conclusion. How convenient it would be to dismiss John Corntel as quickly as that. A mistake. A grievous misunderstanding. *I thought that you ... and you thought that I ... oh, let's forget it, shall we ... let's go back to being friends as we were before ...*

But it wasn't possible. One didn't move from love to friendship. It wasn't like switching off the lights. In spite of everything that had passed between them—her horrified tears, his mortification—she knew she still loved and wanted him, even though she no longer understood him at all.

The opening of the laboratory door roused her from her thoughts, and she looked up from her position on the dais at the front of the room to see that Chas Quilter had come to join the lesson, notebook and textbook under one arm. He smiled his apology for being late and said, "I was—"

"I know. We're addressing ourselves to the three problems on the blackboard at the moment. Catch us up as quickly as you can."

He nodded and took his accustomed place at the second worktable. There were only eight students in the class—three girls and five boys—and the moment Chas settled in and opened his notebook, two of them whispered his name urgently.

Emilia waited only long enough to hear one of them say, "What did they want to know?" and the other ask, "What was it like? Are they easy to—" before she spoke firmly.

"You've a lesson to do. See to it. All of you."

There was a moment of surprised grumbling at the curt instructions, but Emilia didn't worry about what offence she might be giving. That couldn't be helped at the moment. There were considerations beyond the satisfaction of idle curiosity, and the prime consideration was the boy sitting right next to Chas Quilter at the worktable.

Brian Byrne bore responsibility for much of what had happened to Matthew Whateley. He was house prefect of Erebus. It was his duty to see to it that the house ran smoothly, that the boys adjusted to their life at the school, that rules were followed and discipline was maintained and punishments were meted out where necessary.

But somewhere along the line, Brian Byrne had failed, and Emilia could see the burden of that failure weighing on the boy in the set of his shoulders, in his downcast eyes, in the tic that was pulling on the right side of his mouth like a form of palsy. Her heart went out to him.

Brian would face the worst kind of castigation as a result of Matthew Whateley's death. The rebukes he directed towards himself would be bad enough, but those he received from his father would be worse, stinging and chosen with remarkable acuity. Giles Byrne knew how to denigrate people, knew exactly what weapons to use. He especially knew how to find all the chinks in his own son's pathetically insubstantial armour. Emilia had seen him do as much on parents' day last term, running his eyes over Brian's history paper that had been posted with other papers and projects along the east cloister. Byrne had given it barely a minute's evaluation before remarking, "Ten pages, is it?" and then with a frown, "I think you'd better do something about your handwriting if you really expect to go to university, Brian." Then he moved on, dispassionate, uninvolved. As if he were monumentally wearied by it all. A member of the Board of Governors, naturally, could hardly profess an interest that was more marked towards his own son's work than the work of the other pupils.

Emilia had been coming down the cloister and had seen the expression on Brian's face, that blending of hurt, rejection, and shame. She would have gone to him and smoothed past his father's words, but Chas Quilter came out of the chapel at that moment and seeing him, Brian's entire demeanour changed. Within seconds he was talking to Chas, laughing and following him in the direction of the dining hall.

Chas had been very good for Brian. Their friendship had served to draw Brian out of himself, allowing him to move into a world of more self-assured and self-possessed students. But as Emilia watched both boys at the worktable now, each one with his eyes cast upon his own paper, she wondered if Brian's failure with Matthew Whateley would work upon his friendship with Chas. It reflected poorly upon Chas as senior prefect. It reflected poorly upon the whole school. Ultimately it reflected upon his father as well. No matter what happened, Brian stood to lose.

It was, Emilia thought, so damnably unfair.

For the second time that afternoon, the laboratory door opened.

Emilia felt her muscles constrict in automatic reaction: flight or fight. It was the police.

When they entered the chemistry laboratory, Lynley saw that Sergeant Havers had not exaggerated her claim that the building and its rooms had not experienced significant alteration since Darwin's time. The lab was hardly an example of scientific modernity. Gas pipes ran along the ceiling, there were gaps in the parquet floor, the lighting verged upon intolerably dim, and the blackboard was so worn that the problems written on it seemed to melt into the ghosts of hundreds of other problems that lay beneath them.

The eight pupils present sat upon impossibly tall wooden stools, and they laboured at nicked white worktables that were topped by pitted sheets of pine. Small rectangular porcelain basins broke into the surface of these tables as did rusty iron gas jets and copper taps. To one side of this work area, glass-fronted cabinets lined a wall of the room, and they were filled with graduated cylinders, pipettes, flasks, beakers, and a remarkable assortment of corked bottles containing chemicals and bearing hand-printed labels. High on the top of these cabinets, tall burettes were lined up in wooden stands, ready to be used to mix chemicals together a single drop at a time. Such mixing would be done in the fume cupboard on a work top across the room, and it too was ancient, a structure of glass and mahogany with only a rusting fan for ventilation.

The entire laboratory should have been gutted years ago. That it had not been modernised gave evidence of the school's financial situation. It also spoke of the multiple pressures Alan Lockwood faced to keep the school running, to encourage new applicants, and somehow to raise the funds required to bring all the facilities up-to-date.

As if she recognised the implicit condemnation in Lynley's observation, the teacher walked to the fume cupboard and lowered its front window. A filmy residue clouded the glass. She turned back to the pupils who had one by one stopped their work to stare at Lynley and Havers.

"You've problems to complete," she informed them and crossed the room to the door. "I'm Emilia Bond. The chemistry teacher. How may I help you?"

She spoke crisply, with assurance, but Lynley did not miss the fact that a pulse beat rapidly in her throat.

"Inspector Lynley, Sergeant Havers, Scotland Yard CID," he replied, although he could tell from the young woman's behaviour that the introduction was largely unnecessary. Emilia Bond knew quite well who they were and, undoubtedly, why they had come to her laboratory. "We'd like to have some time with one of your students, if we may. Brian Byrne."

Every eye save the teacher's went to a boy who sat next to Chas Quilter. He did not immediately look up but rather kept his attention on the notebook open in front of him, over which he held a pencil. It did not move.

"Bri," Chas Quilter murmured.

At this, the boy raised his head.

Lynley knew that Brian Byrne, as an upper sixth student, would have to be either seventeen or eighteen years old, but he looked both unaccountably younger and older at the same time. The youth came from a rounded face without the emerging definition of features, the toughening of skin, or the incipient lines at mouth and eyes that were the signs of approaching adulthood marking the faces of his peers. On the other hand, the maturity came from an odd combination of hairline and physique. The former was already receding and would probably leave him bald before he was thirty years old. The latter was muscular, like a wrestler's body that had been developed through the use of weights.

As Brian began to slip off his stool, Emilia Bond spoke. Her body moved slightly, an unconscious block between Brian and the police. "Is this necessary, Inspector? The lesson ends in less than thirty minutes. You can't see him then?"

"I'm afraid not," Lynley replied. He made a final survey of the room. Three girls: two leggy, long-haired, and attractive, and a third resembling a timorous mouse. Five boys: three nice-looking and well-built, one very scholarly with spectacles and a slightly humped back, and Brian Byrne somehow the odd man out.

Brian joined them at the door. Lynley nodded his thanks to Emilia Bond.

"If you'll take us to your room," he told Brian, "I think we'll have the privacy we need."

The boy said only, "It's this way," and preceded them down the corridor and out of the building.

Erebus House was directly across from the science building, with Mopsus House to the west of it, Calchus House just to the east, and beyond it, Ion House, the home of the sixth form social club. They walked down a path, crossed a stretch of pavement down which cars, small lorries, and minivans could make deliveries to the buildings, and went into Erebus House by the same door that they had used earlier that day.

Brian's room was on the ground floor, adjacent to the door that gave access to the private quarters of John Corntel, the housemaster. Like the other rooms in the building, Brian's was not locked. He shoved open the door and stepped back to give Lynley and Havers entrance before him.

The room was fairly typical boarding school fare. It would be euphemistically called a bed-sitting room in the school prospectus, an appellation whose verity depended upon the presence of a single bed, a chair, a desk, and three bookshelves along with the requisite pressed-wood cupboard and a small chest of drawers. The reality was that it was little more than a cell with a single leaded casement window, one pane of which was broken. A black sock had been stuffed into the gap to keep out the cold. The air smelled of wet wool.

Brian closed the door behind them without speaking. He shifted from foot to foot, shoved one hand in his trouser pocket, and waited, jiggling some coins or keys.

Lynley was in no hurry to begin the interview. He examined Brian's choice of room decoration as Sergeant Havers took a seat on the narrow bed, removed her jacket, and brought forth her notebook.

The walls, Lynley saw, were sparsely adorned. They held only a small collection of photographs. Three were of school athletic teams—the rugby first fifteen, the cricket first eleven, the tennis first six. Brian was featured in none of them, but it took only a moment to ascertain the common element in each picture. Chas Quilter. The senior prefect was also the subject of a fourth photograph, this one with a girl held to his side, her arms round him, her head resting on his chest, and the wind blowing their hair about and scuttling brilliant clouds across the sky. A girlfriend, no doubt, Lynley thought. It was an unusual picture to find hanging in another boy's room.

Lynley pulled the chair from beneath the desk and gestured Brian into it. He himself remained standing, leaning one shoulder against the wall near the window. The only view it provided was of a bit of lawn, of an alder just beginning to leaf, and of the side door of Calchus House.

"How does one get into the sixth form social club?" Lynley asked.

The question obviously took the boy by surprise. His eyes—an indefinite shade somewhere between blue and grey—darkened as the pupils enlarged in reaction. He didn't immediately respond.

"The initiation?" Lynley prompted.

Brian's mouth twitched. "What does that have to do—"

"With Matthew Whateley's death?" Lynley asked and smiled. "Nothing at all, as far as I know. I'm merely curious. Wondering whether schools have changed much since I was at Eton."

"Mr. Corntel went to Eton."

"We were there together."

"You were mates?" Brian's eyes flashed to Chas' pictures.

"Fairly close ones at the time, although we'd lost track of one another through the years. These aren't the best circumstances under which to renew a friendship, are they?"

"Rotten to have to renew it at all," Brian said. "Good friends should stay good friends."

"Chas is that to you?"

"My best friend," he said frankly. "We're going up to Cambridge together in October. If we're accepted. Chas will be. His marks are good and he'll do well on his A-levels next term."

"And you?"

Brian lifted a hand, wiggled it back and forth. "Not a certainty. I've plenty of brains, but I don't always use them as well as I could." It sounded like an adult's evaluation of him, something that would be written home to a parent.

"Your father could help you get into Cambridge, I assume."

"If I wanted his help. I don't."

"I see." That was admirable enough, a determination to make it on his own without the considerable influence that a man of Giles Byrne's reputation could wield. "And the initiation to the social club?"

Brian grimaced. "Four pints of bitter and"—his face flushed hotly— "getting sauced, sir."

The expression was unfamiliar to Lynley. He asked for elucidation, and Brian continued, giving an awkward laugh.

"You know. Putting hot sauce—or deep-heating rub—on your . . . *you* know." Warily, his eyes went to Havers.

"Ah. I see. That's getting sauced? Rather uncomfortable, I'd think. Are you a member of the club? You've gone through the initiation?"

"Sort of. I mean, I went through the initiation but I got sick. Still, I'm in." He frowned, as if realising what he had just done in admitting to the fact of an initiation at all. "Did the Headmaster ask you to suss this out, sir?"

Lynley smiled. "No. I was curious."

"It's just that we're not supposed to do that sort of thing. But you know how schools are. Especially here. There's not much else to do."

"What does the social club do when it gets together?"

"Parties. On Friday nights usually."

"All the upper sixth pupils belong?"

"No. Just people who want to."

"What happens to the rest of the upper sixth?"

"They're losers, aren't they? They keep to themselves. Don't have mates. You know."

"Was there a party this past Friday night?"

"There's a party every Friday night. This one was smaller than usual, though. Lots of the upper sixth were gone for the weekend. Lower sixth and fifth as well. There was a hockey tournament in the North."

"You didn't want to go?"

"Too much prep. And an exam this morning that I was cramming for as well."

"Lord. I remember how that is. Did that upper sixth party Friday night keep you from seeing to the younger boys here in Erebus House?" Even as he asked the question, Lynley hated himself for the ease with which he had drawn the boy to this point. There had been nothing clever about it, just an admission of similar background and experience to form a loose bond, then each question drawing him further and further out of the protective shell everyone wore—guilty or innocent—when questioned by the police.

"I was back by eleven." Brian became guarded with this response. "I didn't check on them. I just went to bed."

"When you left the sixth form club, were there other seniors there?"

"A few."

"Had they been there all along? Had anyone left the party at all during the evening?"

Brian was no fool. His face told Lynley that even if he had not done so before, he saw the direction the questions were taking. He hesitated before saying, "Clive Pritchard was in and out. He's a bloke from Calchus House."

"A prefect?"

Brian looked wryly amused. "Not prefect material, if you know what I mean."

"And Chas? Was he at this party?"

"He was there."

"All along?"

A moment for thought, for recollection, for a decision about truth or deception. "Yes. All along." The spasm that jerked his lip betrayed him.

"Are you sure about that? Was Chas there every moment? Was he there when you left?"

"He was there. Yes. Where else would he be?"

"I don't know. I'm just trying to get at the truth of what happened here on Friday when Matthew Whateley disappeared."

Brian's eyes clouded. "Are you thinking Chas had something to do with that? Why?"

"If Matthew ran off, he had to have some reason for doing so, didn't he?"

"And you see *Chas* as the reason? Sorry, sir, but that's rot."

"It may be, which is why I'm asking whether Chas was in the social club for the entire evening. If he was there, he could hardly have been seeing to Matthew Whateley."

"He was. He was there. I saw him every moment. I never took my eyes off him. He was with me most of the time anyway. And when he wasn't . . ." Brian stopped talking abruptly. His right fist closed. His lips whitened as he pressed them together.

"So he left," Lynley said.

"He didn't! It's just that there were some phone calls for him. Maybe three. I don't remember. Someone came and got him and he went to the front of Ion House where the phone is and took the calls there. But he was never gone long enough to *do* anything."

"How long was he gone?"

"I don't know. Five minutes, ten minutes. No more than that. What could he have done in that time? Nothing. And what difference does it make? None of the calls came before nine o'clock and everyone knows that Matthew Whateley ran off in the afternoon."

Lynley saw the fine edge of the boy's control, and used it by asking, "Why did Matthew run off? What happened to him here? You and I both know that behind closed doors things go on in a school that the Headmaster and the staff either don't know about or turn a blind eye to. What happened?"

"Nothing. He just didn't fit in. He was different. Everyone could tell. Everyone knew it. He never got the picture that one's mates are important —more important, the most important . . . For him, it was lessons and prep and getting ready for university and nothing else. Nothing."

"So you knew him."

"I know all the boys in Erebus. That's my job, isn't it?"

"And save for last Friday, you do your job well?"

His face closed. "I *do*."

"Your father pushed Matthew for the governors' scholarship. Did you know that?"

"Yes."

"How did you feel about it?"

"Why should I have felt anything? He promotes a student every year for the scholarship. This year, his protégé won. So what?"

"Perhaps that made it difficult for you to smooth Matthew's way into the life of the school. He was from a different background than most of the boys, after all. It would have taken some effort on your part to see that he felt at home here."

"What you really mean is that I was jealous of Matthew because of my father's interest in him, so I didn't lift a finger to make it any easier for him to fit in. In fact, I made him so miserable from the first that he finally couldn't stand it and ran off and got himself killed in the process?" Brian shook his head. "If I put the heat on every boy that my father took an interest in, I'd be spending all of my time at it. He's looking for another Eddie Hsu, Inspector. He won't rest until he finds one."

"Eddie Hsu?"

"An old Bredgardian that my father tutored." Brian smiled, an expression of bitter pleasure. "Until he killed himself, that is. In 1975. Just before his A-levels. Haven't you seen my father's memorial to Eddie in the chapel? It's hard to miss. 'Edward Hsu . . . beloved student.' My father's been looking for his replacement ever since. He has a real Midas touch, does Dad. Except that everything he touches dies on contact."

A sharp knock sounded on the door. "Byrne! Let's do it! Hey! Let's go!"

Lynley didn't recognise the voice. He nodded at Brian who said, "Join the party, Clive."

"Hey, let's be-bop over to . . ." The other boy froze when he saw Havers and Lynley. But he recovered quickly, saluted, and said, "Oh ho! Here be the coppers, I'd guess. Nabbed you at last have they, Bri?" He rolled onto the balls of his feet.

"Clive Pritchard," Brian said by way of introduction. "Calchus House's finest specimen."

Clive grinned. His left eye was slightly lower than his right, and its lid drooped lazily. In conjunction with the grin, this had the effect of making him look a little bit drunk. "You know it, lad." He gave no further notice to the police. Instead, he said, "We've ten minutes to get to the field, laddie, and you've not even changed. What's happening to you? I've a fiver riding that we'll smash Mopsus and Ion, and all the while you're sitting here having a natter with the cops."

Clive himself was dressed not in the school's uniform, but in a blue tracksuit and jersey striped in yellow and white. Both were extremely tight-fitting, serving to emphasise a build that was not muscular but wiry. He looked like a fencer and moved quickly, with a fencer's agility.

"I don't know that I . . ." Brian looked at Lynley questioningly.

"We've enough information for now," Lynley replied. "You're free to go."

As Sergeant Havers stood and moved towards the door, Brian walked to his cupboard, opened it, and pulled out a tracksuit, gym shoes, and a blue and white jersey which he selected from three that were hanging on hooks.

Clive stepped forward. "Not that one, Bri. Criminy, you're getting thick, aren't you? We're in yellow today, unless you're planning to join the Ion boys' team. I know you and Quilter are each other's dolly-bird, but let's have a bit of house loyalty, shall we."

Stupidly, Brian looked down at the garments in his hands. His brow creased. He stood motionless. With an impatient grunt, Clive took the jersey from him, pulled the yellow and white one from the cupboard, and handed it over. "*Can't* be with Quilter this afternoon, lovey pie. Come on. Bring your gear. Change in the sports hall. We've a field of pretty boys waiting to be coshed. And hardly time to see to them all. I'm living hell with a hockey stick. Have I told you that? Mopsus and Ion are the sinners and they're about to meet their retribution. Pritchard-style." Clive mimed the action of smacking Brian's shins.

Brian winced, then smiled. "Let's do it," he said and allowed Clive to dance him from the room.

Lynley watched them go. He did not overlook the fact that neither boy met his eyes as they left.

9

"Let's look at what we have," Lynley said.

In response, Sergeant Havers lit a cigarette and settled comfortably into her chair, a Schweppes tonic water in front of her.

They were in the public bar of the Sword and Garter, a cramped little pub in the village of Cissbury, threequarters of a mile along a narrow country road from Bredgar Chambers. The Sword and Garter had already proved itself to be an inspired choice for their conversation prior to heading back to London. Considering its proximity to the school, Lynley had shown the publican Matthew Whateley's photograph—not really expecting any recognition from the man. So it was with some surprise that he saw the publican nod his shaggy head, that he heard him say, "Aye. Matt Whateley," without the least hesitation.

"You know the boy?"

"I do. He visits regular with Colonel Bonnamy and his daughter. They live just a mile or so beyond the village."

"His daughter?"

"Jeannie. She's in here—sometimes twice a week—with Matt. They stop now and then when she drives him back to the school."

"They're relatives of the boy?"

"No." The publican pushed the Schweppes across the bar and followed it with a glass in which rested two pieces of ice. He opened a cupboard, rooted around for a bit, and came up with a battle-worn metal teapot into which he dropped three sad-looking tea bags. "It was all part of the Bredgar Brigade. That's what I call them. Do-gooders. Matt's one of them, but not as bad as the usual lot." He disappeared through a door to the left of the bar and returned a moment later with a steaming kettle. He poured hot water into the teapot, dunked the tea bags five times, and removed them. "Milk?" he asked Lynley.

"Thank you, no. What sort of do-gooders?"

"School calls them Bredgar Volunteers. I call them do-gooders. They visit the house-bound, do work in the village, help out in the forest. You know the sort of thing. Lads and lasses choose what volunteer work they want to do. Matt chose visiting. He got assigned Colonel Bonnamy to visit. Regular bantam, the colonel is, too. Matt's had his hands full with visiting there, I should say. Earning his stripes, dealing with Colonel Bonnamy."

So part of the puzzle had been fitted into place with the identity of the woman to whom Matthew had been writing his letter. Jean. The colonel's daughter. Beyond this, the publican's conversation revealed that Matthew's disappearance and death were still facts that Bredgar Chambers had managed to keep concealed. No doubt Alan Lockwood would be gratified to know that.

Now Lynley and Havers sat at a small table by a window overgrown with honeysuckle not yet in bloom. The sunlight that filtered through the vine and into the pub was tinted green by leaves. Lynley stirred his tea thoughtfully as Sergeant Havers read through the first few sections of her notes. She yawned, rubbed her fingers through her hair, and rested her cheek on her hand.

As Lynley watched her, he thought how ironic it was that he had come to depend upon having Havers as his partner. Initially he had believed that no one could possibly be less likely to suit him. She was prickly, argumentative, easily given to anger, and bitterly aware of the enormous gap that existed between them, an impassable chasm created by birth, by class, by money, by experience. They could not have been more antithetical, Havers struggling with a fierce determination to rise out of a working class neighbourhood in a grimy suburb of London while he moved effortlessly from his home in Cornwall to his town house in Belgravia to his office at New Scotland Yard. But their differences went far beyond mere background. Their perceptions of life and humanity occupied two opposite ends of the spectrum as well. Hers was ruthless, without sympathy, suspicious of motives, and based on distrust of a world that had given her nothing. His was laced with compassion, rich with understanding, and based almost entirely upon a guilt that insisted he reach out, learn, expiate, rescue, make amends. He smiled at the thought that Superintendent Webberly had been absolutely right to put them together, to insist they remain in partnership even at moments when Lynley believed it was an impossible situation that could only grow worse.

Havers drew in on her cigarette and let it dangle from her lips as she began to speak from behind its plume of grey smoke. "How well do you know the housemaster, sir? John Corntel?"

"Only as a schoolmate, Havers. How well do schoolmates ever know one another? Why?"

She dropped her notebook to the table and tapped upon a page for emphasis. "When he was at the Yard yesterday, he said that Brian Byrne was in Erebus House Friday night. But Brian himself said that he was in the sixth form club in Ion House and that he didn't return to Erebus until eleven. So John Corntel's lying to us. But why lie about something so easy to verify?"

"Perhaps Brian told him he was in the house."

"Why would he do that when any other pupil at the sixth form party Friday night could place Brian there?"

"That's assuming another upper sixth pupil would do so, Havers. I don't think you can make that assumption."

"Why?"

Lynley mulled over an explanation of the peculiar system of honour that governed the behaviour of pupils in an independent school. "It doesn't happen," he said. "In a school like this, the pupils' first loyalty is to their mates, not to a code of conduct or a set of rules. Generally no one ever sneaks—no one tells tales about another who breaks the rules."

"But this afternoon, didn't Brian Byrne do a bit of sneaking on Chas? He said that Chas left the sixth form party to take some telephone calls."

"Hardly a violation of school rules. And, after all, I did push him into making that admission." He went back to the previous point she had been making. "Where are you heading with John Corntel?" Havers stubbed out her cigarette, reached for the pack to have another, but gave up the idea when Lynley said, "For God's sake, Sergeant. Have a bit of mercy, will you?"

She pushed the pack away. "Sorry. If Corntel thought Brian Byrne was doing duty in Erebus House that night, it seems that he could have got that idea only two ways. Either Brian told him he was doing duty—which seems unlikely, since Brian freely admitted to us that he was at a party—or Corntel himself wasn't in the house and merely assumed that Brian was."

"Where do you place John Corntel?"

Her teeth pulled on the inside of her lower lip. She answered delicately. "There was something so odd in the way he described Matthew to us yesterday, sir. Something—"

"Longing? Seductive?"

"I'd say. Wouldn't you?"

"Perhaps. Matthew certainly seems to have been a beautiful child. But tell me how you see John Corntel involved."

"Matthew wants to get away from the school. Corntel has a car. He helps him do so. Isn't that where you were heading when we spoke to the Headmaster?"

Lynley contemplated the ashtray on the table. The acrid smell of burnt tobacco was like a siren, beckoning, charming, impossible to resist. . . . He shoved the ashtray towards the window. "Someone seems to have helped him escape. Perhaps Corntel. Perhaps someone else."

Havers frowned, leafed through her notebook, paused to read. "Why did Matthew want to get away? We thought earlier that it had to do with fitting in, didn't we? He was different, working class. How would he get on with these nits and nobs? And he didn't get on, did he? He got cold feet when he was supposed to visit the Morants and spend a weekend hobnobbing on some country estate. So he nicked an off-games chit and did a scarper to keep from facing the fact that he was different from the other boys when the Morants examined them all together. That's what it looked like to me after listening to John Corntel yesterday. And I can understand why Matthew might feel exactly that way. Like a specimen. Or a charity case. But this Harry Morant he was supposed to visit . . . He's a top-drawer lad, sir. And it seems clear that Harry's as anxious to be gone from this place as Matthew was. Upper class or not. Why?"

Lynley recalled Smythe-Andrews' bitter words about the school. He thought about the significance of Arlens' fainting. "It could be bullying."

What had it been called? *Pleb-bashing.* Making sure the fresh-faced new boys didn't get cheeky, didn't get the wrong idea about their menial place in the school hierarchy. Every school had been outlawing bullying for years. Expulsion was the price the bully paid if he was caught tormenting another pupil after he had been warned off doing so.

"So Matthew runs to escape a bully," Havers said. "He puts himself into the hands of someone he trusts, only to find that the person he's turned to is worse than a bully, is . . . What? A sexual pervert? God, that makes me ill. Poor little bloke."

"There may be more to look at, Havers. The family doesn't appear to have much money. Kevin Whateley carves tombstones, his wife works in a hotel. To get Matthew into the school, they had to bring themselves to the attention of Giles Byrne. Giles Byrne knew Matthew—"

"And has been seeking a replacement for this Edward Hsu, from what Brian told us. But surely you don't think a member of the Board of Governors . . ." Havers reached for her cigarettes and, with an apologetic glance at Lynley, lit one. "There's something, to be sure." She went back to her notes. The paper crackled. Across the room, the publican was polishing the bar with an oily-looking rag. "John Corntel told us yesterday that one of the members of the Board of Governors was at the school when Mr. and Mrs. Whateley arrived. Do you think that could have been Giles Byrne?"

"It's easy enough to find out, isn't it?"

"If it was Giles Byrne, who knows what sort of hidden agenda he had in putting Matthew up for the scholarship, sir. And why did Edward Hsu kill himself just before his A-levels? Did Giles Byrne put a move on him? Did he seduce him? Has he been spending the last fourteen years looking for another nice piece of boy-flesh to have?" Her eyes snapped to Lynley's. "What did it say across that photo of the train in Matthew's dormitory?"

" 'Choo-choo, little poof.' "

"Inspector, you don't think that Matthew was somebody's nancy boy, do you? He was only thirteen! Would he even know his sexual orientation at thirteen?"

"He might. He might not. Or he might not have been given the choice."

"Jesus Christ." It sounded like a prayer.

Lynley thought about his previous night's conversation with Kevin Whateley. He said to Havers, "Matthew's father told me that within the last few months he'd become withdrawn, introspective. As if he were in a trance. Clearly something was bothering him, but he didn't want to talk about it."

"Not to his dad. But to *someone,* surely."

"From what you've told me, it sounds as if he may well have talked to Harry Morant."

"He might have. But I don't think young Harry intends to open his mouth about anything."

"Not yet. He needs time to think, I should guess. Time to decide whom he can trust. He's not about to make the same mistake Matthew made."

"Do you think he knows who killed Matthew, sir?"

"He may not. But he definitely knows something. I'd bet on that."

"Then why didn't you want to talk to him today?"

"He's not ready, Sergeant. Harry needs a bit of time."

For the last forty minutes, Harry had been waiting in the porter's office on the east side of the quad. He sat on the room's sole ladder-back chair without speaking, the tips of his shoes reaching only far enough to graze the stone floor. His hands braced against the seat, and his eyes remained on the pegboard behind the bruised wooden counter. From this dangled an assortment of keys—to vehicles, to buildings, to houses, to rooms—and they caught the afternoon sunlight glowing in through the window, winking like bronze and silver and gold. The porter was at his desk behind the counter, sorting the post, looking vaguely military in the uniform he wore. Everyone knew that the uniform was an affectation. A school porter hardly needed to dress like one of the Chelsea Pensioners. But it contributed an air of dignity to the manner in which the porter carried out his duties. So no one ever complained about it.

To Harry, however, the uniform was an obstacle which created distance between the porter and the rest of the world, although he couldn't have put this feeling into words. He knew only that the porter held everyone at bay with his military tone, his military bearing, and most of all his military clothes. At the moment, Harry didn't want to be held at bay. He needed someone. He needed a confidant.

But it could not be this man who paused in his duties towards the post and honked his nose loudly into a crumpled handkerchief. He would not do.

The office door opened and the Headmaster's secretary popped her head in. Myopically, she squinted about—as if the person she sought might be perched upon a shelf or hanging among the keys. Finding this was not the case, she dropped her eyes to Harry.

"Mr. Morant." She said his name like frost. "The Headmaster will see you now."

Harry forced his hands to release their grip upon the seat of the chair. He followed the woman's tall, spare figure out of the office, down a dim corridor that smelled of coffee, and into the Headmaster's study.

"Harry Morant, Headmaster," the woman said before she left, closing the door behind her.

Harry felt all at sea on the deep blue carpet. He had never been in the Headmaster's study before, and since he knew why he was in there now, he didn't give himself over to examining the room. Punishment was the order of the hour. A slap. A caning. Some sort of hiding. All he wanted was to get it over with, without tears if possible, and be on his way.

The Headmaster, he saw, was not wearing his gown, and Harry did take a moment to decide whether he had ever seen him thus ungarbed before. He didn't think so. But when he considered it, he realised how awkward it would be for Mr. Lockwood to strap him with his gown flying round his arms and legs. It would be absurd. No wonder he'd removed it.

"Morant." The Headmaster seemed to speak from a great distance. He was standing behind his desk, but he may as well have been on the moon. "Sit down."

There were a number of chairs in the room. Six stood round a conference table; two others faced the Headmaster's desk. Harry didn't know which one he was supposed to take, so he remained where he was.

He couldn't remember ever being this close to the Headmaster before. Even though they were separated by an expanse of carpet, by two chairs and the width of a desk, Harry could still see details, and he didn't much like them. A shadow of new whiskers made the Headmaster's skin look blue-black. His neck was pimply and reminded Harry of the skin on a badly plucked chicken that he'd seen once in the window of a Chinese restaurant in London. His nostrils flexed every time he inhaled, like a bull about to charge. His eyes went from Harry to the window to Harry to the window, as if he were wary of an eavesdropper's presence outside beneath the sill.

Seeing all this, Harry steeled himself to get through the interview, to say nothing, to reveal nothing, and above all not to cry. Crying always made everything worse.

"Sit down," the Headmaster repeated. He opened his hand in the direction of the conference table, so Harry chose a chair there. Again, his feet did not quite reach the floor. Mr. Lockwood joined him, pulling a chair out from the table, turning it to face Harry, and sitting down himself. He crossed one leg over the other, carefully pinching the crease in his trousers. "You didn't go to your lessons today, Morant."

"No, sir." It was an easy enough reply, made without lifting his eyes from Mr. Lockwood's shoes. Just inside the left instep was a crust of mud. Harry wondered if the Headmaster knew it was there.

"Did you have an exam you were afraid to take?"

"No, sir."

"A paper or report that was due?"

There *had* been the history panel. He had been more than prepared to do his section of it. That had nothing to do with his skipping his lesson. Still, it seemed a logical hook onto which he could hang the excuse for his behaviour. How hard could the Headmaster beat him for that?

"History panel, sir."

"I see. You weren't prepared?"

"Not as well as I ought to be, sir." Harry heard himself become practically eager when he said, "I understand. It was naughty. You must cane me, mustn't you?"

"Cane you? What are you thinking of, Morant? We don't cane boys at this school. Where did you get that idea?"

"I thought that . . . I'd a message that you wanted to see me, sir. The senior prefect was the one who found me in the sculpture garden. I thought that meant . . ."

"That the senior prefect had reported you for a beating? Does that sound like Chas Quilter to you, Morant?"

Harry didn't reply. The backs of his knees began to prickle. He knew what the expected answer was, but he couldn't force his lips to form the word, nor could he force himself to say it. The Headmaster went on.

"Chas Quilter told me that he found you in the garden. He said you seemed terribly upset. It's about Matthew Whateley, isn't it?"

Harry heard the question and knew only that Matthew's name couldn't pass his lips in any way. He knew that if he said it once, if he allowed Matthew access to his consciousness, the floodgates would open, it would all come pouring out. After that there would be nothing but oblivion. He knew it. He believed it. It was the only reality in his life at the moment.

The Headmaster was continuing to speak. He was trying hard to sound soothing, but Harry had heard that kind of insincere compassion before. He felt the undercurrent of urgency beneath Mr. Lockwood's words, the way his parents sounded when they were trying to be understanding while all the time a quarter-hour late for a golf game.

"You and Matthew were mates, weren't you?" the Headmaster was asking.

"We were in Model Railway."

"But he was a special friend to you, wasn't he? Special enough to be invited for your birthday with all the other boys this last weekend. That sounds like more than just knowing him."

"I suppose. We were mates."

"Mates talk to one another, I imagine. Don't they?"

Harry felt the prickling move from his knees to his spine. He saw where this was heading. He sought to avoid it. "Matt never talked much. Not even during games in the afternoon."

"But you knew him in spite of that? Well enough to want him to go along to your house and meet your parents and your brothers and sisters?"

"Well . . . yes. He was . . ." Harry squirmed. His resolve weakened. Perhaps he could tell the Headmaster the truth. It wouldn't be so bad. It wouldn't take much. "He helped me out. That's how we were friends."

Mr. Lockwood leaned towards him. "You know something, don't you, Morant? Something Matthew Whateley told you? Why he ran away?" When he spoke, Harry felt the Headmaster's breath on his face. It smelled of a mixture of lunch and coffee. It felt very hot.

Want a grind, nancy boy? want a grind? want a grind? Harry stiffened to escape the memory.

"You know something, don't you? Don't you, boy?"

Want a grind, nancy boy? want a grind? wantagrind?

Harry braced himself against the back of the chair. He couldn't. He *wouldn't*. He offered the Headmaster the only words possible.

"No, sir. I only wish I did."

It was half-past five when Lynley and Havers reached Hammersmith. A cold wind was blowing off the Thames, scattering the damp pages of a newspaper along the pavement. A sodden photograph of the Duchess of York lay in the gutter, a tyre print corrugating her left cheek. Round them, the neighbourhood noises swelled and receded much like the ebb and flow of the tide, and the omnipresent scent of exhaust fumes funnelled along the street from the flyover's burden of rush-hour traffic. Darkness was fast approaching, and as they walked towards the river, the lights on Hammersmith Bridge came on, casting a glow against the untroubled surface of the water.

Without speaking, they descended the steps to the embankment, pulled up the collars of their coats, headed into the wind, and made their way to the fisherman's cottage next to the Royal Plantagenet pub. Its front curtains were drawn, but dim lamplight shone against the material like a pool of amber. They entered the low tunnel between the cottage and the pub, and Lynley rapped on the door. Unlike the response to his knock last night, footsteps approached within seconds, a bolt was drawn, the door was pulled open. Patsy Whateley stood before them.

As on the previous night, she wore the nylon dressing gown with its coil of slithering, demonic dragons. The same green slippers were on her feet as well, and her hair was disarranged, inexpertly tied back from her face with a shoelace, once white but now discoloured to grey. When she saw them, she lifted a hand as if to smooth back her hair or to straighten the gaping neckline of her dressing gown. Her fingers and palms were crusty with flour.

"Biscuits," she said. "Mattie did like his biscuits. Took them down to school in his tuck box at half-term, he did. He liked gingers the best. I was . . . today . . ." She looked at her hands, rubbed them together. A fine shower of dust drifted from them to the floor. "Kev went to work this morning. I should have, shouldn't I? But I couldn't. It seemed so final. And I thought if I made the biscuits—" Somehow, miraculously, Matthew would appear at the cottage to eat them. Not dead any longer. Not irretrievably lost. But alive again. And home with his mother, where he belonged. Lynley understood.

He introduced Sergeant Havers. "May we come in, Mrs. Whateley?"

She blinked. "I wasn't thinking, was I?" She shuffled back from the door.

Freshly baked biscuits filled the sitting room with the combined fragrances of cinnamon, ginger, nutmeg, and cooked sugar. But the air in the room was itself very cold. Lynley walked to the corner where the electric fire sat and switched it on. It hummed faintly as its bars came to life.

"Getting late, isn't it?" Patsy noted. "You've not had your tea, I expect. Let me get some. And the biscuits . . . I've made too many for Kev and I to eat. So you'll have some. Do you like ginger?"

Lynley wanted to tell her not to trouble herself, but he knew that she was determined to adhere to a course that would hold off the inevitable process of mourning as long as possible. He didn't reply as she went to the shelf that held her teacups.

"Have you ever been to St. Ives?" she asked, caressing the handle of one of the cups.

"I grew up not far from St. Ives," Lynley said.

"You're Cornish?"

"After a fashion."

"Then you shall have the St. Ives cup. And for the sergeant . . . Stonehenge. Yes, Stonehenge will do. Have you been there, Sergeant?"

"On a school trip once," Havers said.

Patsy picked up both cups and their saucers. She frowned. "I can't think why they've fenced Stonehenge off. Years ago you could walk across the plain and there it was. Just standing there. All those rocks. So quiet. Just the wind. But when we took Mattie to see it, it was only from a distance. Someone said that once a month they let you walk among the stones. We meant to take Mattie back so he could do it. We thought there was time. We didn't know . . ." She raised her head. "The tea." She moved towards the rear of the cottage, through an open door that led into the kitchen.

"I'll help you," Havers said and followed her.

Left alone in the sitting room, Lynley wandered to the shelf beneath the front windows. He saw that since the previous night, two additional sculptures had been added to the collection. They were entirely different from the posturing nudes among which they rested.

Both were marble, and as Lynley studied them, he was reminded of Michelangelo's belief that the object being created from stone was simply imprisoned within the rock itself, that the duty of the artist was to act as liberator. He remembered seeing such a sculpture in Florence, an unfinished piece in which the head and torso of a man seemed to writhe to free itself from the marble. These two pieces before him were much like that, save for the fact that the emerging figures were themselves polished and buffed— suggesting completion—while the rest of the stone was left in its natural state.

Small, rectangular pieces of paper were taped to the base of each sculpture, and Lynley read the uneven handwriting that scrawled across them, *Nautilus* upon one and *Mother and Child* on the other. *Nautilus* was carved from dusky pink marble, and the shell of the mollusc rose out of the stone in a slow, smooth curve that seemed to have neither beginning nor end. White marble had been used for *Mother and Child:* two heads bent together, the suggestion of a shoulder, the shadowy form of a single arm embracing and protecting. Each was a metaphor, an intimation of reality, a whisper rather than a raucous shout.

Lynley couldn't believe that the creator of the nudes had made such a quantum leap forward in his art. He bent, touched the cold curve of the shell, and caught sight of the initials chiselled into the very bottom of the stone. *M.W.* He glanced at the nudes, saw *K.W.*

carved into them. Father and son could not have had a more different artistic vision.

"Those're Mattie's. Not the nudes, I mean. The others."

Lynley turned. Patsy Whateley was watching him from the kitchen doorway. Behind her, a kettle whistled with shrill brevity, followed by the sounds of Sergeant Havers seeing to the tea.

"They're lovely," he replied.

Patsy's slippers slapped against the thin carpet as she joined him at the shelf. This close to her, Lynley caught the biting odours of her unwashed body, and he wondered with an irrational catch of anger what sort of man Kevin Whateley was, that he would leave his wife to face the first full day of this agony alone.

"Not finished," she murmured, gazing fondly upon the mother and child. "Kev brought them in last night. They were in the garden with Kev's other work. Matt started them last summer. I can't think why he never finished them. It wasn't like him not to finish something he began. He always was a finisher. Never could rest until whatever he was doing was done. That was Mattie. Up half the night working on this project or that. Always promising to be off to bed in a tick. 'In a tick, Mum,' he'd tell me. But I'd hear him moving round in his room till half-one in the morning. Still, I can't say why he didn't finish these. They would've been quite nice. Not as real-looking as Kev's, but quite nice all the same."

As Patsy spoke, Sergeant Havers came out of the kitchen carrying a plastic tray which she set on the metal-legged coffee table in front of the sofa. Among the teapot, cups, and saucers sat a plate of the promised ginger biscuits bearing telltale signs of having been part of a batch left too long in the oven. Serrations scored their edges where a knife had been used to remove burnt portions.

Sergeant Havers poured, all of them sat, and they spent the next few moments seeing to their tea. As they did so, heavy footsteps passed the front of the cottage, made the turn into the tunnel, and stopped by the door. A key was thrust into the lock, and Kevin Whateley entered. He stopped short at the sight of the police.

He was filthy. Dust covered his thinning hair and creased into the wrinkles on his face, neck, and hands. Exertion and sweat had dampened it there, so it blotched his skin with uneven patches. He wore blue jeans, a denim jacket, and workboots, all of which were equally covered by grime. Upon seeing him, Lynley recalled what the boy Smythe-Andrews had told him about Kevin Whateley's profession as a tombstone carver. It seemed inconceivable that Whateley had managed to face that sort of work today.

The man pushed the door closed and said, "Well? What you have come to tell us?" When Whateley took a step forward into the light, Lynley saw that his forehead had been cut recently and dirt crusted fresh wounds that should have been bandaged.

"You mentioned yesterday that Matthew received a scholarship to Bredgar Chambers," he said. "Mr. Lockwood told us that one of the Board of Governors, a man called Giles Byrne, put Matthew forward for it. Is that correct?"

Kevin crossed the room and selected a biscuit. His fingers left a shadow of dirt on the plate. He did not look at his wife.

"True enough," he said.

"I was wondering how you happened to select Bredgar Chambers and not some other school. Mr. Lockwood indicated that you reserved a place for Matthew when he was eight months old. Bredgar Chambers isn't unknown, of course, but it's not Winchester or Harrow. Or Rugby. It's the sort of school men send their sons to, to maintain a family tradition. But it doesn't seem to be the sort of school one would select out of the air, without having done some research into it. Or without having been solicited."

"Mr. Byrne recommended it," Patsy said.

"You knew him prior to putting Matthew forward for the school?"

"We knew him," Kevin said shortly. He walked to the fireplace and turned his attention to the narrow mantelpiece upon which sat an opaque green vase, empty of flowers.

"Through the pub," Patsy added. Her eyes were on her husband's back, mute with an unspoken appeal. He continued to ignore her.

"The pub?"

"I worked there as barmaid. Before Matthew," she explained. "I changed to an hotel in South Ken. I didn't want . . ." She smoothed the material of her dressing gown. The movement caused one of the dragons to ripple menacingly. "Didn't seem right that Mattie's mum should be a barmaid. I wanted to do right by him. Wanted him to have more of a chance than ever I did."

"So Giles Byrne was someone you knew from the pub. A local pub? The one next door?"

"Down the mall a bit. Place called the Blue Dove. Mr. Byrne came in there just about every night. Could be he still does. I've not been there in ages."

"Not there," Kevin said. "Not last night, at least."

"You went to the pub to see him last night?"

"Yeah. He'd been at Bredgar yesterday afternoon when Mattie went missing."

It seemed unusual that a member of the Board of Governors would be at the school on a Sunday afternoon. As if reading this thought, Patsy Whateley said:

"We rang him, Inspector."

"Always took an interest in Mattie, he did." Kevin sounded as if he were defending their decision to call in a member of the Board of Governors. "He could make sure we didn't get a runaround from the Headmaster. So he met us there. Fat lot of good it did. With everyone insisting that Mattie'd run off. And everyone shifting blame onto everyone else. And no one bloody willing to ring the police. Fucking sods."

"*Kev* . . ." Patsy said his name like a plea.

Whateley swung on his wife. "What would you have me call them? High and mighty Mr. Lockwood and that bum-boy Corntel. Should I thank them that we've lost our Mattie, girl? Is that what you want? We'd be getting it right then, wouldn't we, Pats?"

"Oh, Kev . . ."

"He's *dead*! Damn you, the boy's dead! And you expect me to thank my betters for seeing to it, don't you? While all the time you bake biscuits to serve to the sodding police who don't give a toss about Mattie or us! He's just a body to them. Don't you see that yet?"

Patsy's face crumpled under her husband's words. She managed only to say, "Mattie does love his biscuits. Ginger the best."

Kevin cried out once. He flung himself away from the fireplace, threw open the door of the cottage, and left. Havers crossed the room quietly and closed the door.

In the brown and yellow plaid chair, Patsy Whateley twisted the sash of her dressing gown, which had fallen open to reveal one plump thigh. Blue veins knotted against pasty skin.

It seemed indecent to Lynley that they should stay any longer, knowing that it would be an act of mercy to leave the Whateleys to themselves. Still, there was more to be learned and little enough time in which to learn it. Lynley knew he was being governed by a cardinal and relentless rule of policework. The sooner one gleaned information after an untimely death, the more likely it was that one would solve the crime. There was no time to lose, no time to soothe, no time to smooth over the rocky path of the Whateleys' grief. He despised himself for doing so, but still he pressed on.

"Giles Byrne came often to the Blue Dove. Does he live here in Hammersmith?"

Patsy nodded. "On Rivercourt Road. Just a bit down from the pub."

"Not far from here?"

"A walk is all."

"You knew each other? Your sons as well? Did Matthew and Brian know one another prior to Matthew's going to Bredgar Chambers?"

"Brian?" She seemed to be searching for a way to connect the name to a memory. "That would be Mr. Byrne's son, wouldn't it? I remember him. He lives with his mother. Has done for years. Mr. Byrne's divorced."

"Could Matthew have served as a replacement for Giles Byrne's own son?"

"I can't think how. Mr. Byrne hardly ever saw Mattie. Perhaps he might have run into him on the green if he was out for a stroll and Mattie was playing there. Mattie often did. But he never mentioned seeing Mr. Byrne that I recall."

"Brian told us that his father once tutored a boy called Edward Hsu. He said that his father had been looking for a replacement for Edward Hsu since 1975. Do you know what that means? Could Matthew have been a replacement for a boy Giles Byrne was perhaps overly fond of?"

Patsy reacted to the question with an infinitesimal movement that Lynley might have missed had he not been watching her hands. They clutched the dressing gown, then relaxed. "Mattie didn't see Mr. Byrne, Inspector. Not that I knew. Not that he told me."

She sounded both insistent and convinced, but Lynley knew that children rarely tell their parents everything. He reflected upon what Kevin Whateley had previously informed him about the change in Matthew's behaviour. An explanation existed for it somewhere. Change does not occur without a force behind it.

There was only one area that he had not touched upon with Patsy Whateley, and he came to it gently, realising the pain it would cause her.

"Mrs. Whateley, I know how difficult this is for you to accept, but it appears that Matthew did indeed run away from the school. Or at least that he wanted to run away and made some sort of arrangement with someone who . . ." He hesitated, wondering why he was having such trouble getting to the point. Havers did it for him.

"Someone who killed him," she said quietly.

"I can't think that," Patsy Whateley replied, giving her attention to Havers. "Mattie wouldn't run off."

"But if he were troubled, if he were being bullied—"

"Bullied?" Her head swivelled to Lynley. "Whatever do you mean?"

"You saw him on holidays. Was he ever bruised? Was he marked in any way?"

"Bruised? No. Of course not. Of *course* not! Don't you think he'd tell his mum if someone was bullying him? Don't you think he'd confide in his own mummy?"

"Perhaps not. Not if he knew how important it was to you that he stay at Bredgar Chambers. He may not have wanted to disappoint you."

"No!" The single word was so much more than mere denial. "Why would anyone bully my Mattie? He was a good boy, a quiet boy. He did his lessons. He followed the rules. Tell me why someone would bully Matt!"

Because he didn't fit in, Lynley thought. Because he wouldn't follow traditions. Because he wasn't shaped to fit the mould. And yet there was more to what had happened at Bredgar Chambers than was represented by a list of Matthew Whateley's class differences. It spoke to Lynley from the eyes of Smythe-Andrews, from Arlens' fainting, and Harry Morant's refusal to go to his lessons. They were all afraid. But, unlike Matthew, they were not afraid enough to run away.

The narrow brick house on Rivercourt Road was dark. In spite of this clear indication that no one was home, Kevin Whateley pushed fiercely through the gate, mounted the steps, and pounded the brass knocker against the door. Even as he did it, he knew it was a futile effort, yet still he knocked. The noise grew louder, echoed in the street.

He *would* see Giles Byrne. He would see him tonight. He would rail and storm and scream and torment the one man who was responsible for Mattie's death. Kevin's fist clenched. He beat it on the door.

"Byrne!" he shouted. "Sod you, bugger! Come out here, damn you. Open this door! You queer! You fucking queer! Hear me, Byrne? You open up! Now!"

On the corner across the street, a narrow shaft of light hit the pavement as a door was opened cautiously and someone looked out. "Steady on," a voice called.

"Bugger off!" Kevin shouted. The door hastily closed.

Two large pottery urns stood on either side of the porch, and when no one from within the Byrne house gave answer to his summons, Kevin's eyes fell upon them, and then upon his hands. He grabbed one urn, heaved it onto its side, shoved it down the neat steps. It sprayed soil and leaves across the tile, crashing and shattering on the swept front path.

"Byrne!" Kevin shouted. The name caught on a laugh. "See what I'm doing here, Byrne? What's that, chum? Want more of the same?"

He fell upon the second urn, found purchase for his hands along its raised lip, and smashed it into the white front door. Wood splintered. Soil flew up into his eyes. Shards of broken pottery struck at his face.

"Had enough?" Kevin shrieked.

He found that he was panting, that a pain caught at his chest like the point of a spear.

"Byrne!" he wheezed. "Damn you . . . Byrne . . ."

He sank onto the top step, into the soil. A crescent piece of the broken urn bit into his thigh. His head felt heavy, his shoulders sore. His vision was blurred, but clear enough to see that next door a slender young man had come out of a house and walked along the pavement to peer past the pyracantha bushes that served as border between the properties.

"You all right, mate?" he asked.

Kevin fought for air. "All right. Okay," he replied.

He pushed himself to his feet, coughing against pain, and stumbled through soil and debris to the gate. Leaving it gaping open upon the mess, he made his way towards the river and the Upper Mall. Ahead of him the branches of an enormous chestnut were silhouetted against the night sky. Kevin blinked at the tree.

I can climb it! Watch me! Watch me, Dad!

Come down from there, Mattie. Break your neck, son. Or fall into the river.

Into the river? I should love that! How I should!

Mum wouldn't think much of it, would she? Come on, down with you. And no nonsense about it.

Down he would come, never truly in danger since he'd only managed to climb to the first branch, but perfectly safe now with both his feet on the ground.

Kevin tore his eyes from the tree, plodded in the direction of the Blue Dove and the green that lay a short distance beyond it. He tried to look at nothing as he walked. He tried to forget where he was. He tried not to realise that every step he took brought him only closer to another part of the neighbourhood that reminded him of Mattie. Especially the river.

Like the few remaining unrestored cottages on the Thames, their own cottage had a passage to the water, remnant of a way of life long dead when the fishermen used it as easy access to their livelihood. It was in a far corner of the cellar—a door leading to a tunnel and a set of stairs that dropped beneath the embankment to the river below. How many times had he warned Mattie off opening that door? How many times had he explained the dangers of a tumble down those worn stone steps?

As many times as he'd told him to be careful about dashing across the street, to stay away from the Great West Road, to keep off the wall that separated the Lower Mall from the river, to cover his eyes with goggles before he ever placed drill to stone, to keep the radio far enough away from the bath. They were loving admonitions, patiently given, all designed to protect the boy from harm.

Yet even as he mouthed these tender warnings, real danger had lurked, waiting to pounce. As much as he had loved his son, Kevin had not seen what that danger was. He had been beguiled into believing that it did not exist, beguiled by Giles Byrne. He and Patsy had caved in to the man's logic, his wit, his superior experience. Damn him to hell.

Mattie hadn't wanted Bredgar Chambers. He'd asked repeatedly not to be sent away. But they'd done it to him anyway, Kevin telling himself that the boy's reluctance to leave Hammersmith was an indication that the apron strings holding son to mother had to be cut. Well, they'd cut them now, hadn't they? No worry that Mattie might cling to his mother any longer. No chance of that.

Mattie. Kevin's eyes smarted. His throat ached. His chest swelled to bursting. He fought it all.

Can I have my own stone to carve sometime, Dad? I've an idea for a piece and ... Let me show you. I've drawn a bit of it here.

How could he be dead? How could that swift, sweet life be over? How could they survive without Mattie?

"Ooooh, mate, looks like you've been mucking round with the pigs!"

The drunken voice roused him. On a bench at the edge of the green, a man slumped in the darkness, drinking from a bottle in a paper bag. He leered at Kevin. He sneered for a smile.

"Piggy pig," the drunk warbled. "Piggy, piggy, piggy, pig!" He laughed and waved the bag in the air.

"Bugger off," Kevin replied, but the words trembled.

"Ooooh, weepy piggy pig!" the drunk responded. "Weepy, weepy piggy pig! Crying 'cause his trousers is covered with muck!"

"You bloody—"

"Oooooh, I'm frightened! I really am! Frightened of the weepy *weepy* piggy pig. What have we got to cry about, piggy? Lost our sow? Lost our piglet? Lost our—"

Kevin lunged at the man, his fingers driving towards his throat. "Bloody bastard! Shut your mouth!" he screamed and began to pound at the face beneath his own. He felt bones crack, felt his knuckles split upon teeth.

The contact was good, the pain was right. And when the drunk's knee came up savagely into Kevin's groin and the agony shot up through his body, that was good as well. He loosened his grip, fell to the ground. The drunk staggered up, kicked Kevin in the ribs, ran off in the direction of the pub. Kevin remained where he was, his body pounding, his heart hammering.

But he did not cry.

10

Deborah St. James was curled into the worn leather chair next to the fireplace in her husband's study. Although her hands held a stack of photographic proof sheets and a magnifying glass, her attention was on the golden-blue lick of flames upon wood. A glass of brandy stood on the table next to her, but other than to breathe in its heavy, vinous scent, she had not been able to touch the drink.

Following Lynley's early morning visit, she had spent most of the day alone. Simon had gone out to a meeting shortly before lunch, from there to an engagement at Chelsea Institute, from there to a session with a team of solicitors who were preparing to represent the defendant in a murder case. He had not wanted to keep any of the appointments and had been in the process of surreptitiously cancelling the first of them when she had come upon him doing so and prevented him, knowing full well that he was putting aside his work so that he could be there in the house should she need him that day.

She had reacted angrily, insisting that she wasn't a child, that he stop trying to coddle her. But anger was a guise she adopted to hide the extent to which her inner turmoil needed release, a release that she knew could only come from telling him the truth. It was upon truth that they had once promised one another that they would lay the foundation for their marriage. She had blithely agreed, believing that one small, ugly secret from the past would not be enough to undermine what they had together. Yet it was doing so now, and this morning, faced with the pained confusion with which Simon greeted her words, she had seen the first unmistakable fissures in their relationship.

His departure had been achingly remote. Coming to stand in the doorway of her darkroom, dressed in his navy suit, his ungovernable hair curling past the collar of his shirt, a briefcase in his hand, he had said little enough.

"I'm off then, Deborah. I shouldn't think I'll be back in time for dinner if this meeting at five is anything like the previous one I had with Dobson's barrister."

"All right. Yes." *My love.* She had wanted to add that, but the chasm between them was far too great. Had it not been there, she would have gone to him and brushed unnecessarily at the shoulders of his jacket, would have smoothed back his hair, would have smiled to feel his arms come round her in automatic reaction, would have lifted her mouth eagerly for his kiss. His hands would have moved to caress her, and her response would have been loving and quick. In another time, under different circumstances. But now, only distance allowed her to protect him, and his proximity was the single most dangerous inducement to speaking at last.

A car door slammed in the street outside, and she went to the window. In spite of everything, she hoped it was Simon even as she knew it probably would not be. It wasn't. She saw the silver Bentley parked along the kerb and Lynley climbing the five front steps to their door. She went to admit him.

He looked exhausted. Tiny lines made etchings at the corners of his mouth.

"Have you had your dinner, Tommy?" she asked him as he hung his overcoat on the rack in the hall. "Shall I ask Dad to fix you a tray? It's no trouble, and I should guess it's high time that you . . ."

She hesitated when he turned to face her. She knew him too well for him to conceal the manner in which murder took its toll upon him. She read it in his eyes, in the set of his shoulders, in the flicker of despondency that passed across his face.

They went into the study where she watched him pour a small whisky at the bar. "How miserable a case like this must be for you. I only wish there was *something* . . . I've thought and thought about it. Surely there's a detail I've failed to remember . . . something that will help you . . . And I ought to be able to remember. I keep telling myself that."

He tossed back the drink and returned the crystal tumbler to its tray. He tapped its rim restlessly.

"Simon's not here," she went on. "One of those days of endless meetings, I'm afraid. I don't know when he'll be back. Tommy, are you sure you're not hungry? Dad's in the kitchen. It'll just take a moment—"

"What's happening to you, Deb?"

The question was unexpected, spoken in kindness. With its tender pressure against her defences, Deborah felt the cold finger of panic touch her. Above all else, saying nothing was imperative.

"I was just going over my proof sheets from the trip." As if to give this statement veracity, she returned to her chair, sat down, and picked up the photographs once more. "As I was printing the proofs, I *did* wonder if they might be of use to you, Tommy. I mean the pictures from Stoke Poges. Not the rest. I'm sure you're not interested in Tintern Abbey."

Lynley's eyes were on her far too long for comfort. He moved Simon's lumpy ottoman nearer her chair, taking that as a seat for himself. Deborah reached for her brandy and drank at last. The liquor felt like fire shooting through her throat.

"I've wanted to tell you how sorry I am," he said. "But there's been no chance. You were in hospital. The next thing I knew, you were off on your trip. Deb, I know what the baby meant to you. To both of you."

She felt the tightness of encroaching tears. He didn't know. He never would. "Please, Tommy," she managed.

The two words apparently sufficed. After a moment, he took the photographs and removed his spectacles from his jacket pocket. He used her magnifying glass to indicate a picture. "Stoke Poges. St. Giles' Church. The problem is that Bredgar Chambers is in West Sussex, fairly dead on the button between Horsham and Crawley. But by no stretch of the imagination is it in a direct line to Stoke Poges and that churchyard. So the killer had to have chosen it deliberately. But why?"

Deborah thought over the question. There did seem to be something after all. . . .

She went to the desk and found her copy of the rough manuscript of the book that her photographs were intended to illustrate.

"Just a moment . . . I remember . . ." She brought the manuscript back, sat down, and began leafing through it to find Thomas Gray's poem. Having done so, she skimmed the stanzas, exclaimed, and handed the manuscript to Lynley. "Look at the epitaph," she said. "The first part."

He read the first four lines aloud.

"Here rests his head upon the lap of Earth.
A youth to fortune and to fame unknown;
Fair Science frowned not on his humble birth,
And Melancholy marked him for her own."

Lynley looked up at Deborah. "It's hard to believe," he said. "I'm not even sure I want to believe it."

"How well do the lines fit that little boy?"

"Perfectly." Lynley removed his spectacles, stared at the fire. "Line by line, it's all there, Deb. Matthew's head was on the earth when you found him, wasn't it? He certainly had neither fame nor fortune. His birth was humble—more than humble, I dare say. In recent months, he'd become morose, melancholy. His father described it like being in a trance. Noncommunicative."

Deborah felt a shiver of apprehension. "Then Stoke Poges was chosen deliberately."

"By someone who had a vehicle, someone Matthew knew, someone with a perverted interest in little boys, someone who knew the poem well."

"Do you know who it is?"

"I don't think I want to." He pushed himself off the ottoman, paced the distance to the window and back. And again to the window. He rested his hand on the sill and looked out into the street.

"What happens next?" Deborah asked him.

"The autopsy has got to give us more. Fibres, hairs, deposits of some kind to explain where Matthew was from Friday afternoon until Sunday. He wasn't killed in that field. He was dropped in that field. So for at least twenty-four hours, perhaps more, he was a prisoner somewhere. The autopsy may give us an idea where. And a sure cause of death. Once we have that, we'll have a clearer direction."

"But don't you have a direction now? Because from what you were saying—"

"It's not clear enough! I can't make an arrest on the strength of a poem, ownership of a car, position of trust at the school, and the curious manner of describing a little boy to me. Not to mention being head of English, a literature master into the bargain."

"So you *do* know," Deborah said. "Tommy, is it someone you . . . ?" She saw the answer on his face. "How dreadful for you. How perfectly awful."

"I *don't* know. That's just it. He has no clear motive."

"Except the curious manner of describing a little boy?" She reached for her photographs and chose her words with care. "He'd been tied up. I could see that. There were abrasions, places where the skin was raw and chafed. And the burns . . . Tommy, it's the worst sort of motive. What's making you afraid to face it?"

He swung round from the window. "What's making *you* afraid?" he demanded.

The words buffeted the brittle calm that their few minutes of conversation had allowed her to develop. She felt her skin blanch.

"Tell me," he said. "Deborah, for God's sake, do you think I'm blind?"

She shook her head. Of course he wasn't blind. He saw far too much. That had always been at the root of the problem. He persisted.

"I saw how the two of you were acting this morning. You were like strangers. Worse than strangers."

Still she said nothing. She willed him to stop speaking. But he went on.

"You're removing Simon from the grief, aren't you, Deb? You believe he feels no loss or at least that it doesn't compare to yours. So you're cutting him off. You're cutting everyone off. You want to suffer alone, don't you? As if it's your fault. As if you're being punished."

She felt her face betray her and knew she had to divert the conversation. She sought direction in vain.

Somewhere in the house, the dog began barking, excited yelping that generally meant a demand for reward for some trick performed. She heard her father's answering laughter.

Lynley left the window and went to the wall of her photographs across the room. Deborah saw him looking at a small black and white study, one of her earliest efforts, taken shortly after her fourteenth birthday. In it, Simon lay in the garden on a chaise, covered by a wool blanket, his crutches at his side. His head canted to the left, and although his eyes were closed, his face was a revealing study of despair.

"Did you never wonder why he leaves this hanging here?" Lynley asked. "He could remove it, you know. He could insist you replace it with something else, something more uplifting, something soothing."

"Something false." ·

"But he won't do that, will he? Have you ever wondered why?"

She saw it. She knew it. It lay at the centre of what she loved about her husband. Not physical strength, not spiritual virtue, not unyielding and implacable rectitude, but a willingness to accept, an ability to continue, a determination to struggle on. Those qualities in him spoke to her eloquently from the backward infinity of their lives together.

What irony, she thought, *that it should have turned out like this. With both of us damaged.* But in Simon's case, he'd had no control of the car or the accident itself. While she had had perfect control. She had made the decision to maim herself, because it had seemed easier at the time, because she had sought convenience in her life.

"I'm crippled," she said simply.

Lynley recoiled from the word and the implications it had always held in his life. "That's nonsense, Deb. You don't know that. You can't."

But she did.

When he arrived home, Lynley found the day's post where it usually was, on the upper left corner of his desk in the library, weighted down by an oversized magnifying glass that Helen had given him as a joke some years ago when he'd received his promotion to detective inspector.

"The game's afoot, my dear Lynley," she had announced, plopping a large gaily wrapped package onto his desk. The magnifying glass had been inside it, along with a meerschaum pipe and a deerstalker.

He had laughed to see them, to see her as well. That was always his reaction to being in her presence.

He'd gone a long time without giving actual definition to what he was and what he felt when he was with Helen Clyde. There had seemed no need to admit to the obvious. With her, he was simply the best he could be—witty, articulate, intelligent, alive. She had somehow managed to engender within him all that was good. If he knew tenderness, it was owing to her willingness to reach out to him when he felt dejection. If he knew compassion, it was because she had shown him how deep was the well of her own sweet kindness. If he knew honesty, it was because she refused to accept anything less, from him or from herself. If he stood complete, coming to terms with his past and willing to face the future, Helen had given him the strength to do so.

What she had not given him was patience. What she had not given him was her ability to live a single day at a time, allowing life's possibilities to grow and develop. He wanted her—now, today, tonight—in every way conceivable, in a consuming possession of her body and her spirit. He ached to have her, and two months' separation had done nothing to mitigate the intensity of that desire.

The expense of spirit in a waste of shame. . . . But lust was not the cornerstone of what he felt for Helen. It never had been.

Lynley picked up the post and walked to the rosewood table where he kept his decanters. He poured a whisky and flipped through the envelopes, looking, as he had been doing for the past two months even without thinking, for one bearing an odd, Greek post-mark. It was not there. In its place were bills, circulars, theatre advertisements, a letter from his solicitors, another from his mother, a third from his bank.

Returning to his desk, he slit open his mother's letter and read through the light chitchat that comprised her loving attempt to urge him away from loneliness. Two of the mares were about to foal; three calves had arrived far earlier than expected but the vet had seen to them and all was well; the Pendykes were sinking a new well on their farm; his brother Peter was recovering from flu; Aunt Augusta had visited for an unendurable three days. And how are you, Tommy darling? We've seen so little of you since January. Why not spend a weekend here? Bring a friend. . . .

Someone moved along the corridor outside the library, humming a spirited rendition of one of the more popular tunes from *Les Misérables*. Denton, Lynley thought. His valet was a great fan of London theatre. The door opened, brushing softly against the deep pile of the carpet. The humming swelled dramatically, then choked to a stop altogether as Denton entered the room and saw Lynley at his desk.

"Sorry," Denton said with an abashed grin. "Didn't know you were home."

"Not planning to leave me for the stage, are you, Denton?"

The young man laughed and brushed at his coat sleeve. "Not a chance of that. Have you had your dinner?"

"No, not yet."

Denton shook his head. "Quarter to ten, my lord, and you've not had your dinner?"

"I got caught up in things. Forgot all about it."

Denton didn't look convinced. His eyes fell upon the post. Since he had been the one to bring it up to the library, there was no doubt that he knew what letters it contained, and what it did not. He said nothing, however, other than to enquire if his lordship wanted an omelette or soup or some fresh ham salad.

"An omelette would be fine, Denton. Thank you," Lynley replied.

He wasn't hungry, but picking round a plate of eggs would at least maintain a semblance of normality.

Denton looked pleased. He began to exit and then apparently remembered why he had come into the room in the first place. He removed a folded paper from his pocket.

"I was going to leave this on your desk. You had a call from the Yard just after nine this evening."

"What sort of call?"

"A message someone took for you but thought best to pass on before tomorrow. The porter from Bredgar Chambers was trying to reach you. A bloke called Frank Orten. Seems he went out to the rubbish fire on the campus and found a school uniform there. A blazer, trousers, shirt, tie. Even shoes. The whole lot. He thought you might want to come round and have a look at them. He says he's certain they're the dead boy's clothes."

11

Frank Orten lived in an asymmetrically shaped lodge just inside the gates of the school. A broad bay window—shaded by a plane tree—projected towards the school drive, one pane open to the morning air. From this issued the steady wailing of a child. It was the first sound Lynley and Havers heard as they got out of the car and approached the lodge entry.

As if he had been watching for them, Orten opened the door before they had a chance to ring the bell. He was already dressed for his workday, in a quasimilitary uniform designed to incorporate the colours of the school. His bearing was ramrod stiff, and his eyes snapped over them in an evaluative examination. "Inspector. Sergeant." He nodded sharply, approval given, and jerked his head in the direction of a disarranged sitting room to his left. "Come in."

Without waiting for a response, he led the way, and planted himself before a stark stone fireplace above which hung a mirror framed in flaking gilt and spotted with age. The back of Orten's head was reflected in it, as were the brass sconces at the other side of the room that cast oblongs of light up against the walls but did little else to dispel a gloom created by the room's northern exposure and its single narrow casement window.

"Bit of a mix this morning." Orten indicated with a flick of his thumb the sound of continued weeping which came from behind a partially closed door to the right of the entry. "My daughter's kids are with me for a few days." A woman's soothing voice attempted to smooth over the troubled waters, but the child's wailing rose to hysterical heights, countered by the high-pitched shriek of another child's angry accusation. Orten said, "A moment please," and left them to join whatever fray was in progress. "Elaine, can you get his—" The door closed behind him.

"Domestic bliss," Havers commented, sauntering over to examine three excessively verdant plants on a carved chest beneath the window. She fingered a leaf experimentally. "Plastic," she announced and wiped the dirt from her fingers.

"Hmm." Lynley was evaluating the room. The furniture consisted of a heavy sofa and two chairs upholstered in a colour that compromised between brown and grey, several tables holding lamps whose shades were askew, and wall decorations of a military nature. These hung above the sofa—two maps and a commendation—but their frames were dusty, and a cobweb dangled from one of them. Children's toys were scattered across the floor, as were copies of *Country Life* with pages looking crumpled and sticky, as if the magazines had been used as mats beneath food. Everything about the room served as a suggestion that no woman shared Frank Orten's life at the lodge.

Nonetheless, when Orten returned to the sitting room, a middle-aged woman followed him. The porter introduced her as Miss Elaine Roly—he was careful to emphasise the *Miss*—and added the information that she was matron of Erebus House, as if this would logically explain her presence in his lodge at this hour of the morning.

"Frank's not much good with the grandchildren alone," Elaine Roly clarified, rubbing her hands down the front of her dress as if in a quest for wrinkles. "Shall I be off, Frank? They seem to be settled now. You can send them up to Erebus after a bit, if you like."

"Stay." Orten appeared to be accustomed to speaking in monosyllabic commands, accustomed to being obeyed as well.

Elaine Roly complied cheerfully enough, choosing to sit next to the window, seemingly oblivious of the fact that the milky light striking the chair spotlit her in an unattractive fashion. She was at the same time austere and monochromatic, Quakerish-looking, like a creation from the mind of Charlotte Brontë. She wore a plain grey dress with a wide lace collar. Her shoes were black, crepe-soled, and sensible. Small stud earrings comprised her only jewellery, and her greying brown hair was pulled back from her face and pinned at the nape of her neck in the fashion of another century. Her nose, however, was shapely and pert, and the smile she directed at Lynley and Havers was genuinely warm.

"Have you had coffee this morning?" she asked them, turning in her seat. "Frank, shall I—"

"No need," Orten replied.

He picked at the braid on the lapel of his uniform jacket. It was, Lynley saw, frayed at that spot, as if Orten reached for it often.

"The message I received last night indicated that you've found some clothes," Lynley said to him. "Are they here in the lodge?"

Orten wasn't prepared to comply with such a direct approach. "Seventeen years, Inspector." His tone suggested this was a prefatorial statement. Lynley saw Sergeant Havers' impatient movement of the shoulders, but she went to the sofa where she opened her notebook and thumbed through the pages, making rather more noise than the effort required. Orten went on. "Seventeen years I've portered here. Nothing like this. No disappearance. No murder. Nothing. Bredgar Chambers has been fine. The best. No doubt of it."

"Other students have died, however. The chapel bears witness to that."

"Died, yes. But murdered? Never. Bodes ill, Inspector." He paused to harumph and then concluded meaningfully with, "Can't say I'm surprised."

Lynley chose not to explore the innuendo. "Yet the suicide of a student must bode ill as well."

Orten's hand went to the school ensign embroidered in yellow upon his breast pocket. His fingers reached for and plucked at the crown that floated above the sprig of hawthorn. A single gold thread was unravelling from it, beginning to destroy the entire design.

"Suicide?" he asked. "You're saying Matt Whateley's a suicide?"

"Not at all. I was speaking of another student. If you've been here seventeen years, you must have known him. Edward Hsu."

Orten and Elaine Roly looked at one another. Lynley couldn't tell if their reaction implied surprise or consternation.

"You must have known Edward Hsu. You, Miss Roly? Did you know him? Have you been here long enough?"

Elaine Roly's tongue darted out to wet her lips. "Twenty-four years this month, sir. I began as a kitchen skivvy. Waited on the masters in the common room, I did. Worked my way up. I've been matron of Erebus the last eighteen years. And proud to say it."

"Was Edward Hsu an Erebus boy?"

"He was. Edward was Erebus."

"A favourite of Giles Byrne, I understand."

"Mr. Byrne tutored Edward during the half-terms and holidays. He's done that for years. He always picks a boy from Erebus to help out special. He's an old boy from Erebus himself, and he likes to do something for the house when and where he can. A fine man, Mr. Byrne."

"Quite close to Edward Hsu, from what Brian Byrne tells me."

"Brian would remember Edward, I imagine."

"You must work closely with Brian since he's house prefect of Erebus."

"Closely?" Her response was studied. "No. Not what I would call closely."

"But since he's house prefect and you're matron there—"

"Brian's a bit difficult," she interposed. "A bit hard to read. A bit too caught up in . . ." She hesitated delicately. In the next room, the children began another fracas, this one milder than the last, but possessing the promise of escalation. "House prefects need to stand on their own two feet, Inspector," Elaine Roly said.

"Brian can't do that?"

"House prefects should be boys who aren't needy themselves."

"Needy in what way?"

"For friendship. For approval. Anxious to be liked. That doesn't work well in a prefect. Never has. Never will. How can a lad discipline younger boys if he's so intent upon being liked by one and all? And that's Brian for you. If I'd had anything to do with it, he'd not have been selected."

"But doesn't the fact that Brian Byrne became a prefect indicate that he had someone's strong approval in the first place?"

"Indicates nothing." Orten cut the air with his hand. "Only who the father is, and what the Headmaster does when the Board of Governors tell him to jump."

A piece of china clattered to the floor in the next room. A howl accompanied it. Elaine Roly got to her feet. "Let me see to that, Frank," she said and left them.

Orten spoke again as soon as the door closed behind her. "Works hard, does Elaine. John Corntel doesn't come near to appreciating the kind of matron he has in that woman. But you've come for the clothes, not to hear about Corntel. Come along with you both."

He led them out of the house, about fifty yards along the main drive to where a secondary lane, bordered thickly by lime trees, veered off to the right. Orten marched ahead of them, his blue cap pulled low upon his forehead. They walked without conversation, Havers reading through her notebook, underlining here and there with a vague, growling mutter while Lynley at her side drove his fists into the pockets of his trousers and thought about Frank Orten's and Elaine Roly's statements.

The structure of any institution generally made it a place where people at all levels jockeyed for whatever power seemed within their grasp. That was no different here than it was at the Yard. While it seemed reasonable to conclude that a school's headmaster would wield the most influence, Orten's words suggested otherwise. The Board of Governors—and any examination of the board led inescapably to Giles Byrne—seemed to weigh heavily in the balance of power. Matthew Whateley had to fit into the picture somewhere. Lynley was sure of it. He'd been chosen for the governors' scholarship, after all, perhaps against the wishes of the school's headmaster. He'd been sent to live in Erebus House, where Byrne himself had once been a student. As had Edward Hsu. There was a rudimentary pattern in all of it.

The unmistakable, acrid odour of smoke became more pronounced as they reached a fork in the lane. Frank Orten led them once again to the right, but Lynley paused, looking down the other fork at the buildings a short distance away. He recognised the back of the science building and the four boys' houses. Calchus was the closest.

"What you want is this way, Inspector," Orten said impatiently.

The right fork was some twenty-five yards long, and it dead-ended at a large doorless shed. This housed three minibuses, a small tractor, an open-back lorry, and four bicycles, three of which sported flat tyres. Only the roof and walls protected the school's utility vehicles from inclement weather, for the windows were paneless, and if the front of the building had ever been hung with doors, they had long since been removed. It was a decidedly unattractive structure.

Frank Orten said, "Essentials are last to be seen to and worked upon these days. Spit and polish on exteriors to catch the public eye, and to hell with what parents aren't likely to see."

"The school's in disrepair," Lynley remarked. "We couldn't help noticing that yesterday."

"But not the theatre. Or the sports hall. Or the chapel. Or that smart sculpture garden people seem to fancy so much. Or anything else that might be looked at on parents' day. And those'll keep enrollment up, won't they?" He gave a bark of sardonic laughter.

"The school has financial trouble, I take it."

"You take it dead-on." Orten paused in his march, looking west where through the lime trees the distant chapel caught the morning light. The hollow sound of a bell began its call for morning prayer. It resembled a dirge. Orten turned away with a shake of his head. "Time was, Bredgar was the best of the lot. Pupils off to Cambridge—to Oxford—as fast as they could go."

"That's changed?"

"Well changed. But I'm not the one to speak of it." He smiled bitterly. "Porters know their place, Inspector. The Headmaster sees to it I'm reminded of mine often enough."

Without waiting for a reply, Orten strode off the paved lane at the edge of the vehicle shed and led them round the corner of the building into a scarred plot of land where the school's rubbish was burned. It was an area redolent with the odours of smoke, damp ashes, burnt weeds, and clippings. These emanated from a cone-shaped pile of smouldering debris. To one side of this pile sat a green wheelbarrow with the clothing in question lumped inside it.

"Seemed best to leave it where it was," Orten said. "Not on the fire, but as close as possible."

Lynley scanned the ground. The soil was hard-packed, threaded with mangled, beaten weeds. While footprints showed upon it, the impressions left were too vague to be made any decent use of— here a toe print, there a heel, here part of a sole. There was nothing substantial.

"Have a look at this, sir," Sergeant Havers said from the side of the pile nearest the vehicle shed. She had lit a cigarette, and she used it to gesture at the ground. "Decent print, that. Woman's?"

Lynley joined her and squatted to look at the print. It had sunk into the softest area near the fire, where a layer of ash had formed a muddy bed. He saw by looking that it was a gym shoe, probably typical to the wardrobe of every person on the campus. "Possibly a woman," he admitted. "Or one of the younger boys."

"Or an older lad with small feet." Havers sighed. "Where's Holmes when you need him? He'd crawl through this muck and have the case solved in a quarter-hour."

"Soldier on, Sergeant," Lynley replied.

As she continued her examination of the area, Lynley went back to the clothing in the wheelbarrow. Frank Orten stood to one side, gazing in the direction of the vehicle shed. His own lodge stood at the other side of a large expanse of open field beyond it.

Lynley reached for his spectacles, put them on, and pulled several neatly folded plastic bags out of his pocket. He donned latex gloves, although even as he did so, he realised the uselessness of such precaution. By now the clothes had so many contaminants upon them after a period on the rubbish heap followed by a night in the wheelbarrow, that it was ridiculous to assume that any usable evidence might be gleaned from them once they were turned over to a forensic team.

There were seven items altogether, their charred exteriors filthy with soot. Lynley looked at the blazer first. It bore no name tag, but ragged threads along the neckline gave indication that one had been removed. This same applied to the trousers and the shirt. He looked up when he came to the tie and saw the pair of shoes beneath it.

"How did you happen to find all this?" he asked Frank Orten.

Orten's eyes shifted to him in preparation for his answer. "I do the burning on Saturday afternoon. Always have. Always make certain the fire's well out before I go on to other things. Noticed on Saturday night that it'd sprung up again. Came to have a look."

Lynley straightened slowly. "Saturday night?" he repeated. "*Saturday* night?"

The man's face was guarded. "Saturday night," he replied.

Across the rubbish pile, Lynley saw Sergeant Havers stop her exploration, toss her cigarette to one side. One hand went to her hip. "Matthew Whateley was reported missing on Sunday," she said. Lynley saw that her face was flushed. "And you never got round to mentioning these clothes until *Monday* night even though you'd found them on Saturday? Why's that, Mr. Orten?"

"Thought it was a bit of a prank when I first saw the fire. When I went out to check on it, it was dark. I just shovelled some soil onto it to put it out. I didn't see the clothes then, not until the next day. Didn't think much about it at the time. Didn't know a boy'd gone missing until Monday morning."

"But even then, we were here most of the day yesterday. Didn't you even think to tell us *then*? Do you know what kind of position suppressing evidence puts you in?"

"Didn't know it *was* evidence," Orten retorted. "Still don't."

Lynley spoke. "Yet when you phoned Scotland Yard, you made mention of the fact that the clothes belonged to the dead boy, didn't you? They were quite specific about that part of the message." He watched the man, saw the single spasm of a muscle in his cheek. "Who convinced you of that? Who persuaded you to phone the police? Miss Roly? The Headmaster? John Corntel?"

"No one! Now you've seen what you've come for, I've work of my own." That said, Orten spun on his heel and moved swiftly back the way they had come. Havers was after him in an instant.

"Wait," Lynley said.

"But—"

"He's not going anywhere, Sergeant. Give him time to simmer."

"Time to cook up a flaming good story about why he waited till Monday night to report a piece of evidence he'd found on Sunday!"

"He's had plenty of time for that already. A bit longer isn't going to improve on what he plans to tell us. Look at this."

He held out a single sock on his palm, flipped it inside out, and pointed to the tag attached to it. It had been badly blackened by the fire, but it was still legibly the number *4*.

"So these *are* Matt Whateley's," Havers said. "But where's the other sock?"

"Either burned in the rubbish pile before Orten got to it or, if we're lucky, dropped somewhere on the way to the pile."

Havers watched as Lynley began to bag each article of clothing. "We've an entirely different case now, don't we, sir?"

"In part, yes. All Matthew's clothes are accounted for. Leisure clothes, games clothes, school clothes. Unless we want to assume that for some bizarre reason he left the campus stark naked on Friday afternoon, we have to conclude that he never intentionally left the campus at all. Someone spirited him away."

"Alive or dead?"

"We don't know that yet."

"But you've a guess, haven't you?"

"Yes. I've a guess. Dead, Havers."

She nodded, exhaled moodily. "So he wasn't running away."

"It doesn't look like it. But if he wasn't running away from something, we've a docket of questions unexplained at the moment. His father said he'd changed over the past few months, he was moody. Then there's Harry Morant and whatever's at the root of his unwillingness to talk to you. On top of that, consider Wedge, Arlens, and Smythe-Andrews when I interviewed them." Lynley picked up the plastic bags and handed two of them to Havers. He removed his spectacles and peeled off the latex gloves. "The question is, if Matthew Whateley wasn't running away from this school last Friday afternoon, what was really going on?"

"Where to begin?" Havers asked.

Lynley looked towards the lodge across the field. "I think Frank Orten has had enough time to simmer."

Rather than use the lane, they returned to the lodge by edging along the one hundred yards of open field that separated the porter's vegetable garden, his garage, and his house from the vehicle shed and the rubbish fire beyond it. Choosing this direction, they ultimately followed a neat brick path between garden and garage that took them to the back door of the lodge. Elaine Roly admitted them into the kitchen.

Unlike the sitting room, it appeared to have benefitted from a recent cleaning, for work tops were spotless, fresh curtains hung at the window, and the only dishes in the sink were obviously from that morning's breakfast. The odour of bacon grease hung in the air, its source a frying pan that stood on the stove, a slice of bread sizzling within it.

Elaine Roly turned off the burner beneath the frying pan and forked the fried bread onto a plate which already held two poached eggs. She said, "He's in here, Inspector," and indicated that they should follow her into the dining room.

This was where the children had been squalling earlier, and they were continuing to do much the same now, one from a highchair upon which he banged a tin cup insistently and the other from the floor in a corner of the room where he beat his heels against the carpet and his fists against his forehead, all the time shrieking, "No! No! No!" Neither appeared to be more than four years old.

Frank Orten was bent over the highchair, inexpertly wiping the last bit of breakfast from his younger grandson's face with a damp cloth.

"Have these eggs, Frank," Elaine Roly said. "You've not touched your coffee. I'll see to the little ones. Time they had a bit of a wash." That said, she lifted the one from the floor and the other from his highchair. The older boy poked at the lace collar of her dress, but she stoically ignored his jabbing fingers and carried both yelping children from the room.

Orten pulled a chair back from the table, sat, and made short work of his eggs and bread. Lynley and Havers took chairs themselves, saying nothing until the porter pushed his plate to one side and gulped some coffee.

"What time did you notice that the rubbish fire had been rekindled?" Lynley asked.

"Twenty past three in the morning." Orten lifted his coffee mug. *Gramps* was painted on it in bright blue letters. "I had a look at the clock before I went to the window."

"You were awakened by something?"

"Not asleep, Inspector. Insomnia."

"So you heard no noise?"

"None. But I smelled the smoke and went to the window. Saw the glow. Thought that the fire had reignited somehow, so I went to have a look."

"You were dressed?"

His fractional hesitation seemed without purpose. "I got dressed," he said. Without being prompted, he continued. "I went out the back, through the field. Not by way of the lane. Got there and saw the flames had begun to grow fairly strong. Blasted idiots, I thought. Some sort of prank the senior boys were pulling, without thinking of the danger should the wind come up. So I took a shovel and used it to put the fire out."

"Are there outdoor lights you might have switched on?"

"Lights on the front of the vehicle shed, yes, but they were off and there are no lights to the side. It was dark. Told you that earlier, Inspector. I saw no clothing then. Main concern was to get the fire out."

"Did you see anyone, notice anything out of the ordinary aside from the fire itself?"

"Just the fire."

"Was it unusual that the lights on the vehicle shed were off? Are they normally kept on at night?"

"Normally, yes."

"What do you make of that?"

Orten looked in the direction of the kitchen, as if he could see through its walls for an answer that might be in the vehicle shed across the field. "I suppose if the lads were playing a prank, they'd want the lights off so they'd not be seen, wouldn't they?"

"And now that you know it wasn't a prank?"

Orten lifted a hand and dropped it back to the table. It was a gesture indicating acceptance of the obvious. "Same thing, Inspector. Someone not wishing to be seen."

"Not a prankster, but a killer," Lynley said thoughtfully. Orten made no reply, merely reaching for his cap that lay like a centre-piece upon the table. The letters *B.C.* decorated the front of it, yellow upon blue, but they were soiled here and there, needing to be cleaned and restored to their original colour. "You've been at the school for years, Mr. Orten," Lynley went on. "You probably know it better than anyone. Matthew Whateley disappeared on Friday after-noon. His body wasn't found until Sunday evening. We've good reason to believe it was dumped in Stoke Poges on either Friday or Saturday night. Since we have the boy's clothes, and since his body was nude when it was found, we can assume he was nude when he was taken from the school and that he was probably taken after dark. But the question is, where was he from the time he failed to show up at games after lunch on Friday until he was taken?"

Lynley waited to see how Orten would react to the implicit invitation to be part of the investigation. The porter looked from Lynley to Havers and pushed himself a few inches back from the table. The movement gained him not only physical distance but an intriguing degree of psychological distance as well.

He answered openly enough, however. "There's storage areas, I suppose. A wing of them beyond the kitchen, near the masters' common room. More in the technical centre. More in the theatre. Trunk rooms in the houses. Attics as well. But everything's locked."

"And the keys? Who has them?"

"Masters have some."

"Keys that they keep with them?"

Orten's eyes flickered momentarily. "Not always. Not if they have too many to carry about in their trousers."

"What do they do with them, then?"

"Hang them in their pigeonholes, usually. Right outside the masters' common room."

"I see. But surely those aren't the only keys to the buildings and the rooms. There must be duplicates should any get lost. Master keys, even."

Orten nodded, but it was as if his head was automatically doing what his mind intended him not to do at all. "I've a set of all the school keys in my office up in the quad. But that office is kept locked, if you're thinking that anyone could get in there and pinch them."

"Even now, for example? Is it locked now?"

"I imagine the Headmaster's secretary's unlocked it. She'd do so if she arrived before me."

"So she has a key to it."

"She does. But you're hardly suggesting the boy was nabbed by the Headmaster's secretary, are you? And if not her, who's going to go in in the middle of the schoolday when I'm not about and pinch some keys? With no way of knowing what door the keys will open? Not much good that would do, I say. Keys I have in my office aren't marked with anything more than a single word. *Theatre. Technical. Maths. Science. Kitchen.* No way to tell what room in any building the key would open. Not without looking through my code book. So if someone pinched keys, someone took them from the pigeonholes in the entry outside the masters' common room. And since *that's* kept locked, the only person who could have done the pinching was one of the masters."

"Or anyone else with access to the masters' common room," Lynley pointed out.

Orten countered in a manner that implied how improbable he believed his own words. "Headmaster. Skivvies. Wives. Who else?"

The porter. Lynley didn't say it, but he saw it wasn't necessary. Orten's cheeks had begun to redden even as he listed the possibilities.

Lynley and Havers paused by the Bentley, Havers to light a cigarette and Lynley to frown at her for doing so. She looked up, caught his expression, and held up a stubby-fingered hand in admonition.

"Don't even say it," she warned him. "You know you're longing to rip this right out of my mouth and smoke it down to the nub. At least I'm honest about my vices."

"You parade them," he replied. "You broadcast them to the world. Is *virtue* even part of your vocabulary, Sergeant?"

"I chucked it along with *self-control.*"

"I might have known." He gazed at the main drive that curved gently to the left beneath a giant beech tree, and from there to the secondary lane leading off towards the vehicle shed, the boys' houses, and the science building. He dwelt upon the information Frank Orten had given them.

"What's up?" Havers asked.

Lynley leaned against the car, thoughtfully rubbed his hand against his jaw, and tried to ignore the scent of tobacco smoke. "It's Friday afternoon. You've nabbed Matthew Whateley. Where will you keep him, Sergeant?"

She tapped cigarette ash onto the pavement, playing it about with the toe of her badly scuffed brogue. "I suppose it depends upon what I wanted to do with him. And how I wanted to do it."

"Carry on."

"If I wanted to have a bit of physical fun with him—the sort of thing that the school's resident paederast or a paedophile might well be chuffed by—I'd take him where there's not the slightest chance that he'd be heard if he didn't enjoy the activity as much as I did."

"Where would that be?"

She scanned the grounds as she answered. "Friday afternoon. All the boys are on the playing field. Games going on. It's after lunch so I'd stay away from the kitchen where the skivvies are doing their cleaning up. Boys might be coming and going in the houses. Girls as well, in Galatea and Eirene. So I'd go for one of the storage areas. In the theatre, perhaps. Or in science or maths."

"Not in one of the buildings in the main quad?"

"Too close to the administration wing, I'd say. Unless . . ."

"Go on."

"The chapel. The vestry. That rehearsal hall next door."

"All fairly risky for the type of encounter you have in mind."

"I suppose. But say it was a different kind of encounter. Say it was only a bit of a nab to scare the lad. On a bet. For a joke. Then I'd take him to a different place. It wouldn't have to be remote at all. It would just have to be frightening."

"Such as?"

"Climb up the bell tower and onto the roof. Perfect if he's afraid of heights."

"But hard to manage if he's struggling, wouldn't you say?"

"If he's duped into following someone he trusts—or someone he admires, or has no reason to fear—then he might go along. He might be told to do so. He might think he's been given an order that he has to obey, never knowing that the person who's giving it has something altogether different in mind when they reach their destination."

"It comes down to that, doesn't it?" Lynley said. "Destination. Chas Quilter showed you the school yesterday. Have you a good idea of its layout?"

"Fairly."

"Then do some prowling. See if you can ferret out a place where Matthew might have been kept for at least a few hours in perfect secrecy, no one the wiser."

"Think like a paedophile?"

"Whatever it takes, Sergeant. I'm going to search out John Corntel."

She dropped her cigarette to the ground and crushed it out. "Were those thoughts connected?" she asked him.

"I hope not," he replied and watched her set off down the main drive.

He walked back to the secondary lane which would take him to Erebus House and John Corntel's quarters. He had only got as far as the fork, however, when he heard his name called. Turning, he saw Elaine Roly hurrying towards him, rearranging the lace collar of her dress as she donned a black cardigan. Large spots of water darkened the dress itself.

"Trying to wash the little ones," she said in explanation, brushing at the spots as if this would dry them. "I'm not much good with boys that young, I'm afraid. When they get a bit older, I can manage them fine."

"As you've done in Erebus House," Lynley replied.

"Yes. Indeed. Are you heading there now? I'll walk with you, shall I?" She began to do so. Lynley said nothing to her at first, waiting for her to say something that would explain why she had called out to him. Certainly her purpose could have nothing to do with an impulsive desire for companionship in a walk up the lane. She pulled at the buttons of her cardigan, as if checking to make sure each was firmly sewn onto the wool. He heard her sigh. "Frank didn't tell you about his daughter, Inspector. You'll think he's hiding something. I can see you're clever enough to know when someone's not being completely straightforward with you."

"I did think there was more to his story."

"There is. But it has to do with pride, not with hiding. And there's his job. He does want to protect his job. That's understandable, isn't it? The Headmaster isn't the type to overlook an absence when one's supposed to be on duty. Even if it's an emergency with no time to let Mr. Lockwood know the details." She was speaking quickly.

"Saturday night?" Lynley asked.

"He wasn't *lying*. He simply wasn't telling you everything. But he's a good man. Frank's a fine man. He's not involved in Matthew's disappearance."

Through the trees that lined the lane, Lynley saw that the pupils were leaving the chapel, some coming out the front doors of the school, heading south in the direction of the theatre and technical centre. They were talking and laughing. As he watched them, it seemed to Lynley that the death of one of their number should have affected them more, should have sobered them, should have allowed them to see how brief a span of time was allotted them. It didn't, however. That was the way of the young. They were always convinced of their own immortality.

Elaine Roly said, "Frank's divorced, Inspector. I doubt he'd tell you that. It wasn't a pleasant situation, from what little he's told me. While he was stationed at Gibraltar, his wife took up with a brother officer. Frank was a bit of an innocent at the time. He never suspected a thing until she asked for a divorce. He was bitter about everything. He resigned his commission, left his two daughters with his wife in Gibraltar, and returned to England. He came right here to Bredgar Chambers."

"How long ago?"

"Seventeen years. Just as he said earlier. The girls are older now, of course. One lives in Spain. But the other—the younger girl, Sarah—lives in Tinsley Green, on the other side of Crawley. She's been troubled for years, married twice, divorced twice. She's dabbled a good bit in alcohol and drugs. Frank thinks he's responsible, since he deserted her and her sister. He puts himself on the rack over that.

"Sarah phoned Frank on Saturday night. He could hear the children crying. She was crying as well, talking about suicide. That's Sarah's way. She'd had a row with her current boyfriend, I should think." Elaine Roly reached out, touched Lynley's arm lightly for emphasis. "Frank went to his daughter on Saturday, Inspector. He was supposed to be on duty. He didn't think to tell the Headmaster where he was going. Perhaps he didn't want to, for he'd only been with her on Tuesday—his regular night off—and the Headmaster might have drawn the line at another evening away from the school, mightn't he? So when Frank got the call, he simply panicked and left. It was just as well."

"Why?"

"Because when he got to Tinsley Green, Sarah was unconscious. He got her to hospital just in time."

The information explained Orten's reticence this morning. But even if the veracity of Elaine Roly's story was sustained by a few quick telephone calls, Lynley saw that the matron of Erebus House had inadvertently added another twist to the events of the past weekend at Bredgar Chambers. For Tinsley Green was not more than two miles from the M23 and the great system of highways that led to Stoke Poges.

"Have the children been here with him since Saturday night?"

Innocently, she blackened him. "Not exactly. Directly after he sent for an ambulance, he phoned me from Sarah's cottage and asked if I would fetch the children from her neighbour. She's an elderly woman—very fond of Sarah—but she couldn't be expected to see to the boys overnight. So I went for them myself and kept them in my flat in Erebus until Sunday afternoon."

"You went to Tinsley Green yourself?"

"Yes. That's right."

"How did you get there?"

"In my car." She added hastily, "The Headmaster didn't . . . Mr. Corntel knew. I went to his rooms. I told him everything. He's a fine man, Mr. Corntel is, and he gave me leave to go straightaway as long as the house prefect and the senior boys knew so that they would be available should any of the younger boys need me. Not that giving Brian Byrne additional responsibility is ever a wise idea, as far as I'm concerned. But as this was an emergency . . ." She lifted her shoulders in a regretful shrug.

"It sounds as if it was no secret that you were going off campus. How did Mr. Orten hope to keep his trip to Tinsley Green from the Headmaster if you were being so above board about your own?"

"Frank didn't intend it to be a secret, Inspector. He was going to tell Mr. Lockwood eventually. He still intends to do so. Except that when Matthew Whateley disappeared, it hardly seemed the time or the place to bring up a few hours of absence. I expect you agree with that."

Lynley sidestepped her request for reassurance. "When he saw that the rubbish fire had been rekindled Saturday night—early Sunday morning, really—I imagine he'd only just then returned from Tinsley Green."

"Yes. But you see, he didn't want to tell you that. With everything else that's happened . . . Mr. Lockwood doesn't look upon shirking one's duty with a very pleasant eye. And he does seem to be on the cutting edge right now. So in a few days, when Frank feels the time is appropriate, he'll tell him."

"What time did you leave for Tinsley Green?"

"I'm not certain. After nine. Half-past. Perhaps a bit later."

"And you returned at what time?"

"I do know that. It was eleven-forty."

"You drove directly there? Directly back?"

Her fingers climbed from her chest to her throat, touched her lace collar delicately. There was a formality to her answer that indicated she understood the meaning and the suspicion behind Lynley's questions. "I did. Directly there. Directly back. I did stop for petrol, but that's reasonable, isn't it?"

"And Friday afternoon? Friday night?"

There was no mistaking the fact that Elaine Roly now read the questions as an affront. "What about them?" she asked coolly.

"Where were you then?"

"Sorting laundry in Erebus in the afternoon. Watching television at night, in my flat."

"Alone?"

"Quite alone, Inspector."

"I see." Lynley paused to study the building they were passing. *Calchus House* was carved above the door. "What odd names these houses have been given," he remarked. "Calchus, who persuaded Agamemnon to sacrifice his own daughter in exchange for fair wind. The herald of death."

It was a moment before Elaine Roly replied. When she did, her voice was once again friendly, as if she'd made a decision to overlook the effrontery of Lynley's previous questions. "Herald of death or not, Calchus died of mortification when Mopsus proved himself the better man."

"A lesson to be learned everywhere one looks at Bredgar Chambers?"

"It's part of the philosophy of the school. It's worked well."

"Nonetheless, I should think I'd be far happier in Erebus House than Calchus. Rather primeval darkness than the herald of death. You said you've been there eighteen years."

"Yes."

"How long has John Corntel been housemaster?"

"This is his first year. And a *good* job Mr. Corntel has done. A very good job. And he would have continued to do a good job had not . . ." She stopped. Lynley looked at her, saw how her face had settled.

"Had not Matthew Whateley happened on the scene?" he enquired.

She shook her head. "Not Matt. Mr. Corntel was doing a fine job with Matt, with all the boys, until he got distracted." She said the last word like an execration, and she needed no prompting to continue. "Miss Bond. She's had her eye on Mr. Corntel since the day she arrived on this campus last year. I noted that the minute I saw her. He's marriage material as far as she's concerned and she means to have him. Make no doubt of that. Little witch wants to turn him inside out. And has done so, if you want the truth from me."

"But you say that in spite of Emilia Bond, Mr. Corntel has managed to do a fine job. No troubles with Matthew?"

"None at all."

"Did you know Matthew yourself?"

"I know *all* my boys, sir. I'm matron. I do my job."

"Is there anything special you can tell me about Matthew, something you noticed that others might have overlooked?"

She thought about this only a moment before saying, "Just his colours, I suppose. All those tags that his mum used to help him with his colours."

"The numbers in his clothes? I noticed them. She must have worried about his appearance a great deal to take that kind of trouble. Most lads, I imagine, don't bother to notice what they're putting on from one moment to another. Did Matthew actually follow his mother's directions when he dressed?"

The matron looked at him in some surprise. "He had to, Inspector. He didn't know his colours."

"Didn't know—"

"Colour deficient, they call it. He couldn't see colours properly at all. Especially the school colours. He had the most trouble with them. His mum told me as much on parents' day during Michaelmas term. Worried that when his clothes were laundered the tags would fall off and Matt would be in a dither about what to put on in the morning. Evidently they'd used the number system for years at home, with no one the wiser."

"And anyone the wiser here?"

"Just myself, I should guess. Perhaps the boys in Matt's dormitory if they took note of his dressing in the morning."

And if they had . . . The boy's problem with colours could have been a source of painful teasing, the sort of ragging that cuts even as it wears the guise of camaraderie. It was just one more detail that made Matthew Whateley different from his peers. But surely, Lynley thought, not different enough to kill.

12

 "John, we must talk. You know that. We can't go on avoiding one another like this indefinitely. I can't bear it."

John Corntel didn't want to look up. He didn't want to respond to the tentative pressure of her hand upon his shoulder. He was sitting in the student memorial chapel and had been doing so since the end of the morning service, hoping its stillness might act as a surrogate for inner peace. It had not happened. Instead, he felt only a numbness that seemed to grow from within his body, having nothing to do with the frigid air of the chapel. He said nothing in response to Emilia Bond's words. Instead, he let his eyes drift from the marble angel atop the altar to the heartfelt memorials that lined the walls. *Beloved student,* he read. *Edward Hsu, beloved student.* What a marvel it was to read those words, to recognise in them the connection that could exist between two people when one wanted to teach and the other to learn. He could not help thinking that had he himself loved his students more, had he given them the devotion he had mindlessly directed elsewhere, he would not be in such turmoil now.

"I know you've no lesson until ten o'clock, John. We must talk."

Corntel realised that there was no way to avoid it. This final confrontation with Emilia had been brewing for days. He had only hoped to put it off a bit, to have more time to marshal the thoughts and the words that would serve to explain the inexplicable to her. In a week, he might have managed to gather the resources he needed to carry the conversation off without breaking. But he knew that he should have realised earlier that Emilia was not the type of woman to wait placidly for him to come to her.

"There's no place for us to talk right now," he told her. "We can't talk here."

"Then we'll walk. There's no one on the playing fields at this hour of the morning, and no one to overhear."

Her manner seemed determined, but when Corntel looked at her—standing in her oversized black gown next to the pew in which he was sitting—he saw that the natural colour of her face was gone, that her eyes were bloodshot, that the skin round them was swollen. Seeing this, he felt something beyond himself for the first time in days, a vague pinprick of empathy that momentarily pierced his armour of despair. But then that feeling faded, leaving the two of them much as they had been before, separated by an abyss that words alone could not bridge. She was so young—too young. Why had he failed to realise that before?

"Come with me, John," she said. "Please. Come with me."

He supposed that he owed her at least a brief conversation. Perhaps it was ridiculous to assume that a few more days of preparation—a few more days of avoiding her—would make this final time together any easier or more bearable for either of them.

"Very well," he said, and got to his feet.

They left the chapel and crossed the quad, passing beneath the statue of Henry Tudor, nodding to members of staff and to the occasional pupil, walking through the far west doors.

Corntel saw that Emilia had been right, as usual. Aside from a groundsman trimming the grass at the trunk of one of the chestnut trees at the playing field's edge, there was no one else about. He wanted to make the conversation easier for them both, but it had long been his curse to be incapable of starting a sensible conversation with any woman. So he struggled for a question, for a comment, for anything. He found nothing. Instead, she was the first to speak, but the words she said did nothing to ease the strain between them, even though they might well have done so had she spoken them to a different sort of man.

"I love you, John. I can't bear to see what you're doing to yourself." Her head was down, her eyes on the ground, watching her feet scuff messily through the grass. The top of her head did not even reach his shoulder, and looking at her pale, soft hair, Corntel was reminded of the delicate spun glass that his mother brought out at Christmastime to make into clouds round the angels that she always hung on a twisted piece of driftwood.

"Don't," he replied. "It's not worth it. I'm not worth it. You know that now, if you didn't before."

"I thought that was the case at first," she agreed. "I told myself that you had duped me for a year, that you'd been pretending to be a different man altogether from . . . Friday night. But I've not been able to convince myself of that, John, try as I might. I do love you."

"No."

"I know what you've been thinking. You think I believe you killed Matthew Whateley. After all, it fits, doesn't it? What could fit better? But I don't believe you killed him, John. I don't believe you even touched him. In fact"—she looked at him and then smiled gently—"I'm not altogether sure you were aware of Matthew at all. You've always been a bit absent-minded, you know."

She was attempting to alleviate the heaviness and tension. But her words rang false.

"It makes no difference," Corntel said. "Matthew was my responsibility. I may as well have killed him. Once the police find out the worst about me, I'll be rather hard pressed to convince them of my innocence."

"They won't find out from me. I swear it."

"Don't. You may find that promise impossible to keep. Thomas Lynley's no fool. He'll be talking to you soon enough, Em."

They had come to the centre of the playing fields. Emilia stopped walking and faced him squarely. A light wind played in her hair.

"Don't you think he's clever enough to realise that if you went into London to ask for his help, you'd hardly be the one responsible for Matthew's disappearance in the first place? No matter what else he discovers about you, he's not likely to forget that, is he?"

"On the contrary, what better device could there possibly be? To wear the guise of innocence, the killer asks the help of the police. I've no doubt at all that Thomas has run into that sort of behaviour before. Be assured he's not removed me from his list of suspects simply because we share an old school tie. Matthew Whateley was tortured, Emilia. *Tortured.*"

She reached for his arm. "Do you think he'll believe that *you* took the boy off campus? That you tortured him, murdered him, dumped his body in a churchyard, and returned to the school, without a hair out of place, and with so little conscience in the matter that you were able to go to the police yourself and request their help?"

He looked down at her hand, so small and white against the black of his gown. "You know it's possible, don't you?"

"No! You were curious, John. Nothing more than that. It's no sign of anything. The only reason you think it *is* a sign is that I panicked. I was silly. I acted like a little fool. I didn't know what to do."

"You didn't know *me*. Not completely. Not until Friday night. Well, now you know the worst, don't you? What do we want to call it, this thing that you know, Emilia? An illness? A perversion? What?"

"I don't know. I don't care. It has nothing to do with Matthew Whateley. More, it has nothing—*nothing*—to do with us."

Corntel heard the conviction with which she spoke and admired her for it even as he knew that there was in reality no *us* any longer. He doubted that there had been one in the first place. He admired, as he always had, her forthright honesty. He admired her willingness to risk herself for him, to throw away pride and even common sense for the sake of what she believed was love. But he knew that had love once been possible between them—and she *had* stirred and reached him as no other woman ever had—it had died on Friday. She might lie about it now, when she was feeling lost and needed to regain at least something of the friendship that had been theirs before, but her face on Friday had mirrored the truth. Love does not always die slowly between a man and a woman. Sometimes it's extinguished in an instant. He meant to tell her all this, but did not have the chance.

"John," she said, "Inspector Lynley's coming this way."

The drama students were working on make-up design. They had begun the project the previous week in one of the classrooms on the west side of the theatre, and now they were spread throughout the complex's four dressing rooms, creating artistic reality from a conception put upon paper, preparing themselves for the theatre master's critical evaluation.

Chas Quilter was among them, feeling, as he usually did, a bit at odds with the level of enthusiasm and pleasure with which the other students generally addressed themselves to any assignment. Today his discomfiture was worse than usual, since browsing through make-up boxes, experimenting with wigs and beards, testing out the effect of a particular shade of eye shadow or pancake had stimulated the group to new heights of excitement, an excitement he simply could not share. Yet he understood both their devotion to the task and their joy in completing it, even if he could not feel it himself. They were, after all, taking theatre studies as part of their A-level course work, determined to make their way from universities onto the London stage. He was doing drama only as an optional extra, having signed up for the course as a means of staying busy during his final year at Bredgar Chambers. For him, the class was a means of forgetting. It had worked for the most part. But it was not working at all today.

Clive Pritchard was the reason. He and Chas had been assigned a dressing room together—an outcome of the alphabetical curse of their surnames—and there was no third party present to alleviate the storm-trooper effect of Clive's repellent personality.

His make-up design acted as the most cogent illustration of his nature. While the other pupils, explicitly following the theatre master's instructions, had selected characters from Elizabethan tragedies round whom they would paint their faces, Clive had entered a world of his own invention, turning himself into a cross between Quasimodo and the Phantom of the Opera, the former apparently giving him the opportunity to fit a hideously long, dangling earring through the hole which he had driven through his earlobe by means of an upholstery needle in October.

Chas remembered the circumstances in the upper sixth social club, with Clive drinking whisky from a flask which he had smuggled out of his grandmother's home during the first half-term. As he drank, he grew louder, more cocksure, more belligerent. His entire demeanour demanded attention and, failing to get it through mere braggadocio concerning a tattoo which he had carved into his inner arm with penknife and india ink during the recent holiday, he captured his audience by means of a more realistic display of his propensity towards self-mutilation. Obviously he had come prepared to do so, since an upholstery needle was not generally among the items found in a schoolboy's kit. But Clive had produced and used it upon himself without flinching. Chas recalled the sight of the slick, curved needle boring into Clive's earlobe and emerging on the other side. He had not known an ear could bleed so profusely. One of the girls had fainted. Two others had been sick. Clive smiled and smiled like a madman through it all.

"So. You like?" Clive spun from the mirror and displayed his handiwork, a sparse-haired wig, newly rotting teeth, the flesh beneath his right eye bulging and putrescent, small corks flaring his nostrils to skeletal dimensions. "This goes one better than your pansy Hamlet, Quilter. Admit it."

Chas didn't have to admit the obvious. He'd chosen Hamlet because of the ease of designing the make-up. It required the simplest transformation, his colouring being acceptable for the Danish prince in the first place. There was neither art nor talent involved in what he'd done to his face, but he didn't care. His heart wasn't in the exercise anyway. His heart had been in nothing for months.

Clive danced like a boxer from foot to foot. "Come on, Quilter. Admit it. This mug's enough to make those birds in Galatea House pass out at the sight. Then when they do . . ." He laughed and thrust his pelvis forward suggestively. "It's sort of like necrophilia to do it to a bird when she's knocked out cold. Nothing like it, Quilter. But you know that already, don't you?"

The words danced their way past Chas' consciousness. He thought only how glad he was that Clive did not feel enough familiarity to use his Christian name. It was a positive sign, something which told him that in spite of everything, he wasn't yet entirely lost.

"Hey, I could do some creeping with this, couldn't I, Quilter?" Clive was asking. He demonstrated by slinking round the room, ducking beneath the make-up tables, peering stealthily into mirrors, whipping a rack of costumes in front of him and dashing them away from his shifting eyes. "I go across campus. It's dark, see?" He chose a cloak from the rack, draped it round his shoulders, and acted out the scene as he described it. "I could choose Galatea House for a glimpse of old Cow Pitt and his wife, but that's not what I have in mind tonight. No, not tonight." He grinned. His eyeteeth were long, extremely lupine. "Tonight I choose to look in on the Headmaster. I explore the truth. Does Lockwood really hump with his clothes on? Does he hump his wife or does he prefer one of the more delectable little third formers? Or does he select a different girl from Galatea or Eirene every night of the week? And do they say to him as he pumps like a dog, 'Oooh, *oooh*, Headmaster, I just love it when you stuff me. You're such a man!' Only *I* will know for sure what's going on, Quilter. And if they look up from their panting and howling and see my face in the window—if they see *this* mug—they'll never know who's looking in on them, will they? They'll only shriek like the devil and know they've been caught at last!" He whirled the cape to one side and stood, legs spread, hands upon hips, head thrown back.

The opening of the dressing room door saved Chas from having to make a reply. Brian Byrne entered. Clive lunged at him with a howl, then fell back laughing when Brian started.

"Holy Jesus! You should see your face!" Clive took up the cape again and struck a pose. "What say to this, Bri?"

Brian shook his head slowly, an admiring smile growing wider on his face. "Amazing," he responded.

"Why aren't you in lessons, laddie my lad?" Clive moved to the mirror and tried out a number of scowls.

"I'm in the San," Brian answered. "Terrible headache. You know."

"Ah, fondling our Mrs. Laughland, son?"

"No more than you, I dare say."

"No more than anyone." Clive winked lasciviously and gave his attention to Chas. "Save perhaps young Quilter here. Gone in for celibacy, haven't you, mate? Setting a good example for all the lads and lasses, like the senior prefect ought." He pulled at the skin beneath his eyes, stretching it viciously but giving no sign of pain. "A bit late for that, wouldn't you say? We're living in a veritable den of iniquity."

Chas dropped his eyes to the make-up box on the table beneath the mirror. The colours there swam before his vision: a palette of eye shadows, an open case of blushers, two tubes of greasepaint. All of them lost definition momentarily.

Clive was continuing to speak. "Christ, Christ! What a piece I had Saturday night, Bri. You should have been with me and had a go yourself. Some little Sharon on her way through Cissbury. Met her outside the pub and got into her pants and showed her what's what. 'Ooooh, baby,' she was shrieking. 'Oooh, yes, yes, yes!' That's the way I like 'em. On the ground, in the dirt, and screaming for more." He did a little dance step. "What I wouldn't give for a fag right now!"

Brian grinned, reached into his blazer pocket, pulled out a packet of cigarettes. "Here." He tossed them. "You can have the rest."

"Great stuff, Bri! Thanks!"

Chas found his voice. "Don't smoke them in here, will you?"

"Why not?" Clive asked. "Will you put me on report? Get me warned off by Lockwood?"

"Just use some sense. If you have any."

Clive stiffened. He opened his mouth to speak, but Brian interceded.

"He's right, Clive. Save them for later. Okay?"

Clive's eyes went moodily from Chas to Brian. "Yeah. Right. I'm off, then. Thanks, Bri. For the fags. You know." He left the room. In a moment, Brian and Chas heard him calling out to several other theatre pupils who had gathered on the stage. The girls shrieked appropriately at his appearance. The make-up, evidently, was a smashing success.

Chas brought a fist to his lips. He closed his eyes. He felt nausea overcome him in a surge, like a wave. "How can you stand him?" he asked.

Brian pulled a stool over and sat down. He shrugged, smiling affably. "He's not all bad. Just a lot of show. You've got to understand him."

"I don't want to understand him."

Brian reached out, brushed at the shoulder of Chas' shirt. "Powder," he explained. "You've managed to get it everywhere. Down your trousers as well. Here. Let me see to it."

Chas stood abruptly. He moved away.

"Holiday's not far off," Brian said. "Have you decided if you'll come with me to London? Mum's off to Italy with one of her men, so we'll have the place to ourselves."

There had to be an acceptable excuse, Chas thought. There had to be a reason. He couldn't find one. Any that he gave would speak of rejection, and that would engender anger. He couldn't risk that. He sorted through a tangle of thoughts that were becoming progressively more difficult to control.

"Brian," he finally managed to say, "we have to talk. Not here. Not now. But we have to talk. I mean really talk. You need to understand some stuff."

Brian's eyes rounded. "Talk? All right. Of course. Wherever. Whenever."

Chas rubbed his damp hands against the sides of his trousers. "We have to *talk*," he repeated.

Brian rose and grasped Chas' shoulder. "We'll talk," he replied. "What else are friends for?"

Emilia Bond offered to find someone to stand in for John Corntel during his fifth form English lesson at ten o'clock, so Lynley and the English master returned to the private quarters of Erebus House. They entered not through the main door that the boys would use but through the smaller, secondary door at the west end of the building. A brass plate hung upon it, engraved with the single word *Housemaster*.

The quarters were a surprise to Lynley. Stepping into them was like being swept back to that postwar period when furnishings were meant to be declared "sensible." Heavy sofas and chairs with antimacassars upon their arms; maple tables of graceless line; lamps whose shades had no distinction; framed flower prints upon the walls. That every piece was of quality workmanship, there was no doubt. But the overall effect was one of age, as if the rooms had been decorated by an elderly woman concerned about maintaining a proper image.

Corntel's study repeated this theme, with a squat desk, an overlarge three-piece suite covered in floral cretonne, and a drop-leaf table upon which stood a pottery jug and a full ashtray that filled the room with the smell of charred tobacco. That last item seemed one of the two contributions Corntel himself had made to the decorating of his home. The other was his collection of books, and they took up a great deal of space. They were arranged upon shelves; they were stacked in piles under the desk; they were crammed into narrow crannies on either side of an undecorated fireplace.

Corntel pulled back the curtains which had been partially drawn to cover the windows. Lynley noticed that the study looked out upon Calchus House, and that a pathway between the two buildings passed not twenty feet from the window. There would be little privacy in this room, save with the curtains drawn.

"Coffee?" Corntel offered and motioned towards a cupboard recessed into the wall. "I've an espresso machine if you'd like to try some."

"Thank you."

Watching the other man go about the business of making the coffee, Lynley recalled Elaine Roly's words. *Little witch wants to turn him inside out. And has done so, if you want the truth from me.* He applied Roly's allegations to John Corntel's present state, questioning whether a relationship existed between the matron's words and the housemaster's condition.

Never had he seen a man wear such a thin veneer of protection. Emotions roiled just beneath the surface. They evidenced themselves in his eyes which refused to hold contact with Lynley's own, in his hands which snatched at objects clumsily as if receiving inaccurate data from his brain, in his shoulders which hunched shell-like round him, in his speech which failed at modulation. It was hard to believe that Corntel could be reduced to such ill-hidden anxiety merely out of love for a woman, unrequited or otherwise. And something in the manner in which Emilia Bond had looked at the man when Lynley had come upon them in the playing fields suggested that if love led the vanguard that assaulted the walls of Corntel's peace, it was not unrequited at all. That being the case, the problem became one of identifying the crucial element that lay at the heart of John Corntel's affliction. Lynley thought he recognised it well enough. One usually does recognise the symptoms of disease in a fellow sufferer.

"What was the name of that boy at Eton who was so good at escaping the duty master?" Lynley asked. "You know the one. No matter who it was on night or weekend duty, he always knew exactly what the routine would be—when rounds would be made, when doors would be checked, when a surprise visit was due to a house. Do you remember him?"

Corntel was sliding the small metal coffee holder into the espresso machine. He locked it into place. "Rowton. He claimed to have ESP."

Lynley chuckled. "He must have. He was never wrong, was he?"

"All that talent wasted just to slip into Windsor to see some bit of fluff. Did you know that? He got her pregnant eventually."

"I can only remember him being harassed by the other boys about examinations. If he had ESP, damn it all, why couldn't he use it to see what old Jervy had put into the history trial for next Tuesday?"

Corntel smiled. "How did Rowton always put it? 'It don't work like that, mates. I only see what these blokes do, or what they're going to do, not what they think.' Someone would argue that if he could see what they were going to do, he could damn well see the examination, since writing an examination is *doing* something, after all."

"And Rowton's response was an intimate description of Jervy writing out his examination, as I recall. Complete with details of Mrs. Jervy coming in to interrupt him, wearing a Mary Quant miniskirt and white vinyl boots."

"And nothing else." Corntel laughed. "Mrs. Jervy always dressed five or six years behind the times, didn't she? Lord, how Rowton could lead one a merry chase with his stories. I haven't thought of him in years. What made you do so?"

"The idea of a duty master. I was wondering who was duty master here this past weekend, John. I was wondering if it was you."

Corntel made an adjustment to the espresso machine. Steam hissed out. Coffee began to flow into a glass carafe. He didn't reply to Lynley's remarks until he had poured two demitasses, arranged them with milk and sugar on a tin tray, and placed this on the drop-leaf table. He pushed the ashtray to one side but did not empty it.

"You're clever, Tommy. I didn't even see that coming. Have you always had such an affinity for policework?"

Lynley picked up a cup of coffee and carried it to one of the armchairs. Corntel followed. He moved a guitar to one side—Lynley noticed that two of its strings were broken—and sat on the sofa. He'd left his own coffee on the table.

"Matthew Whateley was a boy from this house," Lynley answered. "You were responsible for his welfare. He somehow got lost in the cracks last weekend. All that's true, isn't it? But something tells me that what you're feeling over this goes beyond the responsibility inherent to your position as housemaster. So I wondered if you were also supposed to be duty master this weekend, responsible for the security of the entire school."

Corntel's hands dangled limply between his legs. He seemed without defence. "Yes. You know the worst now. Yes."

"I take it that you didn't patrol the grounds at all."

"Will you believe me when I say I forgot?" He looked at Lynley directly. "I'd forgotten. It wasn't actually my duty weekend. I'd traded with Cowfrey Pitt some weeks back and I simply forgot."

"Cowfrey Pitt?"

"The German master. Housemaster of Galatea, one of the girls' houses."

"Why did he want to trade? Or was it your idea?"

"His. I don't know why. I didn't ask. It didn't matter to me anyway. I'm always here unless it's a holiday, and even then sometimes . . . You don't want to hear this. You know it all now. I forgot to patrol. It didn't seem so bad at the time. Most of the children were gone. They had exeats. There was the hockey trip. But if I had only been doing my duty, I might have caught Matthew Whateley trying to slip off. I know that. Still, I didn't patrol. There it is."

"How often are you supposed to patrol the school on a weekend?"

"Three times Friday night. Six times on Saturday. The same on Sunday."

"On a regular schedule?"

"No, of course not. There'd hardly be a reason to patrol, would there, if the pupils knew exactly when I'd be coming by?"

"Do all the students know who the duty master is?"

"All the prefects know. They're given a list each month. They report to the duty master if something's not right, so naturally they have to know who the duty master is."

"Would they have been told that you and Cowfrey Pitt had exchanged duty?"

"The Headmaster would have told them. The exchange was cleared through his office. These things always are." Corntel leaned forward, cradling his forehead in one hand. "Lockwood doesn't know I failed to patrol, Tommy. He's looking for a scapegoat. He has to find one, you know, lest he be named it himself."

Lynley avoided the issue of Alan Lockwood. "I have no choice but to ask the next question, John. You failed to patrol the school on Friday night. You failed again to do so on Saturday. What were you doing? Where were you?"

"Here. I swear it."

"Can someone corroborate that?"

The espresso machine hissed out a spout of steam. Corntel went to unplug it. He remained in that corner of the room, head bent, hands curved round the glass carafe.

"Emilia Bond?" Lynley asked.

A sound escaped Corntel's lips, distant cousin to a cry. "I'm pathetic. What you must think of me. I'm thirty-five years old. She's twenty-five. There's no sense in this. There's even less hope. I'm not what she thinks. I'm not what she wants. She doesn't understand. She *won't* understand."

"You were with her Friday night? Saturday as well?"

"That's the devil of it. Part of Friday. Part of Saturday. But not the entire night. So she can't help you. Don't ask her. Don't involve her in this. It's bad enough between us as it is."

Corntel spoke insistently. His tone was a plea. Hearing this, Lynley reflected upon the penalty a housemaster would pay if Alan Lockwood knew that a woman had spent part of the night in his rooms. Beyond that, he reflected upon Corntel's desire to leave Emilia uninvolved in the situation. This wasn't the nineteenth century, after all, with Emilia Bond a woman whose virtue needed protecting at the cost of a man's professional future. Neither was likely to face permanent perdition for spending a few discreet hours in the other's company. There was something else here, something beyond the woman's presence in Corntel's rooms. Lynley could sense that probability unmistakably, like a clear and present danger. He sought a way to bring it into the open. As far as he could see, the only hope of Corntel's speaking to him with any real honesty lay in the fact that the two men were alone. No notes were being taken. The interview wore at least the appearance of a conversation between old friends.

"I take it you've had some sort of row," Lynley said. "Miss Roly isn't very happy with the impact Emilia's had on your life."

Corntel raised his head. "Elaine's worried. She's been queen of Erebus for years. The last housemaster was unmarried as well, and she can't bear the thought that a housemaster's wife might come along and usurp some of her authority. I ought to tell her she has nothing to worry about. There's no possibility of a marriage here." His shoulders heaved. In a moment he turned round and faced Lynley again. His eyes were red-rimmed. "None of what happened to Matthew Whateley had anything to do with Emilia. She didn't know the boy."

"But you do admit that she was here, in this house?"

"With me. That's the extent of it."

"Yet she does know other boys from Erebus. Brian Byrne, for example, is one of her upper sixth chemistry students. I saw him in her laboratory yesterday afternoon. And he's your house prefect."

"What has that to do with anything?"

"I'm not certain, John. Perhaps nothing. Perhaps everything. You told me that Brian was here in the house Friday evening. Brian himself told me that he was in the upper sixth social club most of the night."

"I thought he was here. I didn't check."

"Not even later? Not after Emilia left?"

"I was upset. I wasn't thinking. I didn't check on anything once she left."

"Do you know whether she actually left the building at all? Did you see her leave?"

Corntel's face, already ashen, seemed to lose even more colour as he took in the meaning behind the question. "Good God, you can't be suggesting that *Emilia* . . ."

"Only yesterday she tried to protect your house prefect from being questioned, John. What am I to think of that?"

"It's her *way*. She doesn't believe anyone's capable of evil. She can't even see it. She doesn't even think—" Again he stopped himself short of admission.

"She doesn't think . . . ?" Lynley prompted.

Corntel came slowly back to the couch and stared down at it as if trying to decide whether to remain standing or to sit. He reached out and touched a worn spot on its arm.

"How could you possibly understand?" he asked dully. "Viscount Vacennes. Earl of Asherton. When has anything you ever tried met with less than success?"

The unfairness of the words—their utter inaccuracy—struck Lynley to the quick. The fact that he had not been expecting to hear them struck him to silence. For the first time since the interview had begun, he wished for Sergeant Havers' presence, for her ability and willingness to cut past emotions and ruthlessly carve right into the heart.

"It's the truth, isn't it?" Corntel was asking bitterly.

Lynley found his voice. "Far from it, I'm afraid. But I can't expect you to know that, John. Not at a distance of seventeen years."

"I don't believe that."

"Your disbelief doesn't alter the truth."

Corntel's eyes moved away from him. Then they returned. His body shook with a convulsive tremor.

"We started out last year merely as friends," he said. "I've never been much good round women, but it was different with Emilia. She was easy to talk to. She listened. Always she had her eyes right on my face. Other women had never been like that, in my experience. They always seemed to be after something. Talking to me, yes, but with their minds on something else so that soon into the conversation I wasn't able to think of a reasonable thing to say to hold their attention. But Emilia"—his expression grew soft, reflective—"if Emilia was after anything at all, I imagine she was after my soul. I think she wanted nothing more than to know me through and through. We even wrote to each other on holidays. It's easier, I find, to say things in writing, easier to be more of what one really is. That's how it is in my case, anyway. So I wrote to her and I talked to her. About my father, about the novel I long to write and probably never will, about music I love, about things that seem important in my life. But not about everything. Just the things that made me look good. Even now I think that had I told her everything—all those nasty little secrets about ourselves that we hide—she might not have wanted me."

"Nasty little secrets usually count for nothing set aside love," Lynley noted.

"No. That's not true." Corntel spoke with resignation, a statement oddly without self-pity, considering how he continued. "Not really, Tommy. Oh, perhaps in your case. You've far more to offer a woman than I. But in my case, when the mind and the spirit and the body are revealed in all their inadequacy, there's not much there."

Lynley remembered the boy who strode across the schoolyard at Eton, head and shoulders above the rest, a King's Scholar assured of a brilliant future. "I find that hard to believe," he said.

Corntel seemed to read his mind. "Do you? Was my performance that fine? Shall I lay some phantoms to rest for you now?"

"If it helps. If you wish."

"Nothing helps. I don't wish. But Emilia's nothing to do with Matthew Whateley's death, and if laying phantoms to rest is the way to convince you, then so be it." He looked away bleakly. "She was here Friday night. I should have seen at once why she had come and what she wanted, but I didn't. Not soon enough to stop things from getting out of hand and ending miserably and upsetting us both."

"I take it she came to make love with you."

"I'm thirty-five years old. *Thirty-five years old.* Can you of all people know what that means?"

Lynley saw the only possible connection and put it into words. "You'd never made love to a woman before?"

"*Thirty-five.* How pathetic. How puerile. How obscene."

"None of those things. Just a fact."

"It was disastrous. Try to imagine the details so I needn't fill them in. Do that much for me, will you? Afterwards, I was humiliated. She was upset, weeping but trying to excuse everything as her fault. Believe me, Tommy, she was in no frame of mind to do anything but return to her own rooms. I didn't see her leave Erebus, but I can't think why she would have done anything else."

"Where are her rooms?"

"She's tutor at Galatea House."

"So Cowfrey Pitt might be able to corroborate her comings and goings?"

"If you don't believe me, yes, ask Cowfrey. But her rooms aren't near the private quarters, so he may have no idea where she was."

"What about Saturday night? She was here again?"

Corntel nodded. "Trying to make things right. Trying to . . . How does one go back to being friends after a scene like that, Tommy? How does one recapture that which twenty minutes of steamy, futile grappling on a bed have utterly destroyed? That's why she was here. That's why I forgot to do my rounds as duty master this past weekend. That's why I didn't know that Matthew Whateley had run off. Because I couldn't act the man the first time in my life that I had the opportunity."

Matthew Whateley had run off. It was the second time Corntel had said it, and there were only two possibilities for the misinformation. Either he knew nothing about the clothing Frank Orten had found upon the rubbish pile, or he was playing it safe and sticking to the established story until offered a new one by the police.

13

It was just eleven when Lynley met with Sergeant Havers in what Bredgar Chambers labelled the Big Schoolroom on the south side of the main quadrangle. This was the original teaching facility on the campus, a white-walled chamber with oak wainscotting and an elaborate vaulted ceiling. Windows were set high into the south wall of the room, and beneath them hung the portraits of every headmaster the school had known since Charles Lovell-Howard had first been given the reins of authority in 1489.

The room was empty at the moment, with a vague pulpy odour of wet wood permeating the air. When they closed the door behind them, Sergeant Havers crossed to the windows and sauntered along the line of portraits, following the school's history until she came to Alan Lockwood.

"Only twenty-one headmasters in five hundred years," she marvelled. "When one comes to Bredgar Chambers, it looks like one comes to stay. Here. Look at this, sir. The bloke just before Lockwood was head for forty-two years!"

Lynley joined her. "That goes some distance to explain Lockwood's need to keep Matthew Whateley's murder under wraps, doesn't it? I wonder if any other boys were murdered while under the tenure of earlier headmasters."

"It's a thought, isn't it? But all of the heads had boys die, didn't they? Girls as well. The memorial chapel is ample proof of that."

"Quite. But a sudden, unexpected death due to war or illness is one thing, Havers. One can hardly cast blame upon anyone for that.

A murder, however, is something else. One looks to cast blame. One must."

Voices rose and fell outside the room as they spoke. Dozens of footsteps pounded down a stairway. Lynley opened his pocket watch.

"Morning break, I should imagine. What have you found in your ramble through the school?" He looked up to see Sergeant Havers staring at the window, frowning. "Havers?"

She stirred. "Just thinking."

"And?"

"It's nothing. Just what you said about blame. I wondered who takes the blame when a student commits suicide."

"Edward Hsu?"

"Beloved student."

"I've gone back to him myself. Giles Byrne's interest in him. His death. Gile Byrne's interest in Matthew Whateley. *His* death. But if Matthew Whateley were indeed killed at this school last Friday or even last Saturday, how can we assign blame to Giles Byrne? Unless, of course, he was here. Rather doubtful, but worth looking into."

"Perhaps not him, sir."

"Who? Brian Byrne? If you attempt that, you lose the connection you're trying to establish in the first place, Sergeant. Edward Hsu killed himself in 1975. Brian Byrne was perhaps five years old at the time. Are you casting blame for a suicide on a five-year-old boy?"

She sighed. "I don't know. But I keep going back to what Brian said about his father."

"Temper that with the knowledge that he dislikes his father. Didn't you get the impression that Brian would be only too happy to deride Giles Byrne, given the opportunity to do so? And we gave him that yesterday, didn't we?"

"I suppose." Havers wandered the length of the room to the dais at the east end, over which was carved in bas-relief an elaborate depiction of Henry VII on a destrier caparisoned, ready to charge. Beneath this stood a refectory table and chairs, and she pulled out one of these and plopped down into it, splaying her legs out in front of her.

Lynley joined her. "We're looking for a place where Matthew Whateley might have been confined from Friday afternoon to Friday night—perhaps even Saturday night—when he, or his body, was removed. What have you come up with?"

"Little enough. Storage and supply rooms by the kitchen which we have to discount, since he disappeared after lunch and too many people would have been working in that area. There are two old lavatories there that don't look as if anyone uses them regularly. Filthy inside, toilets broken as well."

"Any sign of recent occupation?"

"None that I could see. If he was in there, whoever had him was careful to make sure no trace was left behind."

"Anything else?"

"Trunk rooms in all the houses, but they're kept locked and only the housemasters and the matrons have the keys to get into them. Attics above the drying rooms in the houses as well, but each of them is padlocked. And again, only housemasters and matrons have the keys. Storerooms in the science building and an enormous tank of water above the aquariums where one could certainly have drowned Matthew Whateley, but not held him captive for long. Unless he was bound and gagged and his killer knew that no one would be about for the rest of the afternoon. Beyond that, the theatre has dressing rooms and storage rooms behind the stage, and a lighting booth above it. If no performance was scheduled and if someone had access, I should imagine the theatre's our best bet, Inspector. Pupils were in there this morning—I saw our Chas Quilter, by the way, looking as if Yorick had just come back from the dead and he wasn't too pleased at the prospect—but if it was empty after lunch on Friday, it's as good a place as any to have held Matthew Whateley. Especially considering its distance from the playing fields where the students were gathered."

"But how would one gain access, Sergeant? It seems to me that the theatre—with all its props, equipment, costumes, and so forth— would be one of the most securely guarded buildings at the school."

"Oh, it would be locked, all right. But that's no problem at all. I looked into that before I began. Frank Orten told us that keys are kept in two locations—in his office and in the pigeonholes outside the masters' common room. His office is unlocked during the day, so if Orten wasn't about for the moment, anyone could slip in unnoticed and grab the keys marked *theatre* and hope for the best. And if daylight is too risky for a manoeuvre like that, at night a credit card or some other suitable piece of plastic is all that one would need to break into the office in less than fifteen seconds. Their security's pathetic. I can't believe they haven't been robbed blind."

"What about the pigeonholes outside the masters' common room?"

"Worse," she replied. "Frank Orten told us the common room is kept locked, didn't he? With only the masters and the skivvies having keys? Well, it wasn't locked this morning. I walked right in. And the pigeonholes are not only conveniently labelled with each master's name, but I'd say a good fifty percent of them had keys hanging right in them. All one would need to know is what master used what keys. Then, just pop round the common room and bob's-your-uncle."

"We're wide open once again. Everyone had access. Everyone had means."

"Who had opportunity?"

"To grab Matthew after lunch and stow him somewhere until he could be dealt with? Who *didn't* have opportunity?" Lynley thought about the question himself. Something John Corntel had said pricked at his memory. "Let's find Cowfrey Pitt," he said.

Although the morning break had not yet ended, the German master was not with the other teachers in the common room. Instead, Lynley and Havers found him in his classroom on the first floor of the west side of the quad. He was writing in a barely legible scrawl across the blackboard, sloppily slashing umlauts here and there like a private form of Morse code. When Lynley said his name, he continued writing and did not turn from the board until he had completed the job to his satisfaction. He illustrated this point by stepping back from his work, surveying it critically, erasing a few words, and rewriting them with little improvement. Then he gave his attention to his visitors.

"You're the police," he said. "Don't bother to introduce yourselves. Your reputations have preceded you. I've a lesson in ten minutes."

He delivered this information indifferently, brushing flecks of chalk from the sleeve of his gown. The gesture spoke of a less than believable concern for his appearance, for the gown he wore was more grey than black, crusted along the shoulders with both dandruff and dust.

Sergeant Havers shut the door and stationed herself next to it. She gave Pitt the benefit of a look that managed to be expressionless at the same time as it was completely judgemental. It told the German master that his lesson might be scheduled in ten minutes, but it would begin when the police deemed it appropriate, and not before.

"This shouldn't take long," Lynley said to Pitt. "Just a few points to clarify, and we'll be on our way."

"I've an upper sixth group coming in here, you know." Pitt offered this bit of news as if it would determine the length of the questioning he was about to endure. At the door, Sergeant Havers leaned against the wall, suggesting a sort of permanency. As if reading this, Pitt said, "So. Clarify, Inspector. Clarify. Please do. Don't let me stop you."

Lynley walked to the window. The room looked out over the quad, and directly opposite it the bell tower rose, giving access to the roof, its very height a temptation that, no doubt, no Bredgardian schoolboy eager to prove his mettle had ever been able to resist.

"What can you tell me about the off-games chit that got Matthew Whateley released from the soccer game Friday afternoon?"

Pitt remained behind his desk. He pressed his knuckles to its surface. They were cracked and looked sore. "Little enough. It was the regulation form from the San. With his name on it. Nothing else."

"No signature?"

"Judith Laughland's, you mean? No. No signature."

"Is that regular procedure, to receive an off-games chit with a boy's name but no signature from the San sister to verify its authenticity?"

Pitt moved from foot to foot. One hand went to his fringe of oily hair. He pulled at a single stiffened lock that curled behind and beneath his left ear. "No. She usually signs them."

"Usually. But this one wasn't signed."

"I've said that, Inspector."

"You did nothing to check on it, though?"

"That's right. I didn't check."

"Why not, Mr. Pitt?"

"I didn't have the time. I was running late and had to get out to the game myself. I hardly thought about it. Matthew Whateley had bunked off games before. Some three weeks ago, in fact. If I thought anything at all when I saw the new chit, it was that he was up to that trick again and I'd see to him later. But I forgot to do so. If there's a crime in that, arrest me."

"What happened three weeks ago?"

"He'd an off-games chit—this one signed by Laughland—that he brought to me himself. If you ask me, he was faking that one, trying to look sick and working on a cough to make it authentic. But if Laughland bought into it, who am I to complain? So off he went."

"Where?"

"To bed, I presume. To his room. Or to the day room. I've no idea. I didn't follow him."

"I'd think seeing a second off-games chit on Friday, so soon after the other, would have made you immediately suspicious, Mr. Pitt. Especially if this one wasn't signed and the earlier one was."

"Well, it didn't. There it is. I just gave it a quick look and put it in the rubbish." Pitt took a piece of chalk from his desk. He rolled it in his palm, using his thumb to guide it. Outside, a bell rang, the five-minute warning before the next lesson.

"You were running late, you said. But this was after lunch, wasn't it? Had you been off the grounds?"

"I'd been to Galatea. I was . . ." He sighed, but looked tense and sounded more defensive than defeated. "All right. If you must know, there was a row with the wife. I lost track of time. The only reason I stopped by my pigeonhole and saw the chit at all was that I was carrying a stack of papers to my room. I saw the time on the bell tower and realised I wouldn't be able to make it to the classroom and then back to the playing field before the boys started tearing up the lawn."

"But to be just a few minutes late? What sort of crime is that, Mr. Pitt, that you would drop everything and run out to the field?"

"Crime enough for Lockwood. Especially in my circumstances. With a wife who likes the bottle just a bit too much. Do you want me to be any clearer, Inspector? I'd more on my mind than Matthew Whateley."

Pupils called to one another outside in the hall. Sergeant Havers maintained her position by the door. Pitt looked in her direction, dropped his chalk onto the desk.

"I've a lesson," he said with terse insistence.

Lynley responded placidly. "I take it that you and Mr. Lockwood don't get on." He could see Pitt's reaction in the muscles round his eyes.

"Lockwood's looking to sack me because I don't fit the picture of what he has in mind for Bredgar Chambers. He's been trying to build a case for dismissal since first we met."

"Unsuccessfully, it seems."

"The problem he faces is that in spite of my wife and in spite of my appearance, I'm good in the classroom, and the number of my pupils who do well in their A-levels proves it. So he's stuck with me. And stuck with the fact that I know a bit more about him than the average master does." Pitt offered the last sentence in a manner to encourage further enquiry along those lines. Lynley was willing to play along.

"Such as?"

"I know his background, Inspector. I've made it my business to know it. He wants to sack me and I've no intention of giving up without a fight. So I've one or two items I can pull out of my hat if the Board of Governors decide to sit in judgement on my competence."

Pitt possessed fine expertise in playing out his information for maximum effect. Lynley had no doubt that he used this same method when dealing with superiors and colleagues. It couldn't make him a likable man, or a man pleasant to deal with.

"Mr. Pitt," Lynley remarked, "as you've said yourself, you have a lesson this hour. We'd get through this interview a bit more quickly if you got to the point."

"There is no *point*, Inspector. Just that I know all about Lockwood's second-class performance at the University of Sussex, about his interesting live-in arrangement with three young ladies before he married Kate, about his job in the last state school that would have him where his colleagues finally sent him to Coventry because he snitched on them to aggrandise himself every time they stepped out of line. The Headmaster would love to sack me, Inspector, if he could only be sure I'd hold my tongue and not tell the Board of Governors everything I know about him."

"You've apparently managed to uncover quite a bit."

"I go to conferences. I meet other teachers. They talk. I listen. I *always* listen."

"Yet this is a relatively prestigious school. How did Lockwood manage to become headmaster if his background is as black as you paint it?"

"By carefully adjusting the facts here and there. By climbing over the wounded. By sucking up to people who could help his career. For a price, of course."

"Giles Byrne?"

A look of approval passed across Pitt's face. "You're a quick study. Bravo. Why do you think Matthew Whateley was given the governors' scholarship in the first place? Not because he was the best or the brightest. He wasn't. He was very average. A nice boy, but average. That's all. There were half a dozen other candidates more deserving than he. The decision rested with the Headmaster. But Giles Byrne wanted Matthew. So Matthew was selected. *Quid pro quo.* And Byrne was able to illustrate for the other members of the Board of Governors exactly how much power he really does wield. He's like that, you know. But then, aren't we all? Power's an intoxicant. Get a bit, want a bit more."

Certainly the aphorism could be true in Pitt's life. Knowledge was power, and he'd wielded enough in the last few minutes to derogate the Headmaster in every way he could, as if blackening the man's reputation somehow did something to improve his own, as if placing the focus of their conversation on Lockwood would eliminate the chance of its coming to rest upon another, closer, more tender area.

"You traded duty weekends with John Corntel," Lynley pointed out. "Why?"

"My wife had expressed an interest in seeing a play in Crawley. I wanted to humour her, so I asked John to trade."

To keep her away from the bottle, no doubt, Lynley thought. He asked, "What play did you see?"

"*Otherwise Engaged.*" Pitt smiled thinly at the irony of the title. "An older play, I know. But we'd not seen it before."

"Friday night? Saturday?"

"Friday," he replied.

"And on Saturday?"

"On Saturday, nothing. We stayed in for the evening. Watched television. Read. Even tried to have a conversation with one another."

"Did you see Emilia Bond during this time? Friday or Saturday?"

The question piqued Pitt's interest. He cocked his head. "Not at night. I saw her during the day, of course. She lives in Galatea House. It's hard to avoid her. But I didn't see her either evening. And as I recall, her door was closed when I walked through the building." Seeing the alteration in Lynley's expression, Pitt went on. "I *do* check on my girls, Inspector. I'm housemaster, after all. And frankly, they bear a great deal of watching."

"Ah."

Pitt coloured. "That's not what I meant."

"Perhaps you might explain what you meant."

Outside the classroom door, a raucous burst of laughter told them Pitt's upper sixth group were getting restless. Neither Lynley nor Havers made a move to admit them into the room.

"They're unnecessary trouble on the campus, Inspector. Provocation. Temptation. I've seen two of them expelled in the last year for licentious conduct—one with a *groundsman* if you can believe that—and another slither off in the sort of disgrace that her parents euphemistically labelled 'transferring to another school.' " He gave a snort of laughter. "That's just at Galatea House. God knows what they're up to over in Eirene."

"Perhaps that's due to having a housemaster and not a housemistress," Lynley noted. "It must be difficult keeping watch over girls when there are certain conventions of privacy required of you."

"It wouldn't be difficult if Emilia Bond did her job with a bit more care, would it? But I can't depend upon her, so I do it myself."

"In what manner?"

Pitt bristled openly. "I've no interest in sixteen- and seventeen-year-old girls. What does this have to do with Matthew Whateley's death? I only knew him in games. So why don't you toddle off and find someone to talk to who can tell you something of value, Inspector? I'm not that person. This is a waste of time for all of us. I know little enough about policework, but it seems to me that you ought to be looking for someone who likes to dandle young boys. Frankly, I'm not your man. And I don't know who is. I'm only glad to say . . ." His brows knotted suddenly.

"Mr. Pitt?" Lynley asked.

"Bonnamy," he said.

"I've heard the name. Matthew visited him as part of his job with Bredgar Volunteers. Why do you mention him?"

"I'm in charge of the Volunteers. I know the man. Before Matthew, we'd never been able to place a pupil with Bonnamy and have either of them survive more than a single visit. But he liked Matthew from the first."

"Are you suggesting Colonel Bonnamy's the man who liked to dandle little boys?"

Pitt shook his head with a jerk. "No. But if someone at the school was after Matthew that way, the boy might have confided in Colonel Bonnamy."

This was, Lynley admitted, a distinct possibility. Yet what could not be overlooked was the fact that Pitt had manufactured several potential smokescreens during their conversation. They took the form of his allusions to Alan Lockwood, his references to Giles Byrne, his dissatisfaction with Emilia Bond, and now Colonel Bonnamy's friendship with the murdered boy. Once again at Bredgar Chambers, there was too much information being given out in an interview, as if the appearance of ostensible assistance would gloss over the ineradicable stain of guilt.

Lynley looked towards Havers who still guarded the doorway. "Let them in, Sergeant," he told her.

She swung the door open. Four pupils entered at once, three boys and a girl. They looked at neither their teacher nor the police detectives, but instead directed furtive glimpses back into the corridor with mischievous grins. A second girl began to enter the room but she was suddenly snatched backwards, lifted off her feet, and carried into the doorway by a misshapen, hunched figure wearing a black cape and hideous make-up.

"Sanctuary!" he roared, twirling around with the struggling girl in his arms. "Esmeralda! Sanctuary!" He staggered forward three steps and dropped to his knees. His grasp on the girl did not loosen.

The other pupils laughed as the boy bent his head and nuzzled his face into the girl's neck, smacking his lips, smearing both her jersey and her skin with his make-up.

"Let me go!" she shrieked.

Cowfrey Pitt interceded. "That's quite enough, Mr. Pritchard. We've benefitted enormously. You've at least made us thankful that the film was silent."

Clive Pritchard released his grip on the girl, and she rolled onto the floor. She was small and unattractive, with sharp, bony features and a spotty face. Lynley recognised her from his visit to Emilia Bond's upper sixth chemistry lesson the day before.

"You little—" She grasped her yellow jersey. "Look at what you've done! I'll have to have this cleaned!"

"You loved it," Clive responded. "Close as you've ever been to a man, wasn't it?"

She leapt to her feet. "I ought to—"

"Enough." Pitt didn't need to raise his voice. His black tone was sufficient. "Pritchard, get rid of that ridiculous make-up. You've ten minutes to do so. And eight pages of translation by tomorrow for this fascinating display you've regaled us with. Daphne, you're excused to see to your appearance as well."

"That's *it?*" Daphne shrilled, fists balled at her sides, her face screwed up so that her eyes disappeared. "Eight pages of translation? That's to be his punishment? You think he'll do it?" She didn't wait for an answer. "Keep *away* from me, you bastard!" she hissed at Clive and pushed past him to get out of the room.

Lynley looked towards Sergeant Havers but saw that he had not needed to take the trouble of giving her so much as surreptitious direction. She had seen the opening herself and followed the girl.

Barbara Havers did not usually feel any compunction about using a moment of emotional upheaval to press forward to an advantage when she was working on a case. But as she followed Daphne down the corridor, up a short stairway, and into a lavatory, she found herself reluctant to do so. She knew the reason. Whether she wanted to face it or not, like called out to like from the person of this undersized teenager with her dishwater hair, her crooked posture, and her concave chest. Even though there were no actual physical similarities between them, they were both misfits. They might well hail from different social strata—even in her anger, the girl's accent told Barbara that—but their isolation within those strata was identical, nonetheless.

From the door, Barbara watched the girl run water into one of the basins. The room smelled of disinfectant. It was very cold. A small green bar of crusty soap lay on the basin's edge. Daphne lathered her hands with it, grimaced, and rubbed at the greasepaint on her neck.

"Bastard," she flung at the mirror through clenched teeth. "Filthy little bastard."

Barbara joined her, offering a neatly folded handkerchief. "Use this," she said.

The girl took it, said, "Thanks," and scrubbed it across her skin. "Is he always like that?"

"More or less. Pathetic, isn't he? Anything to get just a bit of attention."

"Whose attention?"

Daphne rinsed the handkerchief and worked it against her jersey. "Anyone's. I hate him. Bastard." She blinked quickly.

"Does he go after you like that very often?"

"Clive goes after *anyone*. But he likes to try me best because he knows that I've no . . . The filthy prick. Rotter. Thinks he's such a swell."

"I know the type. God's gift."

"He pretends it's all for a bit of fun, doesn't he? All a big joke with me too stiff to laugh with the others. But what *they* don't know is that when he's got me on the floor, he's holding me against his . . . so I can feel how big . . ." She bit her quivering lip. "It's a turn-on to him. He makes me sick!" She bent over the basin. Her stringy, limp hair dangled down to hide her face.

Barbara saw the dynamics of the relationship easily enough. Victimiser and his victim. "Why don't you report him?"

"To whom?"

The question was filled with bitterness, presenting an opportunity in two simple words. Barbara took it, careful to sound disinterested. "I don't know. I didn't attend a school like this. But if you're hesitant about one of the adults knowing—and I can see why you might be. It's embarrassing, isn't it?—surely another pupil . . . perhaps someone with influence . . . ?"

"D'you mean Chas Quilter, our sainted senior prefect? Our stellar example? Don't make me laugh! They're all the same here. Putting on a front. Acting the part. Chas is no different. He's worse."

"Worse than Clive? Hard to believe, that."

"Not at all. Not—at—all. Hypocrisy is always worse than igno-rance." Daphne ran her fingers roughly back through her hair.

Barbara felt the quick surge of excitement, but she spoke casu-ally. "Hypocrisy?"

It didn't work. At the question, the girl remembered herself and quickly withdrew. Even now, the tradition-bound call of loyalty was stronger than the need for revenge. She folded the handkerchief and handed it over.

"Thanks," she said. "I can't do much with the jersey, but at least the mess is off my skin."

The nature of her response to Barbara's question made further subterfuge unnecessary. There was nothing to be lost by a frontal assault. "You're in Miss Bond's upper sixth chemistry, aren't you?"

"Yes."

"You live in—"

"Galatea."

"She's tutor there. You must know her fairly well."

"No better than her other pupils know her, I imagine."

"Such as Chas, you mean? Or Brian Byrne?"

Daphne looked perplexed at this line of questioning. "I've no idea. Miss Bond's nice to everyone, isn't she?"

"You must see her in the house a great deal if she's the house tutor."

"Yes. Well, no. I just . . . I don't know. I must see her here and there. I don't think about it when I do."

"And this past weekend?"

Comprehension swept across the girl's face. She looked beyond Barbara to the doorway. "Mr. Pitt's waiting for me. Thanks awfully for the handkerchief."

Barbara let her go, remaining behind to reflect on the only piece of information that seemed viable—her remark about Chas Quilter and hypocrisy. That the senior prefect was not all that he seemed had been evident from the first moment they had stepped into Erebus House and seen its disorder. Even before that, a casual remark tossed over the shoulder of a passing boy—*sod you, Quilter*—spoke of some sort of cancer that ate at both the prefect's authority and his position at the school. But that cancer lacked a clear definition. Whether it had anything at all to do with the death of Matthew Whateley remained to be seen.

*   *   *

Colonel Andrew Bonnamy and his daughter lived less than a mile from the village of Cissbury, in one of a cluster of five cottages partially hidden from the passing lane by a privet hedge in need of trimming. Like the other structures, the Bonnamy cottage was small, half-timbered, with wattle-and-daub infilling that was whitewashed but showing signs of age. Cracks etched its surface like geological faults, threading upwards from the foundation and creeping towards the roof. Chestnut trees shadowed this, tall and angular with branches that dipped down to scrape against the tiles.

When Lynley and Havers pulled into the narrow drive to one side of the cottage, they saw a woman descending a slope that led to an orchard beyond it. She was wearing a faded denim skirt, a navy windcheater zipped to her throat, and heavy workshoes. In one hand she dragged a rubbish sack behind her while the other held secateurs and a rake. As she approached them, they saw that her face was stained with disregarded dirt. They saw also that she had been weeping recently, for her tears had left tracks against her skin. She appeared to be about forty years old.

Seeing Lynley and Havers, she dropped the rubbish sack by a stack of firewood and came towards them, rake and secateurs still in hand. She had not, Lynley noted, worn gloves for her gardening, so her hands were grimy. Dirt made black crescents under her nails.

Lynley produced his warrant card and introduced himself and Havers. "You're Jean Bonnamy?" he asked. "We've come to talk to you and your father about Matthew Whateley."

She nodded. Her throat worked furiously but failed to prevent a sound from escaping. It was like a whimper. "I phoned the school this morning to leave a message that I would be late to pick him up today. They put me through to Mr. Lockwood. He told me. Matt always came to us on Tuesdays. To see my father. And I suppose to see me as well, although I'd not really considered that at all. Until today." She looked down at the tools she was carrying. Clods of earth and broken twigs were embedded on the prongs of the rake. "So sudden. Unexpected. I can't bear the thought that he died so young."

Immediately Lynley understood the nature of the information Alan Lockwood had given Jean Bonnamy. "Matthew Whateley was mudered."

Her head came up sharply. She tried and failed to repeat the word, managing at last to say only, "When?"

"Probably Friday or Saturday. We won't know for certain until we have the autopsy results."

Dazed, she leaned the rake against the trunk of a chestnut, dropped the secateurs next to it, and reached out herself for the solid reassurance of the tree. "Mr. Lockwood didn't . . ." Her voice became importunate, tinged with anger. "Why didn't he *tell* me?"

The question was moot, with a dozen different explanations. Rather than explore them with the woman, Lynley merely asked, "What did he tell you?"

"Virtually nothing. That Matthew was dead. That the school was waiting for details. He hurried me off the phone by saying that he'd get back to me as soon as he could give me a 'complete report.' He said he'd let me know when the funeral was, so Dad and I could go." Tears welled up in her eyes, spilling over in a rush. "*Murdered?* He was such a sweet little boy." She wiped the sleeve of her wind-cheater against her wet face. It smeared the dirt and stained the material. Seeing this, and looking from it to her filthy hands, she said unnecessarily, "I'm a sight. I had to work. I had to do something. Dad wouldn't talk. He's . . . Just for a few minutes, I had to get out of the house. And the orchard needed attention. It seemed best that we each be alone for a bit. But he doesn't know the worst. How can I tell him?"

"He has to be told. It's important that he know. We need to speak to him about the boy, and we can't do that if he doesn't know the truth."

"I'm afraid it will kill him. No. I know you're thinking how dramatic and ridiculous that kind of statement is. But my father isn't well, Inspector. Did they tell you that at the school?"

"They told me only that Matthew visited him as part of the Bredgar Volunteers."

"He had a stroke ten years ago in Hong Kong when he was with the army. He resigned his commission, and since my mother was already dead, he came to me here. He's had three more strokes since then, Inspector. Each time he's expected he'll die. But he hasn't. And I . . . we've been together so long now, I can't bear the thought that anything . . ." She cleared her throat.

"If he knows the boy's dead, he already knows the worst, doesn't he?" Sergeant Havers asked the question in her usual forthright manner.

Jean Bonnamy seemed to recognise the truth behind Havers' words, for after a moment's thought she nodded slowly and said to Lynley, "Let me go in to him first. Will you wait here a moment?"

When he agreed, she left them, going up a wooden ramp at the rear of the cottage and entering through a door there.

"How long do you think Lockwood intends to try to keep a lid on this?" Havers asked Lynley when they were alone.

"As long as he can get away with it, no doubt."

"But he's being irrational. The newspapers will pick up the story eventually, if they haven't already. We've a thirteen-year-old boy who was found nude, murdered—tortured—in a graveyard miles away from both his home and his school. We've a story that hints at perversion, homosexuality, sadism, kidnapping, and God knows what else. How on earth does Lockwood think he's going to keep all that quiet?"

"I don't think he's concerned that the story be kept quiet as much as he's concerned that Bredgar Chambers not be mentioned in any part of it. If he could keep the school out of it, no doubt he'd be the first to shout the information from the nearest street corner. But since he can't do that without involving the school, he can't do anything but obfuscate the truth from whomever isn't directly involved."

"All for the sake of the school's pretty reputation?" Havers scoffed.

"And for his own. 'Who steals my purse,' Havers. Lockwood's no fool. He knows how much of his future is tied up in his name and his reputation. Both of them are tied inextricably to Bredgar Chambers."

"And if it turns out that someone Lockwood placed in a position of responsibility is our killer . . . ?"

"Then I should imagine he'll have a difficult time explaining to the Board of Governors how he made such an error in judgement."

"And then he's gone? The first headmaster at Bredgar Chambers not to die with his boots on?"

Lynley smiled wryly. "In a word, Sergeant."

Jean Bonnamy called to them from the top of the ramp. "We're ready for you, Inspector."

If the style of building had not indicated the age of the cottage, the kitchen they entered would have done so. Its ceiling was low and cross-beamed in oak in the fashion of the late fifteenth century, and its oddly shaped, uncurtained windows were set into walls more than twelve inches thick. It was a room in which one stepped back in time, to a period in which life was neither nicely packaged nor convenient. Lynley had the impression that Jean Bonnamy preferred it this way. A large pot on the Aga, emitting the scent of fresh vegetable soup, seemed verification of this fact. She paused there to stir the mixture with an age-darkened wooden spoon before leading them through a low doorway into a sitting room beyond.

This was obviously her father's demesne, for memorabilia of his life in Hong Kong filled it, represented by photographs of junks in the harbour at sunset, a large collection of carved jade and another of ivory, an antique sedan chair with side curtains of heavy, faded brocade. Even the wide-mouthed fireplace had been relegated a position in the overall theme of the room's decoration, for it held a dragon, a creature of papier-mâché head and red silk body, the sort that leads parades down city streets on Chinese New Year.

In spite of this museumlike array of objects, the room smelled largely of dog, and the offender—a coal black retriever with greying snout and rheumy eyes—lay on a blanket in front of an electric fire. He stirred only to lift his head slowly when Lynley and Havers entered the room.

Next to the dog, Colonel Bonnamy sat in a wheelchair with his back to the door. He faced a low cherrywood table on which a set of chessmen indicated that a game was in progress. There was no evidence of a fellow player.

"Here's the Inspector, Dad," Jean Bonnamy said. "And the Sergeant."

"Devil take them," Colonel Bonnamy replied. His speech was perfectly clear, unimpaired by his stroke.

His daughter went to the wheelchair and grasped its handles. "I know, Dad," she said quite tenderly and swung the chair round to face the room. She was careful not to disturb the table on which the chess pieces sat.

Although Jean Bonnamy had told them of her father's strokes, she had not prepared them for what apoplexy had done to ravage him. Even had his health not been impaired, he would have presented a far from soothing aspect. Hair grew out of both his ears in great grey tufts. Huge dark freckles looking much like scabs covered his bald head. His nose was bulbous, and on its left nostril grew a misshapen wart.

Continued ill health had exacerbated this dreadful appearance. The strokes had affected the left side of his body, so his facial muscles were pulled down into a permanent sneer and his left hand was frozen into a claw with cuticles growing the length of his fingernails. In spite of the electric fire heating the room, he wore thick shoes, a flannel shirt, wool trousers. A mohair blanket lay across his knees.

"Please. Sit down, Inspector, Sergeant," Jean Bonnamy said. She removed a stack of newspapers from a slip-covered sofa and returned to her father to push his chair closer to the police. A rattan stool stood on the other side of the chess table, and she fetched this and sat next to her father, her hand on the arm of his wheelchair. She had yet to wash from her work in the orchard, and the proximity of her hand to her father's chalky claw made her seem at once both slovenly and uniquely alive.

"How does one become involved with the Bredgar Volunteers?" Lynley asked. "It's my understanding from talking to Mr. Pitt at the school that Matthew wasn't the first Volunteer to visit here."

"First one with any sense," Colonel Bonnamy muttered. He coughed and gripped the arm of his chair with his good hand. His right arm shook.

His daughter spoke. "Dad's a bit of a curmudgeon when he wants to be. Don't deny it, Dad. You know you are. I thought it would be a good idea for him to have some company other than myself. I'd read about the Volunteers on the notice board at church, so I phoned the school and made arrangements. This was summer term last year."

"Fools they all were, till Matt," her father added, head bent forward and eyes on his lap.

"We tried six or seven of them. All ages. Boys and girls. None of them worked out, save Matt. He and Dad got on from the start."

"Today." The Colonel's voice hardened. "He was to come here today, Jeannie. The chessmen were just as we left them Tuesday last. Just as we *left* them. And you say"—he raised his head with a visible effort and looked at Lynley; his eyes were grey, sharp with intelligence—"murdered. *Murdered?*"

"Yes. I'm sorry." Lynley leaned forward. Next to him, Sergeant Havers rustled through her notebook. "He was found in Stoke Poges, Colonel Bonnamy. His body was nude. There was evidence of torture. But his clothing was left on the school grounds."

The Colonel assimilated the facts quickly. "Someone on staff then. Some hidden bum-boy pretending to be holier-than-thou. That's what you're thinking, isn't it?"

"We don't know what to think. Initially, it seemed that Matthew had tried to run off and had got picked up hitchhiking by someone who abused him for pleasure and then murdered him when he was through having his fun."

"There was no running off for a lad like that. Matt Whateley was a fighter." He fussed with the blanket across his knees. His daughter adjusted it, tucking it in round his legs. "Not the kind of fighter they'd be used to at that school. But a fighter all the same."

"What sort of fighter?"

Colonel Bonnamy pointed to his temple. "The sort that fights with his brain."

"You seem to have been closer to the boy than most," Lynley said. "Did he confide in you?"

"He didn't need to confide. I could see well enough. I could tell."

"But, as you said, you got the impression that he fought with his brain."

"Chess," the Colonel replied.

Apparently Jean Bonnamy felt the response did nothing to clarify her father's description of the boy, for she spoke. "Dad taught Matt to play chess. And no matter how difficult it was for the boy, no matter how many times Dad won, he refused to give up. I don't think he even felt discouraged. He'd just march in here every Tuesday afternoon, set up the board, and have another go at it."

"Fighter," her father declared again.

"In all this time, did he talk to you at all about the school? About his lessons? About his friends? About his teachers?"

"No. Only that his marks were good."

"Dad kept on him about his marks," Jean Bonnamy added. "We both talked to him about what he wanted to do with his life."

"I got the impression that Mum and Dad wanted the traditional sort of thing," the Colonel said, "although Matt didn't speak much about them. I think they were pushing him towards science, law, architecture, finance. That would be typical of their heritage. A career like that upholds the honour of the whole family. Mum, Dad, grandparents, everyone. But little Matt was an artist at heart. And that's what he spoke of. When he talked of school and of the future, he spoke of art."

"Dad encouraged him," Jean Bonnamy said. "Matt promised him one of his sculptures someday."

"A boy ought to be what he wants to be, not what his parents decide for him. But these families are so much like that. I've seen it a hundred times. Total respect for the parents. Complete submission of the personality. Become what you are told to become. Marry whom you are told to marry. It's part of their culture. There's no getting round it. Unless, of course, the child has a mentor who can guide him through the worst of his parents' disapproval when he sets out on his own way."

As he listened, a dawning realisation was setting upon Lynley. But it was tinged with the growing comprehension that, however incongruous the idea might seem, no matter the light Colonel Bonnamy was going to shed upon Matthew Whateley's life and his death, the case was about to become convoluted beyond his expectations. He felt a growing trepidation as the Colonel continued to speak.

"At least Matt benefitted from the fact that only one parent would have been caught up in this family-honour business and all the blasted tradition tied to it."

"Only one parent?" Lynley asked.

The Colonel nodded. "The mother. I never met her, but the name *Whateley* hardly suggests that his father's Chinese. So I assume it's his mother. We didn't speak of it. I should guess it was hard enough for Matt being a mixed race child at that fancy school of his without having to discuss it when he wasn't there."

Next to him on the sofa, Lynley sensed Sergeant Havers' movement. He himself wanted to spring to his feet and pace the room and fling open the windows and rush out the doors. He did none of this. Instead, he forced his mind back to the photographs he'd seen of the boy, recalling the dark hair, skin that was the colour of blanched almonds, delicate features, eyes nearly black. Eyes . . . eyes that were full and wide and not Chinese. Welsh perhaps. Even Spanish. But certainly not Chinese. It was impossible. It made no sense.

"You didn't know Matthew was mixed race, Inspector." Jean Bonnamy spoke softly.

Lynley shook his head, more in confusion than negation. "Have you a picture of the boy who visited you?"

She got to her feet. "I'll fetch it."

When she left the room, the Colonel spoke. "I'd say if you're looking for a killer, you might start with the bigots. The sort of people who can't stand to be in contact with someone a bit different. Ignorant people. The kind who have to obliterate what they can't understand."

Lynley heard the words but could think only of the impossibility of Matthew Whateley's being anything other than what he had been presented from the very beginning—the son of Kevin and Patsy Whateley, scion of a working class family, scholarship recipient, railway enthusiast.

Jean Bonnamy returned with the photograph which she handed to Lynley. He examined it and nodded at Havers. "The same boy," he said and looked back at it again. In it, Matthew and the Colonel sat hunched over the chessboard. Matthew's hand was extended, as if caught in the act of moving one of his chessmen, but his face was turned towards the camera, and he was smiling much the same smile that had been on his face in the photograph Lynley had seen of him on the banks of the Thames with Yvonnen Livesley, his Hammersmith friend.

"I've met Matthew's parents," Lynley said to the Colonel. "Neither is Chinese."

The Colonel appeared neither disconcerted nor taken aback to hear this news. "The boy was mixed race," he said conclusively. "I lived in Hong Kong for thirty-five years. I know when I'm looking at a mixed race child. To you, Matt might well look Occidental. But to anyone who's spent time in the Orient, the boy was half Chinese." His eyes moved moodily to the fireplace and lingered on the head of the garish dragon. "Some people like to crush what they can't understand, the way you'd smash a spider with the heel of your shoe. That's what you ought to be looking for. That kind of ugliness. That kind of hatred. The sort that says white Britannia is supreme and anything else is beneath contempt. You look at that school. I dare say that's where you'll find it."

There was too much to think about, too much to evaluate. Yet points still needed elucidation, especially in the face of what Lynley thought he knew to be the truth about Matthew Whateley's family. "Did Matthew speak to you about any of this? About his family's background? About meeting with some sort of prejudice at the school? About trouble with a teacher or a student or a member of staff?"

The Colonel shook his head. "He spoke only of his marks. And only when I asked. And nothing else about the school at all."

"But there was the motto, Dad," Jean Bonnamy interjected. "You've not forgotten that." She went back to her stool, speaking to Lynley. "Matthew had seen the school's motto somewhere—in the chapel, in the library. I can't recall. But he was quite taken with it."

"I've not seen the motto," Lynley said. "What is it?"

"I don't know what it was in Latin, but he'd managed to get a translation from someone, and he brought it to us," Jean Bonnamy replied. "It had to do with honour. He was most—"

"I'd forgotten that, Jeannie," the Colonel interrupted pensively. " 'Let honour be both staff and rod.' Those were the very words. He was quite taken with them. Wanted to spend the afternoon talking about what they meant. *Honor sit et baculum et ferula.*"

"Odd topic of conversation for a thirteen-year-old boy," Sergeant Havers commented.

"Not for this boy," the Colonel replied. "Honour's in their blood. It's at the heart of their culture."

Lynley wished to avoid that area of dispute. "When was this discussion? What brought it up?"

The Colonel looked at his daughter for help. "When, Jeannie?"

"Perhaps a month ago? Hadn't they been talking at school—in a history lesson?—about Lady Jane Grey? And dying merely for the sake of a belief, for the sake of religion? Wasn't that it? Because I remember Matt asking whether you believed that honour required one to do what was right. You asked him what brought that idea into his head out of nowhere. He said Lady Jane Grey and her decision to die rather than accept the dishonour of renouncing her religion."

Her father nodded slowly. "He wanted to know what we thought was more important, a code of honour or a code of behaviour."

"You said there was no difference between the two, didn't you?"

"That I did. But Matthew disagreed." The Colonel looked at the picture which Lynley had returned to Jean Bonnamy. "That was the Occidental in him speaking. But his Chinese blood told him they were one and the same."

Lynley felt a stirring of irritation at the continual references to a bloodline whose existence had no foundation in any fact. "Yet you never spoke to him about being Chinese. In spite of your own evident love for the culture."

"No more than I would speak to you about the old Norse blood that gives you your lovely hair, Inspector. We're all of us part and parcel of another culture, aren't we? Some are merely nearer to that other culture in time than you and I are. But all of us spring from another source. Accepting that is accepting life. It's the people who can't accept it that become the destroyers. That's all I can tell you."

Clearly it was the Colonel's way of ending the interview, and Lynley could see the strain that the conversation had wrought upon the man. His limbs were shaking. His eyes were heavy-lidded with fatigue. There was no point to pushing for further information. He got to his feet, expressed his thanks to the old man, and, with Sergeant Havers, followed Jean Bonnamy out the way they had come in. None of them spoke until they were on the drive once more.

"Let me ask you this, Miss Bonnamy," Lynley said. "It's not to give you pain but to come to some sort of understanding of why your father believes Matthew Whateley was Chinese. Your father's had four strokes. He can't have escaped unaffected from them."

She looked past him to the privet hedge. Three birds were splashing happily in a puddle of water at its base.

"It's all in his head?" she asked with a smile. "I wish I could make it easier for you, Inspector. It *would* be easier if I'd only agree, wouldn't it? But I can't. You see, I lived in Hong Kong until I was twenty years old. And the moment Matthew Whateley walked into our cottage last September, I knew without a doubt that he was a mixed race child. So it has nothing to do with my father's mind or whether he's in possession of his faculties. Because even if he isn't, it doesn't matter. I'm certainly in possession of all of mine." She rubbed at dirt that was trapped in the lines crisscrossing her palms. "I wish I could change just a few things, however."

"What?"

She shrugged. Her lips trembled, but she controlled them and spoke calmly. "When I took him back to school last Tuesday night, it was late. I drove him past the porter's cottage and I was going to take him directly to the door of Erebus House. But he had me stop at the road to the vehicle shed because it was easier to turn my car around there. He said he could walk the rest of the way. He was thoughtful like that. That was Matthew."

"That was the last time you saw him?"

She nodded and continued, as if her words would act as a form of exorcism for sorrow. "I let him out of the car. He started to walk off. Then a minibus came along the lane and its lights struck Matthew. I remember that quite well because he heard the bus and turned. He waved goodbye to me. And he smiled." She wiped at her eyes. "Matthew had the loveliest smile, Inspector. When I saw it last Tuesday, lighting up his face, I knew how dear he'd become to me. I only wish now that I'd told him."

"We found a draft of a letter to you among Matthew's belongings. Did he write to you last week?" Lynley took the piece of notebook paper from his pocket and handed it over to her.

She read it, nodded, and handed it back. "Yes. I received a note like this on Friday. Whenever he had dinner with us, he wrote a note of thanks. Always."

"He makes reference to a boy who saw him. Evidently you got him back to the school after curfew."

"He and Dad were quite involved in a game and time got away from all of us. I phoned Matthew on Wednesday to make sure there'd been no trouble. He said one of the older boys had seen him."

"Had he been reported to the Headmaster?"

"Evidently not. At least not yet. I think Matt intended to speak to the older boy anyway. To explain where he'd been."

"Would Matthew have faced disciplinary action for being out after curfew even if he was with you?"

"Apparently. The students are supposed to be responsible enough to get themselves back to campus on time, no matter the circumstances. That shows maturity, I suppose."

"The punishment had Matthew been caught after curfew?"

"He might have been confined to the house for a week. Perhaps warned off. I can't think they'd do anything else to him."

"But to the other boy?"

Jean Bonnamy drew her eyebrows together. "The other boy?"

"The one who saw Matthew."

"I don't understand."

It was a twist to the circumstances which Lynley had not seen until this moment. He had previously thought only in terms of Matthew's house prefect—Brian Byrne—not reporting a boy missing during bed check. But now he saw an added dimension. If Matthew Whateley had been out after curfew on Tuesday night, so had someone else.

14

"This thing tastes like sawdust, Inspector! It's disgusting. Must've been made last week. Fresh sandwiches! Ha! Someone ought to put that bloke in the nick for false advertising." Crumbs from her cheese sandwich powdered the front of her maroon pullover. Sergeant Havers brushed at them with a scowl, distributing them generously onto the floor of Lynley's car. He said her name in useless protest. She shrugged. "We could've stopped. We could've gone to that pub. Fifteen minutes to eat wouldn't exactly put us in the dock for dereliction of duty."

Lynley inspected his own selection, roast beef and tomato, and saw that both were rather too green to be considered wise for consumption. "It seemed a good idea at the time," he said.

"Besides," Havers groused now that she had his agreement, "we've not exactly got a reason to go rushing back to the school, have we? As far as I can tell, working through this flaming case is like stepping into quicksand. We're up to our necks now, and all it's going to take is one more blasted detail that creates one more blind alley and down we go. Suffocating."

"Rather a lot of mixed metaphors, Havers."

She scoffed. "*You* tell me what we've got. We started out with class differences. Matt Whateley running off because he couldn't fit in with the la-di-da types at the school. Then we decided it was bullying, with Matt running off because he was afraid of some tough who was pushing him about. Then we went in for homosexuality and perversion. And *now* we're playing with racial bigotry. Not to mention someone being out after curfew. Now, there's a fine motive for murder." She pulled out her cigarettes and lit one defiantly. Lynley lowered his window. "I don't know where we're heading with this muck any longer, and I'm getting to the point that I don't even know where the hell we've been."

"The Bonnamys confused the issue, didn't they?"

Havers blew out a stream of smoke. "Chinese. *Chinese?* It's not a go, Inspector. We both know that. We've a sick old man with an overactive imagination and a heart back in Hong Kong. And in the same house a lonely spinster daughter with fancies of her own. They see a dark-haired little boy who reminds them of the past and without any questioning, they assume he's part Chinese."

Lynley did not disagree. "It's pushing things. But there's something more to evaluate here, Sergeant."

"What?"

"The Bonnamys don't know Giles Byrne. They don't know that he was once devoted to a Chinese student at the school—Edward Hsu. Is it mere coincidence that out of the blue they would tell us they're sure Matthew Whateley was part Chinese?"

"Are you saying that the fact that Matthew was Chinese—accepting that as truth for a moment, which I don't, by the way—was what attracted Giles Byrne to him in the first place?"

"It's a thought, isn't it? Because isn't it peculiar that both Edward Hsu and Matthew Whateley are dead? Not only the two students with whom Giles Byrne was involved, but two Chinese students."

"If you want to accept that Matthew Whateley was Chinese. And if he was, *who* was he? Patsy Whateley's son, the product of an affair that her husband doesn't know about? Kevin Whateley's son, taken in and loved by the sainted Patsy? Who *was* he? What's his story?"

"That's what we'll have to find out. Only the Whateleys can tell us."

He made the turn onto the school drive. At the porter's lodge, Elaine Roly was struggling to put Frank Orten's younger grandson into an antique pram while the other child, disregarded for the moment, threw pebbles at the lodge's bay window. Elaine Roly didn't look up at the sound of the car's passing.

"I should think a bit of time with those two would put her off Frank Orten for good," Havers commented, stubbing out her cigarette in the ashtray. "Do you think she's after him, Inspector?"

"She may be. But from what we saw this morning, he doesn't appear to be encouraging her, does he?"

"Well," Havers said casually in a manner that told Lynley he had inadvertently given her an opening that she intended to use, "when it comes to love, some people don't need to be encouraged to hang on, do they?"

He ignored the question and accelerated the car. They swept down the drive and parked at the front of the school. When they entered the main foyer, they saw that the chapel door stood open and that the choir was gathered in the nave. Today the boys wore their school uniforms rather than the cassocks and surplices that had lent them such a celestial air the previous day. They were obviously engaged in some sort of rehearsal, for in the middle of what Lynley recognised as one of the choruses from the *Messiah,* the choir master stopped them impatiently, blew three separate notes upon a pitch pipe, and made them begin again.

"Getting ready for Easter, aren't they?" Sergeant Havers said. "Under the circumstances, that's a bit much for me. Glories and hallelujahs and one little bloke murdered right under their noses."

"But surely not by the choir master," Lynley replied. He was watching the rehearsal, his eyes seeking and finding the senior prefect.

Chas Quilter was in the last row of boys. Lynley observed him, brooding over what it was about the prefect that had caused him to feel such a twinge of apprehension from the first moment of their meeting. The choir master stopped the boys again and said, "Let's go on with Mr. Quilter's solo now. Have you the place, Quilter?"

Lynley turned away. "Let's rout out Mr. Lockwood, Havers."

Across the foyer from the chapel, two doors admitted visitors into the administrative wing of Bredgar Chambers. One door led into the porter's office, the other into a corridor decorated with trophies won by the school's victorious athletic teams. They walked the length of this to the Headmaster's study, where Alan Lockwood's secretary was working at a word processor. Seeing them, she got to her feet with an alacrity that suggested flight rather than welcome. Behind a closed door across the hall, the murmur of conversation rose and fell.

"You're wanting the Headmaster," the secretary announced. "He's in a meeting at the moment. You'll wait in his study." That said, she brushed past them, opened Lockwood's study door, and motioned them inside. "I can't say how long the Headmaster will be" was her final cool comment before leaving them.

"Nice lass, that," Havers commented when they were alone. "Has all her instructions down, doesn't she? Red carpet treatment and all."

Lynley took the opportunity to examine the photographs and

drawings that documented the school's history on one of the study walls. Sergeant Havers joined him.

The photographs spanned the last one hundred and fifty years, with fading daguerreotypes representing the earliest pictorial records. Across the decades, schoolchildren gathered at the base of Henry VII's statue; they lined up in neat rows in front of the school; they marched in columns across the playing fields; they rode in heavy-wheeled wagons along the school drive. They were uniformed and clean and smiling, one and all.

"Notice anything about them, Sergeant?"

"No girls until recently," she replied. "Thank God for the latter half of the twentieth century."

"Yes, there's that. And something else."

She went from picture to picture. She pulled at her chin. "Minorities," she commented. "Where are they?"

"Just the occasional face. Not unusual two hundred years ago. But surely a bit odd in the last ten years."

"So we're back to bigotry?"

"I don't think we can dismiss it yet, Havers."

"I suppose it's something to play with. Why not give it a try?"

They turned from the wall as the study door opened. But it was not Alan Lockwood who entered the room. Rather, it was his wife. She carried a large arrangement of flowers in a shallow bisque bowl.

Her steps did not falter when she saw Lynley and Havers. She merely smiled fleetingly at them, nodded hello, and took the flowers to the table that sat in the alcove created by the wide bay window.

"I brought these for the council room," she explained pleasantly. "Flowers make a room so much more welcoming, and since Alan is meeting with parents there, I thought that the flowers . . ." She rearranged three tuberoses. Their sweet fragrance was heady in the close air. "I'm afraid I didn't get them ready in time. The meeting's well under way. So I've brought them in here." She moved aside the silver candelabrum at the table's centre. "It's a bit much, isn't it? Both the candelabrum *and* the flowers." She frowned, looked about the room, and took the candelabrum to the fireplace where she placed it on the mantel. It partially obscured the Holbein portrait. Apparently satisfied with this arrangement, she nodded and tucked a strand of grey hair back into place above her forehead. "I do all the flowers for the school. From our conservatory. But I've told you that, haven't I? Sometimes I can't remember what I've said and what I haven't said to people. The first sign of senility, Alan tells me."

"Hardly." Lynley smiled. "Just a lot to remember. I should guess you speak to dozens of people every day. That's a lot to keep straight."

"Yes, of course." She went to her husband's desk and needlessly straightened a stack of folders that lay there, perfectly straight in the first place. The activity suggested that she had come into the study with a purpose other than delivering flowers.

"He works so hard and gets so tired that he doesn't always think before he speaks, Inspector. Things slip out in irritation. Like that remark about senility. But he's a good man, my Alan. A very good man. Decent. Respectable." She found a pencil tucked between two of the folders and neatly lined it up with a pen. "Alan's not appreciated as he ought to be. People don't know what he does behind the scenes, and he doesn't tell them. That's not his way. He's across the hall right now, meeting with four sets of parents whose boys might otherwise go to Eton or Harrow. Rugby. Westminster. But he'll convince them to choose Bredgar. He does that all the time."

"That must be the most anxious part of a headmaster's job," Lynley remarked. "Seeing to it that enrollment stays at a steady level."

"But it's more than that to Alan," she replied. "He's determined to bring the school back to where it was just after the war. That's his mission. Before Alan came, enrollment was off. Exam results were deteriorating, especially the A-level results. But he intends to do something about that. He has already. The new theatre was his idea, Inspector. A way of attracting more students to the school. Well, the right sort of students, naturally."

"Was Matthew Whateley the right sort of student?"

"I gave him violin lessons. Before Bredgar, I played with the London Philharmonic. I suppose you didn't know that. No one does, really. It's not something one drops into conversations with the masters' wives. But I gave it up because it does take some effort to be a proper headmaster's wife, doesn't it? And Alan needed me. As did our own children, of course. We've two small boys in primary school. Has Alan spoken of them? I play with Bredgar's orchestra now, and give lessons here and there. It's not quite the same"— she smiled with regret—"but it's something. Keeping one's hand in."

Lynley was not oblivious of the fact that she had avoided his question. "How often did you see Matthew?"

"Once a week. He didn't practise quite as much as he should have. But that's fairly typical of boys, isn't it? Although I dare say I did expect more of a scholarship child."

"It was an academic scholarship, not a music scholarship, wasn't it?"

"Yes. But one hopes a scholarship student will be a bit more well-rounded, Inspector. Matthew wasn't really the brightest boy to apply for the scholarship."

"You knew the other applicants?"

"Not exactly. Only what Alan made mention of at dinner. He always said that Matthew wasn't quite what Bredgar Chambers was looking for. Of course that wasn't Alan's fault. Nor was it his fault that Matthew was selected for the scholarship, so he can't be blamed at all for his death, can he? He felt he had to—"

"Kathleen."

Lynley and Havers swung round to see that Alan Lockwood had entered the room. He stood at the doorway, his face livid.

Hearing him, Kathleen Lockwood closed her mouth slowly. She swallowed. "Alan." One hand fluttered towards the table. "I've brought you flowers. I thought to have them in time for your meeting, but I didn't. So I brought them in here."

"Thank you." He stepped to one side of the door, his message clear. She read it, and without a look at either Lynley or Havers, she left the room. Lockwood shut the door behind her and faced the detectives. He gave them the benefit of a cold, evaluative examination before he went to his desk and stood behind it, wise enough to realise that he projected both authority and confidence by remaining on his feet.

"I've been made aware that your sergeant has spent most of the morning prowling about the grounds, Inspector," Lockwood said. Each syllable sounded brittle. "I'd like to know why."

Lynley did not answer at once. Rather, he went to the table, drew out one of the chairs, and waited as Sergeant Havers did likewise. Neither of them sat. The Headmaster watched them. A vein throbbed in his temple. He crossed the room to the window and pushed it far open.

"I'd appreciate an answer," he said.

"That's understandable." Lynley's reply was perfectly pleasant. He indicated another chair. "Please sit down, Mr. Lockwood."

For a moment, Lockwood looked as if he would refuse. But after a marked hesitation he sat at the table, across from them. Since the study faced east, the afternoon light did not hide his face as the morning light had done on their previous visit.

"Your porter found Matthew's school clothes on the rubbish pile," Lynley explained. "Since the boy's clothes are all accounted for now, it seems reasonable to conclude that Matthew was removed from the school nude."

Lockwood's eyes grew dark. "That's absurd. *Absurd*."

"Which part? The clothes being found or Matthew being taken from the school nude?"

"Both. And why wasn't I told about the clothes? When did Orten—"

Lynley interrupted. "I should imagine Mr. Orten thought it a matter best left to the police. We've a killer at large. There's no telling who it might be."

Lockwood's response was icy. "What exactly are you telling me, Inspector?"

"That Sergeant Havers has spent a good part of the morning looking for a place where Matthew might have been held securely from Friday afternoon when he disappeared until he was removed and taken to Stoke Poges."

"Impossible. One can't hide a child here."

Lynley recognised that Lockwood could hardly do anything save deny plausibility. He pointed out to the Headmaster that keys were available and security was poor.

Lockwood countered adroitly. "There are six hundred pupils in this school, Inspector. Not to mention members of staff. Can you actually believe that this boy was kidnapped, held hostage, murdered, and that afterwards his nude body was somehow transported off the grounds? All without anyone's being the wiser? That's the most ridiculous thing I've ever heard."

"Not when you consider the full circumstances behind the disappearance," Lynley said. "Whatever transporting occurred, it's reasonable to conclude that it would have been done in the dead of night when everyone was asleep. Additionally, it was a weekend. How many students had exeats? How many were off at the hockey tournament I've been hearing about? How many remained behind? How many staff members were actually here? We both know how deserted a school can be on a weekend, Mr. Lockwood. Now that we know Matthew was here, we're going to have to start questioning the staff. The local police will have to be brought in for this."

"That's unnecessary, Inspector. If any questioning of staff needs to be done, I'll see to it myself."

Lynley's response did much to clarify Lockwood's position in the investigation. "Where were you Friday night, Headmaster?"

Lockwood's nostrils flared. "I'm a suspect, I suppose? No doubt you've a motive signed, sealed, and delivered."

"In a murder investigation, everyone's a suspect initially. Where were you Friday night?"

"Here. In the study. Working on a report for the Board of Governors."

"Until what time?"

"I don't know. I didn't notice."

"And when you had completed your work?"

"I went home."

"Did you look in on any of the houses on your way?"

"Whatever for?"

"You pass directly by the girls' houses—Galatea and Eirene—to go home, don't you? It seems reasonable to wonder if you looked in on them."

"Reasonable to you, perhaps. But not to me. And certainly not on a Friday night. As you said, those are the girls' houses. I'm hardly going to prowl about them at night."

"But you could go in if you wanted to. No one would think it odd to see you."

"I've better things to do than check up on my housemasters. They do their jobs. I do mine."

"What about Ion House where the sixth form social club is? The older pupils who don't leave the school gather there on Fridays, don't they? Did you never look in on them?"

"The pupils police themselves. They don't need me to do it for them. You know that as well as I do. That's what the prefect system is all about."

"You have confidence in your prefects, then?"

"Utter. Absolute. They've never given me a cause to doubt them."

"What about Brian Byrne?"

Lockwood made an impatient movement with his shoulders. "We've been over this ground before, Inspector. Brian hasn't given me cause to be sorry he's a prefect."

"Elaine Roly seems to think he's a bit too needy himself to be an effective prefect."

"Needy? What on earth—"

"Needy for friendship and approval. Not the best choice to watch over other boys."

Lockwood looked amused. "That's the pot and the kettle. If anyone's needy for friendship and approval, I'd say Matron Roly heads the list herself. It's Roly who spends most of her free time trying to worm her way into Frank Orten's affections. As if that old misogynist would ever look at another woman after his wife dumped him. As for Brian Byrne, he became a prefect the way everyone else did. A member of staff nominated him."

"Who?"

"I'm afraid I don't recall." Lockwood reached out and touched an Easter lily that was part of his wife's arrangement of flowers. He played his fingers along the stem. Seeing him do so, Lynley marvelled at the manner in which the body told the truth even when the intellect attempted to lie.

"Is your wife considered a member of staff?" he asked. "After all, she's in the school orchestra. She gives music lessons. Even if she isn't paid for doing so, surely she has an honorary staff position. Surely she has input into decisions. Decisions like—"

The flower snapped from its stem. "All right. Kathleen nominated Brian. I asked her to do so. Giles Byrne wanted his son to be a prefect. Is that what you're so set upon knowing? It hardly has any bearing on Matthew Whateley's death."

"Did Giles Byrne want his son to be prefect of any particular house?"

"Erebus. That's not a crime. It's Byrne's old house. I consider it logical that he'd want his son to live there."

"Mr. Byrne seems to have a number of connections to Erebus, doesn't he?" Lynley queried. "He himself lived there. His son lives there. Matthew Whateley—his nominee for a scholarship—lived there. And earlier, Edward Hsu lived there as well. What do you know about Byrne's relationship with him?"

"Just that he tutored the boy, and that the memorial in the chapel was placed there by Byrne. He was fond of Edward Hsu. But that was long before my time."

"And Edward Hsu's suicide?"

Lockwood did not disguise his irritation. "You can't be suggesting there's some connection here? Edward Hsu died in 1975."

"I'm aware of that. How did he die? Do you know?"

"Everyone knows. He got into the bell tower, climbed onto the chapel roof, and threw himself off."

"Why?"

"I don't know."

"Have you a file on him?"

"I hardly see the relevance—"

"I'd like to see it, Headmaster."

Lockwood pushed himself forcefully away from the table. Without replying, he left the study, and snapped at his secretary in her office outside. When he rejoined them, he carried a manila folder open across his left palm. There were very few papers within it, and Lockwood went through these quickly, pausing to scan a letter written on onionskin.

"Edward Hsu came to us from Hong Kong," he said. "His parents were still living there as recently as 1982, according to this letter. They'd been considering setting up a scholarship in his memory, but evidently nothing came of it." Lockwood read on. "They sent Edward to be educated in England as his father had been educated. His entrance exam results are high. He seems to have been a gifted student. He probably would have made a great success of himself, but he never got as far as his A-levels to prove it. There's nothing else here, but no doubt you're determined to see that for yourself."

Lockwood handed over the file. DECEASED was written diagonally across it in large red letters. Lynley read through the scant material himself, finding nothing more save a photograph of Edward Hsu as he must have looked upon entering Bredgar Chambers as a thirteen-year-old. He raised his head. Lockwood was watching him.

"There was no note to indicate why the boy took his life?" Lynley asked.

"Nothing, as far as I was ever told."

"I was noticing all the photographs on your wall. It was interesting to note how few minority pupils you've had here through the years."

Lockwood's eyes moved to the pictures, then back to Lynley. His expression was unreadable. He said nothing.

"Have you ever considered what Edward Hsu's suicide might imply?" Lynley asked.

"The suicide of one Chinese student in five hundred years of this school's history hardly implies anything to me. And I see no connection whatsoever between that death and the death of Matthew Whateley. If you do, perhaps you'll be so good as to point it out to me. Unless, of course, you're going to bring up Giles Byrne again, and his connection with both boys. But if you do that, you might connect Elaine Roly to both of them as well. And Frank Orten. And anyone else who was here in 1975."

"Was Cowfrey Pitt here then?"

"Yes."

"And did the Bredgar Volunteers exist then?"

"Yes. *Yes.* What on earth does this have to do with—"

Lynley cut him off. "Your wife spoke highly of the attempts you've been making to build enrollment in the school, Headmaster. And to improve exam results. But you'd have to be careful what kind of student you allowed in, wouldn't you—on a scholarship or otherwise—to keep those exam results high?"

Lockwood rubbed his palm across a patch of angry, razor-worn skin on his neck. "You have an irritating habit of skirting issues, Inspector. Hardly behaviour I'd expect from the police. Why don't you ask me what you want to ask me and avoid all the subterfuge?"

Lynley smiled. "I'm merely wondering if Giles Byrne called in a debt that didn't work out in your plans for the school. If you were intent upon sending as many students as possible to Cambridge or Oxford—or at least more students than had been sent there since the war—you probably wouldn't appreciate having a less gifted student foisted upon you."

"Matthew Whateley wasn't foisted. He was *chosen*. In a fair process involving the entire Board of Governors."

"Involving Giles Byrne in particular?"

Lockwood's temper flared. "You listen to me," he hissed. "You handle the investigation. I'll run the school. Is that clear?"

Lynley got to his feet. Havers did likewise, stowing her notebook back into her shoulder bag. At the study door, Lynley stopped.

"Tell me, Headmaster. Did you know that John Corntel and Cowfrey Pitt had exchanged duty weekends?"

"Yes. Have you a problem with that?"

"Who else knew?"

"Anyone. Everyone. It's no secret. The name of the duty master is posted outside the dining hall and in the masters' common room."

"I see. Thank you."

"What does that have to do with all this?"

"Perhaps everything. Perhaps nothing." Lynley nodded a farewell and, with Havers, left the room.

They didn't speak until they were out of the building, pausing on the drive next to Lynley's car. Eight starlings swooped past them, cutting the afternoon air with the rush of their wings, alighting in the larger of the two beech trees that stood like sentinels upon either side of the lane that led off the school grounds. Lynley watched their flight.

"What's next?" Havers asked.

Lynley roused himself from his observation of the birds. "Matthew Whateley's real background. Whatever it is. We need to know it for a certainty before we go on."

"The bigotry angle, then," she said, squinting up at the chapel roof. "D'you suppose that's why Edward Hsu killed himself, sir?"

"As provocation, racism is insidious enough, isn't it? A boy alone, away from his family, caught in an environment that's alien to him, one in which he's not as comfortable as he would like to be."

"Sounds like Matthew Whateley, doesn't it?"

"It does, Sergeant. That's what concerns me."

"You're not thinking Matthew Whateley killed himself and all of this is some sort of elaborate hoax, made to look like a murder?"

"I don't know. We need the postmortem from Inspector Canerone in Slough. Even the preliminary results should tell us something, give us some sort of direction."

"Until then?" Havers asked.

"We do our best. Let's see what the Whateleys have to tell us about their son."

As usual, Harry Morant was the last boy to hang up his games clothes in the drying room of Calchus House. It was a habit of his. He always dawdled behind the others when games were over for the afternoon so that he wouldn't have to crowd into the drying room with everyone else.

It wasn't the jostling of all the boys that bothered him. Rather, it was the overpowering smell of sweat and dirty clothes. This odour was intensified by the room's saunalike temperature, the product of hot water pipes running horizontally along one wall of the small room. If Harry waited until the others had already made use of the drying room, he could draw a deep breath outside the door, fly inside to hang his clothes and towel over one of the pipes, and fly out again without ever having to breathe in the stench that he had once heard the matron fondly call "pure boy." So he always took his time about washing, about changing his clothes, about wandering slowly to the southwest corner of the building where the drying room was tucked out of sight.

He trudged in that direction now, his hockey kit and towel dangling limply in his hand. His feet felt heavy. His shoulders ached. In his chest was a hollow that seemed to grow larger with every passing hour. Something gnawed within him to create that hollow, and it seemed to Harry quite reasonable to conclude that the gnawing would continue until fear and grief and responsibility ate their way greedily right through his flesh, leaving only his bleeding corpse behind. He vaguely remembered reading about some American killer being sentenced to die in the electric chair and saying to the judge who had pronounced the sentence: "You can't kill me. I'm dead already." That's how Harry was beginning to feel.

At first it hadn't been like that at all. Fear had kept him quiet then. For it hadn't taken long for the word to filter down among the third formers that Matthew Whateley had been tortured before his death. Since Harry wasn't a particularly brave boy, the terror of encountering a similar fate had been enough to ensure that he said nothing to anyone. But fear had soon been replaced by grief, engendered by the knowledge that he himself had played a major role in the drama of what had happened to his friend, engendered by the memory of Matthew's determination to be of assistance in the nightmare that had become Harry's life at Bredgar Chambers. Because of this knowledge, responsibility tore at him, devouring both his heart and his conscience. In combination with both dread and sorrow, it was enough to make Harry long only for an end to everything. So he found himself more and more feeling like that wild-eyed American killer, and there was a form of blessing to that. If he was already dead, nothing could harm him any longer.

At the end of the corridor, he took in a deep breath, held it, and pushed open the drying room door. The heat from the water pipes rose like a wall before him. He edged into the room.

It wasn't too much larger than a cupboard, with stained plaster walls, a grey linoleum floor, and a ceiling largely taken up by a padlocked trap door upon which numerous wads of chewing gum had been fashioned into the letters *f-u-c* and the beginning of a *k* by a student who had climbed up the rusty metal wall ladder to reach it. One dim bulb above the door provided light, and in this meagre illumination Harry saw not only that little space was left on the water pipes for his own clothes, but that many of the other garments had been haphazardly thrown into the room in such a rush that they now lay in sweat-sodden piles upon the floor. Matron wouldn't like that. Nor would their house prefect. It would be punishment for all if the room were not straightened up.

Harry sighed, gagged in a breath of the foetid, hot air, and shuddered as he picked up the nearest pile of garments and began to hang them on the pipes to dry. They felt clammy in his hands, and an underlying stickiness clinging to them troubled his memory. It was as if once again, in this fractured moment, his fist was pressed against the sweat-drenched jersey covering the chest that held him pinned to the floor in the darkness.

Want a grind, nancy boy, want a grind, want a grind?

Harry cried out. He looked for escape, flinging clothing on the pipes as quickly as he could.

Want a grind, nancy boy, want a grind, wantagrind?

His grip tightened on the garment he held. There would be no rescue, not from this, not now. Whether he told or not, the outcome would be the same. It was inevitable. It was his due.

His eyes dropped to his hands, which had begun to twist and wring a navy sock. Unlike the other clothes in the room, it was completely dry, and his fingers pulled upon it, making contact with a small patch of cotton that was sewn into the wool. Harry examined this. The number *4* had been written onto the cotton tag.

He stared at it. It was hard to keep secrets at a place like Bredgar Chambers. He had heard this morning with everyone else that Matthew Whateley's school clothes had been found in the rubbish pile by the porter's lodge, partially burned. But not all his clothes, Harry saw now. Not everything had been there.

He swallowed. His mouth was dry. Here was something. *Something.* It wasn't sneaking, wasn't telling, wasn't even taking a risk. Not exactly. But it was something. Perhaps enough to fill the hollow in his chest. Perhaps enough to make the guilt and the sorrow go away.

He looked at the open door furtively. The corridor was empty. Boys were doing their prep. He didn't have much time before the house prefect would come looking for him, wondering why he wasn't in the day room where he belonged. Sitting on the floor, Harry untied his shoe, stripped off his sock, and put Matthew's on. It was a different shade from his own, so he put his own sock back on to cover it. His shoe was a bit snug as a result, but it didn't matter. Matthew's sock was safe.

Now there was only deciding who to trust.

15

When Patsy Whateley answered the door and Lynley saw that she was still wearing her yellow dressing gown with its mass of dragons, he asked himself why he had not earlier connected the dressing gown with what the Bonnamys had said about Matthew. The gown was obviously of a Chinese design, and seeing this seemed to give momentary credence, however unwarranted, to everything the Bonnamys had claimed.

Patsy Whateley looked at them for some moments without apparent comprehension. In the late afternoon, light was failing quickly and since the cottage curtains were drawn and no lamps were on in the sitting room, she stood in deep shadow, her features obscure. She pushed the door wide open and placed herself squarely in the gap, arms flaccid at her sides. Her dressing gown gaped open to reveal part of one breast sagging from her chest like a half-empty flour sack. Her feet were bare.

Sergeant Havers was the first to speak. She moved into the cottage as she did so. "Are you alone, Mrs. Whateley? What have you done with your slippers? Come, let me help you."

Lynley followed her inside and shut the door. That done, he became instantly and unavoidably aware of the foul, fishy odour that Patsy Whateley's unwashed body was lending to the cottage air. While Sergeant Havers did her best to straighten the woman's inadequate clothing, finding at least one of her slippers near the plaid chair, Lynley saw to the lights and cracked open one of the front windows to give at least some relief to the overpowering stench.

Sergeant Havers was speaking to Patsy Whateley as she worked at retying the cord round the woman's thick waist. "Isn't there someone we can ring, Mrs. Whateley? Have you relatives nearby? Is your husband at work?"

Patsy didn't respond. Lynley observed her in the light, noting the crusty skin that surrounded her eyes, the lack of colour in her face, the large circular stains beneath her armpits. Her movements were sluggish. He went into the kitchen.

It had not been cleaned or straightened since Patsy Whateley had baked her biscuits on the previous day. The biscuits lay scattered across the work tops, among the mixing bowls in which batter had hardened into irregular concretions. Utensils were everywhere— spoons, bowls, spatulas, cups, baking sheets, an electric mixer. They sat on the stove top, on the table, on the work top, and in the sink. This was partially filled with filmy water.

Lynley found the kettle sitting lopsided on a burner and carried it to the sink. Sergeant Havers joined him.

"I'll do this, sir," she said. "Perhaps I can find something for her to eat as well. I imagine she's not had anything since Sunday morning."

"Where's this woman's husband?" Lynley heard himself demand. He felt Sergeant Havers' eyes upon him.

"We each deal with loss in a different way," she responded.

"But not alone," he snapped. "There's no need for her to be alone."

Havers turned off the tap. "We're all alone, Inspector, when it comes down to it. With only a flaming illusion that we're anything else." She put the kettle on the stove and went to the refrigerator. "There's a bit of cheese in here. Some tomatoes as well. I'll see what I can do."

Lynley left her and returned to the sitting room where Patsy Whateley was slumped into the chair. Passing the electric fire, he saw the second of her slippers beneath it, and he took it to her, kneeling in front of her to slide it onto her unwashed foot. Holding her heel in his hand for a moment and feeling the hard, scabby surface of her skin, he was struck by unaccountable sorrow.

As he rose, she spoke. She sounded hoarse, as if it was a struggle to speak at all. "Slough police won't give me Mattie back. I rang them today. But they won't let us have him. So we can't even bury him."

Lynley sat on the sofa. The counterpane that had covered it previously lay in a heap on the floor. "You'll have Matthew back as soon as the autopsy is completed," he told her. "If the police get a backlog of work, it can take a few days. They run some lengthy tests."

Patsy plucked at the sleeve of her dressing gown. A crescent splatter of biscuit batter had dried to the material. "No point to that, is there? Mattie's dead. Nothing else matters."

"Mrs. Whateley." Lynley had never felt so useless. Fruitlessly he sought words of comfort, but he found nothing save a single piece of information that might give her some insubstantial relief. "You were right about Matthew."

"Right?" She licked at dry, chapped lips.

"We found his school clothes this morning. We're fairly certain his death occurred at Bredgar Chambers. You were right. He didn't run away."

The information seemed to give the woman a small degree of solace, for she nodded, and looked towards the boy's picture on the sideboard in the dining area. "Mattie wasn't a runner. Knew that from the first, didn't I? He wasn't brought up to run away if things were a trouble to him. Faced things head-on, did Matt. But I don't see why anybody would want to kill my boy."

It was this question that they had come to Hammersmith to address. Lynley sought a way to lead into it. His eyes passed over the room, coming to rest on the shelf beneath the front windows on which stood the souvenir cups and the marble sculptures. *Nautilus,* he saw, had been removed, but *Mother and Child* stood next to a nude woman who lay in an oddly contorted position with her back arched and her breasts pointed towards the sky. The mother and child, he saw, were linked together in stone by the curve of the mother's arm, an eternal conjunction, unbreakable and infinite. It was the metaphor he needed. His eyes on the sculpture, he asked the question.

"Have you any brothers and sisters, Mrs. Whateley?"

"Four brothers. A sister."

"Do any of your brothers have difficulty with colours as Matthew did?"

She looked perplexed. "No. Why?"

Sergeant Havers returned to them from the kitchen. She carried a tray on which she had assembled two cheese and tomato sandwiches, a cup of tea, three ginger biscuits. She set this in front of Patsy Whateley and urged a quarter of a sandwich into her hand. Lynley waited until Patsy had begun to eat before he went on.

"The inability to tell the difference between colours is a sex-linked characteristic," he explained. "Mothers pass it on to their sons. In order for Matthew to be colour deficient, he would have had to inherit that tendency from you, his mother."

"Mattie knew his colours," she said in weak protest. "Just a few he had trouble with."

"Blue and yellow," Lynley acknowledged. "The school colours at Bredgar Chambers." He guided her back to the central point. "You see, for you to be a carrier of a sex-linked characteristic—in this case, the inability to tell blue from yellow—your mother would have to be a carrier as well. That being the case, it would be unlikely that all four of your brothers would have escaped being affected, because it's a genetic mutation, something that gets passed along in the chromosomes when a child is conceived."

"What's this to do with Mattie's death?"

"It has more to do with his life than his death," Lynley said gently. "It suggests that Matthew wasn't your natural son."

Her hand still held the sandwich, but she dropped her arm to her lap. Part of a tomato slipped out and streaked red against the yellow of her dressing gown. "He didn't know. Mattie didn't know." She got up abruptly, letting the sandwich fall to the floor. She went for Matthew's photograph and brought it back to her chair. As she spoke, she gazed upon it, clutching the frame. "Our boy, was Mattie. Our real boy. It never made a bit of difference to us that he was born to someone else. Not a bit of difference. Never. He was ours from the time he was six months old. Such a good baby. Such a love, was Mattie."

"What do you know about his background? About his natural parents?"

"Little enough. Only that one of his parents was Chinese. But that made no difference to me or to Kev. He was our boy, was Mattie. Right from the start."

"You'd been able to have no children of your own?"

"Kev can't have children. We tried for years. I wanted to have that artificial thing, but Kev said no, said he wouldn't have me carrying another man's child, no matter how it was managed. We tried to adopt. Years and years. But no one would let us." She looked up, leaving the picture at rest in her lap. "Kev had trouble finding work that would last in those days, and even if he had, adoption folks didn't find a barmaid suited to be a mum."

Lynley saw how the puzzle was being completed and asked his next question, even though it was mere formality, even though he knew in advance what the answer would be. Circumstances had been conspiring to prepare him to hear it in a hundred different ways over the last two days. "How did you come to adopt Matthew?"

"Mr. Byrne—Giles Byrne—arranged it."

Patsy Whateley delineated the history of their relationship with Giles Byrne: how he had come into the Blue Dove regularly from his home a short distance away on Rivercourt Road; how he had come to know the barmaid through their nightly chats; how he seemed willing to listen to Patsy's tales of being rejected by adoption agencies; how he told her one night that a child was available if she didn't object to the fact that he was mixed race.

"We went to a solicitor's office in Lincoln's Inn. The baby was there. Mr. Byrne'd brought him. We signed the papers and brought Mattie home."

"That was all?" Lynley asked. "There was no exchange of money?"

Patsy Whateley looked horrified. "Did we buy our boy, you mean? No! We did nothing more than sign papers, we did. And then sign a few more when the adoption was final. Mattie was our real son right from the beginning. We never treated him otherwise."

"Did he know about his racial background?"

"Never. He never knew he was adopted. He was our real boy. Our *real* boy, Inspector."

"So you don't know who his natural parents are?"

"Didn't need to know, Kev and I. We didn't care to know, did we? Mr. Byrne just said he knew of a baby we could have. That's all that mattered. All we had to do was promise that we'd bring the boy up so as to allow him to have a better life than just Hammersmith. That was what Mr. Byrne asked us to do. That's all."

"A better life than Hammersmith? What exactly did Mr. Byrne mean by that?"

"The school, Inspector. In order to keep him, we had to promise to send Mattie to Bredgar Chambers, Mr. Byrne's old school."

"Maybe Giles Byrne's penchant for things Chinese extended to females," Sergeant Havers noted as they turned the corner from the Upper Mall onto Rivercourt Road. "We know he was fond of Edward Hsu. Why not fond of some female Chinese as well? Extremely fond, if you know what I mean."

"I haven't discounted the possibility that he's Matthew's natural father," Lynley responded.

"He won't be admitting that to us in a friendly tête-à-tête, Inspector. Not if he's managed to keep it quiet all these years. He's a fairly well-known public figure, after all. That BBC talk show, the political commentaries, the newspaper column. It might look a bit black against him, mightn't it, if an illegitimate son came to light? Especially a mixed race son that he abandoned. Especially if the mother was considerably younger than—perhaps ruined by—our Giles."

"We can't be sure of anything, Havers, until we see what sort of link, if any, we're forging between Matthew Whateley's parentage and his murder."

The Byrne house was only a short distance from the Upper Mall and the river. It was a three-storeyed, brick Victorian structure, without architectural merit other than that found in its passion for symmetry. This passion expressed itself in a repetition of windows—two on each floor—in the balanced ornamentation upon the front of the building, and in the design of the front door upon which knocker, post slot, and knob all lined up one beneath the other with recessed panels on either side. The door, Lynley saw, had suffered damage recently, for the wood was freshly scarred in several places and its white paint was smeared with streaks of dirt.

In the growing darkness, lights shone in the rooms at the front of the house, both on the ground floor and up above. When Lynley and Havers knocked on the door, it was opened within moments. They were not greeted by Giles Byrne, however, but rather by a beautiful Pakistani woman perhaps thirty years old. She wore a full-length ivory caftan of silk and a beaded necklace fashioned into a collar of gold. Combs held long, dark hair away from her face, and her gold earrings winked in the foyer light. She was obviously not a servant.

"How may I help you?" Her voice was low-pitched, pleasant, like a musical instrument.

Lynley produced his warrant card which she studied. "Is Mr. Byrne in?" he asked.

"Indeed. Of course." The woman stepped back from the door and motioned them to come inside. The gesture drew the sleeve of her caftan back along her smooth, dark skin. "If you'll wait there in the sitting room, Inspector, I shall fetch him for you. Please do help yourselves to a drink." She smiled. Her teeth were small, very white. "If you're still on duty, I shan't tell a soul. Do excuse me, if you will. Giles is working in the library." She left them, running lightly up the stairs.

"Not doing badly for himself in the love and companionship department, our Mr. Byrne," Havers muttered when they were alone.

"Or perhaps she's someone he's tutoring. Because he loves education. A real pedagogue, our Giles."

Lynley shot her a look and nodded her into the sitting room to the left of the front door. It faced Rivercourt Road, comfortably but not ostentatiously furnished with well-made pieces that would stand the test of time and use. The dominant colour was green, present in the pale washed lime of the walls, in the moss of the two sofas and the three chairs, in the rich, summer leaf of the carpet whose thickness muffled their footsteps. Across the top of a walnut piano that stood near the window were displayed an assortment of photographs, and Lynley went to examine these as they waited for Giles Byrne to join them.

The pictures acted as testament to the special gift that Byrne brought to his work as the host of one of the BBC's political talk shows. In them, he posed with an array of governmental notables representative of every possible philosophical bent from Margaret Thatcher to Neil Kinnock; from an ageing Harold Macmillan to the Reverend Ian Paisley to a scowling Bernadette Devlin; from three successive American Secretaries of State to one former President. At the side of each of these, Byrne looked the same—sardonic, mildly amused, neither attached nor devoted to anyone. The fact that Byrne was able to keep his political philosophy hidden was what had made him such a success as an interviewer for the BBC. He attacked a problem or a personality from any angle, acting as no one's advocate. He was a man whose acid wit and rapier tongue had torn apart many a cocksure political bigwig in his time.

"Edward Hsu," Sergeant Havers was saying meditatively.

Lynley saw that she had gone to the fireplace above which hung two watercolours, both views of the Thames. They possessed that delicacy of brushwork and misty etherealisation of detail peculiar to Eastern painting. In one, trees, banks, and brakes rose out of a ground fog and seemed to float as effortlessly as the barge nearby on the water at dawn. In the other, three pastel-clad women took shelter from a sudden rainfall on the porch of a riverside cottage, their picnic left disregarded behind. Both paintings were signed simply *E. Hsu.*

"Nice work, these," Havers said. She picked up a small photograph that stood on the mantel beneath them. "This must be Edward Hsu, then. A bit less formal than that snap of him in the chapel at the school." Her eyes moved round the room several times. She looked back down at the picture, frowning, saying slowly, "Inspector, there's something odd here."

Lynley joined her, took the picture from her hands. In it, Edward Hsu and a very young Brian Byrne posed, smiling, in one of the boats on what appeared to be the Serpentine in Hyde Park. Brian sat between Edward's legs, his little hands over Edward's on the oars.

"Odd?" Lynley asked.

Havers replaced the photograph and walked to a cedar bureau across the room. On it stood a copy of the same picture of Matthew Whateley that they had seen in his parents' cottage. Havers picked this up.

"We have Edward Hsu's picture. We have Matthew Whateley's picture. We have"—she gestured towards the piano—"a good half a dozen toffs and assorted swells. But only that one picture of Brian Byrne, in the boat with Edward Hsu. And what was Brian—three years old then? Four?"

"Nearly five."

The two words had come from the doorway. Giles Byrne stood watching them. In the foyer behind him, the Pakistani woman looked like a study of light and dark in her caftan.

"It's no secret that Brian and I are estranged," Byrne commented as he entered the room. His footsteps were slow. He looked extremely worn out. "At his choice, not mine." Momentarily, he gave his attention to his companion. "There's no need for you to stay, Rhena. You've a brief to work on for court next week, haven't you?"

"I wish to stay, my dear," she replied and moved across the room soundlessly to sit on the sofa. She slipped off a delicate pair of sandals and drew her legs up beneath her. Four thin gold bracelets slid down her arm. She directed her eyes towards Byrne and kept them upon him.

"As you wish, then." He went to a small coaching table on which stood decanters, glasses, and a bucket of ice. "A drink?" he asked Lynley and Havers over his shoulder. When they demurred, he took his time about pouring a straight whisky for himself and a mixture of several spirits for the woman. This done, he turned on the gas fire in the fireplace, adjusted the height of the flame, and carried both drinks to the sofa where he joined his companion.

If all this were an effort to stall for time, to marshal his thoughts, to assemble defences, or to demonstrate that he would control the interview, it also gave Lynley ample opportunity to study the man. Byrne was, he knew, somewhere in his mid-fifties, a man without any distinguishing physical beauty at all. Instead, oddities dominated his appearance. Quirks made him seem a caricature of him-self. He was nearly bald, with a thin fringe of hair that clung wispily to his crown and a tuft like a forelock drooping onto his brow. His nose was too large, his mouth and eyes were too small, and, from fore-head to chin, his face narrowed so dramatically that it resembled a perfect inverted triangle. He was quite tall and thin, and although his clothes appeared expensive—hand-loomed tweed, if Lynley wasn't mistaken—they hung upon him loosely. His long arms dangled from his jacket, emphasising large, knobby-knuckled hands. These were jaundiced-looking, particularly the fingers which, on left and right hand both, bore the stains of nicotine.

As Lynley and Havers sat, Byrne coughed catarrhally into a handkerchief before he lit a cigarette. Rhena reached for an ashtray on the table next to the sofa and held it in her right hand for him. She placed her left hand on his thigh.

"You no doubt know we've come to speak to you about Matthew Whateley," Lynley said to Byrne. "No matter where we've turned in the investigation so far, your name has come up as a recur-ring theme. We know Matthew was adopted, we know that you arranged the adoption, we know that Matthew was part Chinese. What we don't know—"

Byrne's cough broke into Lynley's words. He spoke abruptly once he had it controlled. "What does any of that have to do with the more salient fact that Matthew is dead? A child's been brutally murdered. God knows what sort of paedophile's on the loose. And you're checking into the boy's genealogy as if someone on his family tree might actually be responsible. I don't see how that makes any sense."

Lynley had witnessed Byrne at work often enough to recognise the ploy. He would put the subject on the defensive and batter him with a barrage of comments to which he felt he must give competent answers. Yet Lynley knew if he tried to deal with any of the com-ments, Byrne would move skilfully forward like the verbal swords-man he was, slicing his responses to bits with challenges to their credibility and consistency.

"I've absolutely no idea what it has to do with Matthew's murder," he said in reply. "That's what I've come to discover. I admit that my curiosity was piqued yesterday when I learned that you were once close to a Chinese student who killed himself. Piqued even more when I learned that, fourteen years after that student's death, you promoted another student—this one part Chinese—for a scholarship for which he was not the best qualified. And then that student ended up dead as well. Frankly, Mr. Byrne, in the past two days I've found myself running into far too many coincidences for all this not to be tied together in some fashion. Perhaps you'd like to address yourself to that."

Byrne took in this response from behind the smoke that curled upwards from his cigarette. "The facts of Matthew Whateley's birth have nothing whatsoever to do with his death, Inspector. But I'll tell them to you if that's what you're so intent upon discussing." He paused to tap his cigarette against the ashtray. He drew in on it again before he went on. His voice was raspy. "I knew of Matthew Whateley because I knew—and loved—his father. Edward Hsu." Byrne smiled as if reading a reaction on Lynley's face. "No doubt you were thinking that I was the father, a man with a fatal proclivity for things Chinese. Sorry if the truth's a disappointment to you. Matthew Whateley was no child of mine. I have only one son. You've met him."

"And Matthew's mother?" Lynley asked.

Byrne reached in his jacket pocket, brought out a packet of Dunhills, and lit a second cigarette from the glowing half-smoked stub of the first. This he crushed out in the ashtray, coughing viscously into his hand.

"It was a particularly unsavoury situation, Inspector. Matthew's mother wasn't some attractive little dewy adolescent with whom Edward had become enamoured. Considering the boy's single-minded devotion to his studies, a romantic entanglement with a sixteen- or seventeen-year-old girl was unlikely, to say the least. On the contrary, the mother was an older woman who seduced the boy. For the thrill of the conquest, I should guess, or the gratification of knowing she was still desirable, or the tremendous ego boost of having a younger man want to possess her. Choose which you will. I can only assume her motivation was one of them."

"You didn't know the woman?"

"I knew only what I managed to get Edward to tell me."

"What was that?"

Byrne sipped his whisky. Next to him on the sofa, Rhena sat motionless. Some moments before, her eyes had dropped to her hand on his leg. She kept them there.

"The barest facts. She invited him to tea several times. She professed an interest in his well-being. That's how it began. It ended in the bedroom. I'm sure it was a lubricious kick for the woman to initiate such an innocent into the rites of passion. And what a feather in her cap to be found desirable by a teenager on the brink of manhood. I suppose the only thing she didn't allow for was becoming pregnant by him. But once she was, she used her condition in a failed attempt to force Eddie to get money from his family. Extortion. Blackmail. Call it what you will."

"Is that why he killed himself?"

"He killed himself because he believed the school would expel him if the truth were told. The rules about sexual licence are fairly explicit. But even if that weren't the case, Eddie believed he'd dishonoured his family's name. They'd sent him to be educated at considerable cost. Sacrifices had been made for him, and he had disgraced them."

"How do you know all this, Mr. Byrne?"

"I'd tutored Eddie in written English since he was in the fourth form. He'd been here in my home nearly every holiday. I knew him. I was fond of him. I could see he was depressed in the last few months of his upper sixth year, and I didn't let up until I had the story from him."

"He wouldn't reveal the woman's identity?"

Byrne shook his head. "Eddie would have believed it was honourable to hold his tongue about that."

"I can't think that he didn't see—or wasn't told—how much more dishonourable killing himself would be," Lynley commented. "Especially in a situation that was not entirely of his own devising."

Byrne appeared completely unruffled, in spite of the accusation behind Lynley's words. "I don't intend to argue Eastern culture with you, Inspector. Or with anyone else. I'll just give you the facts. This *woman*"—he gave bitter emphasis to the word—"could have had an abortion without Eddie's ever being the wiser. But she wanted money, so she informed the boy that if he wasn't able to tell his family the truth, she would tell them herself. Or she would talk to the Headmaster to make sure that Eddie did 'his duty as a man.' It was a threat that led either way to disgrace and dishonour."

"Surely even at Bredgar Chambers there were extenuating circumstances," Lynley noted.

"I explained them to him. I told him that it wasn't all his fault, that he hadn't raped this woman, that he had been seduced, that the Headmaster would take this into account. But Eddie couldn't—he wouldn't—see beyond what he had done to himself, to his family, to the school. He couldn't study. He couldn't work. Nothing I said made the least bit of difference. I think he'd decided to kill himself once he learned about the pregnancy in the first place. He was only waiting for the opportunity."

"He left no note?"

"None."

"So only you know the truth."

"I knew what he told me. I didn't pass the story on."

"Not even to the boy's parents? You didn't tell them that they were going to have a grandchild?"

Byrne's answer was weighted heavily by disgust. "Of course not. To tell them that would have made Eddie's death even more sense-less than it already was. He died to protect them from knowledge he believed would hurt them. Holding my own tongue respected his wish to protect them. It was the least I could do."

"But you did more than that, didn't you? You went after the child. How did you find him?"

Byrne handed his empty glass to Rhena, who placed it on the table. "The only piece of information he gave me about the woman was that she'd gone to Exeter to have the baby. I hired someone to track her down. It wasn't difficult. Exeter isn't that large, after all."

"And the woman?"

"I never knew her name. I didn't want to know it. Once I'd discovered that she'd left the baby behind for adoption, I didn't care any longer what happened to the bitch."

"Was she someone from the school?"

"From the school, from the village, from the area. That's all I know. After Eddie's death, all I cared about was somehow making sense out of the waste by seeing to it that his son at least had a decent life. I knew the Whateleys. I arranged for them to adopt the baby."

Still, there was a nagging problem—a snag in Byrne's story—that couldn't be ignored. "Surely there were many people ahead of the Whateleys hoping to adopt a child. How did you manage to pull strings to get past them?"

"A mixed race child?" Byrne scoffed. "You must know that the line of people wanting mixed race children doesn't exactly stretch to infinity."

"And even if it did at that time, I expect you exerted enough power to see to it that the Whateleys got the boy."

Byrne lit a third cigarette from the second. Rhena extinguished the second one for him, removing it from between his fingers and crushing it out in the ashtray.

"I admit that. I don't regret it. They're good, hard-working people without pretensions."

"People willing to submit to your holding on to the reins of power in Matthew's life?"

"If that means allowing me to make crucial decisions about the boy's education and his future, yes, they submitted. They wanted the best for him, after all. They were grateful enough to have him. So everyone won under the arrangement. I could keep my eye on Eddie's son as he grew. The Whateleys finally had the child they longed for. Matthew was placed in a loving home, with a future that went beyond the boundaries of his family's life. No one lost."

"Save Matthew. Save the Whateleys. In the end."

Byrne leaned forward in a quick, angry movement. "Do you think I feel nothing about this boy's death?"

"How much does your son Brian know about the circumstances of Matthew Whateley's birth?"

Byrne looked surprised. "Nothing. Only that Eddie committed suicide. He didn't even know that much for years."

"Brian doesn't live with you during the holidays, does he?"

The other man's face remained impassive. "He used to live with me, but when he went away to school, he decided he'd prefer to spend the holidays with his mother in Knightsbridge. A bit more fashionable than Hammersmith."

"Fashion generally doesn't dictate where a teenage boy will live. I should think he'd prefer to be with his father."

"Another sort of boy might, Inspector, but not Brian. My son and I parted ways nearly five years ago when he entered Bredgar Chambers and discovered that I wasn't about to put up with his constant snivelling about the school."

"Snivelling? About what? Was he bullied?"

"He was ragged, as are all new boys. But he couldn't face it, so he wanted to come home. He wanted to be rescued. He phoned here every night. I finally stopped accepting his calls. I wouldn't consider withdrawing him from the school, and he was bitter about that. So he went to his mother. I suppose he saw it as a way to punish me. But that didn't solve his problem. The last thing Pamela wanted was a thirteen-year-old boy hanging about her flat. She agreed to have him on sufferance only during the holidays. But the rest of the time, he was packed off to the school. I see him there occasionally, but nowhere else."

It was the ill-concealed acrimony behind Byrne's words that prompted Lynley to ask the man how much time he spent with

Matthew Whateley and whether Brian was aware of the depth of Byrne's interest in the boy.

Byrne's quick response indicated his understanding of where the questions were heading. "Can you possibly be suggesting that Brian murdered Matthew because he was jealous of a relationship that I shared with the boy? A substitute son?" He didn't wait for an answer. "I saw Matthew only occasionally—on the green or by the river where he played. His parents kept me apprised of the boy's progress in school, and I interviewed him as part of the procedure to get him into Bredgar Chambers on the governors' scholarship. But that was the extent of my relationship with him. I did what I could for him out of love for Edward. And I don't deny loving Edward. He was a brilliant pupil, worthy of anyone's love. He was like a son. He was more than a son, certainly more than the son I have now. But he's dead, and I didn't replace him with Matthew. What I did for Matthew, I did because of Edward."

"And for Brian?"

Byrne's lips thinned. "I've done what I can. What he'll allow me to do."

"Such as seeing to it that he was made a house prefect?"

"I don't deny that. I thought the experience would be good for him. I pulled strings where I could. He needs it on his record if he wants to go to university."

"He hopes for Cambridge. Did you know that?"

Byrne shook his head. "We don't communicate. Obviously, he doesn't find me the most empathetic of fathers."

Nor, Lynley thought, the most accessible role model. The lack of physical beauty aside, how could any son hope to compete with a father having Giles Byrne's background, his reputation and accomplishments? Not to mention his inexplicable success with at least one beautiful woman.

"What kind of role did you play in getting Alan Lockwood his appointment to the school?" Lynley asked curiously.

"I urged the Board of Governors to offer him the job," Byrne admitted. "New blood was needed. Lockwood had it."

"I expect his presence allows you to have considerably more authority on the Board of Governors now, perhaps more power than you would otherwise have."

"That's the nature of any political system, Inspector. Power."

"Something you like, I should imagine."

Byrne took out his packet of cigarettes and lit up again. "Don't deceive yourself about power, Inspector. It's something everyone likes."

Rain began to fall in earnest as Kevin Whateley passed beneath Hammersmith Bridge onto the Lower Mall. Showers had been threatening all day, and the air had been heavy with humidity. But the sporadic drops that generally presage coming storms had not begun to sprinkle pavement and pedestrians until Kevin emerged from the tube at half-past five to tramp towards the river. Even then it seemed that the weather would not actually break. But as he made his way down Queen Caroline Street, the wind picked up force, clouds scudded across the sky, and within moments a prodigious downpour had begun to glaze both streets and pavements with a fine sheen of water.

Emerging from the shelter of the bridge, Kevin lifted his face to the pelting rain. It came from the northeast, chilled by the unforgiving winds of the North Sea, and it felt like countless icy rifle-driven needles, burning and stinging his cracked and weathered skin. The pain was good.

Beneath his arm he carried a slab of pink marble lightly veined with cream. He had seen it leaning against a large block of granite yesterday morning, earmarked for a memorial to be placed in the small church next to Hever Castle. He had kept his eye on the marble throughout the day, had determined the best time and the best manner in which to pinch it with no one's being the wiser. In the past, he had often taken discarded pieces home from the memorial works. Most of his sculptures had been created from these cast-offs, bits and pieces ruined by the careless handling of a drill or the slipping of a chisel. This, however, was the first time he had taken a stone in pristine condition. Had he been caught in the act, it might have cost him his job. It still might, once a search of the dusty warehouse and work yard proved the marble was missing. But Kevin didn't care whether he was given the sack or not. All the years of toil at tombstone carving had been endured for Mattie. For his benefit, for his welfare, for his future. Now that he was gone, what did it matter where or even if his father worked again?

Rain made the marble slippery. Kevin shoved it more forcefully under his arm. Above him, the tall black streetlamps shattered the dark with a light that the raindrops diffracted like prisms. He passed beneath them, slogging through puddles in his heavy boots, mindless of the cold, heedless of the water that soaked his head and shoulders and seeped into his clothes. He was thoroughly drenched by the time he arrived at his cottage door.

It was unlocked, not even completely latched, and without loosening his grip upon the stone, Kevin shouldered the door open and stepped inside. His wife, he saw, was sitting in the old plaid chair with Mattie's picture on her lap. She stared at it without looking up. In front of her on the coffee table, a plate held some half-eaten sandwiches and three ginger biscuits. The sight of these stirred Kevin to unaccountable anger. That she could even *think* of food . . . that she could even want to make herself a sandwich . . . He felt bitter words of castigation rising in his throat, but he forced them down.

"Kev . . ."

It made no sense that she should sound so weak. She'd been keeping her strength up good and proper with her sandwiches all the day, no doubt. He passed her without speaking and went to the stairway on the other side of the fireplace.

"Kev . . ."

His feet thudded against the bare wood. His sodden clothes dripped water everywhere. Once, the marble slipped and gouged the wall. But he continued to climb, past the first-floor landing and on to the second floor to Matthew's bedroom, a small room under the eaves with a single dormer window through which muted light glimmered from the embankment outside and fell upon the sculpture *Nautilus* which Kevin had carried to this room on the previous night and placed on Matthew's chest of drawers. He couldn't have said why he had done so, only that it seemed fitting that the room be made as much Matthew's as possible now he was gone. Bringing *Nautilus* up was the first step. Others would follow.

Gingerly he lowered the marble slab to the floor, resting it against the chest of drawers. Straightening, he was confronted with *Nautilus* again, and he reached out to touch the stone. He ran his thumb along the curve of the shell, closing his eyes at the feeling of its smooth, cool surface. He traced the entire shape of the mollusc, coming to know the difference between the finished shell and the roughly hewn marble that surrounded it.

It'll be like a fossil, Dad. D'you see in this picture? Like something you'd dig up. Or find embedded in the side of a cliff. What d'you think? Is it a good idea? Can I have a bit of stone to do it?

He could hear the voice, so loving, so clear. It was as if the boy were with him in the room, as if he had never left Hammersmith at all. So near to him now. Mattie felt so near.

Kevin fumbled for the pulls on the top drawer in the chest and jerked it open. His hands were shaking. By clutching onto the drawer, he stopped them from doing so, but that action did nothing to quell his ragged breathing. The rain was beating against the cottage roof, gushing through drainpipes, and for several moments he concentrated on these sounds, allowing them to drive everything else from his mind. He sought control, finding it in focusing on a thin stream of air that seeped from beneath the closed window to cool the back of his neck.

Blindly his hands felt through the few objects in the drawer he had pulled open. He lifted them out, examining them, folding and refolding them, smoothing creases away. Everything was old, no longer used, inadequate or unworthy to be taken to school. Three tattered jerseys Mattie would wear when scouting along the banks of the Thames; two pairs of underpants with elastic gone bad; a miniature railway sign; an old pair of socks; a cheap vinyl belt; a misshapen knitted cap. Kevin's hands dwelt longest upon this last object, picking at the ridges of wool. Effortlessly he pictured Mattie wearing it, pulled low upon his brow, his eyebrows hidden and his nose scrunched up against the scratch of the material upon his skin. Winter, it would be, when the wind howled off the river and beat against the walls. But they would be out in it, the two of them, bundled into their pea jackets, heading for the dock.

Dad! Dad! Let's take out a boat!

In this weather? Y're daft, lad.

No! Let's do it! Say we can! Dad? Dad! Say we can!

Kevin squeezed his eyes shut, as if doing so would put an end to the voice that rang in his ears so joyously, over the sound of the rain, over the groan of the wind, over the rush of water down the eaves to the pipes. Woodenly he turned from the chest of drawers and made his way to Matthew's bed. Mindless of his wet clothes, he sat on the edge, reaching for the pillow which he held to his face. He breathed in deeply, longing to catch the scent of his son. But the pillowcase had been laundered—the sheets as well—and if they smelled of anything, it was of the odour of lemons, an olfactory residue of the detergent Patsy used.

Kevin felt the surge of a grievance at this. It was as if Patsy had known their son was going to die, so she had busied herself in getting everything ready, laundering his bed linen, sweeping out his room, folding his clothes into the drawers. Damn the woman's determination that life be neat and tidy! Had she not been so concerned that everything be scrubbed—including Mattie himself—

there well might have been something left of the boy in this room. Even some scent of him. Damn her to hell.

"Kev?" She stood in the doorway, a lumpy shadow in a rumpled dressing gown. The hem was uneven, pulled up on one side above her knee. The front gaped, sagging open with the weight of her breasts. Stains marred the silk. It was not at all the same garment that Matthew had given her just this last Christmas.

Colonel Bonnamy and Jean said you're to have this, Mum. They said you'd fancy it specially. Do you? Do you fancy it, Mum? I've got these slips as well, you see. But I couldn't quite tell if they matched the dragons.

Kevin searched for a hardness within himself that would prove impenetrable to the force of memory. The boy was dead. *Dead.* Nothing could bring him back.

He saw his wife take a tentative step into the room.

"Police were here again," she said.

"What of it?" He heard his anger.

"Mattie didn't run off, Kev."

Kevin thought he discerned some relief behind her words, some cessation to pain. He couldn't believe it. That she had actually allowed a paltry piece of news to make a difference in the fact that their son was dead. Not just gone away to school. Not just on a visit to a friend's. But dead. Gone. Part of forever.

"Did you hear me, Kev? Mattie didn't—"

"Blast your soul, woman! Do you think I care? What bloody difference does that make to what's happened?"

She flinched but continued to speak. "We did tell the police that he wouldn't run off, didn't we? We were right, Kev. Mattie wasn't a runner. Not our Matt." She took a second step into the room. Her slippers flopped hollowly against the bare wooden floor. "They found his clothes at the school. So they think he was still there when he . . . when he . . ."

Kevin's muscles contracted. His chest tightened. Behind his eyes, the pressure built. It throbbed in his brain.

"Police know all about Matt. They guessed it from him not knowing his colours somehow. They know he . . . he . . . they know he wasn't ours, Kev. I told them how we came to have him with us. About Mr. Byrne. About—"

He broke. "Wasn't ours? Wasn't *ours*? Who was the boy if he wasn't ours, woman? Matt's birth is none of their business. D' you hear me, Pats? None of their fucking business!"

"But they need to know as much—"

"They need to know bloody nothing! There's no point, is there? The boy's gone. He's dead. He's never coming back! And nothing some poncey police detective does will ever change that. D'you hear me? *Nothing.*"

"They have to find out who murdered him, Kev. They must do that."

"It won't bring him back! Damn you to hell, don't you see that? Have you lost what little sense you had? Bloody fool! *Fool!*"

She gave an inarticulate cry, the sound of an innocent animal being struck. "I wanted to help."

"*Help?* Christ Jesus, woman, you wanted to help?" Kevin clutched the pillow. Still dirty from the memorial works, his hands created dark smudges against the pale linen. As did his work jeans on the counterpane.

"You're dirtying up Mattie's bed." Patsy sounded querulous and old. "It'll have to be changed now, won't it?"

Kevin's head flew up. "Why?" he asked, and when she didn't respond, he began to shout, the question ugly with violence suppressed. "Why, Pats? *Why?*"

She didn't reply. Rather, she took a step back towards the door. Her hand reached up for the back of her neck. It was a gesture her husband recognised well, a prelude to pretended confusion, a prelude to escape. He refused to allow it.

"I asked you a question. You answer me."

She stared. In the shadows, her eyes were dark depressions in her face, unreadable, lacking feeling and depth. That she should stand there and talk about dirty bed linen . . . that she should even care to think about laundry right now . . . that she should make sandwiches, drink tea, talk to the police . . . and all the while their son's body lay in storage in Slough, waiting for dissection, giving its beauty to the knife.

"Answer me, woman."

She turned to leave. He surged off the bed, crossed the room in three steps, grabbed her arm, spun her to face him.

"You don't walk out when I'm talking to you. You don't ever do that. You don't *ever.*"

She jerked away. "Let me alone!" Spittle spewed from her lips. "You're mad, Kevin. Sick and mad and—"

He struck her across the face with his open palm. She cried out, struggling to free herself from his grasp.

"No! Don't you—"

He hit her again, fist closed this time, feeling the sharp, brutal contact of his knuckles slamming against her jaw. Her head snapped back. She would have staggered, would have fallen against the door, but his grip upon her arm didn't break.

She cried only, "Kev!"

He shoved her into the wall, butted his head against her chest, savagely pounded her ribs. He ripped open her dressing gown, beating her thighs. He clawed at her breasts.

He filled the air with curses as foul as he could make them. But he did not cry.

16

Rather than use the underground parking, Lynley pulled up to the revolving door that gave access to the reception area of New Scotland Yard. The last of the departmental secretaries and clerks were making their exits for the day, heading towards the entrance to St. James's Park Station across the street. Sergeant Havers sighed as she watched them leave, opening their umbrellas against the rain.

"If I'd only had the sense to choose a different career, I might have had a lifestyle that would allow me regular meals," Havers said.

"But nowhere near the psychic satisfaction one gets from knowing the thrill of the chase."

"Exactly my reaction to Giles Byrne," she replied. "Although *thrill* hardly does it justice. Convenient, wouldn't you say, that he's the only person who knows the reason behind Edward Hsu's suicide?"

"No. There's another, Sergeant."

"Who?"

"Matthew's natural mother."

"*If* you want to believe that story."

"Do we have a reason not to?"

She hooted. "Sitting right there next to him on the couch, Inspector. Giving him a quick squeeze and a feel when the going got tough. Rhena. Wasn't that her name? Don't tell me our Giles doesn't like the foreign ladies. But as to why they like him . . . God, I couldn't even tell you. For all we know, Edward Hsu had a sister or a cousin or a significant someone who got too friendly with our little Giles and once he had his way with her and made our Matthew, he deserted her. Faced with the knowledge that his tutorial god had feet of clay, Eddie offed himself by taking a jump from the chapel roof."

"That theory has some decidedly nice elements, Havers. Something between a Greek tragedy and a medieval morality play. The only trouble I have with it is one of credibility. Do you really believe that the boy would kill himself over discovering Giles Byrne's fatal flaw? Be it infidelity, lack of moral fibre, inability to keep a commitment to duty, or anything else."

"It's a thought. I'd hold fast to it if I were you, sir. Mark my words. Our Giles wasn't telling us the truth. Not by half. And my money's on the fact that little Rhena knew it. He could lie like the devil and get away with it. But she didn't look at us once while he was talking. Did you notice that?"

Lynley nodded, reaching for the door handle. "It was curious, wasn't it?"

"Then what do you think about having a go at looking into his story in Exeter? How many homes can there be that take pregnant women? Wouldn't the birth be registered? We'd be fools to accept Byrne's story at face value."

"We would," Lynley agreed. He pushed open the car door. "Set Constable Nkata on it, Havers. In the meantime, let's see if we've anything from the Slough police."

They dashed through the rain into the reception area of New Scotland Yard. There, two plainclothes receptionists were chatting with the uniformed constable who stood at the barrier that separated the public waiting area from the guarded world of policework. His hands draped over the metal sign upon which black letters demanded the presentation of warrant cards and office passes. As Lynley and Havers reached for their identification, one of the two receptionists spoke.

"You've a visitor, Inspector. Been waiting since half-past four." She nodded towards the wall on which was mounted the illuminated manuscript that celebrated on each page a distinguished piece of duty by a police officer.

On one of the chrome and vinyl chairs beneath this memorial sat a schoolgirl, still in uniform, with a satchel pressed close to her side and held in place by her arm, as if in fear of its being snatched away. She was watching the eternal flame across the room.

Lynley had heard of her, had seen her in the photograph in Matthew Whateley's barn stall at Bredgar Chambers. But he had not been prepared for the fact that she looked far older than her thirteen years. Her skin was tawny, her eyes nearly black, her features perfectly sculptured on her face. Yvonnen Livesley, Lynley thought, Matthew's old mate from Hammersmith.

When he crossed the lobby to the girl and introduced himself, she scrutinised him openly. "Your identification," she said. "If you will." He produced it. She read it. Her large eyes moved from it to his face. Dozens of her beaded plaits clicked together as she stood, nodding in satisfaction. "I've something to give you, Inspector. From Matt."

In Lynley's office, Yvonnen pulled a chair close to his desk. She pushed aside a stack of mail, putting her satchel in its place.

"I didn't hear about Matt until this morning," she said. "One of the blokes at school had it from his mum who had it from her sister who knows Matt's aunt. When I heard . . ." She fumbled momentarily with the satchel's buckle. "I wanted to go home at once and fetch this, didn't I, but the Headmistress wouldn't let me. Even when I told her it was police business. She treated me like a joke." She unfastened the buckle, pulled the satchel open, and placed a cassette tape on Lynley's desk. "Here's what you want, then. Here's the flaming bastard what killed him."

That said, she sat and waited for Lynley's reaction. Sergeant Havers closed the office door and took her place at the second chair.

Lynley picked up the tape. "What is this?"

Yvonnen nodded briskly, as if the question indicated he had passed a test of her private devising. She crossed one leg over the other and tossed back her hair. The beads jangled rhythmically. Reaching into the satchel a second time, she brought out a small tape recorder.

"The tape came in the post just three weeks past," she explained. "Matt sent a note as well, telling me to keep it in the safest place I could find. Told me not to tell anyone about it, not to say I had it, not to say I'd even heard from him at all. He said it was a duplicate of one he had at the school and he'd explain everything when he saw me. That was all. I listened to it once, but I didn't . . . I didn't understand, did I? Until what happened to Matt. Listen."

She took the tape from him and slid it into the recorder. A boy's voice cried out—an indistinguishable word. It was followed by a grunt, a dull thud, and the hollow sound of thumping, as if a body had fallen against a bare floor and was being pounded repeatedly against it. A second cry was muffled. Then someone began to speak, a sinister whisper that was cold with a vicious perversity.

"Want a grind, nancy boy? Want a grind? Want a grind? Oooh, what's this nice little thing in our panties? Hmmm? Let's have a better look . . ."

Another cry. Another voice.

"Leave off. Come on. Leave off. Let him be!"

And then the first voice again, lower pitched in contrast to the second. "Oooh, *you* want some as well? Come here. Have a look."

A third voice, fractured, close to tears. "Please. No."

Then laughter. "You know you want it, nancy boy. You know how you do." The sound of a blow. A cry muffled again.

Lynley leaned forward, switched the tape off.

"There's more," Yvonnen said in a rush. "It gets worse and worse. Don't you want to hear it?"

"How do you come to have this?" Lynley asked in response.

Yvonnen ejected the tape and put it on the desk. "It gets worse," she said again. "When I listened to it first, I didn't understand. I thought . . . these boys, you see. They're at this posh school. And things like this . . ." She stumbled wretchedly. For all the sophistication of her appearance and demeanour, she was indeed only thirteen years old.

Lynley waited until she had regained her composure. "You're not to blame, Yvonnen," he told her. "No one could expect you to understand what any of this meant. Just tell me what you know, as far as you know it."

She raised her head. "Over the Christmas hols, Matt came round to see me. He asked me to show him how to wire a room for sound."

"That sounds an unusual request."

"Not from Matt to me. I play about with bugging devices. Matt knew that. I've been doing it for the last two years."

"Bugging devices?"

"Like a hobby. I started out with just a tape recorder. In a soup tureen in the dining room. But now I use directional mikes. I like sounds. I want to do sound in films or for the telly. Like the bloke in *Blow Out*. Did you see that film?"

"No."

"*He* did sound in films. That's how I got interested. It was John Travolta," she added ingenuously. "I'm dead good at it now. I wasn't at first. The dining room sound from the soup tureen was all echoey, so I knew I couldn't just hide a recorder. I needed something better. Something smaller."

"A bug."

"Just before Christmas I did my mum's bedroom because I thought she might tell her boyfriend what presents I was getting. But the tape was dead boring. Just her moaning and groaning when her boyfriend did it to her and him saying things like 'Oh, baby.' I played it for Matt for a bit of a lark. And a tape of two masters talking at school. *That* one I did with a directional mike. From fifty yards. It was good."

"That gave Matthew the idea of wiring a room at the school?"

She nodded. "All he would say was that he wanted to bug some room at the school and he wanted to know the best way to do it. He didn't have any experience at it, but he was right earnest about getting it done. I thought he was doing it as a bit of a joke, so I told him the best thing would be to use a voice activated tape recorder. I loaned him this old one here. It came back in the post with the tape."

"Did he tell you whose room he was wiring?"

"He didn't tell me who. He just asked how to do it. I told him to hide the mike in a place where he wouldn't get distortion from other noises, where he could still be sure he'd pick up the sounds he was interested in, where it wouldn't be seen. I told him to check out the location in advance and run at least two rehearsals to make sure he got top quality sound. He asked one or two questions and took the recorder with him, but he never mentioned it after that. Then three weeks past, he sent me this tape."

"Did he talk to you much about the school, Yvonnen? About his friends there? About how he was getting on?"

She shook her head slowly. "Just that it was all right. Nothing else. Just all right. But . . ." She frowned, played disconsolately with the buckle of her satchel.

"There's something more?"

"Only that . . . he always changed the subject if I asked him about the school. Like he didn't want to talk about it, but he knew he would if I pressed him. I wish I had."

"Let's see what kind of cobblers we've got. Come on. Let's see. Oooh, little ones, aren't they? Give 'em a squeeze. Will he cry now? What y'think? Will he cry?"

"No! Stop! Please! I shan't—"

Lynley pressed the Off button as Sergeant Havers reentered his office. As before, she closed the door. But instead of sitting, she went to the window. Rain beat a sharp tattoo against the glass. She sipped from a disposable cup she was carrying. Lynley caught the fragrance of chicken soup.

"Did you send her off safely?" he asked.

"Constable Nkata's driving her home." Havers smiled wearily. "He took one look at her, saw the future in an instant, introduced himself, and volunteered for the duty."

"Transparent as usual."

"Nothing new in that." Havers joined him at the desk, slumping onto one of the chairs. She meditated upon the yellow globules of liquid fat that dotted the surface of her soup. With a grimace, she drained the cup and tossed it in the rubbish. "It looks like we've come full circle."

Lynley rubbed his eyes. They felt strained, as if he had been trying to read without his spectacles. "Possibly," he replied.

"More than possibly," she argued mildly. "We've got bullying on the tape. Just where we were yesterday morning, Inspector. You said that the third formers you spoke with seemed afraid, didn't you? Now we know why. Someone was after Matt Whateley on a regular basis. For all the rest of the boys knew, they were next."

Lynley shook his head. He ejected the tape. "I don't see it that way, Havers."

"Why not?"

"Because he told Yvonnen he wanted to wire someone else's room for sound, not his own."

"The bully's room, then."

"I'd agree with you, except there were other voices on the tape, not just the bully and his victim. The voices were young, third formers I should imagine."

"Then who—"

"It has to be Harry Morant. Look how the pieces fit if we argue it's Harry and not Matthew who was being bullied. Whoever did the bullying was breaking school rules, no doubt over a period of time. A school like Bredgar Chambers isn't going to put up with this sort of abuse, so the bully faced certain expulsion if he was found out. Matthew knew about the bullying. Everyone knew. But they were all caught up in the code of behaviour that we spoke of before."

"Not sneaking on another student?"

"Look how that affected Matthew. Kevin Whateley indicated that the boy had become more and more withdrawn during the last term. But Patsy said that there was never a mark on him, so it's safe to say that no one was harming him. Add that to what Colonel Bonnamy told us about the conversation he and Matthew had concerning the school's motto—'Let honour be both staff and rod.' Everything fits. That unwritten code of behaviour demanded that Matthew hold his tongue about the bullying of Harry Morant. But the school's motto demanded that he take action to stop the bullying himself. That was the honourable thing to do. So he withdrew from his parents as he tried to decide how to uphold the school motto at the same time as he didn't violate the unwritten code that was supposed to govern his behaviour among his peers. This tape represents his decision."

"Blackmail?"

"Yes."

"Jesus. It cost him his life."

"It probably did."

Her eyes widened. "Then one of the *pupils* . . . Sir, all of them must know."

He nodded. His face was grim. "If this is the reason behind Matthew's death, I think they've known from the first, Sergeant. All of them."

He reached for the stack of the day's post that Yvonnen Livesley had pushed to one side of his desk. Absently he looked through it, finding the postcard midway through the stack.

Like the other, it had come from Corfu, a photograph of the brilliant white buildings of the Monastery of Our Lady of Vlacherna set against the vibrant blue of the sea. The wooded height of Kanoni rose in the distance. Unlike the other, earlier postcard, however, the message on this one began with no salutation, as if by omitting his name, Helen was managing to do what she had set out to do: distancing herself from him more and more every day.

> Two days of dreary rain! With the only entertainment being a
> prolonged visit to the museum at Garitsa. I know what you're
> thinking. The lion of Menekrates *is* perfectly sweet, but after
> an hour of gazing upon him, one does long for something more
> animate as a diversion. But desperate times call for desper-
> ate measures. I've given myself wholeheartedly to relics and coins
> and bits of temple under glass. I shall be so cultured that you'll
> hardly know me upon my return. H.

Aware that Sergeant Havers' eyes were on him, Lynley shoved the card into his jacket pocket, trying to keep his face indifferent, trying to refrain from rereading the last three words, trying to keep himself from hoping they meant that Helen would at last bring her Greek exile to an end.

"So," Havers said breezily with a nod at his jacket pocket, "nothing new on that score, I take it?"

"Nothing new."

As he spoke, a sharp knock at the door heralded the entrance of Dorothea Harriman, secretary to Lynley's divisional superintendent. She was dressed for her evening's departure in typically Walesian fashion, wearing a tailored green suit, white blouse, a triple strand of cultured pearls, and a curiously shaped hat sprouting green and white feathers. Beneath it, her hair was cut to match the Princess' latest style.

"Thought I'd catch you still here," she said, leafing through a stack of folders she cradled in one arm. "This lot was phoned in for you this afternoon, Detective Inspector Lynley. From"—her refusal to wear spectacles caused her to squint down at the scrawl across the front of the folder—"Detective Inspector Canerone. Slough police. Preliminary autopsy results on—" Again the squint. Lynley got to his feet.

"Matthew Whateley," he finished, extending his hand for the folder.

"Is Deb home as well?" Lynley asked as he followed Cotter up the narrow stairway in the St. James house. It was nearly eight o'clock, an unusual time for St. James still to be working in his laboratory. To bury himself in forensic tasks into the night had long been his habit in the past, but Lynley knew he had given that up in the last three years that marked his engagement and his marriage to Deborah.

Cotter shook his head. He paused on the stairs, and although most of his face was unreadable, he could not keep the concern from his eyes. "Been out most of the day. Some Cecil Beaton exhibit at the Victoria and Albert she wanted to see. Shopping as well."

It was a poor excuse. The Victoria and Albert Museum was long since closed for the day, and Lynley knew Deborah well enough to know how little she relished browsing through department stores. "Shopping?" he asked sceptically.

"Hmm." Cotter continued climbing.

They found St. James bent over one of the comparison microscopes, making minute adjustments to the focus. A camera was attached to it, in preparation for documenting whatever two objects he was currently examining. Near the window—closed against the undulating pattern of the continuing rainfall—his computer was rhythmically spilling out sheets of paper upon which graphs and columns of numbers were printed.

"Lord Asherton's 'ere to see you, Mr. St. James," Cotter said. "Will you be wanting coffee, brandy? The like?"

St. James raised his head. Lynley saw with a jolt that his thin face was drawn, as if marked by sorrow and drained by fatigue. "Nothing for me, Cotter," he replied. "For you, Tommy?"

Lynley declined and said nothing more until Cotter had left them alone together. Even then, finding a safe foundation upon which to construct a conversation with his friend was a delicate task. There was too much history between them, too many areas forbidden to discussion.

Lynley drew out one of the stools from beneath the worktable and slid a manila folder next to the Zeiss microscope. St. James opened it, scanned the information scrawled on the documents inside.

"These are the preliminary results?" he asked.

"Such as they are. Toxicology shows nothing, St. James. And there's no trauma at all to the body."

"The burns?"

"Made by cigarettes, as we thought. But certainly not enough damage to kill him."

"It says here they've found fibres in the hair," St. James noted. "What sort of fibres? Natural? Synthetic? Have you talked to Canerone?"

"I spoke to him right after I read the report. All he could tell me at the time was that his forensic team were saying the fibres appeared to be a blend. Natural and synthetic. The natural one is wool. They're still waiting for the test results on the other."

St. James gazed thoughtfully at the floor. "From your description I was thinking of the way hemp is treated when it's turned into rope. But that obviously isn't what they're dealing with when they talk of natural and synthetic substances. Especially if they know one of them is wool."

"That was my first thought as well. But the boy was tied with cotton cording, not with rope. Probably heavy shoelaces, according to Canerone's forensic team. And Matthew was double-gagged, St. James. There were fibres of wool in his mouth."

"A sock."

"Perhaps. That was tied in place with a cotton handkerchief. There were trace deposits of cotton on his face."

St. James went back to the previous information. "What are they making of these fibres in his hair, then?"

"A number of hypotheses. Possibly from something he was laid against. Material from the carpet on the floor of a car, an old jacket in the boot, a blanket, a tarpaulin. Virtually anything that's made of or covered by material. They've gone back to St. Giles' Church to take samples inside, on the off chance that the body was kept there prior to being dumped in the field."

"I'd guess that'll be a useless exercise."

Lynley played with an unopen box of slides. "It's a possibility. But I'm hoping against it. Far better for the investigation if the fibres in his hair are from something in the location where he was held captive. And he *was* held captive, St. James. The pathologist sets the time of death between midnight and four A.M. on Saturday. That leaves at least twelve hours unaccounted for, from the time Matthew disappeared right after lunch to the time of his death. He had to be somewhere on the grounds of the school. Perhaps the fibres will tell us where. In addition to that"—Lynley flipped over a page of the report and pointed to a section of inconclusive findings—"they've come up with some sort of trace deposits on his buttocks, his shoulder blades, his right arm, and under two of his toenails. They're putting them all through a gas chromatograph to be certain, but microscopically they appear to be the same thing."

"Again, something from where he was held?"

"It seems a reasonable conclusion, doesn't it?"

"A reasonable hope. You sound as if you're heading in a fairly clear direction at this point, Tommy."

"I think I am." Lynley told him about the tape.

St. James listened without remark, his sombre expression unaltering. But at the end of Lynley's explanation, he looked away. His attention seemed to focus on a shelf across the lab upon which were assembled jars of labelled chemicals, assorted beakers, burettes, and pipettes.

"Bullying," he said. "I thought schools had put an end to that."

"They're trying. Expulsion's the penalty." Lynley added to this, "John Corntel's at Bredgar Chambers. Do you remember him from Eton?"

"King's Scholar in classics. Always with a dozen or so admiring E Block thirteen-year-olds tagging behind him wherever he went. He'd be hard to forget." St. James grasped the report again. He frowned at it and asked, "How does Corntel fit in? Are you heading towards him, Tommy?"

"Not if the tape has any bearing on why Matthew Whateley was killed. I can't see how that could apply to Corntel."

Apparently hearing a measure of doubt in Lynley's answer, St. James took up the role of devil's advocate. "Is it realistic to think the tape's a motive for murder?"

"If expulsion from the school was a consequence of the tape's being handed over to the Headmaster, if that expulsion put an older boy's entire education on the line—destroyed the possibility of acceptance into university—I should imagine a boy desperate to succeed might well be moved to murder."

"Indeed. I see that," St. James admitted. "You're arguing that Matthew was in effect blackmailing one of the older boys, aren't you? And if the tape was made in a dormitory, that does suggest that the tormentor was one of the seniors—lower or upper sixth, I dare say. But have you considered that the tape may have been made somewhere else? Perhaps in a location where this lad—Harry, you called him?—knew he'd be taken, somewhere he'd been taken before."

"There were other voices on the tape, young voices like Harry's. That suggests a dormitory, doesn't it?"

"Perhaps. But these could be voices belonging to lads who may have been present for the same reason as Harry. Victims as well. They didn't sound like participants, did they?" When Lynley admitted that they did not, St. James went on. "Then doesn't that suggest the possibility that Matthew's killer may be someone else entirely, not one of the older boys at all, but one of the men?"

"It's hardly credible."

"Because you *believe* it's hardly credible," St. James said. "Because it's out of the realm of decency and morality. As is all crime, Tommy. I don't have to tell you that. Are you avoiding Corntel? What role does he play?"

"Matthew's housemaster."

"And when Matthew disappeared?"

"He was with a woman."

"Between midnight and four A.M.?"

"No. Not then." Lynley tried to keep from thinking of the manner in which John Corntel had described Matthew Whateley only Sunday afternoon. He tried to keep from drawing conclusions from the manner in which his old schoolmate had lingered over the details of the boy's natural beauty. Above all, he tried to keep from remembering the damning fact of Corntel's sexual inexperience and everything that society taught one to believe about the oddities of virginity in a man of his age.

"Is it the Eton tie that makes you believe he's innocent, Tommy?"

The Eton tie. There was no Eton tie. There could not be in a police investigation. It was inconceivable. "It merely seems reasonable to follow the tape at the moment, to see where it leads us."

"And if it leads nowhere?"

Lynley gave a tired, dismissive laugh. "It won't be the first blind alley in the case."

"It's not to be Argentina after all, Barbie," Mrs. Havers said. In one hand she held a pair of small primary school scissors, the sort whose tips are rounded and whose blades cut with ease through soft butter but little else. In the other hand was a partially bisected grease-stained travel brochure which she waved like a pennant as she continued to speak. "It's that song, lovey. About crying and Argentina. You know the one. I couldn't help thinking that we might be just a bit depressed if we spent too much time there. With the crying and all. So I thought . . . What do you think of Peru?"

Barbara shoved her dripping umbrella into the old, disintegrating rattan stand by the door and shrugged off her coat. The house was overly warm. The air smelled of wet wool held too close to fire. She glanced in the direction of the sitting room door, wondering if the acrid scent came from there.

"How's Dad?" she asked.

"Dad?" Mrs. Havers' watery eyes tried to focus behind the frames of her spectacles. A large fingerprint obscured the right lens. For the second day in a row, she had managed to dress herself, but she had chosen a sagging pair of knit trousers and her blouse was held together by three safety pins. "I thought that Peru . . . they have those sweet animals there. The ones with the big brown eyes and that soft fur. What are they called? I want to call them camels, but I know that's not right. Look, here's a snap of one of them. He's even got a hat on. Isn't that sweet? What's he called, lovey? I can't remember."

Barbara took the picture from her mother. "It's a llama," she said, returned it, and sidestepped her mother's attempt to grip her arm to keep her for more conversation. "How's Dad, Mum? Is he all right?"

"On the other hand, there's the food. And I do worry about that."

"Food? What are you talking about? Where's Dad?" She started down the hall. Her mother trailed at her heels, catching at the back of Barbara's pullover.

"The food's so spicy, lovey. I can't think it would be good for any of us. Don't you remember the paella we had all those years ago for your birthday? It was too spicy. We all got sick, didn't we?"

Barbara's footsteps slowed. She turned to her mother. In the close confines of the cramped hallway, she saw their shadows distorted against the wall—her own broad and ill-shaped, her mother's angular and wild-haired. Just beyond them, the television in the sitting room was showing an old Fred Astaire and Ginger Rogers film at a nerve-grating volume. Fred and Ginger were on roller skates, dancing their way effortlessly round a gazebo. The odour of burnt wool was becoming more pronounced.

"Paella?" Barbara grimaced inwardly at her needless repetition of everything her mother said. It was as if stepping inside her home nightly prompted her own inchoate mental collapse. She compelled herself to speak logically. "What made you think of the paella, Mum? That was at least fifteen years ago, wasn't it?"

Encouraged, her mother smiled, but her lips seemed to quiver with uncertainty and Barbara wondered if her mother read the impatience on her face. This thought brought its usual attendant rush of guilt. Home all day alone with only an ailing husband for company, was it any wonder that the poor woman clung to a few minutes of conversation—no matter how mad—like a lifeline to humanity?

"Does all this have to do with the trip you've been planning?" Barbara asked, and adjusted the shoulders of her mother's cardigan.

The smile took on confidence. "Yes, indeed. It does. You see, you *knew* what I meant. You always do, lovey. We're kindred spirits that way, you and I."

Barbara had more than a few doubts about that. "And you're worried about the food in South America."

"Yes! Exactly right. I was wondering whether we ought to do Argentina *or* Peru. The llamas are sweet and I did so want to see them. But I can't think how any of us shall manage with that food. Our poor stomachs in an uproar from morning till night. So all day I tried to decide . . . I didn't want to disappoint you, lovey. You work so hard. I know our holiday is the only thing you've got to look forward to. And I wanted it to be special this time. But I can't think how we'll manage with the food."

Barbara knew that there would be no escape until they had found a resolution to the problem. Once her mother's mind was set on a particular thought, nothing could dislodge it until she herself was ready to move on.

"You see, it's the llamas most of all," Mrs. Havers murmured. "I did so want to see the llamas."

Here was rescue, Barbara thought. "But we don't have to go to South America to see them, do we? We can see them in a zoo."

Her mother frowned. "Oh, a *zoo.* Lovey, I don't think a zoo—"

Barbara headed her off. "They've a lovely zoo in California, Mum. In San Diego. I think they've a park there where the animals run free. Why don't we think about California?"

"But it's not very *different,* is it? Not like Turkey. Or Greece. Or China. Remember China, lovey? The Forbidden City and all those curious doorways?"

"I think I should like California, Mum," Barbara said with more determination. "The sun. Perhaps the beach. And we'd see the llamas in that park. Why don't you think about it? We could manage the food in California."

California. Mrs. Havers mouthed the word. Barbara patted her shoulder and went into the sitting room. There she immediately found the source of the pungent smell that was permeating the heavy, hot air in the house. A green and blue blanket had been thoughtlessly flung across the three-bar electric fire that blazed at full force in front of the old walled-in fireplace. Wisps of smoke rose from it. It was mere moments away from bursting into flames.

"Jesus, bloody *hell!*" Barbara cried and dashed to tear the blanket away. She hurled it to the floor and ground her feet against four scorched sections that were giving off the worst of the smoke. "What in God's name . . . Damn it all! Dad! Didn't you even *notice*—"

As she spoke, she spun to her father's chair, anger fired by the fear of what might have happened had she not arrived home in time, and by the anxiety aroused by the thought of what might happen in the future. But both words and anger faded when she saw the futility of a lecture on common safety precautions. Her father was asleep.

His jaw was slack. His head hung forward. His unshaven chin rested on his chest. The oxygen tubes were still in place in his nostrils, but his breathing sounded oddly mechanical, as if his lungs were being operated by a crank turning slowly somewhere on his back.

On the television, Fred and Ginger began to sing. Barbara muttered an oath and switched off the set. Her father's breath alternately gurgled and clanked.

Monday's and Tuesday's newspapers had joined the Sunday paper on the floor. Mingled among them were several pieces of crockery: two cups of untouched tea, a plate of pickled onions and bread, a small bowl of half-eaten grapefruit segments. Barbara stooped to gather the newspapers into a pile. The dishes she placed on top of the stack.

"Dad all right, lovey?" Mrs. Havers had come to the doorway. She held a travel album open against her stomach. The trip to Peru was in the process of being disassembled. Large holes gaped in the pages of the album where photographs of Machu Picchu had not easily surrendered to the idea of removal.

"Asleep," Barbara answered. "Mum, you've got to watch him more closely. Can't you remember? He almost set the blanket on fire. It was smoking. Couldn't you smell it?"

Confusion swept across her mother's face. "Dad doesn't smoke, lovey. You know that. He can't round the oxygen. The doctor said—"

"No, Mum. The blanket was on the electric fire. It was too close to the coils. Do you see?" She pointed to the scorched spots that blackened the wool.

"But if it's on the floor, I don't see how—"

"Mum, I put it on the floor. It was on the fire. It was smoking. The whole house could have burned down."

"Oh, I hardly *think*—"

"That's it! You hardly think!" The words were out before she could stop them. Her mother's face crumpled. Barbara's heart twisted with remorse. *It's not her fault. Not her fault!* Barbara searched for words. "I'm sorry, Mum. It's just that this case I'm working on . . . I'm worried. I don't know. Why don't you put on the kettle for tea?"

Mrs. Havers brightened. "Have you had your dinner? I remembered dinner tonight. I put a pork joint in for us. At half-five on the button, just as I used to. I should think it's done now."

Considering the time—half-past eight—it was either charred to cinders or uncooked entirely. Putting a joint in the oven did not guarantee turning the oven on. Still, Barbara forced a smile.

"Good for you. That's very good."

"I can take care of Dad. I can, you see."

"You can. Yes. Would you see to the kettle now? And perhaps you can check on that pork joint as well." She waited until she heard her mother's movement in the kitchen before bending over her father and touching his shoulder. She shook him gently, saying his name.

His eyes fluttered open. He lifted his head, closed his mouth with what looked like a grimace of pain.

"Barbie." One hand rose to greet her. But he lifted it only inches from the arm of the chair before dropping it down again. His head started to droop.

"Dad, have you eaten?"

"Had a cuppa, Barbie. Nice cuppa round four. Mum made it for me. Sees after me, does your mum."

"I'm going to make you something right now," she said. "Can you manage a sandwich? Would soup be better?"

"Don't matter. A bit off my food, Barbie. Feeling a bit knackered."

"Oh God, your appointment with the doctor. I'll phone him first thing tomorrow. I'll take you in tomorrow afternoon. Will that do for you?" She smiled, not the genuine article but a reflection of guilt. "Can you fit that into your schedule, Dad?"

He returned her smile sleepily. "Rang him myself, Barbie. This afternoon. Set the appointment for Friday. Half-three. All right?"

Barbara felt a small degree of relief at this information. Tomorrow would have been difficult to manage in spite of her promise. Friday, on the other hand, seemed a world away. Between now and then, they might have got to the bottom of Matthew Whateley's murder. That would give her a bit of free time. Between now and then, she might have come up with an idea of how to see to her mother. That would give her a bit of peace of mind.

"Lovey?"

Barbara looked up. Mrs. Havers was in the doorway. In her hands was a roasting pan. Barbara's heart sank. The pork joint in the pan hadn't been removed from the paper in which the butcher had wrapped it. Nor had the oven ever been lit.

Perhaps as a form of self-abuse—she didn't know clearly why she made the decision to do it, and she was beyond evaluating the motivations behind her behaviour at the moment—Deborah St. James walked all the way through Chelsea from Sloane Square station, down the King's Road. The rain beat against her, the wind fought to wrestle her umbrella from her hand. She felt her muscles constricting against the cold, and she knew from the sound of splashing and sloshing that her shoes were sodden and her feet were soaked, even though she wasn't aware of any sensation at all beneath her knees.

Buses and taxis hurtled past her, sending spray onto the pavement round her like angry spume. She could have hailed either, from bus stop or kerb, but to do so would have meant shelter and convenience. She wanted neither. Nor did she care particularly about safety, or the inherent foolishness in making such a long walk in the darkness, where not only was she available to passersby wishing to prey upon her but she was also exposed to the potential danger of vehicles roaring by on streets made slick by the rain.

A twenty-five-minute walk took her nearly an hour, and by the time she made the final turn onto Cheyne Row, her body was shaking with great spasms from the cold. When at last she reached her front door, her hands were trembling so violently that nearly a minute passed before she was able to force her key into the lock. She stumbled inside as the grandfather clock in the hall began to sound the time. It was nine.

Leaving both coat and umbrella by the door, she went into the study, her rigid body not yet ready to yield to the warmth of the house. The fire was not lit in the room, and although her intention was to see to it at once, instead she found herself crouching on Simon's ottoman, arms drawn up to her chest, staring at the grate with its neat pile of logs and their promise of heat.

Out of the storm at last, Deborah was honest enough with herself to examine her behaviour and see it for what it was—punishment for her crimes against her husband, blended with an abandonment to the pleasures of a self-pity she despised even as she welcomed it. Agony of spirit demanded concomitant agony of body. She was only too happy to oblige. To take off her wet clothes—even to remove her ruined shoes—would be to ease discomfort. She did not want that.

She had not seen her husband since the morning. Their conversation had been as brief, as remote and formal as their goodbyes had been on the previous day. Simon had not tried to reschedule any of his engagements. He had not offered to stay at home should she need him. It was as if he had finally recognised her desire to build a barrier between them and had decided to allow her to do so. He did not fight against her determination to isolate herself, but she knew that he was not untouched by actions which he obviously did not understand.

In the study, huddled on the ottoman with her hair hanging like wet streamers round her shoulders and down her back, Deborah found herself examining the entire question of deception, dwelling upon the central point that some forms of betrayal were beyond forgiveness. Estranged from Simon all those years ago, separated from him by six thousand miles, yet all the time loving him, she had sought only to forget, to replace the pain of their disjunction with anything that remotely resembled peace. To be loved by someone, to be held, to be caressed, to be the object of passion and the focus of desire. It had all been a way to mask reality, a pretence in which she acted the role of heart-engaged lover and persuaded her emotions to follow along. It had worked for a while; it might have worked forever, had Simon not come back into her life.

She should have waited for him. She should have held herself back. She should have recognised the self-doubt that had driven him away from her for years. But she hadn't. So she had betrayed him, and in doing so she had been false to a love that had drawn them to each other for most of her life, a love that had allowed them to reach beyond mere commonalities and to touch each other's spirit with unmatched intensity and unequivocal joy. If such a love were betrayed by cruelty or impetuosity or even an inability to face the truth, how did one survive? Where did one find the strength to go on?

Her arms tightened round her. Head pressed against her knees, she rocked back and forth to find comfort, but she found only sorrow.

"Havers and I shall go back to the school in the morning and have the Headmaster listen to the tape."

"You've decided the Chinese element is of no merit, then?"

"I haven't dismissed it. I can't do that. But the tape does seem to provide much more of a motive than bigotry. If we can identify the voice—be it a student or a teacher—I think we're a step closer to the truth."

Deborah heard their footsteps on the stairs. In a moment they would walk by the study door. She shrank from discovery, to no account, for they did not pass by, but rather entered the room together, halting just inside the door.

"Deb!" Lynley spoke her name with sharp concern.

She looked up, brushing wet hair off her face, all too aware of the sight she presented. She managed a smile.

"Caught in the rain," she said. "I've been sitting here, trying to work up the energy to light the fire."

She saw her husband go to the bar and pour a brandy. Lynley joined her at the fireplace, reached for the matches on the overmantel, and lit the kindling beneath the logs.

"At least take off your shoes, Deb," he said. "They're soaked. And your hair—"

"She's all right, Tommy." St. James' brief remark gave evidence of nothing, although the fact of the interjection itself—so completely unlike him—spoke worlds that all three of them chose to ignore. He brought Deborah the brandy. "Drink this, my love. Your father hasn't seen you, has he?"

"I've only just come in."

"Then perhaps you ought to change your clothes before he catches sight of you. God knows what he'll do—or think—if he sees you like this."

St. James' tone was kind, a study in revealing nothing save solicitude. Still, Deborah saw Lynley look from her to her husband. She saw his body tense and knew that he intended to speak. She sought to prevent him.

"You're right. I'll just take the brandy with me." Without waiting for a response, she said, "Good night, Tommy," rose, and brushed a kiss against his cheek. She felt his hand close fleetingly round her arm. She knew his eyes were on her, knew that they reflected the extent of his concern, but she did not meet them. Instead, she attempted to make a dignified exit from the room.

Her shoes squished noisily against the carpet. Even dignity was denied her.

St. James descended the stairs to the kitchen. He had not eaten dinner—much to Cotter's loudly voiced disapproval—and he felt an emptiness within him that, while it had nothing to do with food, might at least be disguised by a makeshift meal.

Aside from the household dog and cat, who looked up hopefully from their respective positions in basket and on stove top, neither Mrs. Winston—his longtime cook—nor Cotter was in the kitchen at the moment. St. James went to the refrigerator, opened it, and was joined by the little long-haired dachshund who vacated her basket for the promise of a snack. She came to sit at his feet, managing to look as soulful and ill-fed as possible.

"You've had your dinner, Peach," St. James informed the dog. "Probably three times over, if I know you."

Peach wagged her tail, encouraged that he had recognised her presence. On the stove, Alaska gave a bored feline yawn. St. James took cheese and a chopping board to the work top beneath the kitchen window. Peach followed, ever vigilant of a crumb's being dropped to the floor.

Once the cheese was unwrapped, once the knife was sharpened, St. James gazed down at both without interest. He raised his eyes to the window and what little he could see of the garden a few feet above his head.

There wasn't much to it, yet Deborah had imbued the area with her personality. Flowers grew in abundance at the base of brick walls, their colours and scents changing with the seasons. A flagstone path led from house to back gate, overgrown with great patches of unruly alyssum that Deborah stubbornly refused to pull up. In one corner, an ash tree bore four separate birdhouses and a large feeder in which sparrows fought regularly in the greedy way of small birds. A rectangle of lawn held two chairs, a chaise, and a low circular table, all constructed of metal. So foolish a purchase, he had told his wife. But Deborah loved the intricate workmanship of the pieces and had said that she would see to their upkeep, fending off the rust that was an inevitable part of placing metal furniture outdoors in the London weather. And she had done so, sanding and painting faithfully each spring, as often as not getting as much paint on herself as she did on the furniture. But she was true to her word. She had always been.

St. James felt the knife beneath his hand. His fingers gripped its handle. The wood ate into his palm.

How had it happened, he thought, that he had given a woman such dominion over his life? How had it happened that he had allowed her to see the very worst of his weakness? For indeed she had seen it, defined by the forces that drove him to be the best in his field, to be admired, to be sought after, to be the first expert witness called upon to explain the meaning behind the pattern of a blood-stain or the implication behind the trajectory of a bullet or the interpretation of metallic striations upon a lock or a key. Some would have called this need to be foremost in science the blind drive of ego. But Deborah knew the truth. She knew what void within him had been filled by his work. He had allowed her to see it.

She had been a witness to his helplessness, a companion to the pain that still came intermittently upon his body. She had watched her father place electrodes on his leg to keep the dead muscles from atrophying. She had even learned how to use the electrodes herself. He had allowed this. He had even wanted it—to bring her closer to him, to share what he was with her, to allow her to know him completely. It was the curse of loving, the miserable exercise of living. In the past eighteen months of their marriage, he had thrown himself into it like an inexperienced adolescent, holding nothing back, leaving no corner of himself into which he could retreat in safety. Because he had never thought he would need to retreat. Now he paid.

He was losing her. With each pregnancy that failed, she had withdrawn into herself for a time. He had understood. Although he longed for a child as did she, he knew his need for one did not match her own. So he had been willing to give her the solitude she seemed to require for an act of mourning. He hadn't realised at first that a bit more of her had seemed to withdraw from him with each failure. He had not counted the weeks that would have told him her recoveries were taking longer, her hopes needing more time to rekindle themselves. Now this fourth failure—this fourth non-birth of a beloved child—had done its worst.

He had never thought his marriage would splinter under the weight of children who did not even exist. It was inconceivable, even now. Had she been some other woman, had he known her less well, he might have been prepared for the change that had taken Deborah from him. But of all people in his life, he had always seen her as the single constant.

He looked down at the knife, at the wedge of cheese. Eating was impossible. He put both away.

Leaving the kitchen, St. James returned to the main part of the house. He climbed the stairs. Their bedroom was empty, as were the other rooms on the first floor, so he continued climbing until he found his wife in her old bedroom next to his lab on the top floor of the house.

She had changed out of her wet clothes into a dressing gown, and her hair was wrapped, turbanlike, in a towel. She was sitting on the brass bed from her childhood, looking through a stack of old photographic enlargements which she had taken out of the small chest of drawers.

He watched her for a moment without speaking, allowing the image of her caught by lamplight to fill his heart. Eyes lowered, she held a single photograph in her hand. She sat without motion.

He felt the strong current of desire sweep through him, the longing to hold her, to feel her mouth beneath his, to breathe the fragrance of hair, to touch her breasts, to hear her sigh. Yet never before had he been so aware of the fear of approaching and provoking her flight.

Still, he crossed the room. Rapt in her study of the photograph she held, Deborah did not look up. St. James himself was momentarily conscious only of the gentle curve of her cheek, the tender shadow of her eyelashes on her skin, the rise and fall of her breathing. It was not until he stood next to the bed, not until he reached out to caress her that he noticed the subject of the photograph that so held Deborah's interest.

It was Thomas Lynley. Blond hair caught by sunlight, thin trails of water a sheen on his body as he ran from the sea. He was laughing, one hand outstretched towards the camera, captured in a moment of timeless beauty and effortless grace.

St. James turned from the sight. Desire died. Despair gripped him. Before his wife could speak, he left the room.

17

Lynley watched one expression after another flit across Alan Lockwood's face as he listened to the tape a second time. Each expression chronicled an emotion felt and subsequently repressed. Revulsion, anger, pity, and disgust succeeded one another.

They had gathered in the Headmaster's office, Sergeant Havers lounging in the bay window, Lynley seated at the conference table with the tape recorder in front of him, and Lockwood standing behind one of the chairs, holding securely to the carved shoulder rail. Since the tape had first been played for him, he had said nothing save "Once again, please." He had looked at nothing save the arrangement of flowers which his wife had brought into his office the prior day. Some of the less hardy blooms had begun to wilt. One of the lilies looked bruised.

The voices on the tape rose and fell. The pleading continued. The harassment went on. Lynley blocked it out.

They had arrived at the school shortly before the end of the morning service in the chapel. The choir was just finishing a hymn—the last notes from the organ reverberating down the length of the chapel like a cresting wave—and one of the black-gowned staff was climbing the steps to the octagonal pulpit to do the final reading from scripture. When he turned to face the assembly, Lynley saw that it was John Corntel. From his position by the memorial chapel, Lynley watched the literature master lower his eyes to the Bible and begin to read. He only faltered once.

"Psalm sixty-two," he announced. Above his black gown and dark suit, with the light from the pulpit shining against his skin, his face seemed etiolated. " 'Truly my soul waiteth upon God: from him cometh my salvation. He only is my rock and my salvation; he is my defence; I shall not be greatly moved. How long will ye imagine mischief against a man? Ye shall be slain all of you: as a bowing wall shall ye be, and as a tottering fence. They only consult to cast him down from his excellency; they delight in lies; they bless with their mouth, but they curse inwardly . . .' "

Lynley heard Corntel trip upon the words, right himself, and plunge on to complete the reading. But one line echoed in his mind with as much force as had the organ music only moments before. *They delight in lies.* The rest of the psalm escaped him.

His eyes followed the length and breadth of the church, absorbing its symmetry and beauty. Fresh rain-washed sunlight allowed the stained glass windows to spill colours onto the choir below. Candles glimmered on the altar, each flame creating its own corona. Gold threads woven through the altar cloth reflected this light in a pattern that shimmered like the surface of water. The magnificent reredos looked like ivory, and above it the rose window spread out its ornamental tracery in an intricate web. On both sides of the aisle, schoolchildren knelt in prayer, their heads resting on the backs of the pews in front of them as if in demonstration of piety and prostration. Lining the chapel walls behind them, staff members did likewise. Only the choir remained standing, and at the end of Corntel's reading, following eight notes of crashing introduction from the organ, they began their final hymn. "Praise God from Whom All Blessings Flow" resounded through the chapel. Listening to this, catching the scent of burning candles and old wood, feeling a solid stone pillar pressing against his shoulder, Lynley was reminded of a fragment of the gospel according to St. Matthew. He could almost hear the words, rising above the choir's singing.

Ye are like unto whited sepulchres, which indeed appear beautiful outward, but are within full of dead men's bones, and of all uncleanness.

The pupils began to file out of the chapel—row after row of them, standing tall, their eyes straight ahead, their uniforms pressed, their hair neatly combed, their faces fresh. *They must know,* he thought. *All of them. They've known all along.*

Now he leaned forward and pressed the button on the tape recorder as the torment of the boy ended yet another time with guttural laughter and the sound of weeping. He waited for the Headmaster to speak.

Lockwood pushed away from the chair and went to the window. He had opened it upon their entrance into the room a quarter-hour previously, and now he pushed on it further and let the cold morning air hit his face. He pursed his lips and inhaled like whistling in reverse. He remained in that posture for nearly a minute. Near him, Sergeant Havers looked towards Lynley. He directed his head at the chair next to him. She took it.

"A pupil," Lockwood murmured at last. "A *pupil.*"

An inadvertent underlying note of relief rang past the Headmaster's statement. Lynley understood. Lockwood had made his own quick assumptions about how the tape could complete another part of the puzzle of murder. If a pupil were responsible for Matthew Whateley's death, the onus of blame did not fall so heavily upon the school. A pupil's culpability meant that no paedophile had been lurking unidentified among the staff members. No monster dwelt behind a facade of pedagogical purity. Bredgar Chambers' reputation—and hence the Headmaster's—was safeguarded as long as that was the case.

"What penalty does a boy face for bullying?"

Lockwood turned from the window to answer. "He gets warned off twice. If it happens a third time, he's expelled. But in this case . . ." Lockwood's voice drifted off as he joined them at the table, choosing the chair at its head rather than the more logical one next to Sergeant Havers.

"In this case?" Lynley prompted.

"This isn't an ordinary sort of bullying. You can hear that for yourself. It sounded like an ongoing sort of thing, perhaps a nightly visitation. For that, the boy would be out at once. Absolutely. No doubt about it."

"Expelled."

"Yes."

"What would be the chances of that boy getting into another independent school?"

"No chance at all, if I had anything to do with it." Lockwood seemed to like the sound of finality behind his declaration, for he repeated, "No chance at all," giving separate emphasis to each word.

"Matthew sent this tape to a friend of his in Hammersmith," Lynley informed the Headmaster. "It's a copy. He told her he'd keep the original recording here at the school. So he must have hidden it or given it to someone he thought he could trust, in the hope that doing so would stop the bullying. We think it's Harry Morant who's being bullied, by the way."

"Morant? The lad Matthew Whateley was to visit last weekend?"

"Yes."

Lockwood frowned. "If Matthew had given the tape to a staff member, it would have been turned over to me at once. So I can only assume that if he gave it to anyone—rather than hiding it—it would have to be a pupil. As you said, someone he could trust."

"Someone, at least, he thought he could trust. Someone whose position indicated he *could* be trusted."

"You're thinking of Chas Quilter."

"Senior prefect," Lynley noted. "There doesn't seem to be another pupil more trustworthy, does there? Where is he?"

"This is my usual weekly meeting time with him. I asked him to wait in the library."

"Sergeant?" Lynley directed Havers to fetch the boy. She left the Headmaster's study to do so.

The library comprised one-quarter of the south quadrangle, abutting the Headmaster's study. Within moments, Havers had returned from it with Chas Quilter behind her. Lynley rose to greet the boy and noticed his eyes move questioningly from the tape recorder on the table to the Headmaster, who remained seated at its head. When asked to do so, Chas took a seat at the table himself, a chair next to Lockwood. It was as if by choice of seating, battle lines had been drawn, with the Headmaster and his senior prefect on one side of the conflict, and Lynley and Havers on the other. Loyalty to school, Lynley thought and readied himself to see whether Chas would also show loyalty to the school's motto. *Honor sit et baculum et ferula.* The next few minutes would tell the tale. Lynley played the tape.

Hot blood surged up Chas' neck as he listened. His Adam's apple suddenly became prominent, bobbling ostensibly of its own volition. One hand reached for his ankle, which rested across his knee. His spectacles reflected the morning light from the windows, disks of gold behind which his eyes were hidden.

"Matthew Whateley recorded it," Lynley said at the conclusion of the tape. "He wired a room for sound here at the school. This is a duplicate of the original tape. We're looking for that original."

"Do you know anything about this, Quilter?" the Headmaster asked. "The police believe that the boy either hid the original or gave it to someone for safekeeping."

Chas addressed his answer to Lockwood. "Why would he do either of those things?"

Lynley replied. "Because he believed he had to follow the school's unwritten rules."

"Rules, sir?"

Lynley found the question disingenuous and irritating. "The same unwritten rules that made Brian Byrne reluctant to tell us how many times you left the upper sixth social club on the night Matthew disappeared. Just as you're reluctant now to tell us about the tape."

A minor movement betrayed the boy, his right shoulder pulling back as if by the force of an invisible hand. "D'you think *I*—"

Lockwood interposed with a baleful glare in Lynley's direction. His conciliatory words indicated that the behaviour of the sons of knighted physicians was above reproach, no matter their elder brothers' failures. "No one thinks anything, Quilter. The police aren't here to accuse you."

Next to him, Lynley heard Havers mutter a nearly inaudible oath. He waited for Chas to respond.

"I've not heard the tape before now," the boy said. "I didn't know Matthew Whateley. I couldn't say where he put the tape, or even if he gave it to someone else."

"Do you recognise the voices?" Lynley asked.

"No, I can't say—"

"But it sounds like an upper sixth boy, doesn't it?"

"Possibly. I suppose. But it could be anyone, sir. I wish I could help. I *ought* to be able to help. I know that. I'm sorry."

There was a quick knocking at the door, three light taps. It opened. Elaine Roly stood framed in the doorway. Lockwood's secretary lurked behind her, attempting to prevent the intrusion. But the matron of Erebus House was not to be thwarted. She threw a withering look upon the secretary and marched across the fine Wilton carpet.

"*She* tried to stop me," the matron said. "But I knew you'd want this straightaway." She pulled something from the sleeve of her blouse, saying, "Little Harry Morant gave that to me this morning, Inspector. He won't say where he found it. Nor what he was doing with it. But you can see clear as clear that it belonged to Matthew Whateley."

She dropped a sock on the table. Chas Quilter jerked spasmodically in his chair.

The library smelled largely of pencil shavings and books. The former odour emanated from the electric pencil sharpener that was used by students with more delight and enthusiasm than actual need. The latter drifted from the tall serried shelves of volumes that jutted out from the walls, their ranks broken intermittently by broad study tables. Chas Quilter sat at one of these, finding it inexplicable that he should feel so numb as his world continued to crumble round him, like a building caught in a conflagration that gives itself up, piece by piece, to the flames. He remembered a Latin phrase that had been one of many he had been forced to memorise as a fourth form student. *Nam tua res agitur, paries cum proximus ardet.*

Alone, he whispered the translation into the listening room. " 'For it is your business, when the wall next door catches fire.' "

How true the aphorism was proving. How assiduously he had avoided facing it. It was as if, without knowing, he had been running from that fire for the last sixteen months, yet every path he had chosen only brought him face to face with another wall of flame.

His flight had begun the previous year with his brother's expulsion from the school. How well he remembered the course of those events: his parents' outrage at the initial accusation made against an older son who wanted for nothing; Preston's hot denials and insistence upon proof; his own impassioned defence of his brother at gatherings of supportive but sceptical friends; and then the humiliation attendant to the knowledge that the accusations were true. Money, clothing, pens and pencils, special food brought in tuck boxes from home. It hadn't mattered to Preston. He had stolen without thinking, whether he wanted the item or not.

In reaction to the revelation of his brother's sickness—for it *was* a sickness and Chas knew that—he had run from Preston. He had run from his brother's need, from his shame, from his weakness. All that had seemed important at the time was to disassociate himself from disgrace. He had done so, throwing himself into his studies and avoiding any circumstance during which his brother's name or his folly might arise. Thus, he left Preston alone in the flames. Yet even as he did so, he faced the fire himself, where he least expected to find it.

Sissy, he believed, would be his salvation, the one person in his life with whom he could be perfectly honest, entirely himself. In the months that followed Preston's expulsion from the school, Sissy had learned all of Chas' weaknesses and his strengths. She had learned of his pain and his confusion, of his hard-edged resolve to make up for Preston's mistakes. Through it all she had been there for him during his lower sixth year, calm and serene. Yet as Chas allowed himself to grow closer to her, he failed to see that she was just another wall, that she too would give over to fire and destruction.

So the wall next door had indeed caught fire. The fire had spread. It was time to put an end to the burning. But to do so would put an end to himself as well. If only his own life hung in the balance, Chas knew it wouldn't matter what he did at this point. He would speak without caring what consequences might follow. But his life touched upon other lives. His responsibilities did not end at the boundaries of Bredgar Chambers.

He thought about his father and his generous expenditure of time in Barcelona where each year during his own holidays he offered his services as a plastic surgeon to those who could not otherwise afford to see one, repairing cleft palates, rebuilding the faces of accident victims, grafting skin over burns, reshaping deformities. He thought about his mother and her lifetime of selfless devotion to both husband and sons. He thought about their faces on that final morning last year when they packed Preston's belongings into their Rover and tried not to let the depth of their confusion and humiliation show. They had not deserved such a blow as Preston's fall from grace had dealt them. So Chas had thought. And so he had determined to alleviate their suffering, to replace it with pride. He could do that, he thought, for he was not Preston. He was *not* Preston. He was not.

Yet even as he swore this to himself, words came swimming into his mind without provocation, like incantations in a nightmare. He had read them this morning while waiting for his meeting with the Headmaster, and now he saw and heard them all again. *Acrobrachycephaly. Syndactyly. Coronal suture.* Without wanting to, he heard Sissy weeping. Without wanting to, he felt guilt and grief. Again he faced that burning wall and tried futilely to tell himself it was not his business.

But he failed to convince himself of anything at all save the extent of his personal culpability in the damage he had inflicted upon the people in his life.

Harry knew what was expected of him the moment he walked into the Headmaster's study. Only Mr. Lockwood and the two detectives from New Scotland Yard were there. On the table in the bay window, Matthew Whateley's sock curled like an incomplete question mark. Someone had turned it inside out, and even from where he stood by the door, Harry could see the small white tag and the black number *4* printed upon it.

He had wanted Miss Roly to give it to the police. He had even expected her to do so. But he hadn't thought that Mr. Lockwood would be told, nor had he imagined that his own part in the drama would not end with his handing over Matthew Whateley's sock. Naturally, he'd seen enough detective shows on television that he *should* have realised the police would want to speak with him. But now that he was here, with the tall blond detective leading him to a chair, his hand warm and firm on Harry's shoulder, he wished he had kept the sock to himself or thrown it away or left it where it was for someone else to discover.

All those wishes were in vain and too late. Harry felt waves of hot and cold wash over him as the detective pulled out a chair for him at the table.

He kept his eyes on his hands that were balled into fists in his lap. His right thumb, he saw, had an ink mark on it that was shaped like lightning. It looked like a tattoo.

"I'm Inspector Lynley. This is Sergeant Havers," the blond man was saying.

Harry heard a rustle of paper. The sergeant was getting ready to take notes.

He felt so cold. His legs began to shake. His arms quivered. If he spoke, he knew that his teeth would chatter and that the words themselves would come out distorted by tremors that fast gave way to sobs.

"Matron Roly tells us that you gave her this sock," Inspector Lynley was saying. "Where did it come from, Harry?"

A clock was ticking somewhere in the room. Funny, Harry thought, he'd not noticed it last time he'd been in Mr. Lockwood's study.

"Did you find it in one of the buildings? Or on the grounds somewhere?"

He could smell the flowers in the centre of the table. Mrs. Lockwood grew them. He'd seen her shadowy movements inside the greenhouse that she called her conservatory. He'd even sneaked a look inside once at the long brick paths between rows of plants. She kept a section for flowers, another for vegetables. Pots hung from poles. Water dripped rhythmically. The soil smelled rich.

"Did you have it all along, Harry? It's Matthew's, you know. You *do* know that, don't you?"

His mouth tasted sour. All along his tongue, back into his throat, was a ridge of flavour like rotten lemons. He swallowed against it. His throat was sore.

"Are you listening to Inspector Lynley?" Mr. Lockwood demanded. "Morant, are you listening? Answer him, boy. At once."

He could feel the wood on the back of the chair. It pressed into his shoulder blades. One part of the carving was like a little bulb of pain.

Mr. Lockwood continued. Harry heard his anger. "Morant, I've absolutely no intention—"

The detective made a movement. A sharp, mechanical *click* followed. Then the room was filled with the sound of the voice.

Want a grind, nancy boy, want a grind, want a grind?

Harry's eyes flew up and he saw a tape recorder in front of the detective. He cried out once, tried to cover his ears to block out the sound. But it was no good. The voice continued. The nightmare was real. He stuffed his fingers into his ears. Still, snatches came to him, filled with derision, contempt, and loathing.

Little thing in our panties ... oooh ... have a look ... little cobblers ... squeeze ...

The horror crashed upon him, as if fresh and new, and he began to cry. The tape switched off. He felt strong but gentle hands remove his fingers from his ears.

"Who did this to you, Harry?" Inspector Lynley asked.

Weeping, Harry looked up. The detective's face was implacable, but his eyes were dark, they were kind and compelling. They invited confidence. They demanded truth. But to tell ... He couldn't. Not that. Not ever. Still, he had to say something. He had to speak. Everyone was waiting.

"I'll take you," he said.

Lynley and Havers followed Harry Morant out the front doors of the school. They crossed the car park in front of the east wing of the quadrangle and set off on the path that led to Calchus House. Since pupils were in their lessons, the grounds were deserted.

Harry trotted ahead of them without saying a word, rubbing his arm back and forth across his flushed face as if to obliterate the signs of his weeping. In the hope that the boy might be encouraged to say more than he had said in the presence of the Headmaster, Lynley had managed to convince Lockwood to remain in his study. But aside from that single sentence spoken on a torn cry, Harry had offered nothing else.

He appeared determined to remain mute as long as possible, putting space between himself and the police as he scurried down the path. His shoulders were hunched. He looked furtively from side to side. By the time they were twenty yards from Calchus House, he was nearly running, and he vanished inside before Lynley and Havers reached the door.

They found him waiting in the building's entry hall, a small shadow in the darkest corner by the telephone. Lynley noted that Calchus House had the same floor plan as Erebus House where Matthew Whateley had lived, and like Erebus, it was in need of repair.

Harry waited until they had closed the door before he slipped past them and made for the stairs. He ran up two flights with Lynley and Havers on his heels. At no point did he look back to see if they were following him. Indeed, it appeared that he hoped he might lose them, and he almost did in the upstairs corridor when he made a quick turn into the southwest corner of the building.

They found him standing by a door. He looked shrunken in size, and he kept his back against the wall as if in the fear of being taken unaware.

"In here," was all he said.

"This is where you found Matthew's sock?" Lynley clarified.

"On the floor." He hugged his arms across his stomach.

Lynley eyed the boy, concerned that he might attempt flight. He pushed open the door and looked into the hot, malodorous little room.

"Drying room," Sergeant Havers said. "There's one in every building. God, what a smell!"

"You checked it, Sergeant?"

"I checked them all. They're exactly like this one. And as foul-smelling."

Lynley looked at Harry, who was staring straight ahead. His dark hair had fallen across his brow, and his face looked feverish. "Stay with him," he told Havers and went into the room. He propped the door open behind him.

There was little enough to see, just water pipes hung with clothes on the walls, a linoleum floor, a single light bulb, a padlocked trap door in the ceiling. Lynley climbed the metal ladder built into the wall to check the trap door, his head brushing against the wads of chewing gum that had been used to decorate it. He reached out, grasped the padlock, and jerked down upon it. It pulled easily away from the hasp that served to keep the door closed, and holding it in his hand, Lynley saw what his sergeant had evidently overlooked in her perusal of the room from the floor below. Someone had used a hacksaw on the padlock. Someone had managed to gain easy access to whatever existed above the trap door. Lynley shoved it open.

Above him was revealed a narrow, dark passageway, its walls covered with paint-chipped plaster. At the end of the passage, a warped door was cracked open and a weak beam of light shot out from it, like daylight diffused through a dirty window. Ascending the final steps of the ladder, Lynley lifted himself into the passageway, coughing against the dust which rose like a miasma with his movements.

He had no torch with him, but the light from the drying room below, in addition to that which came from the doorway at the end of the passage, served to show him the footprints that padded back and forth across the floor. He examined them but saw nothing to distinguish them beyond the fact that they were made by athletic shoes, probably male. He sidestepped several fairly decent prints and went to the door at the passage's end.

It was well-oiled and free of dust. The slightest pressure of his knuckles upon it was sufficient to glide it soundlessly open, revealing a small chamber of the sort peculiar to fifteenth-century buildings, a useless space tucked beneath the gabled roof and no doubt long forgotten by those in authority. It had, however, been neither forgotten nor useless to someone.

Three perpendicular windows along the west wall admitted weak light through windowpanes that were filthy from years of neglect. The consequences of this same neglect extended outward from the windows like an insidious web. Stains covered the walls, some from the damp, others looking like the result of liquor hurled in drunkenness or anger, still others in splatters of rusty brown bearing the appearance of blood. Where there were no stains, lewd drawings had been scrawled onto the plaster, male and female figures engaged in a variety of sexual postures. Rubbish lay in piles on the dusty floor—cigarette butts, candy and crisp wrappers, empty beer bottles, a plastic glass, an institutional mug, an ancient orange blanket left in a heap before the fireplace. This contained its own complement of debris as well as a foul mass of ashes that contributed to air that was already foetid with the odours of urine and excrement. On the plain stone mantelpiece, hardened globules of wax fixed four white candles into position. They were stubs only, and the amount of wax that surrounded their bases gave testimony to the frequency with which the room had been used surreptitiously at night.

Lynley let his eyes take in all of this, realising that it represented a preponderance of evidence that would take a forensic team weeks to sort through in an attempt to place Matthew Whateley in the room prior to his death. That the evidence was here somewhere—represented by a hair from the boy's head or a spot of his blood or a scraping of his skin or a fibre that matched one found on his body—was a fact that Lynley did not question for an instant. But the thought of Patsy Whateley's disintegrating condition was building a pressure within him to bring the case to a quick conclusion. It was inconceivable that he might have to wait an arrest upon the slow and meticulous work of a forensic team. For that reason, he returned to the trap door and called down to the drying room, seeking a way to end Harry Morant's persistent refusal to speak. Sergeant Havers came to the door in answer.

"I'd like Harry to see this, Sergeant," he told her. "Give him some help up the ladder, will you?"

She nodded, fetched the boy, and he joined Lynley in the passageway. Hand on his shoulder, Lynley took him to the room and stood him just inside the door, holding him back against his own body. The boy felt as frail as a reed beneath his grasp.

"This is where Matthew was taken," Lynley said. "Someone brought him here, Harry, perhaps having told him that they needed to have a little talk, perhaps having indicated to him that it was time to put an end to grievances, or perhaps having even rendered him unconscious so that it didn't matter what sort of excuse was cooked up. But this is where he was brought."

Lynley turned the boy's head towards a corner of the room where the dust on the floor was most agitated. "I imagine he was tied up in that corner. See how the cigarette butts litter the floor there? He was burnt with cigarette butts, all over his body. Inside his nose and on his testicles as well. I suppose you've heard that. You can imagine what it must have been like for him, smelling his skin burning and feeling the pain."

Harry's trembling was making his body rigid. He gulped for air.

"You can smell the urine, can't you?" Lynley went on. "And the faeces. Matthew wouldn't have been allowed to go to a lavatory, so he would just have had to dirty himself. It wouldn't have mattered much, as he didn't have his clothes on. But that's why the room smells."

Harry's head was flung back against Lynley's chest. He whimpered.

Lynley touched the boy's forehead. It was searingly hot. "It's guesswork on my part, but I dare say most of it's the truth, Harry. That's what happened to Matthew before he died. But only you can tell us who did it to him."

Harry shook his head frantically.

"He knew that you were being bullied. But he wasn't like the other boys, was he? He wasn't an ordinary sort who would look the other way, relieved that he wasn't the one being harassed. He was the sort of boy who couldn't abide cruelty. Besides, you were his mate. He wasn't about to stand aside and let someone continue to assault his mate. So he engineered a method to stop it all. He wired your room. He made a tape. I imagine he did it three weeks ago during Friday afternoon games when he got that off-games chit from the Sanatorium, pretending he was ill. That would have given him time to set up his sound system and to try it out with no one—save you, of course—being the wiser. Once the room was ready, all you had to do was wait for the next visitation at night. And it *was* at night, wasn't it? That's when these things generally happen."

A heaving of the boy's shoulders told Lynley that he had begun to cry.

"After the tape was made, the bullying stopped, didn't it? It couldn't go on. So everyone was safe. If the bully so much as stepped out of line again, the tape would be produced, and he would be finished here at the school. Except that I don't imagine Matthew ever really intended the bully to be expelled. He wouldn't have wanted to do that, no matter how much the bully deserved it. He probably wanted to give the bloke a fair chance to straighten up. So he didn't give the tape to the Headmaster, did he? He gave it to someone else. The only thing he didn't understand was that to a bully the act of aggression is everything. It's an obsession. It's a real need. In order to go back to his harassment, our bully needed that tape. He needed the copy that had been made of it. He brought Matthew here to get them."

A cry escaped Harry's throat. His feet marched in place against the floor.

"Someone's got to break the silence," Lynley said. "Matthew Whateley tried, but his way didn't work. One can't use half-measures when it comes to the truth, Harry. If nothing else, I hope you see that. Matthew's dead now because he tried a half-measure. I want the name of his killer."

"Can't. No. *Can't!*" Harry gasped.

"You can. You must. Give me the name."

Harry writhed in Lynley's grasp. His head fell forward against his chest. His arms came up. He tried to prise Lynley's hands from his shoulders.

"Give me the name," Lynley repeated quietly. "Look at this room, Harry. End the silence. Give me the name."

Harry's head lifted. Lynley knew he was looking at the room one more time—at the filth, at the debris, at the scarred walls with their bawdy drawings, at the rusty stains, at the dust-covered floor. He knew the boy could smell the evidence of Matthew Whateley's terror. He knew he could feel the malevolence that had brought about his death. Beneath his hands, he felt Harry straighten, felt him draw in a breath that scathed the air.

"Chas Quilter," he cried.

18

Eventually they found Chas Quilter in his bed-sitting room. It was not where he was supposed to be. He had a biology lesson scheduled for that morning, and they had gone first to the science building in search of him. Failing to find him there, they had checked the chapel, the theatre, and the Sanatorium before at last making their way to Ion House. It was the northernmost building on the campus, and unlike the other houses, which were perfectly symmetrical, the proportionate balance of Ion was marred by a single-storey addition that jutted out from the east end of the building. A sign on the closed door of this wing read "Upper VIth—Members Only," and seeing this, Lynley decided to have a look at the interior of the upper sixth social club.

There wasn't much to it. It was a large room with a bank of windows that looked out across the lawn to Calchus House. Furniture consisted of four overstuffed sofas, a billiard table, a Ping-Pong table, three initial-carved trestle tables, and a dozen cheap plastic chairs. Against one wall a television stood with a video recorder below it. Nearby a shelf held a stereo system. Running the length of another wall was the bar.

"What keeps the kids from coming in and helping themselves to a pint whenever they feel like it?" Sergeant Havers asked, following Lynley to the bar. "Surely," she noted sardonically, "it can't be honour. Upholding the school rules and all that rot?"

"After the past few days, I wouldn't argue with you about that." Lynley examined the three taps behind the bar. "They appear to be locked into position. No doubt someone in authority has the key."

"Chas Quilter? There's a comforting thought."

Lynley looked towards the windows. He leaned against the bar. "You can see Calchus House from here, Havers. I imagine you can see it from anywhere in the room."

"Save for a tree here and there."

"Most of the path to Calchus is out in the open."

"I see that. Yes." As usual, she followed his train of thought. "So anyone going to Calchus House on Friday evening during the upper sixth party could have been seen from these windows? There are lights on the path, aren't there? And"— Havers riffled quickly through the pages of her notebook—"Brian Byrne told us that Chas Quilter left the upper sixth party at least three times. He claimed it was to take phone calls. But it could have been to slip out another door and see to Matthew. If Brian was sitting right here and *saw* him on the path, he'd want to protect him, wouldn't he?"

"Let's see if we can find him," Lynley answered.

A door at one end of the social club took them into the Ion House common room. Beyond it a corridor led to the stairs. They began to climb these and on the first landing found a charwoman at work with a roaring vacuum cleaner. She directed them to Chas Quilter's room on the second floor, shouting her instructions over the din. The noise faded as they climbed the second flight of stairs, and it disappeared altogether when the corridor door swung shut behind them. Aside from the faint sound of a stereo playing in one of the rooms, the second floor was still.

They followed the music, a haunting combination of sounds produced electrophonically by a Moog synthesizer. It came from behind the sixth door in the corridor. Lynley paused in front of it, listening, before he rapped sharply, and getting no response, let himself and Sergeant Havers into the room.

The bed-sit did not seem typical to an eighteen-year-old boy. Its furniture was standard institutional issue, but the linoleum floor had been covered with a piece of Donegal carpet and the walls had been hung not with the posters or photographs that Lynley and Havers had come to expect but rather with a selection of framed quotations. They formed a circular, sunburst pattern, representing nearly five hundred years of English literature. Spenser and Shakespeare rested hand in glove with Donne and Shaw. The Brownings were present, as were Coleridge, Keats, and Shelley. Byron had a place between Pope and Blake, and central to the arrangement was the final stanza of Arnold's "Dover Beach," this one larger than the rest, and—unlike the others, which were hand-printed neatly upon thick, creamy paper—it was written in calligraphy upon fine parchment. The words seemed to leap from the frame.

> Ah, love, let us be true
> To one another! for the world, which seems
> To lie before us like a land of dreams,
> So various, so beautiful, so new,
> Hath really neither joy, nor love, nor light,
> Nor certitude, nor peace, nor help for pain;
> And we are here as on a darkling plain
> Swept with confused alarms of struggle and flight,
> Where ignorant armies clash by night.

In the lower right corner of the parchment was the signature *Sissy.*

Chas Quilter was seated at his desk, a thick volume in front of him. He appeared to be deep in his studies at the moment, perhaps preparing to begin some work in biology, for as Lynley approached the boy, he saw that the book was a medical text—heavily underscored in dark ink, with notations in the margins. Across the top of the page to which it was open was the heading APERT'S SYNDROME and beneath it a list of medical terms and their attendant definitions. A spiral notebook lay next to this, but if Chas had intended to make a record of his reading, he hadn't got far. Instead of useful biological notations, he had written only "a fiery deluge, fed with ever-burning sulphur unconsumed" in letters that themselves were licked fancifully by a mass of hand-drawn flames. Lynley recognised the source of this contradictory line when he saw it also lying on the desk, open but face downward. *Paradise Lost.*

Chas, however, was looking at none of this. His attention was focused on matters of neither science nor literature. Instead, he was giving it to the perusal of a photograph that stood on the windowsill behind the desk. In it, he himself stood, his arms round a long-haired girl who rested her head against his chest. It was the same picture which Lynley and Havers had seen on Brian Byrne's wall.

Chas started in surprise when Sergeant Havers went to the bookshelves and punched off the tape deck. "I didn't hear—" he stammered.

"We knocked," Lynley said. "You were obviously preoccupied."

Chas closed the medical volume, did the same to Milton. He ripped from his notebook the page on which he had written the line from the poem and crumpled it into a ball. This he kept in his hand. It crackled as he clutched it.

In the cramped confines of the room, Sergeant Havers moved

past Lynley to the bed where she sat, pulling meditatively upon her earlobe. Her gaze upon Chas Quilter was steely.

Lynley went to the bookshelves where the tape deck sat. He punched a button. The music resumed. He punched another button. It stopped. He punched a third button. The cassette ejected.

"Why aren't you in your biology lesson?" Lynley asked the boy. "Have you an excuse from the Sanatorium? Perhaps something like an off-games chit? They appear to be fairly easy to come by."

Chas' eyes were on the cassette. He didn't respond. Lynley continued.

"I don't think you did the actual bullying," he said. "I don't think that's what Harry Morant meant when he gave me your name." He passed the cassette back and forth between his hands. In response, the boy bit his upper lip, but it was a reaction of a single second's duration. Had Lynley not been watching him, he would have missed it altogether. "I think Harry's too terrified to give me the name I want. After what he's been through, and after what happened to Matthew, it's reasonable enough to assume that he wouldn't think himself safe no matter what I or anyone tried to do or say to reassure him. Or perhaps he's still trying to live under some sort of Bredgardian code of honour. One doesn't sneak on another student. You know the sort of thing. But I think Harry believed, even beyond his fear, that he had to give us something. It was the only way he could make reparation for Matthew's death. Which, of course, he feels largely responsible for causing. So he gave us Matthew's sock. And then—up above the drying room in Calchus House—he gave us your name. Why," Lynley asked, placing the cassette on Chas' desk, "do you suppose he did that?"

Chas' gaze followed the cassette, then raised back to Lynley. Without speaking, he opened one of the two drawers in the desk. From the very back underneath a stack of papers and notebooks, he took out another cassette, and he handed it to Lynley.

The boy said nothing, but there was no need for him to do so when his features so explicitly delineated the struggle in which he was engaged. Lynley had seen such a struggle before, more than seventeen years ago at Eton. He had been warned off twice for two bouts of drunkenness. A third bout and he knew he would be expelled. So he had deliberately brought the gin into his room—because somehow gin seemed so much worse than anything else he might choose to drink, so much more indicative of irredeemable dissolution and disgrace—and had drunk nearly half of the bottle. Because he had wanted to be expelled. Because he had wanted to go home. Because the last thing he could continue to face was being cut off from his sister and his brother and his mother while his father lay dying. If expulsion was the only way to get home, what did it matter that his family would be hurt by it, that it would bring an additional misery in circumstances in which they could bear no more? So he had drunk. But instead of the housemaster, it was John Corntel who had found him. He remembered watching the anxiety on Corntel's face as he tried to decide what to do about his schoolmate who lay in a semi-stupor across his bed. To fetch the housemaster would uphold the school rules. To do anything else would put himself at risk. Lynley remembered how he waited in drunken happiness for Corntel to make the move that would ruin him. He remembered his bleak satisfaction when the boy left his room. But when Corntel returned, he had St. James, not the housemaster, with him. Together they disposed of the alcohol, covered up for Lynley, and safeguarded his place at the school.

We live by codes, he thought. We call them our morals, our standards, our values, our ethics, as if they were part of our genetic make-up. But they are only behaviours that we have learned from our society, and there are times to act in defiance of them, to fly in the face of their conventions because it is right to do so.

"We're not talking about having a smoke in the bell tower, Chas," Lynley said. "Nor pinching someone's jersey. Nor cribbing during an exam. We're talking about aggression. About torture. And murder."

Chas raised a hand to his brow. He bent his head to meet it. His skin was the colour of dirty paste. A shudder passed through his body, and his legs pressed together as if for warmth or protection. "Clive Pritchard," he said, and Lynley took the measure of how much the words cost him.

Without a sound, Sergeant Havers opened her notebook and produced a pencil from her jacket pocket. Lynley stayed where he was by the bookshelves. Beyond Chas, he could see the morning sky framed in the window, filled with the blinding purity of great cumulus clouds.

"Tell me about it," he said.

"It was a Saturday night about three weeks past. Matt Whateley brought me the tape and played it for me here in the room."

"Why didn't he give it to Mr. Lockwood?"

"For the same reason I didn't. He didn't want Clive to be expelled from the school. He just wanted him to leave Harry Morant—and everyone else—alone. That was what Matt was like. A decent little bloke. Live and let live."

"Clive knew you had the tape?"

"He's always known. I played it for him. Matt knew I'd do that. It was the only way to get Clive to leave Harry Morant alone. So I had him come up here and listen to it, and I told him if it happened again, I would hand the tape over to Lockwood. Clive wanted the tape, naturally. He even tried to get it. But Matt told me he'd made a duplicate, and I told Clive as much, so he saw there was no point in trying to pinch this one from me. Not unless he could get to the duplicate."

"You told him it was Matthew who had done the taping?"

Chas shook his head. Behind his spectacles, his eyes were bleak. A thin line of sweat beaded his upper lip. "I didn't tell him that. But it didn't take Clive long to figure it out for himself. Matt was Harry's closest mate here at school. They did model railways together. They were always hanging about together. They were both . . . a bit young for their age."

"I can try to understand keeping the tape to yourself once Matthew Whateley gave it to you," Lynley said. "Especially if it put the bullying to an end. I may not agree with your having done that, but at least I can understand. What I can't understand is the past three days. You must have known—"

"I didn't know anything for sure!" Chas protested. "I still don't. I knew Clive had bullied Harry Morant. I knew Matthew made the tape. I knew there was a duplicate. I knew Clive wanted it. But that's *all* I knew."

"When Matthew went missing, exactly what did you think?"

"What everyone else thought. That he'd run off. He wasn't very happy here. He didn't have many friends."

"And when his body was found? What did you think?"

"I didn't know. I *don't* know. I still don't . . ." The boy broke off wretchedly. He slumped in the chair.

"You chose not to know," Lynley said. "You chose not to ask questions. You chose to turn a blind eye to the obvious, didn't you?" He shoved the cassette into his pocket and looked at the display of quotations on the wall. The room seemed stifling. The smell of sweat and nerves burned into the air. "You forgot Marlowe," he told the boy. " 'There is no sin but ignorance.' Perhaps you'd like to add that to your collection."

When the detectives were gone, Chas put his head down upon his arms and finally allowed himself to weep, giving way to an anguish that had taken root from the seeds of his betrayal of his brother, that had blossomed with his loss of Sissy, that had borne fruit—bitter and malformed—in the last eight days of his life.

He had been trying to write about it, instinctively seeking a purgation of the spirit through the means of verse. He had excelled at that once, had littered the surface of his desk with countless poetic panegyrics to and for and about Sissy. But the agonies of the last few days—in conjunction with the torments that had howled in single-minded pursuit of him for more than a year—had silenced that interior voice which had soared within him, which had once so fired his soul and fueled his passion to write. There were no more words that could diminish a suffering which had become such an all-consuming presence in his life that it appeared to have neither alpha nor omega. It was a wretchedness that was monstrous in form, reaching out to attach itself to everything that brushed near the periphery of his life.

How convenient it had been to turn away from Preston, to excuse his abandonment of his brother by declaring it necessary to the salvation of his family's name. But the reality was that in proving himself not only fallible but also deeply troubled, Preston had fallen from the older-brother pedestal upon which Chas had placed him, and his *own* pride was wounded at having been duped by the guise of guilelessness that his brother had worn. So he had refused to speak to him once the charges were verified. He had refused to see him on his last morning at the school. He had refused to answer the single letter Preston wrote him. He had refused most of all to see a connection between this rejection of his brother and the fact that Preston had gone to Scotland and not returned.

In losing his brother, he had turned to Sissy, making her the vital force through which his blood flowed. In seven months she had grown from his schoolgirl friend, to the single safest harbour for his thoughts, to the inspiration of his writing, to the burning obsession that dominated every moment he did not spend in her company. But like his brother, Sissy was gone, destroyed by his selfishness and need, crushed by the force of an impetuosity that he had neither the sense nor the desire to control.

And hadn't that same impetuosity driven the machinery of Matthew Whateley's death? For without a second thought, he had played the tape for Clive Pritchard—he had even taken a secret satisfaction at the expression of astonishment on Clive's face when he realised he had actually been bettered by a little third former who should have been nothing more than an inconsequential ant beneath his

19

Sergeant Havers lit a cigarette without apology, and standing next to her, Lynley did not complain. They were in the council room across the corridor from the Headmaster's study in the east quadrangle. Although the windows looked out upon the cloisters down which both students and staff members passed, their voices amplified by the vaulted ceiling, neither Lynley nor Havers gave them the slightest notice. Instead, their attention was riveted upon the set of photographs Clive Pritchard had given them.

"Holy heaven," Havers said, mixing reverence with disgust. "I've seen . . . I mean, one can't go forever in CID without coming across pornography, can one? So I've seen it. I've *seen* it, sir. But this . . ."

Lynley understood exactly what Havers meant. He, too, had seen his share of pornography, not only as a police officer but also as a curious pre-adolescent, eager to understand, if not to experience first-hand, the mysteries of adult sexuality. Grainy photographs of men and women coupling for cameras in a variety of postures had always been obtainable if one had the money to pay for them. He could remember the guilty schoolboy giggling that accompanied a group perusal of such photographs, the sweat that smeared finger and palm prints across them, and the urgent self-grappling in the darkness that followed. Each boy wondered who would be his first woman and when it would happen and what it would mean if it didn't happen soon.

As unsavoury as those photographs had been with their bleach-haired women of sagging flesh and pockmarked men mounting them with grimaces of feigned pleasure, they were mild and innocuous compared with what lay before Lynley and Havers on the conference table. These photographs addressed themselves to more than mere voyeurism. Both the subjects and the poses in which they had been captured served as a titillation that was masochistic in origin and clearly paedophilic in design.

"This could be Lockwood's worst nightmare come true," Havers murmured. Ash fell from her cigarette onto one of the pictures. She brushed it off.

Lynley couldn't disagree. The pictures were all of nude children and adults, in both cases male, in all cases the child a subject of sexual bondage, under the power of the adult. This power was expressed through the use of weapons as props: a gun to the temple of a child in one picture, a knife pressed to the testicles in a second, a rope binding a blindfolded child in a third, a threatening live wire shooting sparks in a fourth. In all cases, the children performed upon grinning, aroused adults as if forced to do so, like little slave boys in a world of perverted sexual fantasy.

"It verifies Colonel Bonnamy's contention," Havers continued.

"It does that, doesn't it?" Lynley asked. For beyond the egregious attractions of paedophilia implied by the photographs, beyond the prurient interest in homosexuality they revealed, there remained the fact that every picture was biracial, as if each one represented a twisted commentary on the problems inherent to miscegenation. Whites mixed with Indians, blacks with whites, Orientals with blacks, whites with Orientals. Reminded of Colonel Bonnamy's contention about the racist connotation behind Matthew Whateley's death, Lynley knew it was impossible to avoid the connection between the boy's murder and the photographs before them.

Havers drew in on her cigarette and paced to the window overlooking the cloisters and quad. "It looks bad. It does look awful. But if you think about it, sir, there's something too convenient in Clive Pritchard having those snaps in his room. Just as if he was waiting for us to come along and question him so he could put them on the table and divert suspicion away from himself." She examined the end of her cigarette, her eyes narrowed in speculation. "Because without those snaps, things look pretty bad for our boy, don't they? He had easy access to an off-games chit—"

"As had everyone else, apparently, if it comes to that, Havers."

"—which he used so no one would miss Matthew Whateley when he nabbed him. He had access to that chamber above the drying room and seeing as it's in his own house, I'd say that makes it even more likely that he's our man. He had a motive as well. No matter his fancy couldn't-care-less talk about being booted out of Bredgar Chambers, you can't tell me that doesn't cause him some trouble at home."

"I see all that, Sergeant. But I also see what's before us on the table at the moment. Like it or not, we can't ignore either the subject matter of these pictures or the obvious possibility of a connection between them and Matthew Whateley's death."

Havers rejoined him, stubbed out her cigarette in a crystal ashtray in the centre of the table. She sighed, not with reluctant submission to the implicit order from a superior officer but rather with an acceptance of an unpleasantness to come. "Time for a visit with Emilia, I take it?"

"Quite."

They found the chemistry mistress alone in her laboratory on the ground floor of the science building. Her back to them as she worked at the glass and mahogany fume cupboard, Emilia Bond looked shrouded beneath her long academic gown, like a child playing dress-up in Renaissance garb. She peered over her shoulder as Lynley and Havers entered the room and closed the door behind them. The movement of her head ruffled her baby-fine hair like feathers.

"Setting up for a bit of fun," she explained and went on with her work, giving it her full attention.

They joined her. The front glass panel of the cupboard—built like a window—was pulled down nearly all the way, leaving room only for her hands to work deftly beneath it. Upon the cracked, white interior tiles stood a beaker of liquid into which she was adding a solid substance. She stirred the mixture with a clear glass rod and watched as a second, new solid began forming.

"Ammonium hydroxide and iodine," she announced, as if they had come to evaluate her performance. "They form ammonium tri-iodide."

"That's the bit of fun?" Lynley asked.

"Pupils invariably love it. It appeals to the prankster in all of them."

"And the danger involved? What does that appeal to?"

"Danger?" Her forehead creased with confusion.

"You're working inside the fume cupboard," Lynley pointed out. "I'm assuming your chemicals release some sort of gas."

She laughed. "Oh! No, there's no danger involved. Just a lot of mess if one isn't careful. Look. I've made one batch already." From a corner of the cupboard, she pulled forward a petrie dish that contained a small pyramid of yellow powder. She tapped a bit of this onto one of the tiles and pressed it with another glass rod. In answer, the powder popped and splattered up against the glass sides of the cupboard. Some of it landed like bright freckles on Emilia's arms. "It's mostly used for pranks," she admitted with a grin. "Occasionally I like to show my fifth formers a bit of chemical fun. It keeps their attention. Frankly, I'll do *anything* for their attention, Inspector."

She withdrew her hands from the cupboard, closed it, wiped the yellow speckles from her arms with a bit of rag from her pocket, and pushed down the sleeves of her academic gown. "I understand you've found Matthew Whateley's sock." She sounded businesslike. "Does that bring you any closer to the truth?"

In reply, Lynley handed her a manila envelope into which he had placed the photographs. "Perhaps," he replied.

She took the envelope from him, opened it, and removed its contents. She said only, "I should hope—" before, with the photographs in her hand, she walked to one of the work stations and sat on the tall stool in front of it. Her face worked as she looked through the first three photographs on the stack. Her eyes darted from the pictures themselves to her hands which held them. Lynley saw this, his heart growing heavy. At least in this matter, it seemed that Clive Pritchard had been telling the truth.

"My God, how horrible," Emilia murmured. She placed the stack face down, and looked up at Lynley. "Wherever did you get these? What have they to do with—"

"One of the students gave them to me, Miss Bond. He saw you dumping them onto the rubbish fire near the porter's lodge late Saturday night."

Emilia pushed the photographs away from her. "I see. Well. You've found me out." She sounded like a child trying hard to be clever. "They're awful, aren't they, but they seemed harmless enough, and I simply wanted to get rid of them without anyone being the wiser. I took them from one of my students, a boy in the lower sixth, as a matter of fact." She hooked her feet round the legs of the stool as if to keep herself anchored upon it. "I should have reported him. I realise that. But we had a good talk—a terribly thorough talk—and he was awfully embarrassed. In the end, I promised I'd get rid of them. I had no idea—"

"You don't lie well, Miss Bond," Lynley interrupted. "Some people do. To your credit, you're not one of them."

"Lie?"

"Your face is flushed. You've begun to perspire. I imagine your incriminating himself. A fibre. A hair. Something. So he'd get the keys from the porter's office, take the bus, and be careful not to leave his prints anywhere on it."

Lynley couldn't deny the idea's plausibility. He thought again about Thomas Gray's poem, about the stanza that he had read with Deborah St. James, about how it accurately described the boy himself and the manner in which the body had been dealt with. It was hard to believe a pupil would go to trouble like that.

"The problem is poetry," Lynley said pensively and explained Thomas Gray's poem to Sergeant Havers.

She countered with another idea. "What about all the verses on Chas Quilter's wall? He seems fairly familiar with English poetry."

"Where's his motive, Sergeant?"

"There's that," she admitted. "There *is* that, isn't there?"

"We've two clear-cut motives as far as I can see. Clive Pritchard has one."

"John Corntel has the other?"

Lynley nodded grimly. "How can we look past the implications of that collection of photographs?"

"A little clutch-and-feel with Matthew, and oops, he's dead?" Havers asked crudely.

"Perhaps an accident."

"Too tight with the noose? Too liberal with the electricity?"

The entire idea made Lynley feel ill. He shook off the sensation and felt in his pocket for the keys to his car, which he handed to Havers. "Go to Cissbury, Sergeant," he told her. "See what kind of verification you can get on Clive Pritchard's story."

"And you, Inspector?" she asked.

"It's time to face the worst about John Corntel," he replied.

Lynley rounded the side of the chapel as the police van from Horsham pulled to a halt. Three scenes-of-crime men from Horsham CID climbed out, satchels and equipment in hand. Alan Lockwood joined Lynley at the van. The plan was simple. The team would work in the chamber above the Calchus House drying room and move on to the school's minibuses afterwards, dusting for prints, collecting evidence, taking photographs. Lockwood volunteered to show them the way.

After seeing them off in the direction of Calchus House, Lynley re-entered the main school building, crossed the foyer, and walked into the quad. He passed beneath the statue of Henry VII whose unyielding marble features spoke smugly of victory won at the cost of betrayal. The thought of that five-hundred-year-old conquest and the acts of treachery which had made it possible slowed Lynley's steps momentarily, giving him pause to think about his past association with John Corntel and how that past association called out to dictate his behaviour now. Tradition demanded loyalty from him, while treachery only promised to come attended by its faithful companion, regret. Had that not been the lesson learned by those who had betrayed their anointed king on the field of battle? As individuals, their gain had been but a fleeting bagatelle. Their loss was infinite.

Lynley thought of his present predicament with a measure of self-derisive amusement. How easily it was to demand and expect an eighteen-year-old boy like Chas Quilter to cast off the chains of custom and point the finger of accusation at a schoolmate. When the tables were turned, how difficult it was to expect of oneself that same level of unbending moral rectitude. The manila envelope Lynley carried, so insubstantial a physical burden earlier in the morning, felt weighted by lead.

Whited sepulchre to be sure, he thought in disgust and followed the cobbled path to the dining hall.

Its size was vast, a room capacious enough to hold the entire school at once. They were gathering at refectory tables, arranged by house, with the older students at one end, the younger at the other, the housemaster at the head, and the house prefect at the foot.

The noise bordered on intolerable, six hundred pupils shouting, laughing, and talking all at once. All conversation ceased, however, when Chas Quilter mounted the steps of a monastic-looking podium and began to read aloud from scripture. Lynley waited until Chas had finished the brief passage before he crossed to the tables designated for Erebus House. The roar of voices resumed again as food carts were wheeled out from the kitchen.

Corntel had gone to the end of the table where he was shouting some instructions into Brian Byrne's ear. The Erebus House prefect nodded, as if he were listening, but Lynley saw that his eyes followed Chas Quilter as the other boy made his way to the table where the Ion House boys sat. For a moment after Corntel had stopped speaking, Brian's gaze remained fixed on Chas, a tic pulling at a muscle in the corner of his mouth.

By the time Lynley reached John Corntel, the other man had seen him coming. Perhaps reading Lynley's intention upon his face, Corntel suggested that they go to his classroom rather than talk in front of the pupils. It was quite near, he explained, just above, on the first floor in the humanities section.

With a final set of instructions to Brian Byrne, Corntel led the way out of the dining hall. They climbed the worn stone stairs in the west foyer and walked without speaking to Corntel's classroom on the corridor that ran the length of the building, south to north. The room overlooked the vast playing fields on which an abandoned football lay beside a goal post. Lynley looked out the window, noting that the sky was growing progressively darker as storm clouds moved in their direction from the west.

He couldn't decide how to confront his old schoolmate, reluctant to come face to face with an aberration of character that he found both incomprehensible and unquestionably repugnant. There didn't seem to be an appropriate manner in which to begin the conversation. He turned from the window and saw the blackboard.

Phrases covered it. Lynley read through them as Corntel watched him from a position near the door. *Ironic reference to mercy; daughter versus ducats; the price of enmity; moral worth; realistic grievances; repetition of blood imagery.* At the top of the board, Corntel had written, "The villainy you teach me I will execute."

"*The Merchant of Venice?*" Lynley asked.

"Yes." Corntel advanced into the room. The desks were arranged in a horseshoe to facilitate discussion between students and teacher. He stood by one of these, as if waiting for permission to sit. "I've always liked the play. That delicious hypocrisy of Portia. Speaking eloquently of mercy. Knowing none herself."

It was the opening Lynley needed. "I wonder if that's a theme in your own life as well." He went to Corntel and handed him the envelope. A desk separated them, but in spite of its presence—like a convenient bulwark—Lynley could sense the stress in the other man.

Obviously striving for lightness, Corntel asked, "What is this, Tommy?"

"Open it."

As Corntel did so, he started to speak. Whatever words he intended to say, however, passed into nothing when he saw the nature of the photographs. Like Emilia Bond earlier, he pulled out a chair. But unlike the chemistry mistress, he did not attempt to explain away ownership of the pornography.

Instead, he looked stricken. His words explained the source of his pain. "She gave them to you. She *gave* them . . ."

Lynley knew he could spare him at least part of the mortification.

"No. A boy saw her trying to burn them late Saturday night. He handed them over. She tried to deny they were yours."

"She can't lie, can she? Not Em."

"I don't think she can. That's greatly to her credit." Corntel had not looked up from the pictures. Lynley saw that the other man had begun to clutch them. "Can you explain them to me, John? You must know how bad it looks that you had them in the first place."

"Not the sort of thing one wants to find in a teacher of children. Especially under the present circumstances." Still Corntel did not lift his head. As he spoke, he began leafing through the pictures slowly. "I've always wanted to write, Tommy. Isn't that every English teacher's dream? Don't we all say we *could* write that book if we only had the time or the discipline or the energy once our papers are marked? And this—these pictures—they were the first step." He used hushed tones to relay the information, like a man speaking after the act of love. He continued to go through the pictures. "I know I deliberately chose a sensational subject. For ease of publication, that sort of thing. But one has to start somewhere. It didn't seem like such an awfully dishonest way to begin. I realise how little artistic integrity is inherent to such a project. Still, I thought it would give me a foot in the door." His words were growing slower, more dazed, hypnotic. "And then I could go on. I could write . . . write to my passion. Yes, to my passion. That's what good writing is, isn't it? An act of passion. An act of joy. A kind of ecstasy that others only dream of, that others don't even know exists. . . . And these pictures . . . these pictures . . ."

Corntel traced the figure of one of the naked children. He moved a finger to the aroused adult. He played it along the man's muscular thighs to his groin, across his chest, and up to his lips. He went to another picture and did much the same, lingering over the unnatural mating between child and adult with a misty smile.

Observing, Lynley said nothing. He couldn't have found the words had he tried. Corntel may have hidden himself behind the convenient intention of writing a novel. But the truth was exposed in the pulse that beat rapidly in his temple, in the manner in which he ran his tongue over his lips, in the rapture of his voice. Lynley felt a surge of disgust pass over him. It was followed by pity, profound and deep.

Corntel roused himself and saw that Lynley was watching him. He dropped the pictures. They spread out on the desk.

"God," he whispered.

Lynley found his voice. "I've a little boy dead, John, a boy not much older than these in the pictures. He was tied up. He was tortured. He was . . . God knows what else."

Corntel pushed away from the desk and walked to the windows. He looked out at the playing fields. This seemed to give him the courage to turn and begin to speak. "I began collecting the pictures on a trip to London," he said. "When I saw my first one—in a very private section of an adult bookshop in Soho—I was appalled. And fascinated. And drawn to it. I bought it. And then others. At first, I took them out only on holidays, away from the school. Then I allowed myself an evening once a month in my study, with the curtains drawn. It didn't seem so bad. Then once a week. Then, finally, almost every night. I'd look forward to it. I'd . . ." He looked back outside. "I'd have a glass of wine. I'd . . . Candles, I lit candles. I imagined . . . What I told you at first isn't so far from the truth. I imagined stories about them. Stories. I named them. The boys. Not the adults." He went back to the pictures. "This boy was Stephen," he explained, pointing to a child who was bound and gagged on an antique brass bed. "And this . . . this was Colin. And I called this one Paul. And Guy. And William." He reached for another. His courage seemed to falter. "And this one. I called this one John."

It was the only picture in which two adults were featured, both of them abusing a powerless child. Although he had seen it already, there was no escaping the awful weight of meaning behind Corntel's giving the child his own Christian name.

"John," he said, "you need—"

"Help?" Corntel smiled. "That's for people who don't know their disease. I know mine, Tommy. I always have. Look how it's demonstrated in the way I've lived my life. Giving over power to anyone who wanted it—my father, my mother, my schoolmates, my superiors. Never taking action on my own. Incapable of doing so." Corntel dropped the pictures. "Even with Emilia."

"Her story about Friday night isn't the same as yours, John."

"No. It wouldn't be. I'm . . . Tommy, I had to tell you something, didn't I? I knew you'd eventually discover how upset she was when she left me Friday night, so I invented a reason. Impotency seemed . . . I had to, didn't I? And what difference does it make? What I told you was as near to the truth as . . . Shall I tell you now? It was . . . We managed it. Just. She was very kind."

"She didn't act as if it had anything to do with kindness."

"She wouldn't. That's not her way. She's a good person, Tommy. When she saw how difficult it . . . everything was for me, she managed it all. I let her. I gave her control over everything. And when she came back Saturday night and asked for the photographs—demanded them, actually—I gave them over as well. It seemed the best way I could make reparation for who I am, for what I am. Not a normal man, really. Not anything at all."

Lynley wanted to ask Corntel a hundred questions. More than anything, he wanted to understand how a young man possessed of such a brilliant future had evolved into what he saw before him now. He wanted to understand what would make a world of distorted fantasy more attractive than a vital connection with another human being. Part of the answer, he already knew. There was safety in the life of imagination, no matter how deviant that life actually was. There was no risk involved. One's inner being was never really touched, so one's heart would never be pierced or bear scars. But the rest of the answer remained locked in Corntel, perhaps inexplicable even to himself.

He felt a need to offer his old schoolmate some sort of comfort, to lessen his shame at having been thus exposed. He said, "Emilia loves you."

Corntel shook his head. He gathered up the pictures and replaced them in the envelope, which he handed to Lynley. "She loves the John Corntel she created. The real man she doesn't even know."

Lynley descended the stairs slowly. He brooded over each exchange he'd had with John Corntel, feeling as if, for the last few days, he'd become a spectator caught up in a shifting drama in which Corntel acted out several roles from behind a continuing altering mist.

He'd come to London in the role of housemaster, guilt-ridden over the disappearance of Matthew Whateley. There, he had been a man seeking help, accepting full blame for his part in a series of institutional failures that had culminated in the boy's vanishing from the school. But in spite of the guise of cooperation he had worn, he had not been willing to reveal the distraction which had kept him from seeing to Matthew's welfare during the weekend that had passed.

Emilia Bond had been that distraction, and out of Corntel's relationship with her rose the second role he played—the lover plagued by humiliation. No matter the contents of his personal disclosures to Lynley, the emotion behind them was always the same. Whether alleging a failure to perform adequately in bed or confessing that Emilia Bond had guided their lovemaking, it made no difference. Humiliation was the outcome, and under that humiliation was buried a plea for pity and understanding that Lynley had not failed to hear. He recognised it again when Corntel adopted the third role in their drama.

In the collector of pornography, Corntel portrayed the pathetic neurotic. More, in giving his name to one of the children in the photographs, he went a step further. He painted himself as a victim, not a perpetrator, and asked Lynley to believe that such was the case. Yet all of it seemed too convenient at the moment. All of it had fallen into place too well. For although Corntel had developed an elaborate fantasy world round his photographs, Lynley knew that the loneliness of such an existence might have prompted him to seek reality at last. If the reality that was Emilia Bond had proved a disappointment to the man, what was to prevent Corntel from seeking an actuality that more closely resembled the unhealthy world of his dreams? What was to prevent him from making Matthew Whateley part of that experience?

Surely Corntel knew he had not been eliminated as a suspect merely because he had been forthcoming with bits and pieces of his personal torments. Even if Lynley had been able to dismiss his suspicions, Corntel couldn't believe he would do nothing about the photographs tucked under his arm. They should, by rights, go to the Headmaster. Whether or not Corntel was guilty of Matthew Whateley's death, Lockwood should be the one to decide what to do about the man. It was his job, after all. It was his responsibility.

Yet there were other considerations here. Lynley accepted the inevitability of that fact. There was the memory of Eton. There was his drunken stupor and Corntel's decision not to hand him over for expulsion from the school. There was the memory of his schoolmate speaking eloquently in the chapel, writing prize-winning essays, making himself available to help boys less gifted and less articulate than he. There was seeing him clearly in his striped trousers and cutaway, dashing under the arched gateway, late for a lesson but still having time to help the porter wrestle a large package from a lorry onto the ground. There was seeing that quick smile, hearing the shouted greeting from across the schoolyard. There was a shared expanse of history. There was a common experience. There was— and always would be—the old school tie.

Lynley felt the package of photographs under his arm. They cried out for a decision. He could not make one.

"Inspector." Alan Lockwood was standing at the foot of the stairs. "Might I expect an arrest this afternoon?"

"Once the crime scene men—"

"Bugger the crime scene men! I want Clive Pritchard out of this school. The Board of Governors are gathering for a meeting here tonight, and I want this cleared up before they arrive. God knows when Pritchard's family will claim him. Until they do, I won't have him here. Is that clear?"

"Perfectly," Lynley replied. "Unfortunately, all we have at the moment is a tape with his voice on it. We have no evidence that he did anything to Matthew Whateley, and even Harry Morant won't name him as his tormentor. I can't arrest him on the strength of Chas Quilter's identifying his voice, Mr. Lockwood. All I can do is suggest that you keep an eye on him."

"Keep an *eye*—" Lockwood spat. "You *know* he killed that boy!"

"I know nothing of the sort. I make an arrest on evidence, not intuition."

"You're putting six hundred pupils at risk! Do you realise that? If you don't remove that little bastard from the school, anything could happen. To anyone. I won't be responsible—"

"You *are* responsible," Lynley said. "That's the truth of the matter. But Clive knows he's under suspicion. He's hardly going to step out of line now. Especially since he apparently believes that nothing we have so far can tie him to Matthew Whateley."

"What do you suggest I do with him until you've decided you have something substantial upon which you can base your arrest?"

"I suggest you confine him to his room with someone posted outside to see that he doesn't leave it."

"And *that* will be sufficient?" Lockwood demanded. "He's a killer, blast you. You *know* it." The Headmaster pointed to the envelope under Lynley's arm. "And those? What has your investigation managed to uncover about the pictures, Inspector?"

It was, after all, an easy decision. Now, in this moment. For better or worse.

"Miss Bond found them in her classroom," he said. "Apparently a student had left them behind. She didn't know who it was. She thought it best to burn them."

Lockwood snorted. "At least someone has shown a bit of common sense."

It was beginning to rain again when Sergeant Havers pulled Lynley's Bentley to a halt alongside the chapel. She stepped on the brakes so hard that the car lurched forward and swerved to one side, grazing against the bare branches of a row of pruned hydrangeas. Lynley winced and went to join her.

She was just finishing a bag of vinegar crisps. Crumbs and salt sequined the front of her pullover.

"Lunch," she explained to him, brushing the remnants off her chest as she got out. "Two bags of crisps and a glass of bitter lemon. I should get combat pay." She shoved the door closed. "This thing's a monster, Inspector. It takes up half the road. I nearly bashed into a call box in Cissbury and I swear I hit an old milestone just beyond the school. At least, I think that's what it was. Something inanimate and solid."

"That's a comforting thought," Lynley responded, removing his umbrella from the rear seat. Without one herself, Havers joined him under his. "What did you uncover in Cissbury?"

They began walking in the direction of Calchus House. A bell sounded the summons for afternoon lessons. For a few moments they were caught up in the tide of blue and yellow uniforms as schoolchildren hurried past them in the rain. Havers didn't speak until they were alone on the path. "As far as I can tell, Clive's story checks out, sir. The barman at the Sword and Garter saw him by the rubbish bin late Saturday night. He couldn't exactly tell what Clive was doing, but in his words, 'Whatever it was, he was doing it to a bird who seemed to like it well enough.'"

"Are there lights by the rubbish bin?"

Havers shook her head. "And the barman couldn't describe the boy he saw other than in general terms about his size. He didn't know the girl at all, or at least he didn't get a clear look at her. So we *can* say the boy wasn't necessarily Clive."

"It could have been another boy from the school," Lynley agreed.

She took up the idea with an enthusiasm that suggested she had been thinking it over since leaving the village. "Someone Clive knew would be sneaking off to meet a girl in the village on Saturday night. Someone who might have bragged to Clive about his conquest afterwards, including details of the encounter by the rubbish bin."

Lynley saw how her hypothesis didn't quite fit together. "It sounds good enough, but when it comes down to it, Havers, my guess is that Clive's going to hand over the name of that girl. She'll verify his identity. We'll be back to square one. What time did the barman see them?"

"Just after midnight." Havers dragged her feet on the path. After a moment of reflection she said, "Well, there *does* seem to be something in that, sir. Clive's clever. We saw that in the way he chose to use those pictures at just the right moment. I can see him going into Cissbury to arrange an alibi and then coming back to deal with Matthew Whateley's body later. He claims that he saw Emilia Bond when he was coming over the wall from his trip to the village. But he could just as easily have come back earlier, taken the minibus to Stoke Poges, dumped the body, and seen Emilia Bond upon his return. She didn't see him, after all. We've only his word that he saw her when he was climbing over the wall. And if Frank Orten saw the fire round three in the morning, surely Clive had time to do everything."

"Stretching it, Havers."

"A bit. But he could have. He *could* have. And you can't tell me that bloke wouldn't know how to orchestrate a crime. His first words from the cradle were probably 'synchronise your watches.' If you ask me, all we need is some evidence from that room in Calchus House, something more from the minibus, and Clive Pritchard as we know and love him is going to be history."

Lynley frowned, going over Havers' words in his mind. Getting no response from him, she continued.

"I saw Jean Bonnamy in the village as well. Posting some letters. She was a bit done up, Inspector, like she was going to meet someone for lunch."

"Hardly a suspicious activity, Sergeant."

"I know that. But when she's seen to herself, she's not half-bad. Nice hair, nice skin. I had a good look at her. And I couldn't help wondering what she might have looked like fourteen years ago, what she might have looked like to an eighteen-year-old boy."

"Edward Hsu."

"It's possible, isn't it? She's lived in Hong Kong. She has her father's love for things Chinese. She might be Matthew Whateley's real mother. She might have kept track of him all these years. She might even have seen to it that he was sent to their house as a Bredgar Volunteer. We have only Giles Byrne's description of what Matthew's natural mother was like, scheming and money-grubbing. Perhaps she wasn't like that at all."

"Your argument suggests Giles Byrne is more involved in Matthew Whateley's birth than he would like us to think."

"Jean Bonnamy could have known about Giles Byrne through Edward Hsu. She could have gone to him for help. And now, to protect her, Giles Byrne might be lying like the devil."

"We've thought that from the first about Byrne," Lynley agreed. "Perhaps Constable Nkata will find something in Exeter."

"Or nothing," Havers added.

"Then we'll be closer to the truth." Lynley guided Sergeant Havers across the lane to Calchus House. "Let's see what the crime scene team have come up with."

The team were still at work up above the drying room, and the crime scene photographer was just climbing down the metal ladder, followed by one of the other officers.

"Anything?" Lynley asked the second man who was carrying a work case. Above them a vacuum began to howl.

The officer placed his case on the floor, squatted over it, and said over his shoulder, "Just finished dusting for prints. They're hundreds of them. Hairs. Fibres. It's like a rubbish heap."

"How long before you—"

"We don't have the manpower of the Met, Inspector. We'll be sorting through everything for weeks. That's the best we can manage."

Lynley knew how reluctantly Horsham CID had sent their crime scene team to the school in the first place. He chose his words carefully. "We've one of the upper sixth boys under suspicion. If there's anything we can use to tie him to this room, to tie Matthew Whateley to this room . . ."

The man scratched his head, rearranging a haystack of untidy grey hair. "Whateley was . . . how old?"

"Thirteen."

"Hmmm. Does seem unlikely that Whateley . . ." The man removed the top tray from his case and brought out three plastic bags. "These might have belonged to your upper sixth lad," he said. "I'm not certain a thirteen-year-old would have been using them, and I hope to hell an adult would have the finesse to arrange his sexual liaisons in a more attractive environment. Apologies to you, Sergeant. Not a sight for a lady." He dangled the bags in front of their faces. Each contained a used condom. As he continued to speak, he swung the bags back and forth, keeping time to his words. "An old blanket's been used up there as well. We've packaged that already. I've money on its showing plenty of stains. *You* know the sort I'm speaking of, no doubt. Appears the room was used for a bit more than . . . Well"—he grinned lasciviously—"no doubt you take my meaning."

"The drawings on the wall suggest that well enough," Lynley said drily. Havers, he noted, was standing with her arms folded across her chest, her face a stubborn refusal to give in to the Horsham officer's attempt to embarrass her. She was used to it. Women had been in CID for years, but not everyone welcomed them. Lynley drew her into the corridor.

She was quick to speak. "Those fit in with Clive's personality, don't they?"

He nodded. "Anyone who'd have at a girl standing up next to a rubbish bin would hardly draw the line at having her lie down in a bit of dust and filth. And yet, I wonder about Clive's willingness to take precautions against pregnancy, Havers. That seems out of character, doesn't it?"

Havers' face registered the extent of her distaste. "Unless the girl insisted. Although I can't imagine *any* girl in her right mind wanting to . . . up there . . . alone with him . . . Frankly, our Clive made my skin crawl, Inspector. So whoever the girl is, I should guess she goes in for whips and chains. That seems to be Clive's style."

"If we can find her, Havers, we'll have someone who can place Clive Pritchard in that room."

"Affirmation that he knew of the room's existence," Havers concluded. Her eyes widened as she completed the thought. "Daphne!"

"Daphne?"

"The girl he went after in Cowfrey Pitt's German class. If I'm not mistaken about her, she's just the person we're looking for to put the thumbscrews to Clive."

They returned to the administrative offices in the east quadrangle, seeking the current location of the girl whom Clive Pritchard had harassed on the previous day. The Headmaster's secretary had all the pupils' schedules in a file on her desk, but instead of looking through it to seek the information Lynley wanted, she handed him a telephone message and spoke curtly enough to transmit her displeasure at having to come into unsavoury contact with the police.

"Scotland Yard," she said. "You're to phone them." As Lynley's eyes dropped to the telephone on her desk, she added icily, "From the porter's office, if you please."

Frank Orten was not at his desk when they entered his office. The room was unoccupied, a fact that was not lost on Lynley. Hanging against the wall on the other side of the counter that separated Orten's work space from a waiting area designated by the presence of three wooden chairs, keys dangled from a pegboard. Lynley went behind the counter and examined them. Havers remained by the door.

"Minibus keys are there, aren't they?" she asked.

Lynley found them on a hook above which was a label printed with the single word *vehicles*. Other hooks had labels as well, printed with the names of the various buildings: *maths, technical centre, theatre*, etc. The houses were also represented by labels, the two girls' houses—Galatea and Eirene—segregated from the boys' houses on the other side of the board. Havers had indeed been accurate in her assessment of the school's security. It was nonexistent.

The office door opened, and Frank Orten entered. His quasi-military cap was pulled low on his forehead, and his jacket and trousers were spotted from the rain. He hesitated in the doorway, looking from Havers to Lynley to the pegboard of keys.

Lynley spoke. "How often is your office unoccupied like this, Mr. Orten? Would you say it's a fairly common occurrence?"

Orten went to his desk behind the counter. He removed his hat and placed it on a shelf next to a glass jar filled with small pink and white seashells. "Wouldn't say that," he replied.

"At least once a day? Twice? More?"

Orten looked offended. "One goes to the toilet, Inspector. No law against that, as far as I know."

"Leaving the office unlocked?"

"I'm not out of it three minutes!"

"And this time?"

"This time?"

Lynley indicated the state of the man's uniform. "You've been out in the rain. Surely you don't need to go outside to find a lavatory, do you?"

Orten turned to his desk. A large black binder sat upon it. He opened this. "Elaine has my daughter's kids with her at Erebus. I checked on them."

"Your daughter is still in hospital?"

"She is."

"Which hospital is that?"

Orten swung round in his chair. "St. John's. In Crawley." He saw Sergeant Havers make note of his answer. He adjusted his neck against the high collar of his uniform jacket. "What's this?" he demanded.

"Details, Mr. Orten," Lynley replied. "I've come to use your telephone, if I may."

Orten shoved the telephone towards Lynley in a fashion that did not hide his irritation. Lynley dialled the number for the Yard and within moments was speaking to Dorothea Harriman. He did not give her an opportunity to deliver her message. Instead, his earlier conversation with Sergeant Havers in mind, he asked:

"Has Constable Nkata reported in yet, Dee?" On the other end of the line, he could hear Superintendent Webberly's secretary shuffling through papers. In the background, word processor keys tapped and a printer whirred.

"You're in luck, as usual," Harriman replied. "He rang from Exeter not twenty minutes past."

"And?"

"Nothing."

"Nothing?"

"That was his message. 'Tell the Inspector nothing.' Seemed a bit cheeky to me, but that's Nkata's style, isn't it?"

Lynley didn't bother to correct her impression of the constable's message. He understood it well enough. The Exeter investigation into Giles Byrne's story about Matthew Whateley's birth was turning up nothing. Sergeant Havers' intuition was proving accurate.

Harriman was continuing. "You've had some information from Slough police that I thought you'd want, Detective Inspector. They've completed the autopsy. There's a clear cause of death."

"What have they told us?"

"Poisoning," she replied.

Lynley's mind began to race with ideas. It *was* as he had thought: something in the food Matthew Whateley had been given while held in the chamber above the drying room; something he had drunk; something that had worked quickly upon him; something a pupil had access to. . . .

Then Dorothea Harriman spoke again, her words cutting through and destroying the entire direction of his thoughts.

"It was carbon monoxide," she said.

20

It was nearly four o'clock when Detective Inspector Canerone of the Slough CID ushered Lynley into his office, a cramped cubicle furnished in metal and plastic, with a preponderance of Ordnance Survey maps on the walls. An electric kettle—hissing steam from its spout—sat atop one of the three dented filing cabinets, while on another were arranged a child's collection of Beatrix Potter figurines.

"They belonged to my son," Canerone said in explanation. "I couldn't bring myself to throw them away when he moved off with his mum. Tea?" He pulled open one of the cabinet drawers from which he produced a china teapot, two cups, two saucers, and a sugar bowl. "She left this behind as well," he continued, unabashed. "It seemed a shame to leave it all at home where it'll never get used. There's no milk. You don't mind?"

"Not at all."

Lynley watched the other detective make the tea. His movements were ponderous, and he paused frequently as if considering whether a potential gesture were a solecism that might cause him social embarrassment.

"You're working the case alone?" Canerone asked. "That's not typical of the Met, is it?"

"I've a sergeant to assist. She's still out at the school."

Carefully Canerone placed teapot, sugar, cups, and saucers on a tray which he carried to his desk. "You think the boy was killed there." It was a conclusion rather than a point of interrogation.

"I thought so originally," Lynley replied. "But now I'm not certain. It's the carbon monoxide that's thrown me off."

Canerone pulled open the top drawer of his desk and removed a package of digestive biscuits. He placed two on each of the saucers and filled the cups with tea. Handing one to Lynley, he munched on a biscuit and opened a folder that lay in the centre of his desk.

"Let's see what we have." He blew across the surface of his tea and took a noisy sip.

"One usually associates carbon monoxide with cars," Lynley said. "But one *can* be exposed to it—and die from it—in other ways as well."

"There's truth in that." Canerone nodded. "From coal gas. From a faulty furnace. From a stopped-up flue."

"In a room. In a building."

"Certainly." Canerone used a biscuit to gesture at the report. "But the concentration attached to the haemoglobin was high. So the boy was exposed to it in heavy volume. And, I should guess, in a fairly confined space."

"The room I have in mind is quite small. Up under the eaves and above a drying room. Lots of pipes running through it."

"Gas pipes?"

"I'm not certain. Perhaps."

"Then the room's a possibility. But I rather think . . . No. Unless it's dwarf-sized, I don't think it'll work. Not at this concentration in the blood. And not if the lad was the only one to die. You can verify this with our forensic team, but I think you'll find they agree."

Lynley knew he had to adjust his thinking. He did so reluctantly. "Could the boy have died while being transported somewhere in a vehicle?"

Canerone seemed interested in this line of thought. "That's more sensible than the room, to be sure. Bound and gagged in a vehicle— perhaps in the boot—with the driver not knowing that the exhaust was leaking inside to kill the boy. That's a good possibility."

"And when the driver reached his destination and discovered what had happened to the boy, he dumped the body in Stoke Poges and fled."

At this, Canerone shook his head. He popped the rest of his first biscuit into his mouth. "That's unlikely. Lividity had already set in. The body had been moved from the site of death into that cemetery quite some time *after* death. Our man's guessing, at the extreme, twenty-four hours."

"So Matthew would have had to be dead in that vehicle for an entire day before his body was moved."

"A risky business," Canerone pointed out reasonably. "Unless our killer's sure that no one's going to prowl round his car. But whatever the truth turns out to be, it's a certainty that the boy didn't die on the hour's drive between the school and the churchyard." Thoughtfully he tapped the report against his desk. "Perhaps our killer was intent upon taking him somewhere else. Perhaps he reached his destination, found the boy dead, panicked, left the car, and took twenty-four hours to come up with a way to dispose of the body."

"By removing it from his car to another vehicle? A minibus perhaps?"

"There's something in that," Canerone agreed. "I'd say a bit of evidence as well, since one wouldn't want to risk having a body lying openly in a minibus." He turned a page of the report and handed a document to Lynley. "You recall the fibres caught up in the boy's hair? Wool and rayon. What does that suggest to you?"

"Anything. A piece of clothing. Rug from a car."

"Coloured orange." Canerone attended to his second biscuit.

"The blanket," Lynley said.

Canerone raised his head questioningly. Lynley told him about the drying room, about the chamber above it, about the room's contents. "Horsham CID have taken the blanket for analysis."

"Get us a patch of it. We'll see if we can match the fibres."

Lynley had no doubt that a match would be made. The fibres would connect Matthew Whateley to the blanket. The blanket would place Matthew Whateley in the room. If Havers had any luck with Daphne, Clive Pritchard would be associated with the room as well. The circle of the crime was beginning to close, overriding Clive's story about how he spent Saturday night.

". . . the analysis on the deposits under the boy's toenails and on his shoulders and buttocks." Canerone broke into Lynley's thoughts.

"Sorry?"

"We've completed that analysis. It's potassium hydroxide, but its two other names might be more familiar to you. Caustic potash. Lye."

"*Lye?*"

"Odd, isn't it?"

"Where could Matthew Whateley have come upon lye?"

"If he was held, bound and gagged, somewhere," Canerone pointed out, "he would have picked up the lye in that location, I should guess."

Lynley weighed the implications of this against what he had come to know about Bredgar Chambers. As he did so, Canerone continued, his manner affable.

"Every schoolboy knows the basics about lye, that it's used in soap and detergents. So I should think you're looking for a storeroom of some sort. Perhaps a place where the cleaning agents are kept. A shed. An outbuilding." Canerone poured himself a second cup of tea. "Or there's the possibility that he came into contact with the lye in the boot of the vehicle in which he died. If that's the case, you may be looking for a service vehicle, one that does hauling and clean-up for the school."

Canerone went on, and although Lynley made appropriate replies, his thoughts drifted elsewhere. He evaluated the information he had and admitted to himself the possibility that he was twisting the facts to fit a case that he had sketched out in his mind, instead of collecting the facts and building a case upon them. Failing to maintain an objective distance until all the information had been gathered was always the risk of policework. He had walked this perilous route once before, so he recognised his tendency to draw a conclusion too soon. More significantly, he recognised his propensity for letting loyalties from the past colour his interpretation of the present. He put up his guard against that proclivity and forced himself to assess the relative strength of each piece of evidence they had come across.

The danger inherent to an investigation into murder grew out of the need for haste. The more quickly the police gathered pertinent details, the likelier that an arrest would follow. But the attendant hazard was that reality could become easily blurred. The need to fix guilt often resulted in the unconscious suppression of a fact that might otherwise lead in a new direction. Lynley was aware of this. He saw how it was acting upon the investigation now.

The carbon monoxide poisoning had turned the case on its ear. It made the chamber above the drying room an unlikely location for Matthew Whateley's death. If the new reality was that Matthew Whateley had died elsewhere, then the additional new reality was that—no matter how Lynley longed to pin guilt upon him—Clive Pritchard was not only not involved, but also telling the truth. Inexorably, then, that truth led back to the photographs. The photographs led back to John Corntel.

There had to be a way to verify that the room in Calchus House could not have been a source of the poison that killed the boy. Before moving on, that verification had to be made. Lynley knew beyond a doubt the very man who could make it. Simon Allcourt-St. James.

*   *   *

"Tuesday last," Colonel Bonnamy said. The words slurred into one another. That was always the case late in the day when his strength diminished. "Tuesday last, Jeannie."

Jean Bonnamy poured her father less than half a cup of tea. Because he suffered from tremors as he grew more exhausted, a half-cup was all he could manage without spilling, and he refused to allow her to hold a fuller cup to his lips. Rather than suffer the ignominy of being fed and watered like a toddler, he took his tea and his food in smaller portions. His daughter didn't mind. She knew how important dignity was to him, and little enough remained of that once she'd helped him to dress or bathe or get to the lavatory.

"I know, Dad," she replied, but she didn't want to talk about Matthew Whateley. If they spoke about the boy, she would begin to weep. Her father would respond by breaking down himself, and in his condition, that would be dangerous. His blood pressure had been high for the last two days. She was determined that nothing would force it higher.

"He would have been with us yesterday, girl." Her father lifted the teacup to his lips. The shaking in his arm rattled the china against his teeth.

"Shall I play chess with you, Dad? Would you like that?"

" 'N place of Matthew? No. Leave the board be." Her father placed his cup in his saucer. He took a slice of buttered bread from the plate on the table between them. He shivered.

Seeing him do so, Jean realised how cold the sitting room had grown. Darkness was rapidly falling outside—intensified by the continuing rain and the bank of tenebrous grey clouds that pushed from the west—and the gloom of the late afternoon was matched only by the chill that seeped into the cottage like a stealthy intruder.

The electric fire was lit, and their old retriever basked in front of it quite happily. But the heat did not carry across the sitting room to their chairs. Watching her father shiver again, Jean spoke.

"I think we need a fire, Dad. What do you say? Shall I move that old dragon of yours and give us a proper blaze?"

Colonel Bonnamy turned his head to the fireplace where his Chinese dragon rested against two prongs on the grate. Outside, a gust of wind tossed its way through one of the chestnut trees, scraping its branches against the sitting room windows. The retriever lifted its head, listened, gave a deep-throated growl.

"Just a storm, Shorney," Jean told the animal. He growled a second time. Something banged against the cottage. He barked.

"Never liked weather," Colonel Bonnamy said.

The dog barked again. He looked from Jean to the window. Tree branches tapped against it. The rain fell harder. Something rasped the wall. Burdened by age, the dog struggled to his feet, planted them on his blanket, and began to yelp.

"Shorney!" Jean Bonnamy admonished. The animal howled. His short coat bristled.

"Blast it! Enough!" Colonel Bonnamy cried. With his good hand he crumpled a bit of newspaper and threw it at the dog to distract him, but the paper fell short. The dog's barking continued.

Jean went to the window and squinted against the glass, but all she could see was rain streaking the pane and the reflection of the lights in the sitting room. Another gust of wind coughed against the cottage. A sharp clatter followed, as if tiles were tumbling from the roof to the ground. The dog snarled, showing teeth, taking two steps towards the darkened window. As he did so, something banged against the cottage, then slid noisily down the wall.

Over the dog's responding howl, Jean said, "That must have been the rake, Dad. I think I left it outside with the secateurs. When that inspector came yesterday . . . I'd better fetch them before they're ruined. And some wood for the fire as well. Shorney! Quiet!"

"We need no fire, Jeannie," her father protested as she went to the coat rack and pulled on a mackintosh stained with grease. But even as he spoke, a shudder passed through his body. The wind shrieked in the chimney. The retriever bayed.

"We do," Jean replied. "I won't be a moment. Shorney!"

The dog advanced in her direction, but the last thing she intended was to let the old retriever out in a storm. She slipped from the room, closing the door behind her. The lights were not on in the kitchen, so she felt her way across the room and opened the back door.

A blast of cold wind hit her, whipping against her clothes. Rain pelted her wildly. She huddled into her mackintosh and went out.

She had left both the rake and the secateurs in the rear of the cottage, leaning against the wall. They would have fallen in the storm, she decided. That would have been the noise they had heard. She hurried along the cottage wall, turned the corner, and began to search for them in the gloom. Inside the cottage, the dog continued to bark, but the sound was muted compared to the growing roar of the wind.

"Now, where on *earth* . . ." She came upon the secateurs easily enough, fallen to their side next to a clump of lavender. But the rake seemed lost. As she felt along the ground for it, the wind streamed her hair directly into her face so that it stung her eyes and beat against her skin. "Oh, damn!" And over the din, in an attempt to settle the dog, "Shorney! Quiet!"

She pushed herself to her feet, tucked the secateurs under her arm, and made her way along the path to the shed at the far side of the garden where she kept her tools. Yanking the door open, she stepped inside, taking a few moments' respite from the unabated fury of wind and rain. She hung up the secateurs on their hook. The shed door banged shut.

Startled, she cried out, then laughed at herself nervously. "A *storm*," she said.

She thought about waiting until the rain abated before she gathered wood from its shelter next to the shed. But the image of her father shivering in the cold prompted her to action. She, after all, could warm herself quickly enough with a bath and a bit of brandy if she got chilled. She retied the belt of her mackintosh, pulled up its collar, and steeled herself to meet the rain once more. She took a step towards the door, her hand outstretched. On its own, it flew open.

Jean jumped back, gasped. A figure appeared in the doorway, silhouetted against the sky outside. Jean started to speak. "What d'you—"

She saw an uplifted arm. It held the rake. It lashed down furiously, sharp metal tines digging into her neck. She fell. She rolled away. She tried to protect her head. The rake sought her, finding her again and again. She felt her flesh tear. She tasted her blood.

Faintly, at a great distance, the retriever barked in panic.

Lynley watched as St. James made his way with some difficulty up the old wall ladder. The process was both slow and awkward, but as always St. James' face remained impassive as he made the climb. Above him, Lynley knew better than to extend his hand and offer assistance. Still, he felt himself draw a breath and hold it until his friend stood safely in the small corridor next to him.

Lynley handed St. James a torch. "It's here," he said, beaming his own cone of light towards the door at the corridor's end.

It was after six. The building was quiet, empty of boys and staff members during the dinner hour. Only Clive Pritchard remained in

Calchus House, confined to his bed-sitting room with a staff member posted in the corridor outside.

"What kind of heating system do they have?" St. James asked as he followed Lynley into the little room.

"Radiators."

"That's not going to be much help, is it?"

"There's a fireplace, though."

St. James shone his beam in that direction. The scene-of-crime men had removed both ashes and debris. "You're thinking of coal gas, I take it?"

"I'm thinking of anything, at this point."

St. James nodded and examined the fireplace. He lowered himself to the floor and directed his beam up the flue. "But the question is, where would a student get his hands on coal to burn up here?"

"From any of the houses. They all have fireplaces."

St. James shot him a curious glance. "You want this to be the spot, don't you, Tommy?"

"That's why I've asked you to make the determination for me. I like to think I've learned to be a bit more circumspect when I find my objectivity slipping."

"John Corntel?"

"I don't think so, St. James. But I need to be sure."

St. James didn't respond. Instead, he spent a few more minutes looking over the fireplace before he pushed himself to his feet, rubbing his hands together to free them of dust.

"The flue's clean," he said. "That's not your source." He walked to the wall and followed the pipes at its base, playing his light along them. "Water pipes," he said. "None of them are gas." Rain beat against the window. St. James went to it and examined the narrow stone sill. He guided his light along the beams in the ceiling. He flashed it into corners. He directed it along the worn floor. At last he shook his head. "I don't see how Matthew Whateley could have died in here, Tommy. He may have been in here for a period of time—Horsham CID will be able to tell you that—but this isn't where he died. What else did Canerone give you?"

"Lye."

"As in *Macbeth*?"

Lynley smiled. "As in soap."

"Ah. Lye."

"Trace deposits. That's all. It could have come from this room, I dare say, considering what it looked like in here before the scene-of-crime team swept through."

St. James was frowning as Lynley spoke. He said, "I shouldn't think lye would have been kept in here, Tommy."

"Why not?"

"It's too caustic. Anyone handling it would have to be damned careful about it. It attacks glass and clay. Iron as well. It dissolves skin tissues. It's the sort of chemical compound—potassium combined with water—that one might find—"

Lynley held up a hand to stop St. James. The image was planted firmly in his mind. He had seen it, seen her, watched her deft movements. Only hours ago. The sudden horror of contemplating a crime of such enormity momentarily froze Lynley's words.

"What is it?" St. James asked.

He formulated his question. Guilt and innocence rode hand in hand upon his friend's answer. "St. James," he asked, "can carbon monoxide be produced?"

"Produced? What are you asking? We've been up here looking for the means of production."

"I don't mean as a by-product. I don't mean as an accident. I mean produced deliberately. Are there chemicals that can be mixed together to form carbon monoxide?"

"Certainly. Formic acid and sulphuric acid."

"How is it done?"

"By adding formic to sulphuric. That dehydrates the formic—removes the water from it. The result is carbon monoxide."

"Can anyone do it?"

"Anyone with the chemicals and the equipment. You'd have to do it with a burette, to control the flow of formic acid into the sulphuric. But anyone . . ."

"God. My *God.*"

"What is it?"

"Potassium hydroxide. I was thinking of it as *lye,* not as a chemical compound, St. James. Potassium hydroxide. Carbon monoxide. He died in the chemistry lab."

"The fume cupboard," Lynley said. He unlocked the laboratory door with keys supplied by Frank Orten. He groped for the lights. The room became preternaturally bright. Lab tables sprang out of the darkness. Glass-fronted cupboards jumped forward, glittering. Across the room from them, the fume cupboard was closed, the glass that comprised its front and sides still smudged and cloudy as Lynley had first seen it.

St. James went to examine it, pushing up on the sash that served as its front panel. "It looks like a two-metre cupboard," he said, studying everything from the white tiles of its base to the vent in its side. "Two metres tall. One metre in width." He leaned closer to the traces of the deposit which smudged the glass. "I should think . . ." He removed a penknife from his pocket and scraped it against the glass. A residue of white powder dropped into his hand. He brushed it off. "I should think that's your potassium hydroxide, Tommy. If one were going to create it in the lab—and it would be a technical demonstration of what happens when one mixes an alkaline metal with water—it would have to be done in a fume cupboard like this. Not so much because of fumes, but because of the reaction."

"Which is?"

"It bubbles first. Then it explodes, sending up a white powder. In this case, right against the glass of the cupboard."

"So when Matthew Whateley was put inside, he would have picked up the trace deposits from the glass."

"I should think that's how it happened."

"And the carbon monoxide?"

St. James directed his attention to the rest of the lab. "Everything's here. The beakers, the burettes. Look at the chemicals in that cupboard. Each bottle is plainly labelled. And is the cupboard locked?"

Lynley checked this. "No."

"Formic acid? Sulphuric?"

Lynley went through the bottles. There were dozens of them. He found what he was looking for on the bottom shelf of the second cabinet he opened.

"Here they are, St. James. Formic and sulphuric. Other acids as well."

St. James nodded. He pointed to the row of large burettes that were lined across the top of the cabinets. "We've a volume of two cubic metres to fill with gas," he said. "The drain and the vent in the fume cupboard would be blocked off. The boy would be placed inside—bound and gagged. In a corner of the cupboard would be set up one of the wide beakers and the largest burette—a five-hundred-cc one would be the most likely. The formic acid would drip into the sulphuric. Carbon monoxide would form. The boy would die."

"Wouldn't he try to knock over the burette or the beaker?"

"Possibly. But the space is confined. He'd be placed inside the cupboard with little freedom of movement. Even if he did move, I should guess our killer explained to him all the corrosive qualities of the acids being used. So even if Matthew wanted to knock over the beaker—even if he had the room to do so, which I think unlikely— how reasonable is it that he would do it and risk having the acid spill over his skin?" St. James closed the fume cupboard. He turned back to Lynley. "So I suppose the question is: Do you have a suspect familiar with chemicals?"

It was the obvious question. Lynley found himself reluctant to give a reply. Again, disquiet afflicted him. He hadn't wanted to find guilt in John Corntel. But he wanted to place it in this room even less.

The laboratory door opened and Sergeant Havers entered. She was carrying an umbrella which had apparently afforded her little protection from the rain, for her jacket bore great damp patches upon the shoulders and down the back, her trousers were speckled with water, and her wet hair clung to her skull like a cap.

"Simon." She nodded a greeting at St. James before speaking to Lynley. "I was with the Horsham scenes-of-crime team when they got called to Cissbury. So I went with them. It seemed best at the time."

"What's happened?"

Havers told them briefly about the attack upon Jean Bonnamy, about the blood and the rake and the ruin of the woman's face; about her fractured skull; about the manner in which the flesh had been torn from her neck; about the finger she had lost when the rake drove through it; about her father's panic that quickly gave way to shock.

"When she didn't come in from getting wood for the fire, he dialled the emergency number. He didn't know what else to do. She's in hospital in Horsham. Still unconscious when I left."

"What do the doctors say?"

Havers waggled her hand back and forth. "Touch and go, Inspector. She may make it. She may not."

"God."

"That's not all," Havers said.

Lynley looked at her sharply, hearing the bite behind her statement. "What is it?"

"I saw your car out front and went into the quad to look for you. I went into the dining hall. Everyone was talking about it. Chas Quilter's gone missing. No one's seen him since one o'clock."

"It seems he disappeared right after lunch," Havers said as they lifted their umbrellas against the rain. They strode towards Ion

House, matching their pace to the slower gait of St. James. "At least that's the last time anyone claims to have seen him."

"Who saw him last? Who spoke to him?"

"Brian Byrne, evidently. Right before their afternoon chemistry lesson, Chas asked him to tell Emilia Bond that he was going to the Sanatorium for aspirin. After that lesson, Brian went to the San to check on Chas, only to find that he wasn't there."

"After what happened to Matthew Whateley, Brian didn't send up a hue and cry at once?"

"Apparently he spent the next few hours trying to find Chas himself. He's claiming that Chas has been upset about personal problems—Brian either doesn't know what they are or he wouldn't say, and I have my own thoughts as to which is the case. At any rate, he launched his own search. He didn't tell anyone that Chas was missing until everyone noticed it at dinner. I should guess he was covering for him, hoping he'd turn up."

"Where did he last see Chas?" St. James asked.

"Just outside the dining hall. Brian was leaving and Chas was waiting for him on the stairs. He claimed to be feeling unwell—and Brian says that he looked like hell. But again, that could be his attempt to protect him now he's run off and got himself into trouble. Or to protect himself, for that matter. If he suspected that Chas was about to run off, he should have reported him to a staff member."

"What's Lockwood done about it?" Lynley enquired.

A heavy gust of wind blasted against them. Sergeant Havers struggled to hold on to her umbrella. "Like everyone else, he didn't know Chas was missing until dinner."

"With the Board of Governors coming for a meeting tonight, one student murdered, and now a second student missing. This must be *déjà vu* of the worst kind for Lockwood."

"He was doing a Salome when I saw him a moment ago. Your head on a platter, Inspector. That sort of thing. But it isn't *déjà vu*." She had to raise her voice to be heard over the wind and the rain. "The circumstances are identical. Using the San as an excuse and then disappearing. Still, I don't think this duplicates Matthew Whateley's disappearance. I've had a talk with Daphne."

They entered Ion House through the east door which took them into the common room. There they shook off their umbrellas and removed their coats, dropping them over the backs of several tattered armchairs. St. James switched on a lamp. Lynley closed the door to the hall. Havers squeezed some of the water out of her hair and stamped her feet for warmth.

"It seems that Daphne had a second run-in with Clive Pritchard last night. She was crossing from the library to Galatea House when he jumped out from behind a tree and scared the devil out of her. Made a grab. Pressed up against her so she could have a proper feel of his equipment. The same sort of thing we saw him do before the German lesson. So she was ready enough to talk about him."

"And?"

Havers shook her head. "She knew about the chamber above the drying room, all right. She didn't know which building it was in, but she knew the room existed somewhere. There's no secret about that among the pupils, it seems. A number of legends appear to be connected with all the old attics. Hauntings. Ghoulies and beasties and things that go bump in the night. The usual rot."

"No doubt promoted by the administration to keep the pupils from seeking them out," St. James noted.

"No doubt," Havers replied. "Only it didn't work in this case. From what Daphne said, there's one boy who's given the Calchus House room a proper work-out on a regular basis for the last two years. The only problem is that he isn't Clive Pritchard, although I could tell that Daphne would have preferred to put the finger on him."

"If not Clive, then who?"

"Chas Quilter."

"Chas—"

"The same," she said. "I admit that I was prepared to hear that Clive was our man. But I suppose I should have been ready for it to be Chas. Yesterday Daphne alluded to his hypocrisy. That's all she would say at the time. But now Chas has disappeared, her tongue's loosened quite a bit. It seems he was having it off with some bird two or three times a week, mostly last summer term. The girl's not here any longer, and Daphne couldn't say if Chas has found a replacement for her. But as far as I can tell, any number of the ladies would be only too willing to volunteer for the duty."

"Including Daphne herself?"

"A woman scorned?" Havers asked. "I don't think so. She's a misfit, Inspector. She knows Chas Quilter—or any other bloke— would never give her a second look. Combine those two facts and we've a girl—the sort that no one ever notices—who hears and sees more than other people think. You know what I mean."

St. James spoke. "The sort of person people talk in front of because she projects such an air of disinterest?"

"Like part of the furniture. Yes. I think so. So she hears things. She sees things. She files them away."

"One can't escape gossip in a school like this," St. James said to Lynley.

"Especially if the gossip concerns itself with sex," Havers added. "Adolescents have other interests, naturally, but nothing ever quite matches the power of who's-having-a-poke-with-whom. If Chas Quilter was using that chamber to have at the young ladies last summer term, it stands to reason that he would continue doing so now. Probably with more success, since he's senior prefect this time round. And it *does* explain why the senior pupils don't appear to hold him in any particular awe. If he's busy breaking the rules himself, he could hardly demand that they do otherwise."

"So we still have no way to tie Clive Pritchard to that room," Lynley noted.

"That's true enough," Havers replied. "But we *do* have something better, don't we? Another motive for murder. Sexual licence, isn't that what Cowfrey Pitt named it? If the word went out on Chas, he would have been expelled. Out on his ear. What university did Brian Byrne say Chas hoped to attend?"

"Cambridge."

"Expulsion from Bredgar Chambers might have put an end to that."

"You're arguing that Matthew Whateley knew Chas Quilter used the room."

"It was common enough gossip, sir. Something that Matthew might have dropped in a conversation that got back to Chas. Chas already knew Matthew believed in upholding the school rules—he had the audiotape of Clive Pritchard's bullying to prove it. So it was probably only a matter of time before Matthew blew the whistle on Chas himself. But first he might have told the story to someone he knew— someone he could trust—the very same way he had come to Chas about Clive Pritchard. So it wouldn't be enough to eliminate Matthew. That other person would have to be eliminated as well. Just in case she remembered what Matthew had revealed about Chas."

"Jean Bonnamy?"

"That's how I see it."

"But why not her father? Wouldn't Matthew have told him as well?"

"Possibly. But he's old. He's sick. Chas would reason that the shock of an attack on Jean would drive everything else from his mind. Besides, there was a dog in the cottage. Who would want to risk attacking the old man with a dog there to protect him?"

"An old dog, Havers."

"How would Chas know that? He attacked Jean outside. The dog was in the cottage. He could hear him bark, no doubt, but he couldn't see him."

"But we know Matthew said nothing to Jean. Surely she would have told us had he done so."

"We know that, sir. Chas doesn't. All he knows is that Matthew knew her well enough to write her letters. We gave him that information ourselves."

"You seem relatively sure that Chas is our killer."

She sounded impatient. "Everything about it fits, Inspector. He had motive. He had access. He had opportunity."

"Does he have knowledge of chemistry?" St. James asked.

Havers nodded sharply and continued, using her hand for emphasis. "And that's not all. Daphne saw him at the social club on Friday night. Brian Byrne told us that he left the party to take some telephone calls, but it turns out that he didn't tell us everything. He didn't tell us that Chas was in the corridor weeping. He didn't tell us that Chas left the party at ten o'clock and never returned. Brian's protecting him, Inspector. Just as he did this afternoon when he kept it under his hat that Chas was gone. He's been doing that from the first. They all have. You know as well as I that it's part of their flaming code."

Lynley thought a moment. Through the closed door, voices came from the hall. Dinner hour was over. Evening prep would begin within the next few minutes.

"What time was Jean Bonnamy attacked?"

"A bit before five, from what Colonel Bonnamy says. Perhaps a quarter to the hour."

"And Chas was last seen at one?"

Havers nodded. "So he had nearly four hours to develop his plan, get to Cissbury, lie in wait for Jean Bonnamy, attack her, and be off."

Lynley pushed himself away from the chair against which he had been leaning as they spoke. "Let's have a look in his room," he said. "That may tell us where he's gone."

Boys were mingling in the foyer, taking off wet coats and shaking umbrellas as they came in the door. They stood in groups, separated by age, with the youngest closest to the outside door and the oldest nearest the stairs. They were chattering noisily—particularly the third formers by the door who were also engaging in a playful shoving match—but their house prefect brought them to attention as Lynley, Havers, and St. James approached.

"Ten minutes till prep," he shouted. "You know what you're doing."

Hearing this, the boys scattered, some up the stairs, some into the common room, others towards the telephone at one side of the foyer. A half-dozen older boys watched warily as the Londoners passed them.

On the second floor, pupils were ducking into their respective dormitories and collecting textbooks and notebooks for the evening's prep. Next to Chas Quilter's room, two boys engaged in hushed conversation, but they parted quickly when one of them raised his head and saw three interlopers in the corridor. They disappeared into two different rooms at the far end of the hall.

In Chas Quilter's room, everything was much as it had been when Lynley and Havers had spoken to him earlier. The medical volume, the notebook, the copy of *Paradise Lost* were still on his desk. The stereo cassette player still held the music created by Moog synthesizer. The bed was still neatly made. The rug on the floor was undisturbed. Only the photograph on the windowsill had been touched, but it merely lay face down as if the boy had decided that he could no longer bear to look upon it.

Havers was browsing through the pressed-wood cupboard. "Clothes are still here," she said. "His school uniform is missing."

"So it's not his intention to run off permanently," Lynley noted. "That *does* duplicate Matthew Whateley's disappearance, Havers."

"You're thinking that whoever killed Matthew Whateley also attacked Jean Bonnamy and now has Chas?" Havers sounded unconvinced. "I don't see that, sir. Chas Quilter's a big boy. He's an athlete, after all. Nabbing him would hardly be the same proposition as nabbing Matthew Whateley. Grabbing little Whateley was probably like taking a baby from its pram, compared to what grabbing Chas Quilter would be like."

Lynley was at Chas' desk. He touched the books thoughtfully. There was something in Havers' words. A possible connection between what they had learned about the senior prefect in the last twenty minutes and what he had been revealing to them—in bits and pieces—all along. He flipped the medical volume open.

"St. James," he asked his friend, "do you know anything about Apert's syndrome?"

"No. Why?"

"It's a thought . . ." Lynley scanned the page, for the first time reading what Chas Quilter had been reading when they entered his room that morning. The words were dizzying. Lynley tried to assimilate them as, next to him, St. James reached forward and picked up the photograph from the windowsill.

"Tommy—"

"A moment." His eyes swept the text. *Coronal sutures. Syndactyly. Acrocephalosyndactyly. Bilateral coronal synostosis.* It was like reading Greek. He turned the page. A photograph stared up at him. The final piece of the puzzle that was Chas Quilter clicked into place. It was followed immediately by a dawning understanding of the forces of chance and circumstance that had combined to result in the murder of Matthew Whateley.

"Tommy." St. James was saying his name again. His hand shot out to grip Lynley's arm.

Lynley looked up. His friend's angular features were sharp, his expression intense. He was, Lynley saw, holding the photograph from the windowsill.

"This girl," St. James said. "I've seen her."

"Tonight? Here?"

"No. Sunday. Deborah went to her house to phone the police. In Stoke Poges, Tommy. She lives across the street from St. Giles' Church."

Lynley felt his blood begin to pound. "Who is she?"

"She's called Cecilia. Cecilia Feld."

Lynley's eyes went to the wall of framed quotations. To the calligraphic lines from Matthew Arnold. *Ah, love, let us be true to one another.* And the small, neat signature at the bottom, near the frame. *Sissy.* Cecilia. Being true. Waiting in Stoke Poges.

They dropped Sergeant Havers at the hospital in Horsham where she would wait in the hope that Jean Bonnamy might regain consciousness and name her attacker. They drove on through the rain towards Stoke Poges. The continuing storm slowed traffic to a crawl in some places. As the minutes passed and St. James related what little he had heard Cecilia Feld tell the police Sunday night, Lynley felt his sense of urgency grow. It was after eight o'clock when they pulled into the drive of the house across the street from St. Giles' Church.

As they got out of the car, Lynley took up the medical volume that he had removed from Chas Quilter's desk. He tucked it under his arm and followed St. James through the rain.

The house was dark, save for a light that shone at a distance through the translucent glass of the front door. Their first knock brought no response. Nor did their second. It was only when Lynley found the doorbell—half-hidden under a mass of wet Virginia creeper—that they were able to rouse someone inside the building. A shadowy figure approached. The door opened a cautious two inches.

She was small, delicate, a wisp of a girl who looked extremely unwell. But Lynley recognised her from her picture. He produced his warrant card. "Cecilia Feld?" When she nodded solemnly, wide-eyed and mute, he said, "I'm Thomas Lynley. Scotland Yard CID. You've already met Mr. St. James, I believe. Last Sunday night. May we come in?"

"Sissy? Who is it, my dear?" A woman's voice came to them from a hallway to the left of the front door. Footsteps approached. A second figure in shadow joined Cecilia. She was a taller woman—grey-haired and sturdy, with strong, capable hands. One of them sought Cecilia's shoulder and drew her back from the door. She stepped in front of the girl. "May I help you?" With a flip of a switch the porch was instantly brightened, and the light fully exposed the two women in the house.

In spite of the hour, they were both dressed as if for bed, in wool wrappers with slippers on their feet. The older woman had begun to put her hair up in curlers, so her head looked oddly shaped, knobbed on one side and smooth on the other. She scrutinised Lynley's warrant card. Behind her, Cecilia stood against the wall, her arms cradled in front of her, hands cupping her elbows. Beyond them, from a room at the end of the hall, a diffused light shifted and blinked. A television set, Lynley decided, with the sound turned off.

Evidently satisfied with Lynley's credentials, the woman held the door open wider. She introduced herself as Norma Streader—*Mrs.* Streader, she emphasised—and led them to the room from which the shifting light shone. She lit two lamps and used a remote control unit to switch off the television set.

Planting herself on the chintz-covered couch, she said, "What may I do for you, Inspector? Please. Sit down." And then to the girl, "Sissy, I think it's time you had a bit of a lie-down, don't you?"

The girl looked willing enough to leave. Lynley stopped her. "It's Cecilia we've come to see."

Cecilia had taken a position near the doorway, arms still wrapped round her body as if in the need to protect herself. When Lynley spoke, she edged a few inches into the room.

"You've come to see Sissy?" Mrs. Streader repeated. "Why?" She examined them shrewdly. "You're not here on her parents' behalf, are you? They've caused this child enough distress already, and if she wants to stay here with me and my husband, she's welcome to do so. I've made that clear to the social worker, to the solicitor, to the—"

"No," Lynley interposed. "We're not here on behalf of her parents." He looked at Cecilia. "Chas Quilter's disappeared from Bredgar Chambers."

Lynley saw her grip her wrapper. She said nothing. Mrs. Streader spoke quickly. "What do you want with Cecilia, Inspector? You can see she's not well. She shouldn't even be out of bed."

"I don't know a Chas Quilter." Cecilia spoke in a whisper.

Even Mrs. Streader looked surprised by this response. She said, "Sissy."

Again Lynley interrupted. "Of course you know him. Rather well, I should guess. He has your picture in his room at the school. He has the stanza you copied from Matthew Arnold on his wall. Has he been here tonight, Cecilia?"

Cecilia said nothing. Mrs. Streader opened her mouth to speak, but closed it again. Her eyes went from Cecilia to Lynley to Cecilia. Finally she said, "What's this about, please?"

Lynley shifted his gaze to the woman. "Murder."

"No!" Cecilia took a step towards them.

" 'Ah, love, let us be true to one another,' " Lynley quoted. "That was the line you and Chas Quilter clung to, wasn't it? It got you through these past few months."

She dropped her head. Her hair—so lovely in the photograph, so thin and lifeless now—swept forward momentarily to cover her face.

"Has he been here?" Lynley asked.

She shook her head. She was lying. He could feel it.

"Do you know where he is? Do you know where he's gone?"

"I've not seen Chas Quilter in . . . I don't know. Months. Ages."

Mrs. Streader extended a hand to the girl. "Sissy. Sit down. You must. You're not strong."

Cecilia joined her on the couch. Lynley and St. James sat opposite them in the matching armchairs. A coffee table stood between them. On it were two glasses, one empty, one half-filled with a soft drink. Their presence was a revelation of the truth.

"We need to find him, Cecilia," Lynley said. "You must tell us how long it's been since he left you. You must tell us where he is."

"I haven't seen him," she repeated. "I told you. I haven't *seen* him. I don't know anything about him."

"You're protecting him. That's understandable. You love him. But I can't think you'd do that in the face of murder."

"You're talking nonsense."

Lynley leaned forward. He placed the medical volume on the table between them, but he did not open it. "You and Chas were lovers during your lower sixth year, weren't you?" he said. "You made love in the little chamber above the drying room in Calchus House. Late at night. On weekends. When no one was about. You tried to be careful. You tried to take precautions. But you didn't always manage, did you? So you became pregnant. You could have had an abortion, but I don't think that's the sort of people you and Chas are. He wanted to do right by you. You wanted to do right by him, by the baby. So you pretended to transfer out of Bredgar Chambers to another school. Cowfrey Pitt said something about a girl transferring out at the end of summer term last year under questionable circumstances. You must have been that girl. And you did it to protect Chas Quilter. If anyone discovered that he'd made you pregnant, he'd be expelled from the school. His education would be in shambles, and the future you planned to have together would be in shambles as well. But I imagine your parents weren't too pleased when you wouldn't have an abortion and wouldn't name the father, so you had to come here, to a foster home."

"Sissy, my dear . . ." Mrs. Streader reached for the girl, but Cecilia jerked away.

"You don't know anything," she said to Lynley. "Even if you did, I've committed no crime. I've done nothing. Nor has Chas."

"A thirteen-year-old boy is dead, Cecilia. A woman is in hospital with a fractured skull. Several people's lives are in ruins. How much more is going to go into the protection of Chas Quilter's future?"

"He's done nothing. I've done nothing. We—"

"That was almost the case," Lynley agreed. "But you panicked Friday night—was that when you had the baby, Cecilia?—and you phoned the school. Again and again. You needed him, didn't you? Because the future was in doubt. The plans were going awry."

"No!"

"The happy ending you were looking for with Chas had been twisted by a circumstance you hadn't considered. It was one thing to leave the school, to bear a pregnancy without him, even to have his baby and be willing to safeguard his reputation at the cost of your own. There was even a bit of nobility in that. But it was quite another thing when you saw the baby, wasn't it? You weren't prepared for Apert's syndrome." Lynley opened the medical volume. He turned the photograph of the baby towards Cecilia. "The concave skull. The misshapen eyes. The long forehead. The webbed fingers. The webbed toes. The possibility of mental—"

"Stop it!" Cecilia shrieked.

"The child would need years of plastic surgery even to look normal. And the greatest irony of this entire wretched mess is that the best plastic surgeon in the country is Chas Quilter's own father."

"No!" Cecilia flung herself forward, grabbed the book, hurled it across the room.

Lynley pressed her. "Was Chas backing out on your plans, Cecilia? When he found out about the baby, did he want to end his relationship with you?"

"He's not like that. You don't even know him. He loves me. He *loves* me!"

"I don't see how that's possible. He let you leave the school. He let you give up your education. He let you have this baby all alone—"

"He was here. He came. He said he would and he did because he loves me. He loves me!" She began to cry.

"He was here for the birth?"

Cecilia rocked on the couch. She sobbed bitterly, a fist at her mouth, one hand cradling her elbow as if it were supporting a baby's head. Mrs. Streader spoke.

"He came up on Tuesday evening, Inspector."

"No!" Cecilia shrieked. Her hands dug into her hair.

Mrs. Streader's face was soft with compassion. "Sissy, I must tell them the truth."

"You can't! You promised!"

"While it was just you and Chas, yes. But if someone has died. If there's been a murder—"

"You can't!"

Lynley was waiting for Mrs. Streader to continue. As he did so, the words *Tuesday evening* sang in his brain. Matthew Whateley had been with the Bonnamys Tuesday evening. Jean Bonnamy had driven him back to the school quite late. The lights of a minibus had struck him as he waved goodbye. Jean Bonnamy had seen that bus. So whoever had been driving it had no doubt seen Matthew. This, then, had to be the boy to whom Matthew was referring in his note to Jean Bonnamy.

"He came on Tuesday evening," Mrs. Streader continued. "Sissy was already in hospital in Slough. He came to the hospital, but when we knew it would be hours before the baby came, we insisted he go back to the school. It was dangerous enough for him to be away without permission for even a short time. Considering how he'd managed it, it was even more dangerous for him not to return as soon as he could."

"How had he managed it?" Lynley asked, although he was certain what the answer would be.

"He'd taken one of the minibuses."

Lynley saw how it had been done. Breaking into the porter's office was a simple procedure. The keys were available on the wall. By Elaine Roly's admission, Frank Orten had been with his daughter Tuesday night—was with her every Tuesday night—so he wouldn't have been in the lodge to hear one of the minibuses drive by. It was a risk, but Chas had been desperate enough to take it. Enough in love. Enough burdened by guilt. Everything had gone perfectly until he returned the bus . . . only to be seen by Matthew Whateley. Of all persons to see him, no one could have been worse than Matthew, who had already demonstrated his willingness to take action when someone decided to live in defiance of the rules. The problem was that since Chas—the senior prefect—was breaking the rules, Matthew Whateley had no one to turn to if he wanted to serve the cause of honour without breaking the code of silence by which all the pupils lived. He could hardly act on what he knew about Chas in the manner in which he had acted on what he knew about Clive Pritchard. So his only option would have been to tell the Headmaster. Chas faced expulsion because of Cecilia's pregnancy. He faced expulsion because he'd taken the minibus. He faced expulsion because he'd protected Clive Pritchard. Any one of the charges against him might not be enough to seal his fate. All three of them acted in concert to doom him. His future rested in the hands of a thirteen-year-old boy who believed in rules, who believed in honour. The only way he could survive was to eliminate the threat. And on Friday night, he'd done it. Then on Saturday, he'd taken the minibus a second time. He'd dumped the body in Stoke Poges.

"I imagine you were the one who phoned Chas repeatedly Friday night," Lynley said to Cecilia. "You knew about the upper sixth social club. You knew where he would be. Why did you phone him?"

Cecilia wept. "The baby."

"I should guess you needed someone to talk to," St. James said to the girl. "In this kind of tragedy, it only helps if you can talk to someone you love."

"He was . . . I *needed* . . ."

"You needed him. Of course. What could be more reasonable?"

Lynley spoke. "Did he come to you on Saturday, Cecilia?"

"*Please*. Don't make me. Chas!"

Lynley looked towards Mrs. Streader, but she shook her head and with a worried glance at Cecilia said, "I wasn't here Saturday. I . . . Cecilia, tell them."

"Chas didn't. He didn't. He wouldn't. I *know* him."

"If that's the case," Lynley said, "then you no longer need to protect him, do you? If he did nothing save come here to see you, Cecilia, what purpose does it serve to withhold the truth?"

"He didn't!"

"What happened when he came? What time was it?"

Tears blotched her skin. "He didn't! You want me to tell you he killed that little boy. He didn't. I *know* it. I know him."

"Prove it to me. Tell me the truth."

"You'll twist it! I know! But you can't twist this because there's nothing there but what happened. He came here. He was here an hour. He left."

"Did you see the minibus?"

"He left it on the road."

"Not in the churchyard?"

"No!"

"Did he talk about the churchyard?"

"No. *No!* Chas didn't kill Matthew. He couldn't kill anyone."

"But you know the boy's name. You *know* it. How?"

She twisted away from them.

"He's been here. Today. Where did he go? Cecilia, for God's sake, where did he go?" The girl said nothing. Urgently Lynley went on, searching for something that would convince her to part with the facts. "Don't you see? If he's done nothing, as you claim, then he himself may be in danger."

"You're lying," she spat at him.

She spoke the truth. But that no longer mattered. The line that divided truth from fiction was obliterated by death.

"Tell me where he is."

"I don't know. I don't *know*. He wouldn't tell me. I told him I'd never betray him, but he wouldn't tell. He knows you're after him. He didn't do anything, but he knows you think he did. And he laughs at you. He laughs. He said to tell you that he'll lead you on a path of glory. That's what he said. Those were his words. And then he left."

"When?"

"An hour past. So follow his trail, if you want. Follow it."

Lynley got to his feet. Chas' message was burning its way into his skull. He recognised the words. He had seen them when Deborah St. James had shown him Thomas Gray's poem on Monday night.

Lynley didn't want to understand what Chas' message to him meant. He didn't want to reveal his sudden fear to the girl. She had already borne enough.

But Cecilia seemed to read beyond the impassivity on his face. As he thanked her and walked with St. James to the door, she followed them. "What is it?" she asked. "What do you know? *Tell* me!"

Lynley looked at Mrs. Streader. "Keep her here," he said.

He went out into the rain. St. James followed. The door closed behind them, cutting off Cecilia's cries.

From the boot of his car Lynley removed two torches, handing one to St. James. "Hurry," he said and drew up the collar of his coat.

The wind angled the rain into their faces as they rushed down the drive and crossed the country road to the lane leading to St. Giles' Church. It was unlit, deserted, and the beams from their torches reflected upon great pools of water from the long afternoon of storm. Small wind-torn branches caught at their trousers, and mud oozed from verges that were still bare of spring growth.

Lynley knew such a walk would be difficult for his friend. He knew he ought to help him lest he lose his footing. But as he glanced at St. James, the rain beating against his face, the other man shouted, "I'm all right. Go on!" and Lynley broke into a run, driven by that partial line of poetry and its implicit message, driven by the fear he had heard in Cecilia Feld's voice, by the hopelessness he had seen that day on Chas Quilter's face.

The paths of glory lead but to the grave. And hadn't that proved true for Chas? Senior prefect, member of the rugby first fifteen, the cricket first eleven, the tennis first six. Handsome, admired, intelligent. Guaranteed Cambridge. Guaranteed success. Guaranteed everything.

The lych gate loomed in front of him, water streaming off it in sheets. Lynley ducked beneath it, and the beam from his light caught upon a sodden garment lying in a heap in a corner. Lynley picked it up. It was a Bredgar Chambers jacket, once blue but now quite black from the rain. He didn't bother to look for the name tag that would be sewn onto the lining. Instead, he tossed the jacket to one side and plunged out from the shelter of the lych gate once again.

"Chas!" he shouted. "Chas Quilter!"

He ran towards the church in the distance, his feet pounding against the concrete path. He arced his torch from side to side, but it shone upon nothing except ghostly gravestones—slick with water—and grass beaten down by the rain.

Under the second lych gate another garment lay, this a yellow pullover. Like the first, it had been flung into a corner, but one arm had caught upon a nail protruding from the lych gate wall. Eerily, like a spectre, this pointed towards the church. Lynley ran on.

"Chas!" His cry seemed to die in a blast of wind that was howling from the west.

He shot the beam of his light across the graves. He shot it towards the church. He played it on the windows. He continued to run.

"Chas! Chas Quilter!"

The wind had knocked a tree rose onto the path, and Lynley stumbled against it, his trousers catching upon its thorns. He shone the light down, ripped the material away from the bush, and righted himself. As he did so, the beam of his light flashed momentarily on a streak of white ahead. It seemed to be moving.

"Chas!"

He broke away from the path and dashed through the graves towards the figure he saw beneath a widespread yew tree near the southwest door of the church. White shirt. Dark trousers. It had to be Chas. It couldn't be anyone else. Yet the figure up ahead was tall, too tall. And he was turning and turning and turning back and forth. As if taken by the wind, as if struck by the wind, as if dangling in the wind. . . .

"No!" Lynley flung himself the last twenty yards to the tree and grabbed onto the boy's legs to support his body. "St. James!" he shouted. "For Christ's sake! St. James!"

He heard an answering shout. Someone was coming. He squinted against the rain, his heart pounding in his chest. But the figure that hurtled along the path and tore through the graveyard was not his friend. It was Cecilia.

She screamed. She flew across the lawn. She clawed at Chas. She clawed at Lynley, tearing at his arms, biting his hands as she attempted to separate him from the boy.

"Chas!" she screamed. "No! Chas! Don't—"

Her words were cut off as St. James reached them and grabbed her, pulling her away and dragging her back. She tried to beat at him, but he held her arms behind her and pressed her face into his chest.

"Let her go!" Lynley shouted. "Grab the boy. Hold him. I'll cut him down."

"Tommy!"

"For the love of God, St. James. Do as I say!"

"Tommy—"

"We've no time!"

"He's dead." St. James flashed the beam of his light upon Chas Quilter's face, revealing the ghastly colour of the wet flesh, the exophthalmic eyes, the swollen, protruding tongue. He flashed the light away. "It's over. He's *dead.*"

21

Lynley met with Cecilia in her bedroom. Mrs. Streader sat next to the bed, one hand on the girl's arm and the other wiping away her own tears. She murmured Cecilia's name occasionally, but it seemed more to comfort herself than to comfort the girl, who was sedated and rapidly slipping towards sleep.

Outside the bedroom, Lynley could hear St. James and Inspector Canerone talking. Someone coughed. Someone else cursed. A telephone jangled. It was answered on the second ring.

Lynley's heart felt sore. It seemed an additional cruelty to question Cecilia, but he did so anyway, giving ascendancy to the policeman within him and forcing into submission every impulse he had to assuage the girl's pain.

"Did you know Chas was coming to see you this evening?" Lynley asked her. She turned her head to him lethargically. "What did he talk to you about, Cecilia? Did he mention Matthew Whateley? Is that how you knew his name?"

Cecilia's eyelids drooped. Her tongue, looking swollen, passed over her lips. She spoke listlessly. "Chas . . . he said . . . Matthew saw the minibus. He was on the back lane to Erebus and Ion, and he saw. Tuesday night. So he knew."

"Matthew knew that Chas had taken the minibus?"

"He knew."

"You spoke to Chas on the phone Friday night. Several times. Did he tell you he'd taken Matthew to the room in Calchus House?"

"He said . . . no . . . nothing of Matthew. We . . . it was the baby.

I wanted to talk to him about the baby. I had to . . . we . . . to decide what to do . . . If he would just tell his father . . . but he wouldn't. His father . . . he wouldn't tell him."

"He didn't tell you about Matthew? He said nothing about the chemistry laboratory? About the fume cupboard?"

She shook her head weakly. "Nothing of Matthew." A crease appeared between her eyebrows. She sought Lynley's eyes. "But he said . . . someone else knew of the minibus. That it didn't end . . . with Matthew. But that it had to end somewhere. It had to end . . ." Her hand rose to her lips. Tears streaked slowly from her eyes. "I didn't . . . I should have known what he meant. I didn't. I didn't think he would . . . there's the baby. And . . . *Chas.*"

Mrs. Streader wiped the girl's cheeks. She said, "Sissy. Sissy, love. It's all right. There. It is."

"It didn't end with Matthew," Lynley told the girl. "Someone else saw Chas with the minibus that night. A woman. Jean Bonnamy. Did he tell you about her? Did he tell you what happened to her this afternoon?"

"No. Jean . . . He said nothing of Jean. Only that you'd been after him . . . that you wanted him to talk to you . . . to tell you . . . he said you didn't understand. You couldn't know. He felt bound . . ." Her eyelids closed.

"Bound to you? To protect you? As you had done for him?"

She stroked the satin that banded the top of the white wool cover. "Protect. Chas protect," she murmured. "He's like that, Chas is. He'll protect." Her hands relaxed. Her jaw grew slack. She slept.

Gently Mrs. Streader smoothed the girl's forehead. "Poor love," she said. "She's been through it, Inspector. Parents, pregnancy, the birth, the poor baby's deformity. Now this. And she loved him. They loved each other. I had no doubt of that. I've seen the young men come to my house to visit girls they've got in trouble before this. But there was never one who touched the sort of devotion Chas Quilter had for this child. Never one."

"Did you hear any part of their conversation tonight?"

Mrs. Streader shook her head. "They wanted time alone and I gave it to them. You may go ahead and argue that I was derelict in leaving them alone together, after what they'd got up to in the past and the result that's lying like a half-made little lamb in hospital. But I saw no reason to deny them what comfort they could take from each other's presence. There's little enough love in the world, and even less joy. If a few minutes holding one another brought them a bit of peace, what right have I in refusing to allow it?"

"You weren't here on Saturday night when Chas came to see Cecilia?"

"I wasn't. But I've no doubt he was here. Cecilia told me he'd said he would come to her that night, and Chas wasn't a boy who made promises he didn't keep. Just like today."

"Today?"

Mrs. Streader arranged Cecilia's hair against the bedclothes. "He phoned at noon. He said he was coming. *Promised* he was coming. And he was here by four. That was Chas."

Lynley felt his reaction to her words like a reflex working on his muscles. He got to his feet. The light on the bedside table struck the right side of Mrs. Streader's lined face. The rest of her was in shadow. But from what he could read of her expression, Lynley knew that the woman had no idea of the import behind what she had just said.

"Here by four?" he repeated.

"He said he'd hitchhiked. And he must have. He was soaked. Why? Is it important?"

Lynley didn't reply. Instead, he left the room. He sought St. James, finding him in the sitting room with Inspector Canerone and a uniformed constable.

"There's no doubt it's a suicide," Canerone said when he saw Lynley. "The boy came prepared." He handed Lynley the ill-made noose. It had been fashioned from two Bredgar Chambers ties that were knotted together, one blue with thin yellow stripes, the other of an identical pattern but with the colours reversed: yellow with thin blue stripes.

Lynley held them like a snake in his two hands. Yellow on blue. Blue on yellow. It went beyond Matthew. He himself had seen the confusion over colours played out right before his own eyes, but until this moment he'd been distracted by allusions to relationships. He'd been delving for meaning beneath idle talk about hockey rather than recognising a horrible truth. He spoke to St. James. "We need to get back to the school." And to Canerone, "Can your men handle the details here?"

"Of course."

Lynley rolled the ties into a coil which he shoved into his pocket. He said nothing more. Instead, he began assimilating information, dwelling upon the single reality that remained once suspects' motives were discarded and their opportunities were examined. With a nod to Canerone, he left the room.

When they were in the car heading back to West Sussex, St.

James broke into Lynley's thoughts. "What is it, Tommy? You're not thinking it's not a suicide, are you?"

"No. Chas Quilter took his own life. As far as he could see, it was either kill himself or tell the truth. There was nothing else for it. Death seemed the better alternative to him." Lightly, Lynley struck the steering wheel with his fist. "It says it right on the wall of that miserable chapel. I read it. Damn it all, I *read* it, St. James."

"What?"

"*Per mortes eorum vivimus.* Through their deaths we live. The school's blasted memorial to its old boys who died in war. And he bought into it, damn him. He bought into that and into everything else—the code of silence, the demands of honour, the loyalty to his mates. So he killed himself. St. James, he hanged himself rather than tell the truth. Through *his* death, others live. Cecilia said it best. 'He'll protect.' But it works both ways, doesn't it? You don't protect a friend who won't protect you."

"Are you saying Chas Quilter didn't kill Matthew Whateley?"

"He didn't kill Matthew. But Chas is the reason why Matthew died."

Sergeant Havers met them in the school's main entrance hall. She was just leaving the chapel as Lynley and St. James came in the front door. Her clothes were dishevelled, her hair was rumpled, her face looked exceedingly tired.

"Nkata phoned in again from Exeter," she announced.

"Any news?"

"He says that nothing checks out. If there was a Eurasian baby born there thirteen years ago whose adoption was orchestrated by Giles Byrne, no one has heard of it. Everyone said the exact same thing when Nkata explained the situation to them. An adoption of the sort Giles Byrne has described would be a strictly private affair, usually managed by the mother, a solicitor, and the adoptive parents. No one else. That's it. Byrne's story is bunk. But we've a bit of luck connected to that, because the Board of Governors have been meeting in Lockwood's council room all evening. They're still at it right now. Giles Byrne's with them."

Lynley was not surprised by the news from Constable Nkata. It was yet another puzzle piece clicking into place. "How's Jean Bonnamy?"

Havers kicked her shoe against an uneven stone in the floor. "They think she'll make it."

"Still unconscious?"

"Yes and no. She came out of it briefly, before they took her into surgery."

"Was she able to speak?"

"Enough."

"And?"

"She managed to give Horsham CID a description. I was there when they took it. She couldn't see her attacker very well because of the light, but she saw enough. It wasn't Chas Quilter, sir. Nothing matched up. Not the height. Not the weight. Not the body type. Not the hair. No spectacles either, and I can't guess he'd try to attack someone blind. So we've lost our man again."

Lynley shook his head. "We've found him, Sergeant. I've no doubt there'll be a volume of forensic evidence to hold him."

"Are we ready for an arrest, then?"

"Not quite. There's one more question that I'd like to have answered. Giles Byrne's the man to do so."

The meeting of the Board of Governors was concluding as Lynley and St. James entered the administrative corridor. The door to the council room stood open, allowing a yellow haze of stale cigarette smoke to permeate the fresher hallway air. Through this came the sounds of congenial farewells being given, followed by an exodus of eight men and one woman who, talking among themselves, passed Lynley and St. James with little more than a curious nod before going out into the night. Obviously, Lynley thought, the Headmaster had managed to soothe any anxieties the governors had expressed about the disappearance and death of Matthew Whateley.

Alan Lockwood was still in the council room. Seated at the broad walnut table, he was talking with Giles Byrne and pinching the knot of his tie. Coffee cups, carafes of water, and ashtrays surrounded them, and as Lynley and St. James entered the room, Giles Byrne lit a cigarette and leaned back in his chair. Next to him, Alan Lockwood looked hastily at the window that was open a mere three inches onto the cloister. But, perhaps with a view towards politics, he made no move to open it further.

"As to the pending arrest," Lockwood was saying.

Byrne lifted a lazy hand to stop him. "I believe our good Inspector himself can best address that, Alan. If you'd care to ask him about it." He sucked on his cigarette and held the smoke for some seconds in his lungs.

Lockwood's head swivelled towards the door. He shot up from the table when he saw Lynley and St. James. "Well?" The single word was a demand for both information and performance. It also had the ring of apocryphal authority, no doubt produced for the benefit of the man who had been largely responsible for Lockwood's employment at the school.

Ignoring it momentarily, Lynley introduced them to St. James. He went on to say, "Matthew Whateley used to visit a woman in Cissbury called Jean Bonnamy. She was attacked late this afternoon."

"What does that have to do with—"

"She's given the police a description, Mr. Lockwood. There's not much doubt that her assailant came from this school."

"Pritchard's been watched every second. There's no way he could have left Calchus House and got into Cissbury. It's an impossibility."

"It wasn't Clive Pritchard. He's been tangentially involved in everything. There's no getting round that. But Clive was never the prime mover in what's happened at Bredgar Chambers over the past week. He's not clever enough for that. He was merely an unwitting pawn."

"A pawn?"

Lynley advanced into the room. St. James walked to the window where he watched the exchange. "It's all been a bit like a game of chess. I didn't see that at first. But tonight I recognised the similarities. Most especially, I saw how the minor players have been sacrificed from the first to protect the king. Just as one does with pawns and then, of necessity, with rooks and bishops. Only now, the king's dead. I imagine that was the one eventuality that our killer never expected." Lynley joined them at the table. He pushed a coffee cup and a carafe of water to one side. Lockwood was forced to resume his seat.

"What is all this?" he demanded. "Mr. Byrne and I have business to attend to, Inspector. If you've come to play games— "

"Chas Quilter's dead, Mr. Lockwood," Lynley interposed. "He hanged himself in Stoke Poges this evening."

The Headmaster's lips formed the boy's name soundlessly. Giles Byrne spoke.

"How ghastly. Alan, I shall leave you to deal with this. Perhaps a phone call in the morning . . . ?"

"Please stay, Mr. Byrne," Lynley said.

"This obviously has nothing to do with me."

"I'm afraid that's not the case," Lynley said as the man was rising. "It has everything to do with you. It has to do with a pathetic need for love, a need for a tie to another human being. And that, I'm afraid, is entirely bound up in you."

"What are you trying to tell me?"

"That Matthew Whateley's dead. That Chas Quilter's dead. That Jean Bonnamy's in hospital with a fractured skull. All because you can't face a relationship with another human being unless that person promises you perfection."

"That's outrageous."

"You cut your son off when he was thirteen years old, didn't you? Because he snivelled, you said. Because he wasn't enough of a man."

Giles Byrne mashed his cigarette into the ashtray. "And I killed Matthew Whateley for the same reason?" he snarled. "Is that where you're heading? Because if it is, you had better know that I'm not about to listen to this without a solicitor present. And when your game is played out, Inspector, I hope you've some alternative career to turn to because you'll be through with policework. Am I making myself clear? You're not dealing with some puling adolescent now. I advise you to know what you're about before you go any further."

Alan Lockwood spoke unctuously. "I hardly think the Inspector means to suggest—"

"I know what he means to suggest. I know what he's been sniffing at. I know how their minds work. I've seen it often enough to realise when . . ." A movement at the door caused Byrne's angry words to falter.

The man's son stood there, Sergeant Havers behind him. "Hello, Father," Brian said. "How nice of you to let me know you'd be here this evening."

"What's the meaning of this?" Giles Byrne asked Lynley.

Sergeant Havers shut the door. With her hand on his arm, she guided Brian Byrne to the table. He sat, not next to his father but opposite him. At the head of the table, Lockwood loosened his tie. His eyes darted from Byrne to his son. Neither spoke. Someone passed in the cloisters outside the room, but no one looked towards the windows.

"Sergeant," Lynley said.

As she had done earlier for Clive Pritchard, Havers went through the procedure of cautioning the boy. While she did so—the words rising automatically from years of having said them—she thumbed through her notebook. When she finished the caution prescribed by the Judge's Rules, the boy's father spoke. His lips scarcely moved.

"I want a solicitor here. Now."

"We're not here to question you," Lynley said. "That's not your decision. It's Brian's."

"He wants one," Byrne barked. *"Now."*

Lynley said only, "Brian?"

The boy shrugged, indifferent.

"Give me a phone," Byrne said. "Lockwood, a *phone.*"

The Headmaster began to move. Lynley stopped him. "Do you want a solicitor present, Brian? It's your decision to make. Not your father's. Or mine. Or anyone else's. Do you want a solicitor?"

The boy looked at his father, then his eyes slid away. "No," he said.

"For Christ's sake!" his father exploded, one hand slamming onto the table.

"No." Brian was firm.

"You're doing this to punish—"

"No," Brian said.

Byrne twisted towards Lynley. "You've orchestrated this. You *knew* he'd refuse. If you think for a moment that a court of law is going to uphold this sort of procedure, you're mad."

"Do you want a solicitor, Brian?" Lynley repeated evenly.

"I've said. No."

"This is murder, you blasted little ninny!" Byrne shouted. "Have some sense just once in your miserable life!"

Brian's head jerked away. The tic that Lynley had seen plague his lip before now pulled at it in a vicious spasm. The boy pressed his knuckles to his face to control the twitching muscle.

"Are you listening to me? Do you hear me, Brian?" his father demanded. "Because if you think I'm going to sit here and watch you—"

"Get out," Brian said.

His father leaned across the table and grabbed the boy's arm, wrenching him forward. "You think you're being clever, don't you? You've got me so I'll beg. Is that it? Is that what you want? Is that what this performance is all about? Well, you'd better think again, lad. Because if you don't, I'll walk out that door and leave you to face this alone. Is that clear? Do you understand? You'll face this alone."

"Get out," Brian said.

"I'm warning you, Brian. This is no game now. You listen to me.

Damn you, listen. You can do that much. You *are* still capable of that much, aren't you?"

Brian tore himself from his father's grasp. The effort thrust him back against his chair. "Get *out!*" he cried. "Go back to London. Have it off with little Rheva, or whatever her name is. But just get out. Leave me alone. That's what you do best. It always was."

"Christ Jesus, you're like your mother," Byrne said. "Just *exactly* like. With nothing on your mind save a passing interest in what kind of stimulation goes on between other people's legs. You're pathetic. The both of you."

"Then go!" Brian shouted.

"I wouldn't give you that pleasure," Byrne hissed. He reached for his cigarettes, lit one. The match flame trembled. "Ask him whatever you like, Inspector. I wash my hands of him."

"I've no need of you," Brian hurled back. "I've friends enough. Plenty of them."

No longer, Lynley thought. "Chas Quilter's dead," he said. "He hanged himself this evening."

Brian whirled to him. "That's a lie!"

"It's the truth," St. James said from his place by the window. "We've just come from Stoke Poges, Brian. Chas went to see Cecilia first. And afterwards, he hanged himself from that yew tree in the churchyard. You know the one."

"No!"

"I imagine he felt that closed the circle of the crime," Lynley said. "Perhaps he chose the yew tree because he didn't know exactly where you'd put Matthew's body. Had he known which tree you'd left Matthew under on Saturday night, I'm certain that's where he would have hanged himself. It would have been a form of justice that appealed to him. Chas would have wanted that."

"I *didn't* . . ." But the affliction in the boy's voice gave him away.

"You did, Brian. For friendship. For love. As a way of securing the devotion of the single person whom you admired the most. You killed Matthew Whateley for Chas, didn't you?"

He began to cry.

His father said, "God. *No,*" and nothing more.

Lynley spoke gently, like a parent relating a bedtime story and not the tale of a barren crime. "I imagine that Chas came to you late Tuesday night, perhaps even on Wednesday. He'd had a phone call from Cecilia, he'd known she was in labour, and he'd done something terribly foolish in order to go to her. He'd taken the minibus. It was an act of desperation, to be sure, and he was just desperate enough to try it. Frank Orten was gone on his regular night off. Chas wouldn't be missed for a few hours. But when he returned, Matthew Whateley saw him. Chas came to tell you that."

The boy's hands were at his face. He wept against his closed fists.

"He was worried," Lynley said. "He knew Matthew might report what he'd seen. He told you that. He just needed someone to talk to. He didn't intend that anything should happen to Matthew. He probably just wanted your reassurance, the kind of thing friends give each other all the time. But you saw a way to calm his worries, didn't you? At the same time as you won his friendship forever."

"He was my friend. He *was*."

"Indeed. He was. But there was a chance you would lose him when he went to Cambridge, especially if you weren't accepted yourself. So you needed a way to bind him to you, to have a connection with him beyond that tenuous old school tie. Matthew Whateley provided it. As did Clive Pritchard. Clive helped you without even knowing he was doing so, didn't he, Brian? You knew he wanted to find the duplicate tape Matthew had made of the bullying. You knew Matthew was scheduled to go to the Morants'. So I imagine you masterminded the entire scheme for Clive. He would nab Matthew after lunch on Friday and go on to games himself—a bit late, no doubt, but that was probably par for the course for Clive—while you would put an off-games chit with Matthew's name on it in Mr. Pitt's pigeonhole. Everyone benefitted from your plan. Clive was able to have his fun with Matthew—torturing him with lit cigarettes on Friday after games in the chamber above the drying room in order to encourage Matthew to reveal the location of that duplicate tape—Chas would be able to rest easy in the knowledge that all his secrets were safe once Matthew was dead, and you would be able to offer Chas irrefutable proof of your infinite friendship—Matthew Whateley's corpse."

Giles Byrne spoke. "It's not true. It can't be. Tell him. It *can't* be."

"It was clever, Brian. A tribute to sheer, audacious intelligence. You would kill Matthew to protect Chas, but Clive would think he himself was responsible for the boy's death. I imagine you took Miss Bond's school keys from her pigeonhole in the masters' common room. It would be easy enough to do so, and she wouldn't miss them on the weekend. Then late Friday night you fetched Matthew from Calchus House. You took him to the chemistry lab, killed him in the fume cupboard, and returned his body to Calchus House so that when Clive next went to see him, he would find him dead and—not knowing how he died—assume responsibility. He would panic, come to you for advice. And you would offer to dispose of the body. Clive would be grateful. He would even help. He would hold his tongue and protect you, because in protecting you, he would assume he was protecting himself. But Chas knew the truth, didn't he? I suppose you had to tell him. It was the only way to reveal your supreme act of love for him. So he knew. Perhaps not at once. But eventually. When the time was right for you to reap his gratitude."

Alan Lockwood protested. "How could all this have happened? There are *hundreds* of pupils . . . there's a duty master . . . it's an impossibility. I don't believe it."

"Most of the pupils were on exeats. Others were at a hockey tournament. Still others had been partying heavily and were no doubt sleeping off a booze-up. The school was virtually deserted as a result." Even now, Lynley found that he could not add that the duty master—John Corntel—had forgotten to patrol, that Brian probably knew Corntel wasn't alone for the evening, that since his room adjoined Corntel's, he would surely know that Emilia Bond was with him and he would suspect how they would be spending their time, that, as a result, the school was his to do with as he pleased.

"But why?" Lockwood demanded. "What had Chas Quilter to fear from anyone?"

"He knew the rules, Mr. Lockwood. He'd got a girl pregnant. He'd taken one of the school vehicles to go to her. He'd hidden the truth about Clive Pritchard's bullying of Harry Morant. In his mind, he was the strongest candidate for expulsion, and he believed that expulsion from Bredgar Chambers would destroy his future. His mistake was in telling Brian that. For Brian immediately saw how to use it in order to win Chas' love. But Brian didn't take into account that Chas would feel the weight of both guilt and responsibility, not to mention the anxiety of potential discovery. You see, the chance of discovery didn't end with Matthew Whateley's death. Chas found out that the boy had written to Jean Bonnamy about seeing him Tuesday night. He was with us when Sergeant Havers and I found the draft of a letter to her. I've no doubt that Chas spoke to Brian about that. And Brian saw that while he could do nothing to assuage Chas' guilt or lighten the burden of responsibility that weighed upon him, he could do something about the potential for discovery. So he decided to remove the final possibility of endangerment to Chas. He went after Jean Bonnamy, as another gift of love."

Brian looked up. His eyes were dull. "Am I supposed to confirm what you've said? Is that what you want?"

"Brian, for God's sake," his father pleaded.

But Lynley shook his head. "There's no need. We'll have the forensic evidence from the lab, the minibus, and the chamber in Calchus House. We have Jean Bonnamy's description of you, and no doubt we'll find traces of her blood, her hairs, and fragments of her skin on your clothes. We have your knowledge of chemistry. And ultimately, I should guess, we'll have Clive Pritchard telling the truth. Unlike Chas, I shouldn't think Clive's going to be willing to kill himself rather than implicate you in Matthew Whateley's death once he learns how the boy really died. So there's no need, Brian. I've not brought you here for that."

"Then for what?"

Lynley removed the Bredgar Chambers ties from his pocket. He uncoiled them on the table and then loosened the knot that held them together.

"One of these ties is predominantly yellow," Lynley said. "The other is blue. Will you tell me which is which, Brian?"

The boy lifted a hand a few inches off the table. He dropped it weakly, as incapable of making the decision now as he had been when choosing the correct jersey to wear for a hockey game two days before. "I . . . I don't know. I can't tell. It's the colours. I—"

"No!" Giles Byrne lurched to his feet. "God damn you. This is enough."

Lynley stood. He wrapped the ties round his hand and looked down at the boy. He wanted to feel that mixture of rage and glory, that black satisfaction of a murder avenged and a killer sent on his way to the bar of justice. But he knew quite well there was no possibility that even the most rudimentary vengeance might grow from the ruins of the past few days. "When you killed him," he asked heavily, "did you know Matthew Whateley was your brother?"

Sergeant Havers used the Headmaster's study to make the requisite telephone calls to the Horsham and Slough police. They were courtesy calls. The formal exchange of information would come later, after statements were compiled and reports were written.

St. James and Lockwood remained in the council room with Brian Bryne while Lynley went in search of the boy's father. Giles Byrne had left the room only moments after Lynley asked his final question, not remaining to hear Brian's answer, not remaining to face the confusion, the dawning comprehension, and ultimately the horror as each crowded past the other across his son's face.

Brian had seen the reality quickly enough. It was as if Lynley's single question had unlocked a series of memories within him, each one more wrenching than the last. He said only, "It was Eddie. It was *Eddie,* wasn't it? And my mother. That night in the study . . . They were there . . ." before he gave a strangled cry. "I didn't *know. . . .*" He lowered his head to the table, burying his face in the crook of his arm.

After that, the story came out in disjointed pieces, erupting between Brian's wretched sobs. It was not so very different from Lynley's conjectures. Central to the tale was Chas Quilter: whom Brian had accompanied to Stoke Poges late Saturday night; who in his distraction had not noticed the blanket-shrouded figure on the floor in the rear of the minibus; whose need to see Cecilia alone had prompted him to agree wholeheartedly when Brian had offered to wait for him outside the Streaders' house in the bus; who did not know that Brian had used the time in Stoke Poges to dump Matthew's body in St. Giles' churchyard.

Listening to Brian, Lynley saw the manner in which Matthew's murder, committed under the guise of friendship, was in actuality a form of insidious blackmail in which the payoff was to be a lifetime of loyalty and love.

Chas had heard the story of Matthew Whateley's disappearance on Sunday afternoon with everyone else. But unlike everyone else, when given the information that the boy's body had been found in Stoke Poges, Chas knew at once not only the identity of the killer but also the motive behind the crime. Had Brian rid himself of Matthew's body in any other location, Chas might have spoken up to see that justice was done. But Brian was far too clever to allow Chas the option of unburdening his conscience, so he had created a set of circumstances in which Chas' speaking up—or pointing the finger of accusation at anyone else—meant that he would be condemning himself, and condemning himself meant abandoning Cecilia when she needed him most. There was absolutely no way for the senior prefect to win, and no way for him to emerge with a conscience that was not stricken by remorse. So he had removed himself from the game.

Now, with a glance that told St. James to stay with the boy, Lynley left the room. The corridor outside was dark, but at the far end the door to the foyer stood open and beyond it Lynley could see a pale light against the stone floor. The chapel was open.

Giles Byrne was sitting beneath his memorial to Edward Hsu. If he heard Lynley's footsteps, he gave no sign. Instead, he remained upright in the pew. Every muscle of his body seemed painfully controlled.

When Lynley joined him, he spoke. "What's going to happen?"

"Horsham CID will send a car for him. And for Clive Pritchard. The school's in Horsham's jurisdiction."

"And then?"

"Then it's in the hands of the prosecutors."

"How convenient for you that is. Your job is done, isn't it? Wrapped up in a tidy little package. You go on your way, content with the truth having been revealed. The rest of us stay here and deal with it."

Lynley felt an inexplicable need to defend and deny, but he quelled it, too exhausted and depressed to make the attempt.

"She did it all deliberately," Byrne said abruptly. "My wife didn't love Edward Hsu. I'm not sure Pamela has ever loved anyone. But she needed admiration. She needed to see desire in men's faces. In the end, she needed more than anything to hurt me. It always comes down to that, doesn't it, when a marriage is falling apart?" In the half-darkness of the church, Byrne's face looked skeletal, hollowed by the shadows under his eyes and beneath his cheekbones. "How did you know my wife was Matthew's mother?"

"Your story about his birth in Exeter didn't hold true. You denied knowing his mother, yet an adoption couldn't have been arranged as you described it: with only you, a solicitor, and the Whateleys involved. So it came down to only two possibilities. Either the mother was involved in the process of adoption, or she'd abandoned the baby, leaving him to you, the legal—if not the natural—father."

Byrne nodded his acceptance. "She used Eddie for revenge. Our marriage was running thin when he came into our lives. We had so little in common in the first place. I'd been attracted to her youth and beauty, her vivacity. She'd been on the rebound from a broken engagement and was flattered by my devotion. But you can't build a marriage on that, can you? It began to fall apart soon enough. By the time we had Brian—as a way to salvage our relationship—it was as good as over, at least on my part. She was a shallow woman, without much substance. I let her know it."

Lynley reflected on the manner in which Giles Byrne had probably revealed his disenchantment to his wife. No doubt it had been done with little concern about her feelings, little need to spare her pride. Byrne's next words confirmed this.

"She was no match for me in the arena of derision, Inspector. But she knew how I loved Edward Hsu, so she struck back at me through him. To Pamela's way of thinking, seducing Edward would serve two purposes. She would punish me while she proved to herself that she still had some value. Edward was merely an instrument to effect those ends. She used him well, right in my study where she could be relatively certain that I'd walk in on them eventually. Which I did."

"Brian mentioned the study a few minutes ago."

Byrne raised a hand to his eyes, then dropped it. Age showed in his movements; it was underscored by the lines in his face. "He wasn't even five years old. I'd come upon them—Pamela and Eddie—in the study. We had a violent row. Brian walked in on it." Byrne seemed to be watching the play of candlelight upon the melancholy face of the stone angel atop the altar. "I can still see him standing by the door, his hand on the knob, holding on to a stuffed animal and taking it all in. His mother naked and doing nothing about putting on a shred of clothing; his father in a rage, calling her a two-quid whore while she railed at him about his own desire to bed Edward; and Edward, cowering against the cushions of the sofa, trying to cover himself up. And weeping. God, that horrible weeping."

"How soon after that did he kill himself?"

"Less than a week. He left our house that night and returned to the school. I tried to talk to him repeatedly, tried to explain to him that it wasn't his fault. But he believed that he had dishonoured our friendship. It was no matter to Edward that Pamela had set out upon a course of seduction that only a dead man might have been able to resist. As far as he was concerned, he should have been strong enough to resist her. But he wasn't. So he killed himself. Because he knew that I loved him. Because I had been his friend and tutor. Because he had made love to his friend and tutor's wife."

"Then he never knew about the pregnancy at all."

"He never knew."

"Why did your wife carry the child? Why didn't she abort?"

"Because she wanted me to remember the manner in which she'd taken her revenge. What better way for me to remember it than seeing her growing bigger every day with Edward Hsu's child."

"Yet you didn't divorce her at once. Why not?"

"Because of Edward. Had I only had the sense to hide my contempt for Pamela's inadequacies, she would never have sought him out in the first place. Can you understand? I felt responsible for Pamela's behaviour, for Edward's suicide, for the baby's existence. It seemed to me that the only way I could make any expiation at all was to keep Pamela in my life until the baby was born, in the hope that she would tire of the game and give him over to me to dispose of."

"You didn't intend to keep the child yourself."

Byrne glanced at him drily. "Pamela would have clung to that baby like the living embodiment of maternal devotion had she even suspected that I wanted him. As it was, I didn't want him. I just wanted to provide for him."

"I take it that Matthew wasn't born in Exeter."

"In Ipswich. Pamela stayed in a home there, the sort of place where one can discreetly give birth and then move on to better things. Which is exactly what she did as soon as Matthew was delivered. As the father of record, I placed the baby in a foster home while Pamela returned to London, posing as a grieving mother whose infant had been stillborn. She mourned suitably for a few weeks. I filed for a divorce which she didn't contest. Later I returned for Matthew and made the arrangements for the Whateleys to get him."

"Brian never knew about any of this?"

"He never knew. He saw that scene in the study but he didn't know what it meant. And he never met Matthew."

"Until Bredgar Chambers."

"Yes." Byrne looked round the chapel. At the foot of the stone angel, a guttering candle spilled its wax and went out. The scent of its extinguished wick sharpened the air. "I thought it was the right thing to do, sending Matthew to his father's school. Just as I'd done with Brian. Just as is done over and over again. Generations of fathers handing down some sort of pathetic torch to their sons, expecting them to carry it, expecting them to use it to light a world that they themselves have utterly failed to illuminate." Byrne reached for an old hymnal from the back of the pew in front of him. Uselessly he opened it, closed it, opened it again. "I thought it best that he be made into a man. I thought it best not to coddle him. I thought it best that he be made to stand on his own two feet. I thought it *best* . . . He's eighteen years old, Inspector. I'm fifty-four. And I've been sitting here asking a God I don't believe in to let me exchange places with my son somehow. Let this happen to me—the arrest, the trial, the publicity, the punishment. Let me bear this burden for him. Let me at least do that."

Absalom, Absalom, Lynley thought. It was the cry of every father who had stubbornly failed to bind his life and his love to his son. But just like David's mourning the death of Absalom, this sudden flowering of Giles Byrne's solicitude could not change reality. It came far too late.

22

The night's storm had tapered to a drizzle as Lynley pulled the Bentley away from the east entrance to the Bredgar Chambers quadrangle. Ahead of them, the unmarked police car from Horsham CID passed under the trees and disappeared round a curve in the drive. Aside from the lights that glowed intermittently upon the paths between buildings, the grounds were dark and deserted. If a duty master walked a designated round to check upon buildings and the whereabouts of pupils, he was nowhere to be seen.

In the rear seat of the car, Sergeant Havers yawned. "I can understand how Brian got Matthew from Calchus House to the science building," she said. "Poor little bloke probably thought he was being rescued in the middle of the night by his own house prefect. He'd cooperate well enough, wouldn't he, even if Brian hadn't removed the gag or untied his hands. And by the time he realised his saviour was leading him in the wrong direction—to the science building and not to Erebus House—no doubt Brian made short work of tying his feet again. And carrying him into the building. And tossing him into the fume cupboard. But what I can't see is how Brian managed to get Matthew's body from the science building back to Calchus House and then from Calchus House to the minibus the next night without being seen."

"There was no one to see him in the dead of night on Friday," Lynley replied. "Corntel wasn't patrolling the school, most of the pupils were gone, the others were asleep. It's a short enough distance from Calchus House to the science building. Even carrying Matthew over his shoulder, I should guess it took no more than thirty seconds—perhaps less—to dash across the lawn, across the lane, and back into Calchus House. The real risk was on Saturday night, but that was minimised by the fact that Brian was no longer working alone. Clive Pritchard, thinking he himself was responsible for Matthew Whateley's death, was there to help, all the time assuming that Brian was saving him from discovery and never realising the truth was just the opposite."

"The vehicle shed is just down the lane from Calchus House," Havers said thoughtfully.

Lynley nodded. "They took the blanket from the attic, rolled Matthew into it, and carried him down to the vehicle shed. It was late, and as long as they stayed off the lane and kept themselves under the protection of the trees, they ran little risk of being seen. Since the lane itself is a service road and not a main artery of the school, even if they had walked along it carrying the blanket between them, chances are no one would have come along."

"Doesn't that lane go right by the porter's lodge?" St. James asked.

"It sweeps around past it about fifty yards away. But even if Frank Orten had been able to hear the bus at that distance—even if hearing a vehicle might have raised his suspicions in the first place—he was gone that night. The boys knew that. Elaine Roly had told Brian Byrne. And even if Orten had returned while they had the bus, he parks his own car in a garage near the lodge so he wouldn't necessarily know the bus had been taken."

"Then once Clive helped load Matthew into the minibus," Sergeant Havers said, "he was free to skip on to Cissbury, where he established his alibi."

"While Brian and Chas headed for Stoke Poges."

"Rather late to go calling on someone," Havers pointed out. "It must have been well after midnight when they got there."

"But Cecilia knew that the Streaders were spending the weekend with their daughter," St. James added. "She told the police that Sunday night. So it hardly mattered what time Chas arrived, as long as he arrived eventually."

"She knew he would have to hitchhike or take the minibus again," Lynley finished, "so in either case, she wouldn't have been expecting him early."

"What a bloody waste," Havers said in summation. "Inspector, why didn't Chas Quilter just tell the truth? Why did he kill himself? Why did he choose death?"

"He felt trapped, Havers. He saw his situation as hopeless. Beyond that, any move he might have made would have resulted in a betrayal of someone else."

"He wouldn't sneak," she concluded contemptuously. "That's what it came down to, didn't it? That's the sum total of what he'd learned at Bredgar Chambers. To withhold the truth out of loyalty to one's mates. How pathetic. What miserable creatures these places breed."

Lynley felt the impact of his sergeant's words. He didn't respond. He couldn't. There was too much accuracy in what she had said.

They drove past the porter's lodge. Elaine Roly was standing on the narrow front porch, opening a tattered umbrella. Framed in the doorway behind her, Frank Orten held a sleeping child in his arms, the older of his two grandsons.

"How long d'you suppose she'll keep hoping to bag him?" Havers asked as the lights from the Bentley passed over them for an instant. "After seventeen years, you'd think she'd have given up."

"Not if she loves him," Lynley answered. "People give up on all sorts of other things, Havers. But they rarely, if ever, give up on love."

Although it was midnight when the knock sounded on their cottage door, Kevin Whateley and his wife were prepared for visitors. They had received the telephone call from Bredgar Chambers before eleven, so they knew that the Scotland Yard detectives would be paying a final visit to their home that night.

The police brought a third person with them, a whip-thin crippled man who wore a steel brace through the heel of his left shoe and walked with a twisted gait. Detective Inspector Lynley introduced him, but Kevin heard only the word *forensic* before he drifted out of the conversation and sat on a chair at the dining table, divorced from the others who remained in the sitting room. Patsy asked them if they would have coffee. All three refused.

Kevin saw Inspector Lynley's dark eyes taking in his wife, moving over the bruises on her arms, her blackened eye, the tentative manner in which she walked with one arm pressed beneath her breasts as if in the need to protect her ribs. Dimly he heard the inspector's quick question. Patsy's response was calm. It was a fall on the stairs. She even added a creative touch to the story. She'd fallen *up* the stairs, she told them. Can you credit that?

She was careful not to look at Kevin as she spoke. But the

inspector did so. He was, Kevin saw, nobody's fool. He knew what had happened. As did the lady sergeant with him. She put it nicely enough. Is there anyone I can phone for you? A friend, perhaps, that you'd like to visit? It helps, sometimes, to have a friend nearby when you've lost someone you love. Her meaning was clear. Best be out of the house, Pats. No telling what might happen here next.

Patsy did not seem offended by the suggestion. She merely drew her foul-smelling dressing gown round her and took a seat on the vinyl settee. Her bare legs squeaked against the material, drawing attention to themselves. Kevin could see the dark growth of hair like lead tracing upon them.

We've made an arrest, the inspector said. I wanted you to know at once. That's why we've come so late.

The words came to Kevin from a great distance, tingling through his skull and working into his brain. *We've made an arrest.* So it was over.

He heard Patsy's voice but her response to the detective did not register. Nothing registered save the initial statement. *We've made an arrest.* Somehow, that idea suggested a finality that Kevin had not expected. It made Matthew's death quite real. It was no longer the nightmare from which Kevin had hoped he might one day awaken. *Arrest* nullified that. The police do not arrest based upon the occurrence of a nightmare. They only arrest if the nightmare is real.

Kevin didn't know he had got to his feet until he heard his wife say his name. By that time, he was already at the stairs, mounting them numbly, walking in a mist. Below him, he heard the conversation continue. Questions were asked. Names were mentioned. Condolences were expressed. But none of that mattered to Kevin any longer. Only the stairs mattered—climbing them, feeling the wood beneath his feet, turning on the landing, seeking the top of the house.

The door to Matthew's bedroom stood open. Kevin went inside, flipped on the light, and sat on the bed. He looked at everything, making a detailed study of one object at a time, attempting to use each to conjure up a separate vision of his son. There stood the chest of drawers where Matthew would have dressed in the morning, pulling on clothes in a helter-skelter fashion in his rush to be out of doors. There the desk where he would have done his schoolwork and constructed the model buildings for his railway set. There the expanse of corkboard on the wall where Matthew posted photographs of family outings, of locomotives, of holiday memories they all had shared. There the shelf where he kept his books and the tattered stuffed animals too cherished to be thrown away. And the window from which he leaned to watch the boats on the Thames. And the bed in which he slept in safety for thirteen years.

Kevin saw all of this. He studied it. He examined. He memorised. All the time he fought to conjure up the image of his son. All the time he fought to hear Matthew's voice. But nothing came. Only the single word *arrest* and the incontrovertible knowledge that an end had been reached, a finality achieved which he could not ignore.

"Mattie, Mattie, Matt," he whispered. But there was no answer. There was nothing at all save the objects in the room. And they were not his son. Try as he might, he could not bring Matthew forth from the wood and the paper and the glass and the cloth that comprised the environment in which he had lived.

Lookit me, Dad. Watchme, watchme.

Kevin wanted to hear it. The words did not come. Only if he said them himself could they take on life now. But Matthew would never say them again.

We've made an arrest. It was over.

Kevin forced himself to rise from his son's bed and went to the chest of drawers. Leaning against it was the piece of marble he had taken from the tombstone works only last night. He picked it up, carried it back to the bed, laid it across his knees. In his pocket was the pencil he used at work, and he felt for this, grasped it, stared down at the stone.

It seemed to Kevin that sketching the outline of that first terrible word was an admission of defeat, an open assertion that he had failed his son just at the moment when he needed him most. It seemed to Kevin that it meant acceptance, that it meant resignation, that it meant going on. How could he do that? How could he commit such an act of disloyalty? How could he let his agony go?

His hand trembled above the fine, veined stone. "Mattie," he whispered. "Mattie. Mattie. Matt."

He pressed the pencil against the cold marble. He formed the first letter. He sketched the name. Beneath it, the words *beloved son.* Beneath them, the fragile curve of a shell.

"It'll be a nautilus, Mattie," he said. But there was no response. Matthew was gone.

"Kev."

His wife had come into the room. He could not face her. He went on with his work.

"They've gone, Kev. The inspector says we can fetch Mattie now. The police in Slough have done with him."

He could not speak. Not now. Not about Matthew. Not to his wife. He went on with his work. She crossed to the bed. He felt her sit down next to him and knew she was reading what he was writing on the stone. When she next spoke, her voice was tender. She covered his knobby, callused hand with her own.

"He'd like that, Kev. Mattie would like the shell."

Kevin felt the dreadful tightness come over him, felt the swelling of a grief he could no longer control. That she should speak to him still. That she should still love him. That she should be willing to reach out and understand.

He dropped the pencil. He clung for a last moment to the cold solidity of the marble on his lap.

"Pats—" His voice shattered.

"I know, luv," she said. "I know. I do."

He began to cry.

Barbara Havers waited until Lynley had driven off before she walked the remaining distance to her house in Acton. Because of the hour, he had wanted to take her right to her front door, but she had managed to convince him to leave her at the corner of Gunnersbury Lane and the Uxbridge Road, telling him that she needed a few minutes' stroll in the rain-washed night air to clear her head.

Lynley had protested at first. He made no pretence of liking the fact that she wanted to walk home alone through the dark streets of a London suburb after midnight.

Nonetheless, she had insisted, and perhaps he had heard beyond the surface of her words to the resolute need for privacy beneath them. Perhaps, hearing that, he had understood how important it was to her that he not see the conditions under which she lived her life away from New Scotland Yard. He was, after all, an astute observer and he could hardly have failed to notice the degree of decay in some of the neighbourhoods through which they had just driven. In any case, he had reluctantly agreed, stopping the car beneath a streetlight and watching with a frown as she got out.

"Havers, are you certain . . ." He had lowered the window. "This can't be the best of ideas. It's late."

"I'll be fine, sir. Really." She rustled in her shoulder bag, brought out her cigarettes. "See you in the morning, all right?" She said good night to St. James and stepped back from the car. "Go home, Inspector. Get some sleep."

He grumbled a response, raised the window, and drove off.

Barbara stood for a moment and watched the receding rear lights of the automobile mark their progress back into the heart of the city. She lit a cigarette and dropped the match into a puddle of water on the pavement. It sizzled for an instant, leaving a tiny plume of smoke like a miniature cirrus.

The night was oddly quiet. A heavy bank of rain clouds that obscured moon and stars served to muffle sound on the ground below. The only noise that broke into the stillness was the rhythmic slapping of her shoes on the pavement. Even this was muted and absorbed by the damp.

In front of her house, she flicked her cigarette into the wet street and watched as an oily puddle extinguished it. She crossed the patch of earth to the front door, noting that the rain had not managed to alter the rock-hard condition of the ground. Her car was still in the underground parking at New Scotland Yard where she had left it that morning, insisting upon meeting Lynley there rather than letting him pick her up on his way to Bredgar Chambers. As a result, she would have to ride the underground to work tomorrow—a disagreeable prospect but far less disagreeable than it would have been to see the expression on Lynley's face had he had a glimpse of her family's home. It hardly held up to a comparison with his own Belgravia town house.

She climbed the front steps, rooting for her doorkey. Fatigue drained her to weakness. It had been a gruelling day.

The humming struck her the moment she opened the door. It was a mindless sound, two notes repeated over and over, discordantly, with barely a pause for breath. It came from the lower part of the stairway, and Barbara saw a figure crouched upon the second step, arms hugging legs, head upon knees.

"Mum?" she whispered.

The humming continued. Into it her mother inserted a wavering few words. "Don't try to see Ar-gen-*ti*-na."

Barbara went to her. "Mum? Why aren't you in bed?"

Her mother's head lifted. Her mouth curved into a vacuous smile. "There *are* llamas there, lovey. In that zoo. In California. Only I don't think we can go."

Despite the fact that her conscience demanded some sort of apology to her mother for not having let her know how late she would be, Barbara felt the pricking of irritation. Surely her mother knew by now that if she didn't telephone, it was because she was caught up in a case. Surely it wasn't necessary for her to check in like a schoolgirl if the calls of her job kept her away from home for an evening. Surely her father had enough sense left to explain to her mother what Barbara's absence meant.

She became aware of a second noise in the house that she hadn't heard upon entering, the monotone buzzing of the television, tuned in to a station that was off the air for the night. She looked towards the sitting room.

"Mum!" She gave in to exasperation. "Isn't Dad in bed either? Have you let him fall asleep before the telly? For God's sake, you *know* he's got to have some decent rest. He can't get it in an armchair. Mum, you *know* that."

Her mother reached out and caught at Barbara's arm. "Lovey. We can't go, can we? And the llamas are so sweet."

Barbara disengaged her mother's hand. She stifled a curse and went to the sitting room. Her father, she saw, was in his armchair. No lights were on. Barbara switched off the television and started to reach for the floor lamp next to her father's chair. Her hand stretching past his head, she realised suddenly what was wrong in the room, in the house itself. For she had heard the humming. She had heard the buzzing of the television set. But she had not heard the one sound that the years of his illness had accustomed her to hearing. She had not heard her father's laboured breathing. She had not heard it from the door. She had not heard it from the stairway. She was not hearing it now from her position directly next to his chair.

"God. Oh *God.*" She fumbled for the light.

He had probably died sometime in the early afternoon, for his body was cold and rigour had already set in. Still, Barbara lunged for his oxygen, turning valves wildly, muttering a prayer.

If she could only get him from the chair. Onto the floor.

The two-note humming came into the room, accompanying her mother's utterly distracted voice. "I brought him soup, lovey. Just like you said. At half-twelve. But he didn't move. I spooned some for him. I put it in his mouth."

Barbara saw the soup stain on her father's shirt. "God, oh God," she whispered.

"I didn't know what to do. So I went to the stairs. I waited. I waited on the stairs. I knew you'd come, lovey. I knew you'd see to Dad. Only . . ." Mrs. Havers looked in confusion from Barbara to her father. "He wouldn't eat the soup. He wouldn't swallow. I poured some in his mouth. I held it closed. I said you must eat, Jimmy, but he wouldn't answer. And—"

"He's dead, Mum. Dad's dead."

"So I left him to sleep. He needs the rest, doesn't he? You said that yourself. And I waited on the stairs. My lovey will know what to do, I thought. I waited on the stairs."

"Since half-past twelve, Mum?"

"That was the right thing to do, wasn't it, lovey? To wait on the stairs?"

Barbara looked at the lines on her mother's face, at the gaunt cording of her neck, at the vacant expression, at the uncombed hair. All she could think of by way of threnody to greet her father's death was the mental repetition of the same two words: Oh God, oh God, oh God. They summed the count of her emotion. They delineated despair.

"We can't go to that zoo," her mother said. "We can't see the llamas now, lovey."

The telephone startled Deborah St. James out of sleep. It jangled once before being answered hastily in some other part of the house. She reached out automatically, felt the emptiness next to her in the bed, and looked at the clock. It was twenty past three.

Lying sleeplessly in bed, she had heard Simon's return shortly after one, had waited in the darkness for him to come to her, finally falling into a restless sleep herself. Now it was apparent that he had not come to bed—or to their room—at all. Nor had he done so on the previous night, using as an excuse that he had worked late in the lab, that he had not wanted to disturb her and thus had slept in the guestroom.

She felt a dismal emptiness at this second night without him. It left her drifting, growing smaller, more insignificant, more alone. For a moment she lay there trying to feel relief at this division that was keeping him from her. But she could summon only desolation and found in the nighttime telephone call an excuse.

She reached for her dressing gown and pulled it on as she left the room. The house was quiet, but she could hear her husband's voice somewhere above her. She climbed towards it.

By the time she reached the laboratory, he had ended his telephone conversation, and he looked up in surprise when she said his name from the doorway.

"The phone woke me," she said by way of explanation. "Is something wrong? Has something happened?" She thought of his family, of all the possibilities. But while he looked grave, he did not look stricken.

"It was Tommy," he replied. "Barbara Havers' father died today."

She felt her features cloud. "How awful for her, Simon." She walked into the room, going to stand next to him at the worktable. On it, he had spread out a police report in preparation for the job of verifying or nullifying its extensive conclusions. It was a piece of work that would take him several weeks, certainly nothing that he had to begin tonight.

He was distracting himself with his job, distracting himself from having to talk to her. She had wanted it that way. She had clung to the hope that his commitment to his career would keep him so busy that he might simply let her go off on her own and build a separate life from his, so that they might never have to look upon the real heart of the sorrow she had created for them both. Yet now that he appeared to be willing to do just that, she could not endure it, not after what she had seen and recognised on his face when he had looked at the photograph of Tommy two nights ago. She sought something to say to him and found her subject in another's distress.

"I'm so sorry. Is there anything we can do for her?"

"Nothing at the moment. Tommy will let us know. But Barbara's always been fairly private about her family affairs. So I doubt there'll be much she'll let us do."

"Yes. Of course." She reached for the toxicology report, picked it up, and gazed at the jumble of words without comprehension. "Have you been home long? I was asleep. I didn't hear you come in." The lie was casual, conversational, certainly no greater sin than any other on her conscience.

"Two hours."

"Ah."

There seemed nothing more to say. Polite conversation was difficult enough to maintain during the daylight hours. In the middle of the night, with exhaustion claiming the better part of their ability to communicate with an exchange of mere pleasantries that danced across the surface of meaning, it was impossible. Yet in spite of this, she did not want to leave him, and she didn't have to analyse where that feeling was coming from. His face two nights ago had revealed to her that he believed in a fiction that she had to lay to rest. There was only one way to do that, only one way to give him back to himself. She wondered if she would be able to do so. It seemed so much easier to muddle on, to hope that somehow they would get through this time and find their way back to each other with no expenditure of emotion or effort. At this moment, however, that kind of convenient conclusion to their troubles seemed unlikely. More, it seemed cowardly. Yet she could not find the words to begin.

Without apparent reason, her husband began to speak. His eyes on the array of papers and equipment on the worktable, he told her about the case Lynley had been working on. He spoke about Chas Quilter and Cecilia Feld, about Brian Byrne, about Matthew Whateley's parents and their Hammersmith cottage. He described the school. He talked about a fume cupboard and a claustrophobic chamber above a drying room, about the porter's lodge and the Headmaster's study. Deborah listened closely, coming to understand that he was speaking in order to forestall her departure. The realisation gave her hope.

She listened to everything. One hand rested on the worktable near his. The other played on the satin piping of her dressing gown.

"Those poor people," she said when he had concluded. "There's nothing worse . . ." She didn't want to weep any longer. She wanted to put mourning behind her forever, but it wouldn't recede. She forced herself to confront it. "What can be worse than losing a child?"

He looked at her then, his face an engraving of doubts and fears. "Losing each other."

She felt the dread of speaking but made her way past it. "Is that what's happened? Have we lost each other?"

"We seem to have." He cleared his throat, swallowed. Restless, he reached towards a microscope and adjusted one of its dials. "You know"—his words were light, but the effort this cost him was apparent—"it may very well be my fault, Deborah, not yours. God knows what else that blasted accident may have done to me besides take away the use of my leg."

"No."

"Or there could be some sort of genetic defect that I'm passing on so that you can't carry a child full term."

"My love. No."

"With another man, you might—"

"Oh, Simon. Don't."

"I've had time to do some reading about it. If it *is* genetic, we can find that out. I'll have a chromosome study done—a karyotype. After that, we'll know and can decide what to do. Of course, that would mean I couldn't be the father of any of our children. But we could find a donor."

She couldn't bear what he was doing to himself. "Is that what you think I want? A child at any cost? Nor yours, but just anyone's?"

He looked back at her. "No. Not that. Not just anyone's."

It was out then, on the table between them. Even as she wanted to flee from what inevitably had to follow, Deborah still found that she could marvel at the courage it had taken her husband to give his worst fears life. Faced with such unwavering resolution, she was struck to the core by the strength of her love for him.

"You mean Tommy's child," she said.

"You've thought of that, haven't you?" His question was gentle. Hearing it, Deborah felt she could have borne a bitter accusation better than such a display of understanding. Even though, at the root of it, he did not understand, even though he would never understand unless she told him everything. "It would be natural enough," he was continuing reasonably, as if the statement did not tear unforgivingly at his heart. "If you'd only married Tommy as he wanted all those years ago, you might have had a child by now."

"I've not thought of that. I've never once thought of how things might have been had I married Tommy." She stared without seeing at the items on the table, an exercise in summoning up the courage to go on. She knew he didn't believe her denial. Why should he? What other excuse could there be, save regret or remembrance, for her perusal of her photographs of Tommy?

Slowly he began to gather together the police report, clipping papers and putting them back into files. She saw that he'd left one of the computer printers on, and she bought time by going to it, shutting it down, and diligently replacing its cover. When she turned back to him, he was watching her from the pool of light shed by the high intensity lamp on the worktable. She herself was in a cavern of shadow. She knew the darkness served to hide what played upon her face.

"There wasn't a happily ever after," she said. Her palms were sticky. Her eyelids stung. "You and I were in love. We married. I wanted your child. It seemed reasonable to assume that everything would fall into place according to my plans. But things didn't do that. I'm trying to come to terms with the fact that they probably never will. And with the fact that . . ." She felt her own resistance to saying anything more. Her body seemed to harden. She struggled against its protective refusal to let her speak. ". . . with the fact that it's all my fault, really. I did it to myself."

He moved on the stool, making a gesture which served to contravene her words. "It's no one's fault, Deborah. You can't cast blame in a situation like this. I don't understand why you want to."

She averted her face, not so that he couldn't see it, but so that she would not have to see his. Instead, she looked upon the black gaze of the window. Her own reflection dared her to go on.

Her husband spoke again. "Even if you want to assess blame, as I've said, it could just as easily be me as you. That's why I think we should have some tests. Then if I'm the one—if there's a genetic problem—we can go from there." He paused and returned quietly to his earlier theme. "We can find a donor."

"Is that what you want?"

"I want your happiness, Deborah."

The words were both a torment and a challenge, even though Deborah knew he intended them to be nothing more than an avowal of his love. "At what cost to yourself?"

He didn't reply. She turned back to him. He met her gaze with an expression of controlled placidity that was supposed to demonstrate his ability to relinquish the gratification of fathering a child. But his eyes could not carry the burden of the lie.

"No," she said softly. "Beloved. No. There's no need for tests. No need for donors. No need for you to put yourself through any of this. I'm at fault. I know it."

"You can't."

"I do." She remained across the room. It seemed better that way. She didn't know what he would do when he heard the truth, but she felt certain he wouldn't want to be near her. "You see . . . I just didn't think about it at the time. I was only eighteen."

"Eighteen?" he repeated, perplexed. "What are you talking about?"

"An abortion," she said. She went no further. She knew she would not have to. He would complete the rest of the story himself.

She saw him do so quickly. He flinched. His face blanched. He stood abruptly.

"I couldn't tell you, Simon," she whispered. "I *couldn't.* It was the only thing you never knew. So many times I wanted to . . . but I knew what it would do to you . . . what you would think. And now . . . Oh God, I've destroyed us."

"Did he know?" St. James asked numbly. "Does he know now?"

"I never told him."

He took a single step towards her. "Why not? He would have married you, Deborah. He *wanted* to marry you. What would it have mattered to him if you were pregnant? He wouldn't have cared. He would have been overjoyed. You would have been giving him exactly what he wanted in the first place. Yourself and an heir. Why didn't you tell him?"

"You *know* why."

"I don't."

"It was you." She broke. "You *know* it was you."

"What do you mean?" he demanded.

"I loved you. Not Tommy. I loved *you*. Always. You know that." Sobs grew, leaving her incapable of speech. Still, she tried. "I thought . . . it wasn't real to me then . . . and you were always . . . I wanted . . . you were the only one . . . Always. But I was alone . . . and those years when you wouldn't write to me . . . So he came to America . . . You know the rest . . . I didn't . . . he was someone . . ."

She heard him move then, heard his uneven footsteps rapidly strike the wooden floor. For a moment she thought he was leaving the room. It was, after all, what she deserved. But then he was next to her, pulling her into his arms.

"Deborah. God. Deborah." His hands were in her hair, pressing her head against his shoulder. She felt the forceful pounding of his heart. His words were ragged. "What have I done to you?"

She could only say, "Nothing. *Nothing.*"

He held her fiercely. "I did everything wrong. Everything backwards. And you bore the brunt of it all. My fear, my confusion, my doubt. All of it. For three rotten years. I'm so sorry, my love." And then again, lifting her face, "My love."

"The photograph . . ."

"It meant nothing. I know that now. You were looking at the past. That has nothing to do with the future."

It took more than a moment for the import of his words to strike her. His hands were on her face, his fingers wiping away her tears. He said her name. It was a shaken whisper.

Her eyes filled again. "How can you forgive me? How can I ask that of you?"

"Forgive?" He sounded incredulous. "Deborah, for God's sake, that was six years ago. You were only eighteen. You were a different person. The past is nothing. Only the present and the future matter. Surely you know that by now."

"I don't see . . . How can we ever be what we were to each other? How can we go on?"

He pulled her close. "By going on."

A misty rain fell upon the mourners who stood round Jimmy Havers' coffin in South Ealing Cemetery. A plastic-topped shelter had been set up to protect Sergeant Havers, her mother, and a collection of half a dozen elderly relatives of the deceased, but the rest of the group stood beneath umbrellas. A clergyman was intoning a plea for God's merciful judgement, his hands holding a Bible to his chest, mud splattering against the hem of his cassock. Lynley tried to concentrate upon the words, but he was distracted by bits and pieces of a whispered conversation behind him.

"Had to *negotiate* to get him into South Ealing, don' you know. Had to buy the plot *special.* They've had it for *years.* That's their son in the next grave."

"She found him, I hear. Barbie. He'd been dead all day. Her mum was right there and she didn't even *know* he was gone."

"No surprise to me, that. Batty, her mum is. Has been for ages."

"Senile?"

"Just batty. Can't be left alone for ten minutes."

"Cor. What's Barbie to do?"

"Put her away, I'd guess. There has to be *some* home as will take her."

"Not likely to be easy. Just look at the poor thing."

It was the first time Lynley had seen Sergeant Havers' mother. He was still trying to come to terms with the sight of her, and with his own previous reluctance to invade the closed world that was Barbara Havers' life. He had known Barbara for years, had worked with her closely for the past eighteen months, yet every time she had fended off a circumstance that might have allowed him to know her as more than merely a colleague, he had allowed her to do so with very little protest. It was as if, all along, he had taken the full measure of the secrets she was trying to hide and was only too willing to allow her to go on hiding them indefinitely.

Her mother had clearly been one of them. Dressed in an overlarge black coat that dangled round her ankles, she clung to Barbara's arm, smiling, her head cocked to one side. She did not seem to be aware of the funerary rites going on round her. Rather, she cast diffident glances at the group that stood opposite her in a semicircle round the yawning grave, and she whispered to her daughter and stroked her arm. Barbara's only response was to pat her mother's hand, although she attended to her briefly by fastening the top button of her coat and brushing away several grey hairs that lay on its collar. That done, she returned her attention to the clergyman. Her face was composed; her eyes rested on the coffin. She appeared to be giving her thoughts to the service.

Lynley could not. He could ground himself only in the here and now. Prayers for eternity meant less than nothing. He examined the mourners.

Across the grave, St. James held an umbrella over his wife, while Deborah took further shelter in the curve of his arm. Next to them, Superintendent Webberly stood bareheaded in the drizzle, his hands driven into the pockets of his raincoat. Behind him were three other DI's, and next to them the singular black face of Constable Nkata. The small crowd was dotted with other representatives from the Yard. They were here for Barbara. They had never known her father.

Beyond them, a woman in pink plastic gloves was digging industriously in an urn at the side of a marble-topped grave. She paid no attention to the service going on, squishing round in galoshes as if she were alone. She only looked up from her employment when a car approached, its tyres plashing through the puddles along the lane behind Lynley that led from the cemetery's entrance on South Ealing Road. It stopped, motor running. A door opened and shut. The car drove off. Quick footsteps crossed the pavement. Someone had come—quite late—to join the mourners.

Lynley saw that Havers had descried the newcomer, for her eyes moved from the grave to the back of the group and then immediately, as if inadvertently, to him. She averted her gaze at once, but not quickly enough. He knew Havers. He read her well. He realised who had come. Even had he not drawn this instant conclusion from Havers' expression, the faces of St. James and Deborah would have told him. No doubt it was they in the first place who had put through the call to Corfu that brought Helen Clyde home.

And it *was* Helen who stood at the edge of the crowd. Lynley knew it. He could feel it. He did not even need to turn and see her for verification. He would sense her presence in the very air whenever she was near him, to the end of his life. Two months of her absence had made no change in that. Two decades would not do so.

The clergyman ended his prayers, stepped back, and watched the attendants lower the casket. When it was settled, Sergeant Havers urged her mother forward a few tottering steps and helped her throw a handful of spring flowers into the grave. Mrs. Havers had been clutching them throughout the service. She had dropped them twice on the way from the chapel. They were bedraggled now, a flutter of stems and petals without definition any longer. They floated out from her hand, were quickly sodden by the rain.

The clergyman murmured a final invocation for peace and eternal rest. He spoke to Sergeant Havers and her mother. He stepped away. The mourners pressed forward to murmur condolences.

Lynley watched them do so. St. James and Deborah, Webberly and Nkata. Neighbours and colleagues and distant relations. He stayed by the grave. He stared down into it. Dull light winked from the small brass plaque on the coffin lid. Now that he was released from the proprieties required of one during a funeral, now that turning, greeting Helen, and making conversation were all behaviours expected of him, Lynley found that he could bring himself to do nothing at all. Even if he could mouth harmless inanities in an effort to prevent Helen from leaving him again, how could he hope to manage that without his face declaring everything that he wished to conceal?

Two months changed nothing. Nothing at all. They did not lessen his love for her, nor did they do anything to attenuate desire.

"Tommy."

His eyes cast down, he saw her shoes first. Despite his discomfiture, he had to smile. They were, as always, so completely Helen: impractical, beautiful bits of leather offering absolutely no protection from the weather, cut in a fashion only a masochist could endure.

"How on earth can you wear those things, Helen?" he asked her. "They look like misery."

"Agony," Lady Helen corrected. "My feet are so sore that my eyeballs actually hurt. I feel like an experiment for podiatric torture. If a war were on, I'd already have told the enemy everything I know."

He laughed quietly, raising his head to look at her. She was unchanged. The smooth chestnut hair still framed her face. The dark eyes still held his own unwaveringly. The figure was slender, the carriage upright and proud.

"Have you come from Greece this morning?" he asked her.

"It was the first flight I could get. I've come straight from the airport."

Which explained her clothing, light and springlike in shades of peach, entirely unsuited to a funeral. He removed his trench coat and handed it to her.

"Am I that awful?" she asked.

"Not at all. You're getting wet. The shoes look beyond redemption at this point, but there's no reason to ruin the dress."

She shrugged her way into the coat. It was absurdly enormous upon her.

"At least you've an umbrella," he noted. It was dangling from her fingers, unopened.

"Yes indeed. One of those wretched collapsible things. I bought it

at the airport. It's been collapsing quite cooperatively ever since."
She cinched in the coat's belt. "Have you spoken to Barbara?"

"On the phone several times since Wednesday. But not today. Not
yet."

Lady Helen watched the assembled people moving towards Sergeant Havers. Lynley watched Lady Helen. When she turned back to
him suddenly, he felt the heat take his face. Her words surprised
him.

"Simon told me about the case, Tommy. About the school. That
little boy." She hesitated. "It sounded particularly dreadful."

"Parts of it were. The school mostly." He looked away. At the next
gravesite, the woman in the pink gloves was still digging in the urn.
On the ground next to her an azalea waited to be planted.

"Because of Eton?"

How she knew him. How she did. How she always would. How
she could touch him to the core of his being—to his very essence—
without even trying. "I prayed for him at Eton, Helen. Did I ever tell
you that? In the memorial chapel. With those four archangels in each
corner looking down on me and guaranteeing that my prayers would
be heard. I went there every day. I knelt. I prayed. Please, God, let
my father live. I'll do anything, God. Just let my father live."

"You loved him, Tommy. That's what children do when they
love their parents. They don't want them to die. There's no sin in
that."

He shook his head. "That isn't it. I didn't know. I didn't think. I
prayed for him to live. Helen, to *live*. I never thought to pray that he
might be cured. And my prayer was answered. He lived. For six
horrible years."

"Oh, Tommy."

Her warmth and compassion were far too much. He spoke without consideration. "How I've missed you."

"And I you," she said. "Truly."

He wanted to take hope from those four simple words. He wanted
to infuse them with both meaning and promise. Hearing them, he
wanted to risk it all once again, to offer Helen his life, to declare his
love, to insist that she recognise and embrace the union that had
long existed between them. But if they had not allowed him to forget
her for a moment, the past two months without her had at least
taught him a degree of restraint.

"I've a new sherry at home," he said in answer. "Will you try it
sometime and tell me what you think?"

"Tommy, you know I'm a hopeless victim to sherry. It could be decanted right through someone's dirty socks and I'd still taste it and pronounce it delicious."

"In any other circumstance that could be a problem," he admitted. "But not in this case."

"Why not?"

"I've only used clean socks."

She laughed. It lit her face.

Encouraged, he asked, "Will you come tonight?" And then he added hastily, "Or tomorrow. Or later. Of course, you're exhausted from your trip."

"And after the sherry?" she asked him. "What then?"

He let pretence go. "I don't know, Helen. Perhaps you'll tell me about your trip. Perhaps I'll tell you about my work. If it gets late, perhaps we'll scramble eggs and burn them and throw out the lot. Or perhaps we'll just share the evening together. I don't know. That's the best I can do. I don't know."

Lady Helen hesitated. She looked towards Sergeant Havers and her mother. The cluster of people round them was getting thin. Lynley knew she wanted to go to Barbara, knew he himself ought to be standing in that group of people near her and not waiting here for the woman he loved to say something—anything—that would indicate what his future might be. He was irritated with himself. Once again, he had put Helen into an untenable position. His need to *know*, to have instantaneous resolution, would drive her away from him again and again.

"Look. I'm sorry," he said abruptly. "I wasn't thinking. That seems to be a chronic condition of mine. Shall we let it go for now and talk to Barbara?"

Lady Helen looked relieved. "Yes. Let's do that."

She took his arm and they walked towards the group that still stood under the plastic canopy.

"Tommy," Lady Helen said reflectively after a moment. "You know, I'm awfully fond of sherry. I always have been."

"I know. That's why I thought—"

"What I mean is yes. Tasting the sherry. I'd like to do that tonight."

Her hesitancy was a call for caution. Lynley refused to allow himself to misunderstand. He merely said as she had, "And after the sherry?"

"I don't know. Like you, that's the best I can do. Is it enough for you this time?"

It was not enough. It would never be enough. Only certainty would satisfy. But that would not come at once.

"It's enough," he lied. "For now. It's enough."

They joined St. James and Deborah. They waited to speak to Barbara. Lynley took what pleasure he could from Helen's hand on his arm. He drew a measure of contentment from the pressure of her shoulder against his, from her presence at his side, from the sound of her voice. It was not at all what he wanted from her. It never would be. But he knew it would have to suffice for now.